THE VOW

Praise for *The Vow*

2024 American Fiction Awards Finalist in Historical Fiction

"*The Vow* poignantly explores both the rewards and challenges of being a creative woman. With its rich descriptions of eighteenth-century Europe, this novel is a well-researched, timeless look at how powerfully the soul can guide us, both in art and in love."

—Ginny Kubitz Moyer, author of *The Seeing Garden*

"Lovers of art and seekers of the Divine will be especially enthralled by this masterful work set in late-1700s Italy and England—a creative revelation of the painterly life of Angelica Kauffman, a historical, exceptionally accomplished artist. Relive her encounters with celebrities of the time, including Joshua Reynolds, Goethe, and royalty."

—Francine Falk-Allen, author of *A Wolff in the Family*

"In this mesmerizing tale woven by Jude Berman, the intricate dance between ambition and betrayal unfolds with breathtaking elegance. With skillful prose and classical descriptions, Berman paints a vivid portrait of a woman defying the constraints of her time, making this novel an unforgettable masterpiece in its own right."

—Joanne Howard, author of *Sleeping in the Sun*

"A lyrically written, deeply imagined fictional biography of one of the early feminists—the renowned artist Angelica Kauffman, who was close friends with both Joshua Reynolds and Goethe."

—Sara Loyster, author of *The Daughters of Edward Darley Boit*

"In *The Vow*, Berman brings a mostly forgotten eighteenth-century artist breathtakingly to life. Angelica Kauffman was truly exceptional—fierce, independent, beautiful, fought over by patrons and lovers. This graceful and well-researched novel exposes the deepest heart of a passionate woman who makes excruciating choices to keep her spirit free."

—Laurel Huber, author of *The Velveteen Daughter*

"Based on extensive research, *The Vow* uncovers the life of Angelica Kauffman, an artist who vows never to marry but instead pursue her art. Berman imagines rich scenes of Kauffman's struggles as a woman trying to succeed and find love too. An insightful and intimate book that pulls back the curtain on the art salons of eighteenth-century Italy and England."

—Linda Moore, author of *Attribution*

"Swiss artist Angelica Kauffman's quest for immortality—both as an artist and as a woman—underpins her every movement in Jude Berman's compelling second novel, *The Vow*. Berman breathes life into a historical character who dared to break professional and social boundaries. This intriguing and historically accurate novel will delight readers of art history, women's history, and eighteenth-century historical fiction."

—Ashley E. Sweeney, author of *Eliza Waite*

"Jude Berman's *The Vow* brilliantly explores the life of eighteenth-century Swiss artist Angelica Kauffman. In an era when women live with few rights, Kauffman rejects society's restrictions and follows her dream of becoming a successful portraitist and history painter. In a stellar first-person narrative, we share Kauffman's struggles, passions, and successes. If you're a fan of classical art, historical novels, and the roots of feminism, you'll love *The Vow*."

—Susen Edwards, author of *What a Trip*

THE VOW

A Novel

Jude Berman

SHE WRITES PRESS

Published 2024
Printed in the United States of America
Print ISBN: 978-1-64742-788-7
E-ISBN: 978-1-64742-789-4
Library of Congress Control Number: 2024909082

For information, address:
She Writes Press
1569 Solano Ave #546
Berkeley, CA 94707

Interior Design by Kiran Spees

She Writes Press is a division of SparkPoint Studio, LLC.

To the other Wolfgang

Contents

Prologue

can't remember dying. It happened so quickly. So quietly. Like the moment of midnight passing into the morrow. Like a rainbow, its colors already faint, fading into the clouds.

For a long time I thought I was still in my room, the candle flickering by the window, the priest's voice a constant drone as he read the same verse over and again. I don't know why he insisted on "Ode for the Dying." I called out several times but apparently he couldn't hear me.

Then I found myself in a chapel—or perhaps some sort of Egyptian temple. I couldn't be sure in the darkness. Later it seemed I was sitting by a lone pine tree. To orient myself, I tried bringing to mind habitual actions. How much red pigment to mix with the yellow for a sunset. What size brushes to use when painting the eyes, the cheekbones, the hint of a dimple. How long to wait before applying the varnish.

I'm grateful for these simple thoughts. They have kept me steady. Steady enough so I can begin to focus on what is most dear to my heart. On what needs to happen next. On all I must remember.

Venice

One

Venice, 1765

Papa taught me always to look for the brief bath of luminosity at dusk. It never disappoints. This evening, filtered through panes of stained glass, it sets fire to Titian's *Assumption*. The painting, which has been towering over me all day as I worked to copy it, suddenly glows from within. Red robes grow redder, the clouds softer. Heaven a richer gold. Then all the colors explode, engulfing the Virgin in a radiance that rebounds off the sanctuary windows as if they were looking glass.

In a world fabricated of light, I can no longer gauge where I'm standing.

Our Lady's arms, raised toward God, drop to her sides. Long fingers of light reach down and touch me. Her head inclines downward, her gaze meets mine.

Her breath is warm on my face. Within it, a whisper: *Soar beyond what you know. Paint with your soul. Paint for God!*

As quickly as it began, the moment is over.

I, Angelica Kauffman, stand alone again before my unfinished canvas in the Basilica di Santa Maria Gloriosa dei Frari. It is a late afternoon in October of the year 1765, time for the lamplighter to make his rounds.

I become aware of how chilly the sanctuary is, of the insidious dampness that has seeped into my bones. I'm tired, hungry, even a bit irritable. There are so many scenes I long to paint, such vibrant colors swirling in my head. Yet I have little to show for my efforts at the end of a vexing day. *Paint for God?* Really, that would be better left to the angels.

Footsteps echo on the stone floor, breaking the silence. Antonio Zucchi, the lodger with whom my father and I share quarters, is coming toward me with his usual bouncing step.

"Your father's been delayed." His whisper is loud enough to create an echo of its own.

His brusqueness might offend me if I weren't so used to it. My father and I met him in Milan, and our travels have since taken us along parallel paths. A few days after we arrived in Rome, there he was. When we were in Naples, he was in Naples. So it was no surprise when he showed up in Venice. Now that he sleeps in the attic above our apartment and doesn't wait for an invitation to join us for meals, he's practically kin.

I set down my palette, rub my hands to get warm, and begin cleaning my brushes, starting with the smallest yellow one.

He folds his arms and stares at my canvas. "Not finished?"

Unable to deny that, I focus on my brushes.

"You've done *nothing.*"

His tone riles me, as I'm sure he intends it to, but I'm not about to be seduced into another argument. The one last night in the privacy of our home was bad enough. A public outburst—in a church, no less—would be far worse. Without looking up, I run the tip of the yellow brush slowly, deliberately along the edge of my paint box. It doesn't leave any trace of color. I pick up another brush and dip it in mineral spirits.

Even with my head down, I can feel Antonio's glare. It's no secret he harbors at least as much envy as admiration for me. Not only am I fifteen years younger, but the acclaim I've won exceeds anything he could hope to receive for his own craft. His envy grows each time I get a more impressive commission.

I know what he's thinking: Someone as young and idealistic as I needs someone with more worldly discernment—someone like him—to guide and protect me. It's not an idea I've ever encouraged. I don't need anyone directing my career or watching over me like that. Nor in any other way Antonio might fancy. My father provides all the help I need. We're a team: I paint, he handles business. Our income may be meager, but the commissions he has procured for me would be the pride of any artist, let alone a woman.

Abandoning any pretense at a whisper, Antonio gestures toward the altar. "For a girl to presume to do justice to this masterpiece, what a mockery!"

My art a mockery? It's been a slow day, but that's a step too far. And the way he called me *girl*, like it's some kind of incurable disease. My reply is quiet yet firm: "Giuseppe Morosco didn't think so when he gave me the commission. He has confidence in me." *Unlike you*, I think, picking up a russet red brush.

"I'm confident too," he huffs.

But I've heard enough. "You know Papa and I need the money," I say, thrusting my brush close enough to his nose to make him pull back. "Life isn't cheaper here than in Rome or Milan. Even sharing rooms with you, we can barely afford food. Not to mention art supplies. Besides, why shouldn't I create a replica of great art?"

"Next you'll try for a replica of the sun!" He spits out his words, then turns and rushes from the church.

I shake my head as I watch him go. Then I glance at the Virgin. Her arms are raised to the Lord, palms open, eyes locked with his.

There is no sign it was ever otherwise. She's too enraptured to be bothered by our pettiness.

So why should *I* bother? The fact is, despite his bravado, Antonio has little knowledge of history painting or reproductions. When he looks at the Virgin, he doesn't appreciate the brilliant reds Titian used more than two centuries ago, when the church considered such colors scandalous. Nor have I seen him stop—as I often do—beside Titian's tomb here in the Frari to pay his respects to the master. No, Antonio is an artisan primarily devoted to architectural trimmings and decorative ornaments. If he thinks about reproductions, it is to adorn a dinner plate. He'll never understand my dreams and passions.

I inhale deeply. So that's it. One has to live as one sees fit, to paint what one is called to paint. To do anything less—*that* would be a mockery. If I want to paint the sun, I'll paint the sun. And it will be magnificent.

Still, I have to admit, inspiration hasn't been shining on me. For hours, I've gone over and over one small corner of the canvas. Morosco expected the painting yesterday, but my father bargained for an extra day. Now I'm going to disappoint both of them.

As I place my paints in the wooden box with splintered lid I inherited from Papa, the lamplighter and several others enter the church. A young man dressed in black offers a votive candle, then wanders over to inspect my canvas. His tall form hunches a bit too closely over my shoulder, his long blond curls brushing against my cheek, forcing me to step aside.

"For sale?" he asks.

"It's sold already."

A giant ruby flashes on his finger as he adjusts his temple spectacles so he can take in both the original and my copy. I feel his eyes on me too. "Tell the buyer he's fortunate," he says before turning away.

Others approach and discuss my work among themselves. As if I were invisible. I untie my apron and smooth the folds of my skirt as I listen to their reactions. Transformed through a dozen eyes, my unfinished painting becomes a dozen different paintings—all finished, all worthy of praise. *If only one would affix itself to my canvas. Before Papa arrives.* Of course, Antonio will be back too. I'm determined not to argue with him again.

It's hard not to argue with someone who is convinced he knows what's best for you. Or so I've discovered. After supper, it is my custom to wash and dry the dishes while Antonio sits at our rough-hewn table and designs the engraving for a plate. When the dishes are in the cupboard, I join him with my sketchbook. Last night, I was rendering Penelope's hands as they hold Ulysses's bow—gracefully elongated yet strong enough to support the weapon. Her right thumb looked as it should, but the left was at an odd angle.

Antonio stopped to watch. "We should join forces."

I shrugged. "You're welcome to do engravings of my history paintings."

"Not Penelope."

"Why not?"

"The design isn't circular."

"Then adapt it."

But he wasn't satisfied. He wanted me to set aside my sketches and develop a motif for his plates. "They'd fetch a high price," he insisted.

"I've worked all day on a painting that's already sold. Have you forgotten?"

At that, he launched into a diatribe about what's best for me—namely, to stop distracting myself with the vacuous allegories of history painting. And definitely no more replicas.

I pointed out his illogic. Many of his engravings are reproductions of history paintings. As they should be. That's what people rush to purchase. Besides, mythology is a genre of pure passion. Any artist with talent—irrespective of gender—knows that. And surely I have talent. So why should I limit myself?

None of what I said had any effect. Antonio expected his to be the final word. I was just a girl, obligated to listen to him. Having decided how that girl should paint, he badgered me until I heaved a sigh of frustration—which he probably interpreted as an admission of defeat, though it was anything but—and gathered up my sketchbook and chalks and retired to the loft where I sleep.

My thoughts are interrupted by a rustling at my side.

A woman in ivory silk, pearls shimmering in her upswept hair, skirt with the widest hoops I've ever seen, has entered the sanctuary. Obviously a personage of import. Each time she flicks her jewel-studded fan, I inhale rose perfume. It's intoxicating.

She tilts her head and regards my painting.

I sense a compliment forthcoming and prepare to receive it with grace. But before she can speak, our attention is drawn to the front of the church, where two men are engaged in heated debate. As they rush toward us, she steps away.

Papa drops his satchel and reaches for my painting.

My hands fly to protect it. I can only imagine the stories Antonio has fed him.

"What is this?" he cries. "Antonio says you're not painting. I say that's impossible—"

"John Joseph, be gentle!" Now that his criticisms have found an ear, Antonio is ready to jump into the opposite role—the one he covets—as my protector.

But Papa is fixed on my painting. On me. "My darling," he pleads, "tell me it's not true!"

Antonio might have created this scene, but he doesn't have the power to end it. We both know I'm the one who has a special touch with my father, who can say what he needs to hear. Antonio expects that of me now. But I can't find the words. Much as I've resisted it, Antonio has managed to plant a seed of doubt. So what if rivers of color flood into paintings in my mind's eye as I fall asleep? So what if I dream of making masterpieces? It's all useless if I can't create a fair copy.

"Think of our sacrifices!" Papa isn't angry, just afraid. "Your mother and I thought only of your talent, your success. Now it's all in your hands."

I want to throw my arms around him, promise those sacrifices weren't in vain. I myself have vowed the highest sacrifice: to place my art over all else, even over marriage. My art is my life, my love. I work all day, every day, often without stopping for a meal between dawn and dusk. But I don't mind; my art is all that matters. Nothing brings greater joy than to watch a patron behold a finished piece. I want to say I will start at the first light tomorrow and make up for lost time. I'll complete the painting by day's end. But I can't make that promise. It is one thing to love painting, to feel called to the life of an artist; it is something else to live up to others' expectations. The fact they are my own expectations too doesn't help.

"I'm sorry" is all I can say.

Antonio shoots me a look that says, *I warned you not to be a dreamer.*

I stare back at him, then at my father, then at the unfinished canvas. Tears are pooling in my eyes. Another minute and I'll be crying. In public.

Suddenly, the lady reemerges from the shadows. If she's been watching, she gives no indication she witnessed anything unusual. "May I ask a favor?" Her voice is as smooth as the pearls in her hair. Quiet as a lady's voice is supposed to be.

I blink away my tears.

"I need a portrait to remind me of Venice. I'd like this young artist to execute it." She addresses my father as if he were one of her rank. "Would you permit me, sir, to commission it?"

You're so beautiful, I think, *I want to paint you just as you are right now.*

She turns to me, all smiles. "I hope you'll agree to paint a portrait for me."

As I express my gratitude, Antonio draws Papa aside. "It's Her Excellency Lady Wentworth," I hear him whisper, "wife of the British ambassador."

My father thrusts himself forward. "Of course . . . you're most . . ." He trips over his tongue, trying to correct any untoward impressions. "My daughter, Angelica, is widely acclaimed . . ."

"Papa!" I hiss. There is no reason to lose his dignity. Our dignity.

"We . . . we've," he stammers, "just come from Naples—"

"Papa, please! Her Excellency knows."

Lady Wentworth extends her hand. Without hesitating, I place my paint-stained fingers in it. If my rough skin shocks her senses, she doesn't let on. "I thought you might be Angelica," she says. "I've heard so much about you. I just got a letter from Herr Winckelmann praising a portrait you did. I knew I had to have one for myself."

Within a few minutes, everything has been settled. I will go home with her, so she can show me where I'll be working. We will discuss the commission, and if everything is acceptable to my father,

I will begin work straightaway—or as soon as my copy in the church is finished. No one questions whether it will be.

As we walk out of the church, Lady Wentworth and I, and cross the pavement to the waterway, where her gondola awaits, I turn at the last second and glance back. Antonio is in the doorway, staring after us, looking so small against the massive brick building, with its towering campanile. All the bounce has drained out of him.

I know he wants to protest, to make a case that my father must be more careful about where—and with whom—he allows his daughter to go. He wants to explain how wealthy people take a fancy to certain artists because it's the fashion of the day, only to drop them a short while later. But he knows my father too well. Any objections now will be discounted. All Antonio can do is bide his time, hoping for a chance to snatch me back into his world.

You poor fellow, I think as I descend the steps to the water, *even that will be too late.*

I take my seat in the felze of the gondola and pull a thick wool blanket over my lap. Not only will it keep me warmer than just my cloak, but it will hide the stains that, despite my apron, run all the way down my skirt.

While Lady Wentworth attempts to swivel—difficult with her extra-wide hoops—so she can direct the gondolier to arrange her packages, I relax into the pillows. The sides of the felze have been left open, affording a wide view of the canal. Lanterns hanging from the buildings cast their rays over the water, making sparkles dance on the ripples. Under my skin, ripples of joy are doing a dance of their own as I recall the Virgin's words: *Paint with your soul!* I'm not certain how to do that. I just know I want to. And someday, somehow, I will.

For now, I can't wait to start my new commission. No matter that it's only a portrait, not a history painting. I can do it and do it well. The world will see.

I lean over and peer into the water. From this angle, no sparkles are visible. Looking into the depths is like staring into the vast palette of God's unknown. Anything can be created, anything dissolved, in each instant. Before an artist has dipped their brush into paint, no one knows if a masterpiece will be created. Likewise, the life of a painter is unpredictable. This afternoon is proof enough of that.

When all the packages have been stowed, the gondolier shoves off. With one smooth stroke, he cuts through God's palette. *At what point*, I wonder, *does the work of the artist cease, and her life itself begin?*

Two

The oar dips and splashes, rocking our boat as we round the bend away from the church and enter a narrow passageway. On either side, the buildings are like huge ships moored in the water. Though it is late, the canal is bustling with activity. People hang over balconies, brandishing glasses of ale, calling out to neighbors. Children play on their doorsteps, alarmingly close to the water.

Suddenly my gaze is drawn upward.

A solitary figure stands on a low-arching bridge, watching our gondola pass beneath. I recognize the man with fair curls and black coat who praised my painting in the church, the man with the ruby ring. For an instant our eyes meet. Even though it's dark, I have the unnerving sense he can see through me.

A tap on my knee brings me back to the boat.

Lady Wentworth is smiling patiently. A fine mist has settled on her hair, giving polish to the pearls. "So," she says, "tell me about the artist."

I hesitate. It would be easier, I've often thought, if my paintings could speak for themselves. Stories of Greek mythology are what move people. Everyone loves images of sublime beauty and valor, patience and perseverance, grandeur and glory. They love the vision of a perfect world. The personal story of a young woman artist—not so much. That's best kept quiet. Especially if you have as little stomach as I do for people's useless ideas about how she should lead her life.

"I hear you've been an artist since an early age," she prompts.

Her prompt works. In fact, I can't recall a time before I was an artist. Perhaps I was born one, if that's possible. "Yes," I say, slipping one foot out of its shoe and curling my toes on the soft cushion. "Other children bored me. I didn't care for their dolls or spillikins. Drawing on the floor with my father's chalks was much more fun."

"Ha! A child prodigy. I knew it."

She looks at me expectantly, but I don't react. This isn't always a compliment. Many people don't appreciate a prodigy, especially not a girl. "I was born in Switzerland," I say instead. "My parents came to Italy so my father could paint portraits and cathedral ceilings—" I stop, too proud to reveal how poor we actually were. Besides, the life of itinerant artists seeking new commissions and wealthier patrons is hardly within a lady's purlieus. "My parents always looked after me," I say.

"So your father taught you?"

Again I hesitate. "Not exactly—"

"No? How then are you so accomplished?"

With her persistence, my reluctance fades. I do have a reason to tell her about myself: Patrons need to know about any artist they support. All the more so if that artist is a woman, to make sure her talents don't go to waste.

I explain that my father guided me, but he wasn't my teacher. I taught myself by copying masterpieces. When he saw how easily I made copies, he gave me paints of my own and expected a new copy every fortnight. "One can learn so much by studying artists such as Leonardo da Vinci, Raphael, and Correggio," I say, not mentioning—as she undoubtedly knows—that none were women. "Papa's favorite is Leonardo, so I imagined him as my teacher."

"Does your father still paint?" she wants to know.

"He gave up his work so he could focus on my career."

"How generous." She looks at me with a keen eye. "And practical. He knows where the real talent in his family lies."

This time I smile at her compliment. Because it's true. In fact, few know the lengths to which my father went to make sure I received an education—even to the point of facing ridicule himself. In Milan, he was branded an opportunist for foisting a child into the limelight. The artists didn't want a girl studying in the galleries. What if she outshined them? No one wanted to risk that. Yet my father made it happen.

And then there was the rumor I'd snuck into the academy disguised as a boy to draw from live models. An artist in Milan concocted the story to discredit me. Furious, my father did what he could to dispel speculation, but it kept cropping up wherever we went. When we traveled to Florence, he had to go to battle all over again because the artists there refused me entrance to their galleries. They argued I belonged at home, caring for a family, not laboring for money. I'm relieved to see Lady Wentworth is more supportive.

"And your mother?" she says. "Is she in Venice too?"

As I shake my head, I withdraw my eyes to the dark surface of the water.

Mama was always my strongest advocate. Yet she never asked me to paint nor told me to become a painter. In her eyes, her daughter simply *was* an artist. Whenever I brought her a sketch, even a rough one, she set aside what she was doing and admired it.

I often woke to visions of colors swirling in my head. When they wouldn't go away, I cried out.

She rushed to take me in her arms. "They're like paint," she whispered. "Soon you'll put them into the prettiest pictures."

We were living in Milan when she died. For three years, I'd been painting portraits of the nobility. They were unsophisticated pictures, but my clients were too taken by the novelty to notice. And I loved the chance to paint. The fact that I was paid made it even more thrilling.

Then suddenly the thrill was gone. My father and I couldn't bear to stay by ourselves in Milan, so we returned to the hamlet his family called home—Schwarzenberg, in the Bergenz Forest. He slept with the goatherds in Uncle Michel's barn, while I shared a bed with two cousins. Life in the alpine village cut a sharp contrast with what I'd grown accustomed to, and my grief gave way to resentment. One evening, my oldest cousin arrived late for supper. He came straight from the goat shed, smelling of manure, and sat down beside me. When he handed me his plate, expecting me to serve him, it was more than I could take.

"What's next?" I cried. "Will I have to dine with the goats?"

They were harsh words. I knew that as soon as I said them, yet I was too proud to do anything but drop my napkin and flee the room. My father followed. He demanded I apologize, then go to church and confess. Although I often went to church in those days, it was to paint frescos, not to think about my sins. That night, however, I was so afraid for my soul I couldn't sleep.

As it turned out, the parish priest did what my father couldn't: help me find the love beneath my grief. Mama was in heaven, he assured me, but her love would live on forever.

I vowed to attend church regularly, a vow that was immediately challenged by the weather. But I didn't let it deter me. When the roads became impassable by carriage, I rose before daybreak and trudged for three hours in snow over my knees to attend mass. This backbone of faith, I came to see, was my mother's lasting gift.

* *

"She died when I was fifteen," I say as soon as I can speak again. "My father and I have been traveling together ever since."

Lady Wentworth reaches out and touches my arm. "I'm so sorry! That's a difficult life."

"Perhaps. But it suits me," I say, sitting taller. She doesn't need to know how difficult it really is. "There have been strokes of luck as well. Like when the governor of Milan granted me permission to visit the private galleries whenever I wished."

"What an honor."

"Yes. No woman before that could copy in the galleries."

I explain that I painted my first portrait when I was eight. I discovered I could take one look at a person's face and know their true character. My first patron of real importance was the Bishop of Como, when I was eleven. His portrait was so successful that I was showered with commissions. My father had to start refusing some so I wouldn't neglect my lessons. When we moved to Milan, it was the same. After I painted the Duchess of Modena, all the nobility wanted portraits. "Since then," I say, "it's been my livelihood."

"So you will specialize in portraits?"

"Oh no, I want to be much more than a portrait painter!" As I say this, I can't help but notice her raised eyebrows. Like everyone else, she thinks women painters can do portraits—and those interminable still lifes—while history painting is the exclusive domain of men.

I ignore the eyebrows. "I'm going to be a history painter. That's why I've studied Greek and Roman mythology. In Rome, I received commissions for history paintings of Penelope, Coriolanus, and Bacchus and Ariadne. Nothing excites me more than making my own interpretations. And of course the range of color I can use is much greater than for portraits."

"My goodness, I had no idea." Despite her eyebrows, she clearly values spunk. "So you've studied anatomy?"

She's assuming, of course, that to paint male gods and heroes, I must have a detailed knowledge of their anatomy. "That hasn't been possible," I say. "However, I don't believe life drawing is necessary to create aesthetically pleasing figures."

"So how did you learn to paint figures?"

I explain that with my father's help, I devised a method. First I worked on what I could see: the head and hands and feet. The rest I learned from copying plaster reliefs of classical sculptures. I hesitate, but only for a second. "I'd love to paint you as a goddess."

"Which one?"

"Aphrodite, in robes of white and gold." That was how I'd hoped to paint my mother; I don't suggest it lightly.

She smiles broadly. "The goddess of love! With my daughter as an angel by my side."

I'm pleased she speaks my language.

"I'd love for you to be my guide in the galleries," she says as we pass the Doge's Palace, its long row of slender columns and arches like spiderly legs crawling over the dark waters. "If it weren't so late, I'd suggest stopping now."

I tell her I could get used to a life with time to visit galleries just for the fun of it.

"Art lectures are so dull," she says, eyes fluttering to emphasize her point. "I'd rather go with you so I can learn the secrets of each painting."

"I'd love that, my Lady!"

"My dear Angelica," she says with sudden intensity, "if we're to become friends, you must call me Bridget." She holds out both hands, inviting me to withdraw mine from under the blanket and place them in hers.

I do so.

"I'm so happy we've met," she says. "I've always wanted to know what it's like to be a woman *and* an artist. You must enlighten me."

Her warm hands pull me under a spell of intimacy that's hard to resist. I want to lean into her, feel her arms enfold me, as I share with her the world I live in. Yet how can I describe the life of an artist to someone who has no talent of her own? I could say I stand apart, an observer to record history, character, emotion. That I offer my interpretations but don't have the privilege of plunging into life myself. Or perhaps I should say I live more fully than others, that living at the apex of creation heightens color and texture and the very light of which images are born. I'm not sure which is truer. Sometimes I feel separate from the world. Like today, struggling in the church. Other times, it seems art and life will consume me.

Of course, being female complicates all this. Which isn't to say that's how I experience myself when I'm painting. My eyes aren't female when they perceive color. My hand holding the brush isn't gendered. Though I haven't yet figured out what it means to paint with one's soul, I do know it can't be done by a man or a woman. That would be too constrained. I think about this often, but most people don't. They just see me as feminine and flimsy and capricious, incapable of making my artistic mark on the world. And they make sure I don't forget that.

"Tell me," Bridget coaxes, "what do you do when you're not working? An artist's life must be lonely. Who are your friends? And the man at the church—are you engaged?"

Her last question jolts me back to my senses. "I'd never marry Antonio!"

"Antonio?"

"The man at the church. I assure you, I'd never marry him."

"You're right," she says, smiling. "He's too old and not nearly good enough for you." If she is referring to his ill-tempered behavior earlier, she's too polite to do so directly.

"In any case," I say, "I'm not interested in marriage." There is no reason for her to think I'm unmarried because I lack suitors, when the truth is I chose to devote myself to painting. Besides, I'm not willing to give up my right to the money I earn. Not to mention the right to own my paintings. I might as well give up my power to breathe.

Her eyebrows rise again. "Surely someone as attractive—"

"Of course there've been a few," I say, anticipating her point. "But in Milan, after my mother died, I swore off the idea of marriage. So much work is required if one intends to paint masterpieces. As I do. I won't have time for a husband."

"You value your independence."

I nod. "You could say I'm married to my brush."

Bridget throws back her head and laughs with such glee I have to join in. "I'm so happy we've met," she says again. "You're going to be a breath of fresh air in my life—in all of society. As to your wild ideas about remaining a spinster . . . we'll see about that."

Our gondola stops before an iron gate. Willow boughs overhang one side, almost touching the water. A servant swings open the gate, revealing a flight of marble steps leading to a path, illuminated by a string of lanterns, that winds up through a terraced garden.

As we step out of the gondola, the wave from a passing boat catches us. Bridget grabs my arm just in time to save me from a swift dip in the canal. We both whirl around to see who caused the turbulence.

It's the man from the church, looking back at us as his boat speeds into the darkness. I see the faint glint of the ruby on his hand, which he is holding over his heart.

With a giggle, Bridget waves to him. "That's Count Frederick de Horn, a friend of my husband. Intriguing man. He likes to visit us, so you'll meet him soon."

"He's in mourning?"

"His mother died recently."

I want to say he doesn't act like someone in mourning. But I can't substantiate the feeling. "I've met him already" is all I say.

Three

Bridget climbs the steps, and I follow. At the top, we come to a long, narrow reflecting pool; at its far end, two marble goddesses perpetually pour out the contents of their Grecian urns. A servant takes our cloaks as we walk into the entrance hall.

Bridget grabs my hand and leads me through a series of rooms, each more elegantly furnished than the one before, until we come to a room arranged as a gallery. A large painting on a gilt easel occupies the place of honor. "When you spoke of history painting," she says, "I knew you had to see this."

I approach the masterpiece. "Another Titian?"

She nods. "Do you like it?"

It's most likely a copy, but so expertly done I can't tell for certain. The blues of its sky and sea blend with the room's Prussian blue walls, creating the impression we stand within the painting. Ariadne stretches a hand toward her departing lover, while her head swivels back toward Bacchus as he leaps from his chariot, robes lifting like crimson wings behind him. Copy or not, the scene is breathtaking.

"Now, that's true love!" I exclaim.

To my surprise, Bridget is skeptical.

I tell her I know the story well, having painted it for a British patron. Bacchus falls in love with Ariadne after Theseus has broken her heart. My favorite part is when Bacchus, having promised his beloved the heavens, takes her crown and places it among the stars.

"Ah, I wondered why there were stars in a blue sky." Bridget studies the canvas as if viewing it for the first time. It occurs to me she isn't used to the deeper meaning of art. Her pride in this painting is based on the artist's fame.

Since she asked me to be her guide, I explain. "The stars symbolize enduring love—"

"I see *his* love," she cuts in. "But she doesn't love him. Look at her. She still longs for Theseus."

I smile. Clearly Bridget is a quick learner. "Perhaps the artist believes Bacchus's love is enough for both of them. See how Titian has lit up his chest, so he shines like the rising sun. No nearby heart could possibly resist him." I choose my words carefully so Bridget won't think I'm contradicting her. "Surely such love will endure."

Suddenly a clock begins to strike.

"Come!" Bridget says. "The ambassador is waiting, and we're late for supper."

My own first encounter with love was anything but enduring. It was a love affair with music. It happened while my father and I were staying at the Count of Montfort's castle in Milan after my mother's death. Because it was a skill she'd taught me, I began to play the clavichord and sing. During the day, I painted portraits of the count's family; after sundown, I sat at the keyboard.

One evening, as I reached the refrain of a melody, I heard a baritone blending with my soprano. I looked up to see dark curls disappear through the parlor door. "Wait!" I called.

I was halfway to the door when his head poked back in. "You sing like an angel," he said.

Raphael was a musician. And charming. He had a habit of tossing his head so one of his unruly curls would flip over and rejoin the rest. He was staying at the castle for a while and suggested we practice together.

Every evening, we worked on something new, and layer by layer, my grief dissolved in song. Then one night, he thrust some sheets of music into my hands. "Our madrigals are lovely," he said, "but your voice can do much more."

I took one look at the complex notation and passed it back to him.

But he was adamant I was ready for his favorite Monteverdi arias. So we began with Orpheus and Eurydice. After a few weeks, he had us giving open-air concerts in the castle's courtyard. Which meant additional time practicing. I wasn't sure which I liked more: our singing or the kiss he implanted on my lips at the end of each evening.

All this meant less time to paint.

"Come to Rome with me," he coaxed. "You'll have a brilliant career as an opera singer."

"And give up painting?"

"You don't have to. Just shift your focus. Let your art become what your music is now."

He was persuasive. And I was tempted. Maybe it was possible to love both art and music.

He steered me to an armchair in the parlor, across from the clavichord. "Close your eyes and picture yourself on stage. The velvet curtain is rising. Your costume is stunning. When you sing, the crowd is spellbound. Night after night, thousands flock to see you, to hear you. You're a star in the world of opera seria, so full of drama and passion!"

My eyes flew open. "A woman could do that?"

He explained that not all the principal roles go to musici, who have sacrificed their bodies for the sake of a career in opera. Kneeling before me, he took my hands in his and raised them to his lips, kissing first one, then the other. "You'll love it. Besides, the stage offers more money than you'll ever receive as a painter."

I withdrew my hands. "I have to talk to my father first."

Much as I prized my independence, I was seventeen. I needed Papa's consent. However, when I went to him, I discovered Raphael had already persuaded him that opera would give me fame and fortune. Still, the final decision was mine to make.

Deciding between two loves is always difficult. It's hard enough to choose between two people; choosing between two parts of oneself is even harder. So I went to a priest for advice.

"You fell in love with music," he said with a smile. "And you already love painting."

"Yes, father." I couldn't tell if he was laughing at me.

But his reply was serious. "You're fortunate to have two gifts. Few people are so blessed. However, I can say with certainty that you won't be satisfied in the world of the stage. Actors and singers have habits that will tarnish your good name and make it impossible for you to attend mass. Choosing such a life will take you away from your faith."

He spoke to the needs of my soul. If I went to Rome with Raphael, I'd be forced to forget about painting for God. When I explained this to my father, he was easily won over. The difficult moment was telling Raphael.

When I sat down to practice that evening, he strode into the room. He had no idea I'd seen the priest or that my father had changed his mind. "So," he demanded, "when do we leave?"

"I'm not going to Rome," I said, as if there'd never been a question. "I will travel with my father and learn everything I can about painting."

This time when he flicked his unruly curls, all the charm was gone. I'd seen his handsome face for weeks but never noticed how he looked down his nose at me.

So ended my first love affair. It was never a serious flirtation with Raphael; it was a flirtation with music. In the end, it set the course of my life as an artist. I knew every breath God gave me I would use for painting. And there was one unexpected boon. I had taken for granted that it was only a matter of time before I married. Every woman married. It was expected. That changed when I saw how readily my life could have gone in a direction I would have regretted. If Raphael or Antonio—or any other man—were my husband, I would have to submit to his decisions. He could force me to stop painting. That can never be! I am first and foremost an artist. And for that matter, free to flirt with whomever I choose. Even if Bacchus himself placed a crown on my head—or among the stars, should I be so honored—that wouldn't sway my heart.

I smile at Catherine, seated across from me, as I pull my napkin from its swan-shaped ring and lay it on my lap. It's almost an insult to put such exquisitely embroidered linen on my woolen skirt. Before sitting down, I rubbed the worst of the russet red stains from my hands, then folded back my cuffs so the splatters wouldn't be so visible. But my painter's dress is still just that.

Catherine grins back. She was allowed to dine with the grown-ups so she could meet the artist, while her younger brother was whisked off to bed by the governess.

Bridget turns to the ambassador. "Now the children have someone with whom they can speak English."

He immediately addresses me in English, inquiring how I became so fluent.

A short, stout man, he is John Murray. I gathered from Bridget, as we rushed to the dining hall, that he is her second husband. The first, from whom she inherited her title and her wealth, died years ago.

"My mother taught me English, French, and Italian. And of course German," I say, wishing my English was more polished. And that I wasn't gobbling the truffle-laced princisgrass quite so feverishly. My hunger returned with a vengeance at the sight of such lavish food.

"She's also fluent in the language of color," Bridget adds. "I've asked her to paint my portrait. She should paint yours as well."

After dinner, Bridget and I retire to her drawing room to discuss the commission. There will be three portraits: one of her, one of the ambassador, one of Catherine. Everything I need will be provided. All that remains is my father's signature confirming the financial details.

Then it's time to go home. Bridget is about to call a servant to bring my cloak, but stops herself. "What am I thinking?" she exclaims. "You can't leave till you've seen your room!"

We've already decided the Prussian blue room will serve as my studio, so I'm confused.

"I mean *your* room," she says, "where you can take rest whenever you wish."

She leads me up two flights of stairs, across the upper landing, and into a bedroom that is twice the size of the apartment I share with my father. A four-poster bed with pink drapery dominates the décor; pink-and-white satin hangs from the windows. An alcove with a cedar chest serves as a dressing room.

Speechless, I approach the poudreuse and pick up a gold comb. As I run it through a lock of tangled hair, my reflection in the looking glass stares back in astonishment.

Bridget throws open the doors of a tall armoire and lifts out an emerald green gown. "I used to be as slim as you. I'd be honored if you'd wear what no longer fits me. With any needed alterations, of course." Clucking her approval, she lays the gown over my wool outfit, then grabs my shoulders and holds me at arm's length. The gown falls to the floor. "Angelica, are those tears?"

I can't deny it.

"Happy tears, I hope. Or are you Ariadne, mourning a love from your past?"

Smiling through my tears, I bend to retrieve the green bundle. "I think I'm remembering my future. Is that possible?"

Four

Our small kitchen appears to have shrunk. What felt cozy before seems cramped. The rough floorboards don't receive my step the way the ambassador's Persian carpets did; the solitary lamp casts deep shadows that create a dinginess I never noticed before. Antonio has pushed aside their dirty dishes to make room on the table for his engraving, while my father is nailing new soles onto the buckled shoes he's worn since we left Schwarzenberg. They look up in unison when I enter.

Antonio lays aside his burin. "Well?"

"Our friend is afraid you're leaving us for good," my father says with a chuckle, then mumbles under his breath, "God help me, these shoes need more than resoling."

"Don't be silly," I say. "Where could I possibly go?" Out of habit, I begin to clear the table and heat water for their dishes. The two men listen as I describe the gondola ride, the Prussian blue room, the swan-shaped napkin rings, the truffle-laced princisgrass.

Antonio demands a drawing of the swan so he can improve upon the ring's design. After I've scrubbed the dishes, I sit down and oblige him with a sketch.

Meanwhile my father presses for more specifics. This is the first time I've interviewed a new client on my own, and he wants to be sure I covered everything. He listens as I describe the canvas sizes and compositions, as well as payment schedule for each, then praises my business sense and promises to call on Bridget tomorrow to give his signature.

"She's expecting you," I say.

Antonio is pleased with the swan but doesn't share our excitement about the commission. He tries to conceal his fear beneath a barrage of questions: "What about the *Assumption*? Won't you even try to finish it? What will Morosco say? I thought you gave him your word?"

But I'm in too good a mood to let him spoil it. As I pick up a towel and dry their dishes, I explain that the copy will be finished as promised. Morosco will see it was worth the wait. "And guess what?" I say, wheeling around to face them.

"What?" My father is eager for more.

"Bridget gave me a closetful of gowns!"

"Hand-me-downs." Antonio curls his lip. "I hope that isn't how she's paying you."

"Of course not," I say.

"Sounds like she'll pay better than Morosco," my father adds.

"Well, you'd better paint fast," Antonio says. "Before she returns to England."

"She said nothing about leaving," I say with finality, before the idea can take root in my father's mind. England won't be on our itinerary for some time.

My father delivers a friendly cuff to the side of Antonio's head, then retires to his chair by the fireplace. I pull up a footstool so I can lean against his knee while we watch the flames.

"Remember," I say after a while, "how I complained in Schwarzenberg about dining with a goatherd? No one guessed then I'd be dining with the British ambassador."

From across the room, Antonio shoots me a piercing look. "Who says you won't dine with a goatherd again?"

"Say what you want," I shoot back. "I'm the one who dined with the ambassador."

At the first sign of light, I throw open the shutters on the gabled window at the foot of my bed and look out over the city. In Venice, the sun rises and sets to the sound of trumpets. Church bells ring, clocks chime. Listening to this symphony and watching the dawn colors spread across the sky, I know I can finish copying the *Assumption* in very little time.

In fact, as soon as I pick up my brush in the Frari, it flies between my palette and the canvas. The Virgin's figure, the pink clouds, the angels and cherubim—everything comes to life. If the church is cold and dank, I don't notice. Nor does my stomach ask for food. I'm feasting on the thrill of creation.

In the evenings, I'm still full of energy. After an hour of sketching, I stay up to play music, something I haven't done in ages. We don't have a clavichord, but I play my zither and sing. Antonio makes a good-faith effort to set aside his resentment—along with his etching tools—and drums time with his fingers on the table.

At the end of the week, my painting is delivered to Giuseppe Morosco, and the final payment is in my father's pocket. Our hardships are over. After settling the rent and restocking the pantry, I buy a pair of boots for him and some paints for myself. I even willingly set aside my own share of resentments and cook a chestnut pudding, Antonio's favorite.

I will never take on another reproduction. Not if I can help it. This is my vow to myself.

I will paint only portraits and original history paintings. I will live for my passion, for my art. I will discover what it means to paint for God. Whatever people think I might be able to accomplish, I will accomplish that and more.

Five

There are no mistakes. Or so I think as I ride in the carriage Bridget sent to pick me up. It is the morning of the thirtieth of October, my twenty-fourth birthday. How fitting to spend it starting the new painting.

After a heavy nighttime downpour, the sun is out. The horses seem to be prancing higher than usual; even the old cobblestones look fresh and new. I marvel at the perfection of everything. If I wasn't copying in the chilly church, I'd never have met Bridget. If Morosco's painting was finished on time, this new commission wouldn't be mine.

Not that Antonio would see the perfection. In every situation, he looks to expose the lack, the less than, the inevitable loss. Maybe that explains why he never married: He would see only the faults of his bride.

Of course, I won't marry either. But for entirely different reasons.

Resting on the carriage pillows, I allow myself to daydream. One day my father and I will have a house with a large studio and a separate room for people to view my work. My art will be shown in all the major galleries. I'll be free to choose any subject I love. All the Greek gods and goddesses, heroes and heroines, will take up residence in my studio. I'll converse with them, laugh with them, clothe them in every color imaginable.

It doesn't end there. One day a stranger will visit. Though we've never met, the bittersweetness in his eyes is oddly familiar. I can't help but feel he possesses something I've waited a long time for. He walks around my studio and studies all the paintings. Through his eyes, they come alive as never before. And so do I when he reaches for my hand.

Yet this is not a courtship—not in the way people view courtship. No. It's a meeting of free and unfettered spirits, far superior to any marriage. In the eyes of the world, he may be a man and I a woman, but together we are so much more.

Bridget is still in her dressing room when I arrive. A servant offers to take me to the pink-and-white guest room, but I insist on going straight to the Prussian blue room. As Bridget promised, an easel with fresh canvas awaits in the far corner, behind Ariadne and Bacchus. Because it's warm, the windows have been thrown open. Sunlight floods the room.

As I finish preparing my palette, Bridget appears in a gown with floral embroidery and deeply scooped neckline. Her hair is piled high, woven with satin ribbons. She's even more beautiful than before.

She kisses me on both cheeks, enveloping me with rose perfume. "I trust you've found everything you need."

"It's perfect," I say, inhaling her scent as I help her lower herself into a chair by the window. "I hope you don't mind sitting still."

"Of course not." She makes her hands limp so I can arrange them holding her fan half open on her lap. "Patience is a small price to pay to see oneself as a goddess, wouldn't you say?"

I correct her: She won't become a goddess quite yet. First I'll do a sketch; if that pleases her, we'll proceed with the portrait. Only after that will I start on a history painting.

"Even so, I'll be in good company, won't I?" She starts to giggle but stops when she realizes it disrupts her pose. "I mean the company of the great ones you've already painted: the Bishop of Como, the Duchess of Modena, the Count of Montfort, Herr Winckelmann."

Vanity has a funny habit of playing in the minds of my sitters. Most expect me to make them more striking or more beautiful; some want me to make them more famous. Whatever Bridget may want, it will be hard to make her more lovely than she already is. As my chalk caresses the oval of her face, then lingers in the soft hollow of her cheek, before sliding down to stroke her lips, I feel certain no one will be able to avoid falling in love when they see this portrait.

My preference is to work quietly, without the distraction of a conversation. Of course, that's difficult for the sitter. It doesn't take Bridget long to break our silence. "Antonio looked upset when you left with me," she says. "Has he come around yet?"

"He'll have to accept it," I say equivocally. Though he's been amenable of late, I suspect he still harbors resentment.

"The Italians like to keep their art for themselves," she continues, as if neither of us is Italian. In fact, with such an itinerant life, I no longer have a clear sense of my nationality.

"It's pride," I say, speaking about Antonio, not all Italians.

"Perhaps. Or a sense of superiority over British artists. In any case, you'll find we British are better patrons. We'll give you more substantial commissions, pay you more as well."

I tell her I appreciate that and describe the portraits I did for British travelers in Italy. "The one of David Garrick," I say, "was my first work exhibited in London."

"So you've been to England?"

"Only my paintings."

"How sad not to be there and see the public's reaction," she says.

"But you've given me an idea: I'd like to unveil this portrait at our grand ball next month. Can it be ready?"

I tell her it can if I work as late as light permits each evening.

"Even if it isn't," she says, "you must come. All of Venice will be here. You'll meet so many intriguing people."

The way she says *intriguing*, with a glint in her eye, brings to mind the man in mourning. That was how she described him. I've been so busy I had almost forgot about him.

"Can you keep a secret?" she says suddenly.

I assure her I can.

"No one knows yet," she says, "but my husband will be transferred to Constantinople in the new year, while I take the children to England."

This might be a secret, but it's hardly welcome news. When Antonio hears it, he'll have the satisfaction of saying he told me so. Hiding my disappointment, I promise to complete all the necessary sittings before they leave. "Surely," I add, "you'd rather go with him."

"Heavens no!" she exclaims, her fan sliding to the floor as she clasps her hands. "Can you picture me in such a barbarous country? And with children?"

As I pick up the fan and guide her back into her pose, I explain that, for me, Turkey is alluring. The legacy of ancient Greece is very much alive there. Troy, the setting for one of my favorite history painting subjects—the Trojan War—isn't far from Constantinople. I hope my father and I can include that part of the world in our travels.

She chuckles. "You aren't thinking like a mother yet."

I acknowledge I'm not. Nor will I ever be, since I don't plan on marrying.

She gives a little snort. "You'll see it differently soon enough. But that's not what I want to discuss—" She pauses so deliberately that I automatically stop drawing. "Angelica, I'd like you to come to London with me."

I'm stunned.

"It's the best place for your career," she continues. "And for you personally. Our house on Charles Street has plenty of studio space. I'll introduce you to so many new patrons."

"You want me to go to London?" I echo.

She trains her eye on me, watching for the idea to catch hold. She knows all the artists, she tells me: Joshua Reynolds, William Chambers, Joseph Wilton, and so many others. It will be the opportunity of a lifetime. "Since no one knows yet that we're leaving, please don't mention this," she adds. "All I ask is that you think about it."

I turn back to my sketch in an effort to contain my excitement. This is a secret worth hearing! I can't think of anything more momentous than going to England with Bridget. Yet the terms must suit both my father and me. "Your confidence in me is humbling," I say. "But I have duties here."

"I know," she says. "I'm not asking you to shirk your duties. Still, this is the modern age. A woman can be independent—especially someone like you, a gifted artist. You can't be subservient if you want to make your mark on the world."

"I'm not afraid of independence," I say, pleased she values a woman's liberty. "My father always gives his input, but I make the important decisions about my career. It's just that he's getting older and needs me to care for him."

"And you will!" She proposes I accompany her to London so I can get established. When I'm ready, my father can join me; in the meantime, she'll see to it that he is well looked after.

I put down my chalk and face Bridget. "In that case, how could I refuse?"

"I knew you'd agree!" She jumps up and embraces me, bathing me in rose perfume, then announces she can't sit still a moment longer and invites me for tea in the garden. "The ambassador is busy with Count de Horn," she says. "But you'll stay, won't you?"

I tell her my father isn't expecting me until evening.

She is already halfway to the door. "This afternoon, I'm going to the piazza. Perhaps you can put on a nice gown and come with me. Afterwards we can stop at a gallery."

"Today is—" I blurt out.

"Is what?"

I confess it is my birthday. I can't imagine a better way to celebrate.

As we leave the gallery, the lace overskirt on the blue gown I chose from the cedar closet swishes around my ankles like froth on the crest of a satin wave. I'm swimming in sumptuousness. But it's not just the dress. With Bridget, I'm happier than I've ever been.

"Look!" I say playfully, pointing across the piazza. "There's the Virgin."

Shielding the sunlight with her gloved hand, she looks at the steps beneath the central arch of the basilica, where a mother is cradling her infant. Then she laughs in the uproarious fashion I'm learning to recognize as her mark of approval. "You're so right! And there," she says, gesturing to a man behind them, "is Joseph, exactly where he should be." As we walk arm in arm, she finds a mythical or biblical character for each person I point out. It's as though we are gliding through a Renaissance painting, not the modern Venetian piazza.

Wandering farther, we come to a shop selling ornaments. "The owner looks like he stepped out of a Rembrandt painting," Bridget says as she peers inside.

Looking over her shoulder, I recognize Giuseppe Morosco. "He's one of my patrons," I say. "Let's go in."

Morosco looks surprised to see me dressed so elegantly, in such distinguished company. As we inspect his wares, Bridget picks up a silver beaded necklace. She runs it back and forth through her fingers, then hands Morosco a gold piece.

"I haven't forgotten your birthday," she says, easing the chain over my head. "Please accept this as a token of my love."

I vow to wear it always.

In response, she throws her arms around me. As we hug, the chain snaps, sending silver beads cascading across the floor.

"Oh!" she cries. "What have I done?"

"Nothing that can't be fixed," I say, scrambling to gather the beads. "Now your love is everywhere. That must be a good omen, don't you think?"

Six

Antonio's eyes follow me around the kitchen as I prepare pease pudding for supper. "Something is different about you," he says finally. "What is it?"

"She's twenty-four," Papa says. "My child has grown up."

"It's more than that."

I say nothing, having promised Bridget not to mention her—our—trip to London. I intend to tell my father when we're alone.

"What aren't you telling us?" Antonio persists. "Is it some gentleman?"

I repress a giggle. "No."

Antonio takes my giggle as all the evidence he needs: One day at the Wentworth estate and I've been seduced. He slams his hand on the table so forcefully the bowls jump. "John Joseph, you must put a stop to this! Your daughter's reputation will be ruined if you let these people take advantage of her."

My father tries to make peace. "Antonio has a point," he says. "You decided against a career on the stage because you didn't want to risk your good name. Have you forgotten?"

I set the pudding on the table and frown at my father. I know how to conduct myself; he should know that. More importantly, he should have more trust in me. "Nothing dishonorable happened," I say. "Our friend is jealous, that's all."

"Maybe nothing yet," Antonio concedes. "But you're withholding something."

I look from one to the other. Both are genuinely concerned—so much so, they haven't touched their food. Besides, their suspicions aren't completely unfounded, "All right . . ." I say slowly.

"I told you something's up!" Antonio is triumphant.

Surely Bridget didn't mean for me to keep a secret from my family, and Antonio is practically family. "Yes," I say. "But you must swear not to say a word."

They agree.

"Bridget invited me to go to London in the new year."

"Incredible!" my father exclaims. "We've always wanted to go to England."

Antonio is as sullen as my father is exhilarated. I ignore him. As we eat, I convey Bridget's assurance that, with what I can earn in London, we will never want again. I will go with her right away, and Papa will follow. We can spend a few years in London while I make a name for myself, then return to Italy and enjoy our wealth. Rome will always be our final destination.

Antonio's pout turns to panic. "You'll never come back. The ambassador and his wife have bought you. It's your life, your soul, your special talent you are selling," he rants. "You women are all alike: You'll give up everything for a little admiration."

"Stop the nonsense, Zucchi!" For once Papa is stern. "My daughter has a right to her success. If you can't lend your support—"

"I'm sorry," Antonio says before my father can complete his sentence. "It's true. I am jealous, as you said, Angelica. I will always prefer you in your old dress, not borrowed silks. I want you to stay as you are—more at home with goatherds than ambassadors."

I'm tempted to say, *You just want me for yourself, but that will never be.* Instead I accept his apology. I lay a hand on his shoulder and ask that we please set aside our strife for now.

My father welcomes the truce. He lights extra candles to make the kitchen more festive, then pulls out a package and hands it to me. "Tonight we celebrate your birthday. Tomorrow there'll be time to think about London."

Lying in bed, I'm so excited I can't sleep. It was a glorious birthday, ending with the exquisitely carved paint case my father made for me. He watched as I placed in it everything from the old box with its splintered lid. Now it will go with me to London, the city of infinite possibilities for an artist.

When I finally fall asleep, colors swirl in my head, so vivid and unrelenting that I feel like a child again. Just as I am about to call out to Mama for comfort, the colors coalesce into a painting. It is Bridget's portrait.

"Perfect!" she cries when I show her. "Now you must meet the queen."

Some doors swing open, and the queen is ushered in.

She walks straight to me. "Who are *you*?"

I make a deep curtsy. "Angelica Kauffman, Your Majesty."

When I raise my head to see if my work pleases her, she is staring at me unsmiling. I didn't expect that. I'm wearing the emerald gown from Bridget's cedar closet; surely its elegance must please the queen, even if my painting does not.

Then I see it. A large muddy stain runs from the hem up to my waist. And hanging in the air all around us, the unmistakable stench of goat manure.

London

Seven

London, 1766

I stand before the easel in my new studio—the first time I've had a studio to call mine—unable to keep the smile off my face. It's hard to believe I was toiling over copies in a cold church just eight months ago. So much has changed.

Not only is it a pleasant June morning, but the colors on my canvas give ample cause to smile. The greens of field and forest, blues of stream and sky, silvery white where mist meets mountain—all shine brilliantly in Arcadia, land of the gods. As I apply a ruddy blush to the cheeks of two shepherds, I recall my vow to paint the sun. Now that sun is shining on these shepherds' faces. The painting isn't sold yet, but I'm not worried.

We've been in London less than a fortnight and already I feel at home. Antonio took my father to Schwarzenberg in a carriage the ambassador loaned us before leaving for Constantinople. Although I miss my father, I know he's being well cared for.

"I'll write when I find a house big enough for us both," I promised as we parted.

"Have mercy on me!" he exclaimed. "I need a letter before that."

"You worry more than Antonio," I teased. "Of course I'll write as soon as I arrive. But we must be patient. I need to establish a clientele before we can afford our own home. If everything works out, you can come within the year."

So far, everything is working out perfectly. I've been given all I could possibly need to settle into Bridget's stately house on Charles Street. My bedroom is next to Catherine's and looks out over the bustling town. It takes but a minute to run down the back stairs to my studio, an oval room with light streaming through the south-facing windows. It also has a small foyer where clients can wait, and its own side entrance, so they can come and go without disturbing the household.

Not that Bridget seems to care about being disturbed. Never has anyone pampered me so much. She looks after me as she might a younger sister—even a daughter—popping her head into my studio at all hours of the day to see if the servants have refilled the water pitcher, or dropping off a basket of warm crumpets if she thinks I rushed off too quickly after a meal.

She has promised to introduce me to Joshua Reynolds and other artists as soon as she is rested enough. In the meantime, she's spreading word among her friends about the painter she brought from Venice. Some immediately came to request a portrait. Of course, Bridget didn't let them leave until they'd viewed the mother-of-pearl cutlery the ambassador gave her as a farewell present and the ostrich feather hat she herself picked up for a song in Verona.

On the first day of our journey from Venice, we traveled as far as Verona. Having been delayed by heavy rain, it was already dark when we reached our lodgings. I stood in the courtyard as people darted about unloading trunks, carting away luggage, and dodging stray dogs, while the horses stomped impatiently for their feedbags. Traveling with Papa was a much simpler affair.

The governess led Catherine and her brother to bed. With so much to discover, I wasn't ready to follow, so I wandered into the road, deserted at that hour, and from there down a side street. I didn't tell Bridget because I didn't expect to go far. Passing between the rows of houses, avoiding puddles and loose cobblestones, I came to an ancient bridge spanning the Adige River. Its massive yet elegant structure was worthy of a history painting. Maybe a scene from the Trojan War. I walked out to the middle to experience it more fully.

Beneath me, the river was wild, driven by the storm. I closed my eyes and listened to its roar. *My life is like this*, I thought. *Churned up. Yet I feel the power of God in its churning.* I opened my eyes, and raising my head toward the starless sky, reaffirmed my vow to put to use the talents I've been given. To paint for God! Yes, I may laugh and converse and entertain myself along with everyone, but within my heart, I will never forget what really matters.

Just then, a man came out of a tavern and stumbled onto the bridge, so I gathered my skirts and ran back to the inn.

Bridget was waiting. "Where were you? We searched all over!"

I apologized for alarming her. "I was enjoying the night. Isn't it incredible?"

I expected her to share my feeling; after all, she'd done nothing but encourage my freedom. Instead she was stern. "You belong to *our* family now. You can't go running off alone."

"But I've gone off alone my entire life."

"You're a person of consequence now," she said, then softened her words with a wry smile. "There is a price to pay for that privilege."

When she put it that way, without her usual sisterly caring, I knew better than to argue. Artists must defer to the wishes of a patron. Always, in all situations. My father taught me that.

Since that night, Bridget's words have continued to echo in my life. Privilege, it appears, wants to change me in more ways than I imagined. I don't even look the same. Before leaving Venice, I gave all my old, torn, stained frocks to charity; now I wear only the elegant gowns I inherited from Bridget. There's a different one for every day of the week—no, every day of a fortnight. In the studio, I cover each dress with an apron stitched by Bridget's dressmaker.

I'm glad Bridget has seen fit to be more intimate again. At times, I almost forget she's my patron. In the late evenings, she calls me to her bedroom and shows me how to wear my hair more stylishly, twisted over a hairpiece, as she does, or puts the ostrich feather hat on my head so I can see how au courant I look. All the while, she regales me with stories about the famed Mr. Reynolds. With her help, I'll be fully presentable when it's time to meet him. She promises to buy me some of the extra-large pannier hoops that are all the rage. Maneuvering through town in a skirt of such circumference, I'll never fail to remember that I'm a person of consequence.

The door to my studio swings open and Catherine rushes in. A servant follows with a vase of red peonies, which he sets on the table by the window.

She dances around me like a bee around a bouquet. "Who's your secret admirer?"

"I didn't know I had one."

"Please," she coaxes, "tell me. I won't tell a soul."

"Truly, I don't know. But let's find out." I pull a small envelope from the flowers, open it and remove a piece of parchment, and hand it to her.

She stands still long enough to read: "'To my dear Miss Kauffman. Until we meet again. ND.'" She looks at me, puzzled. "Who's ND?"

"I have an idea."

Catherine knows when it's impolite to press further. "Whoever he is, he must admire you," she says, handing back the note. "Mama says you're going to be the most admired woman in all of London."

"As long as they admire my paintings too," I say with a smile. I enjoy Catherine's company, especially since I'll never have a child of my own. She hasn't shown much interest in sketching, but she's always keen to examine my canvases. I ask what she sees now.

She studies the scene, then says, "Those are the children we saw in Verona, the day Mama found her ostrich feather hat."

I tell her I'm painting them as shepherds in Arcadia. When she wants to hear more, I drop into the armchair where I place my sitters and explain: "Pan was the god of shepherds. He had horns and a goat's body and always played his reed pipes." I pause. "Did you know it was because of those pipes that King Midas got ass's ears?"

She giggles as she shakes her head.

"Apollo, the god of truth, played a silver lyre. But the king preferred Pan's pipes because he played from his heart. In a spate of rage, Apollo gave the king ass's ears."

She giggles more loudly.

"He kept the ears hidden. Only the royal barber knew. One day, the barber couldn't hold the secret any longer, so he dug a hole in the ground and whispered the truth into it. Reeds grew up and whispered that truth to the world." I glance at the cuckoo clock on the mantel. The ambassador found it in Germany, and Bridget gave it to me because I didn't own a timepiece. It's about to announce the noon hour. "That's all for now," I say. "I must get back to painting, and your mother must be wondering where you are."

Catherine turns to leave. At the door, she looks back with a frown. "Apollo is the god of truth, and the king told the truth. It was unfair of him to curse the king."

"Sometimes those who love us don't treat us fairly," I say. "But think of the reeds. They lived by the truth. And that truth is what artists can give to the world."

Alone again, I try to concentrate on the shepherds. I want this to be one of my most accomplished history paintings. If it is finished in time, I will submit it to the annual exhibition of the Society of Artists.

But my attention keeps drifting to the parchment on the table.

When I said I have an idea who ND is, I wasn't being entirely forthright. I have more than an idea. *How much time*, I wonder, *before their giver appears himself?*

Eight

The butler stands inside my studio door, one arm stiffly outstretched, the other equally stiff by his side, and announces: "Master Nathaniel Dance!"

A stocky man in a purple coat and plumed hat follows the arm through the door. With a grin almost as flashy as his feather, he whips off the hat and clasps it to his breast. Then he bounds across the room, seizes my hand, and raises it to his lips. As his nose meets my knuckles, his dark eyes twinkle up at me. "I came as soon as I heard you were in London."

"Your peonies were the perfect calling card," I say, flirting back with a lingering smile.

He presses my hand to his lips a second time. "So you haven't forgotten?"

Of course I haven't forgotten. It was New Year's Eve, when my portrait of Bridget was unveiled and I was presented to all of Venetian society, the night I wore for the first time the emerald green gown. It fit without any need for alteration. Poised above its fashionably low neckline was a crystal pendant, borrowed for the evening and hung on the silver beaded necklace, restrung by Bridget's jeweler. The Prussian blue room had been rearranged, and my canvas installed in the place of honor. Ariadne and Bacchus were spending the evening upstairs in one of the guest rooms.

Bridget told me to stand by her portrait so everyone would know I was the artist, but I preferred to stand by the fireplace so I could observe as people studied it. That didn't mean I was unwilling to talk. Far from it. Every few minutes, Bridget brought someone to meet me. Soon a queue formed with noblemen and clergy, politicians and artists, Germans and Italians. I spoke with all and prayed I'd remember their names and titles when next we met. In case I might not, Antonio was stationed off to one side, making note of every encounter.

At one point, I caught a glimpse of a tall man hovering on the landing of the staircase, his blond hair almost white against his dark coat. It was the intriguing Count Frederick de Horn. Though we both frequented the Wentworth estate, we had yet to meet. I sensed he was waiting for me to be free so he could introduce himself.

As it turned out, I was never free. The portrait was a grand success, and more and more people joined the queue. Then, just as I was hearing from Lady Abernathy about how she ran into David Garrick and his wife at the mud baths near Padua, a pair of hands flew across my face from behind, covering my eyes. Reaching up, I half-expected long, thin male fingers with a ruby ring. But though they were male, the fingers were short and stubby. I felt a flicker of disappointment.

"Give up?" It was a familiar English voice.

Disappointment turned to delight as I peeled away the fingers and turned around. "Nathaniel!" I exclaimed. "I thought you were in England!" Lady Abernathy—the personification of discretion when the situation dictated—backed away, as did others who'd been waiting to speak with me. Even Antonio took a step back.

"You're right, I should be in London." Nathaniel's smile twinkled in his eyes. "But before I left Rome, Herr Winckelmann told me you were here, and I knew I had to see you first."

"Next you go to England?"

"Yes. But now I'm here. With *you!*"

"Me and a hundred other people."

Seeing two more guests approach, he offered his arm and nodded toward the ballroom, where a rousing rigaudon had just begun. "You may have a thousand admirers," he whispered, "but don't dance with anyone but me."

"Dance with Mr. Dance?" I teased. "How could I refuse?"

"That rigaudon's still dancing in my bones," Nathaniel says, as we stand in my London studio. He lets go of my hand and careens around the room, like a wild animal trying to escape its tether, almost colliding with my easel.

"Watch out!" I cry. "I think you've made too much of our little dance."

Abruptly, he stops cavorting. "You know, I still have that sketch you did of me in Rome. I plan to hang it over my fireplace."

"That silly sketch? I couldn't capture your likeness because you wouldn't stop clowning." I make my voice stern, but in truth, I'm enjoying his antics. Seeing him romp in my studio narrows the distance between Italy and England.

"I can be such a bad boy," he says with exaggerated regret, eyes twinkling. "We'll have to remedy that."

I ask what he has in mind.

"Come to my studio and let me paint your portrait. Then I'll sit for you. I promise to obey all your instructions. Fair?"

The chance to improve on my sketch is tempting, but I haven't forgotten my father's admonition not to sit for formal portraits. Informal sketches are fine, but a male artist could try to tamper with my reputation in a formal portrait, which then obviously couldn't be unpainted. This isn't something I wish to worry about, yet if it could jeopardize my career, it can't be ignored.

"Tell me first," I say, "how will you portray me?"

Instantly the twinkle leaves his eyes. "What kind of question is that? I'll paint you as the artist you are, so all the world can see your beauty, character, and simple grace."

His sincerity touches me. "When do we start?"

We settle on the following Wednesday afternoon.

After he leaves, I busy myself adding color to the meadow behind the shepherds, dotting it with lily and gentian, violet and coral bell, occasionally stopping to glance at the table by the window. The red peonies have the brightest hues in London on this misty afternoon. Yet they will fade and wither. Even now, they pale in comparison with the flowers blooming in eternal color on my canvas. And with the intensity of the colors surging within me, driving me to paint. Those are the colors I value most.

Still, Nathaniel's mischievousness amuses me, as does our flirtation. Since I'm never going to marry, I can enjoy a little fun. Any independent woman charting her own course in the world needs trusted friends. And, twinkle or not, I see no reason not to trust Nathaniel.

Bridget doesn't appear for supper. Instead, she sends a note saying her health has taken a sudden turn and the doctor has ordered her to bed, with an injunction against excitement of any sort—even conversation. We will have to postpone our outing to Joshua Reynolds's studio. She's sorry because she knows how eager I am to make his acquaintance, and she herself has been looking forward to taking me, but the delay is unavoidable.

I am, I admit, more than a little disappointed. I've grown used to her companionship, to seeing her beauty, inhaling her rose perfume, receiving her sisterly care. I hope, with a little rest, she'll soon be back to her usual self. In the meantime, though, I settle on a routine that suits me. Since the children eat with their governess, I take meals alone in my rooms, which gives me more time to paint. I do portraits in the morning and focus on history painting in the afternoon. Except, of course, on afternoons when I sit for Nathaniel.

At my first sitting, he directs me to a high-backed chair, where he places a wreath of flowers atop my braids and drapes a fox pelt over my shoulders. The fur hangs low over my bodice, which has a high neckline and several layers of lace tight around the throat. I chose it from among the other bodices I inherited from Bridget, based not just on its meticulous stitching but also on its modesty.

He stands back to survey the setup. "The embodiment of elegance," he says. "I like it. Now let's make the woman into an artist."

He picks up a small brush from his easel and puts it in my right hand, which he places atop my left hand so that together they are balancing a closed portfolio on my lap. Because we're in his studio, it's his portfolio. But no one will know that when they view the painting. And view it they will. Portraits by Nathaniel Dance are in high demand, and my image will hang in the finest gallery.

As he gets to work, his eyes fly back and forth between me and his canvas. I feel his glance move from my face to the lace on my neck to my shoulder to my hands. I do my best to stay motionless, but it's not easy. First I feel a slight tickle on my chin, then a bigger tickle in my nostril. Soon a fiery discomfort is prickling in every pore. Yes, other artists have sketched me, but this is different. I can't quite say why. Maybe it's due to our flirtation. Or maybe to the concern that I'm being seen foremost as a woman when really I'm foremost an artist. Either way, I'm not as immune as I thought to the scrutiny of a man's eye. An eye with a twinkle, no less.

"Please," I say, "don't you give your sitters any rest?"

His twinkle turns to a frown. "You look flushed. Are you all right?"

I tell him I could use some water.

The instant he turns away for the water, I feel normal again. No male eye has power over me. When he hands me the cup, I notice he is a bit flushed himself. He's just better at hiding it.

"What did you expect?" I joke, as I sip the water. "You've suffocated me with this fur."

Of course, what I wear for a self-portrait is a different matter entirely. I'm free to paint myself without any need for a high neckline or confining fur. I can go so far as to flaunt my freedom by wearing loose, flowing Grecian robes, and no one will object. Not even Bridget. As soon as time allows, I intend to do exactly that. It will be a self-portrait worthy of a history painter.

Bridget sits in her bed, propped up by a mound of pillows, her lapdog, Constable, curled at her elbow. She has summoned me to say that several weeks of bed rest have paid off, and we can speak again. Her face, always so beautiful, is gaunt and pallid. Not the image of Aphrodite for the history painting we planned. She extends a hand, and I take it in both of mine. Her fingers are icy even on a summer day. I suspect more than the change of climate is to blame.

"I'm sorry, Angelica." She sighs deeply, and the sigh turns into a cough. "We had such grand plans. I'm afraid I've failed you."

"Please," I say, "that's not true." I don't want her to see my presence here as an imposition—or worse, a reason to ship me back to the Continent. "Really, everything's worked out perfectly. I have so many new clients."

"That's good," she says, straining to hold back a cough. "But I wanted to be the one to make the introductions. It's so important to know the right people."

I sit on the edge of the bed and stroke her hand. Her rose perfume, strong as ever, smells rancid. I try not to inhale too deeply. "Everyone's been kind. Just like yourself."

"You don't realize," she says. "Society here isn't like on the Continent. You need to know what is proper and what is not. Do you understand?"

I nod, though I'm not sure I do. Or want to. When I traveled with my father, neither of us paid much attention to social formalities. The whole issue of privilege aside, I'm more interested in finding my way as an artist than in anything else society—or Bridget—might have to offer. Surely she is aware of this. "I've received commissions from your friends," I say. "Lord Exeter and Lady Spencer and Lady Mary Coke—"

She pulls her hand from mine and hoists herself higher onto the pillows. "That's good. But you can't keep wearing my old hand-me-downs. What will people think? As soon as I'm stronger, I must call my dressmaker."

Generous as her offer is, I hesitate. Antonio warned me about just this sort of transaction with a patron. Selling my soul, I think he called it. "I appreciate your kindness," I say, "but I've saved enough for a new wardrobe."

"That's my Angelica, always independent." She smiles as she shakes her head. "I'm glad we can talk again. However, I mustn't keep you from your studio."

Sensing this is Bridget's way of telling me she's too weak to speak more, I express my relief at finding her much revived, then turn to go.

As I reach the door, she stops me. "I may be indisposed, but don't think I have deaf ears."

Her tone is so sharp that I freeze.

"You can't keep secrets in this household. Catherine told me all about your caller."

That can only mean one thing, and it's not something I wish to discuss. I respond as casually as if we were discussing the number of ribbons on my hat. "Oh? Mr. Dance?"

"Indeed, Mr. Da-a-a-nce." The way she pronounces his name, with an exaggerated *a*, suggests he doesn't meet her approval. "His interest in you was obvious on New Year's Eve."

I acknowledge he was in Venice. I don't ask why this matters so much she must speak of it despite her fatigue. Or why it's her business, when I didn't need her to introduce me to Nathaniel.

She raises her brow. "That wasn't the first time you'd met, was it?"

"We met in Rome," I say coolly. As far as I'm concerned, I've accounted for all the ribbons on my hat. Not wanting to leave on a sour note, I offer to fluff her pillows before I go.

But she isn't so easily assuaged. While I work the pillows—and Constable scoots to a safer spot near her feet—she probes further. "Rome. Venice. Now London. Is there a secret agreement between you?"

"Absolutely not." I have to pinch myself to keep my voice from rising. Her accusation irks me more than it should, given how baseless it is. This is the side of Bridget I first saw in Verona. I didn't like it then, and I don't like it now. "He's painting my portrait, and I will paint his. That's all. Under no circumstances will I marry him. Or anyone else."

She settles back on her pillows, which instantly lose most of their fluff. "You may have no intention of marrying, but I'd wager Mr. Dance feels otherwise."

"If he does, he hasn't told me."

"Not yet. And when he does, what then?"

"I'll refuse him."

"And if he doesn't like your refusal?"

"It will still be a refusal."

She looks at me sternly, and I wait to be excused. Having been called back once, I don't want to offend by leaving too soon now. As my father used to say, a patron is always right.

"Well," she says at last, "as long as you're careful."

"I am."

"You can't be too careful," she says with a sigh. "Especially since you've come up in the world so suddenly."

My shoulder blades stiffen at her insinuation. As if I would keep the company of any artist who might befriend me solely because I have rich patrons. As if Nathaniel might do that. "Mr. Dance," I say flatly, "is an honorable man."

"Honorable or not, you can do better." She does her best to stifle a sneeze, then adds, "When I'm healthy again—pray it's soon—I will take you to meet someone who outshines Nathaniel, Antonio, and all the rest."

I take that as my cue to depart.

As I go down the stairs to my studio, I remind myself many things have changed over the past months, but one has not. In Venice, I assured Bridget I had no desire for marriage. Here in London, I'm as free as ever of that desire. Yes, I believe in enduring love, and I work hard to capture its mysteries with paint. In the dark of night, I may even long for a certain bittersweet gaze from someone who knows me as no other does. But none of that will stop me from becoming an artist, fully and consummately. That for me is more than sufficient.

Most evenings, after using the remaining light to do some sketching,

I'm still too wrapped up with work to fall asleep before midnight. When I close my eyes, I'm often overwhelmed by colors swirling in my head. The same colors that flowed onto my canvas during the day haunt me at night. So while everyone else in the house sleeps, I sit at the black walnut desk in my bedroom and write to my father.

I tell him how much I miss him but also confirm that my coming to London was the best move for us. He'll be pleased to see the sums I calculate in neat rows in the leather ledger he gave me. My expenses are quite modest due to Bridget's kindness, while my income is steadily increasing.

When I finally go to bed, it's often still difficult to sleep. The only way to hold the wild colors at bay is to allow my mind to run back to the studio, to let it busy itself adjusting the angle of a skewed shadow, adding highlights to a headdress, making lips more capable of a smile.

At such times, I imagine a knock on the studio door. Before I can answer, a mysterious but somehow familiar visitor lets himself in, walks to the window seat as though he's been there a thousand times. As he looks at my paintings, what is bittersweet in his eyes becomes sweeter. Then we fall silent, and I marvel at how it's possible to commune so fully without uttering a word. Always I fall asleep before he leaves.

Nine

While Bridget remains indisposed, I make time to meet some artists of lesser import than Joshua Reynolds whom I feel free to approach without her introduction. I go first to George Moser, an enamel painter and old friend of my father's from Switzerland, who lives just around the corner from Saint Martin's Lane Academy. His daughter, Mary, is three years younger than me and also an artist. We quickly become friends.

The Mosers are in the habit of holding gatherings in their home, at which artists share sketches and paintings and their latest creative ideas. It's a chance to critique art in a way I didn't experience while traveling with my father. I begin attending regularly. Nathaniel is a regular as well.

When I tell Mary I want to use her image in a painting I'm titling *Prudence Sacrificing to Duty and Enchaining the Wings of Cupid*, she agrees to sit for me. I like creating explicatory titles. Mary, I believe, will measure up to this one.

"I could never succeed as a history painter," she says wistfully during her first sitting.

"Why not?" It's a rhetorical question, and I'm less than prudent for asking. Mary mostly does delicate floral paintings, and she herself appears no less delicate. Suggesting she do history paintings would be like suggesting a daffodil do battle with a winter storm.

"Don't get me wrong," she says. "I may choose to work on

historical subjects at some point. But I'm not sure I have the stamina
to compete in a man's world. Tell me, how do you manage it?"

I'm not sure what to say. I compete with men because I see no
reason to assume my talent is inferior, to think my signature on a
painting less significant. Yet, much like women who publish anony-
mously, many women artists feel the need to conceal their identities.
I've seen history paintings in an exhibition credited only to "One of
the Fair Sex." As if the artist must cower because someone found her
pleasing to the eye. Or thought her gender should be given consider-
ation when assessing the value of her art. "I've always been my own
person," I say after a moment, adding chalk to soften the pointed end
of her nose. "Perhaps because I don't seek a husband, it's easier to
aspire to something greater in life, as men feel free to do."

Mary is shocked. "You don't wish to marry?"

I shake my head, regretting my initial question. Mary is a friend,
but some things are better left unsaid, even between friends. As a
child, I watched other girls clutching their mother's skirts, as I did
with Mama. But that didn't make us the same. Color didn't speak to
them as it spoke to me. Mary is an artist. Yet she is one of those girls.
"I have nothing against marriage," I say. "It's just that I've chosen to
give art the highest place in my life."

"But I want to marry!" she objects. "And have children. When
my husband and I start a family, I might retire as an artist. Are you
implying that limits my work *now*?"

"Of course not." Each of us, I explain, has a different tempera-
ment. I was speaking for myself, not telling her how she should feel.

"Yet we're both women artists, facing the same challenges.
Like"—she gives a little laugh—"Dr. Johnson said."

"You mean when he said that a brush, like a sword, belongs in the
hands of a man?"

"Yes, and that painting portraits is an indelicate pursuit for women."

"Right, because to paint a man's portrait, we must—God forbid—stare into his eyes," I say with a snort. "If Dr. Johnson thinks seeing a man's eyes up close is a problem, he should declare history painting less indelicate than portraits, and therefore most suitable for women."

Mary laughs more freely. "Not to mention that, unless you keep your eyes closed, *sitting* for a portrait is at least as indecent as painting one."

I laugh in agreement, despite my recent experience with Nathaniel. Though Mary is frail in health, she has a sharp wit. She's also easy to sketch because she sits as motionless as the still lifes in her studio. Others might think her face plain, but to me it reveals character; her pensive eyes and patient smile are marks of the prudence I plan to capture.

"I hope you won't be offended," she says. "There's something I want to ask."

"What is that?"

"I heard you dressed as a boy in Milan to attend life drawing classes. Is it true?"

Abruptly I set down my chalk. I didn't think that old rumor had followed me to London.

She takes my silence as confirmation. "O Angelica," she gushes, "I wish I had your courage!"

I'm about to deny it, but her response gives me pause. What if my father had actually disguised me as a boy? I would have loved those classes! It might have taken courage, but it would have been worth it because I would have learned so much about the human figure. And so easily. Not to mention the satisfaction of tricking those stodgy artists. Suddenly I wish all that had happened. But sadly it didn't. So I set

Mary straight and explain that history painting doesn't require one to draw from live models. "Tell me," I say, picking up my chalk again, "from whom did you hear that rumor?"

"My friend Henry Füssli."

"I don't think I've met him. He sounds German."

"He's Swiss—a writer who aspires to be an artist."

"Has he attended your gatherings?"

She flushes as she explains that he used to come all the time but now rarely does.

"Don't keep him away for my sake," I joke. "I won't accuse him of spreading rumors."

But Mary isn't laughing. When I ask if I've said something wrong, she shakes her head. "I'd like you to meet him," she says finally. "I'd value your opinion."

I'm about to ask why my opinion matters, when I catch on. Mary is enamored with a man who no longer—if he ever did—returns her affections. No wonder she's reticent. She needs more than an opinion; she needs my help. Then it occurs to me that I have the independence and impartiality to do that. So I make a proposal. "Let's prepare a special invitation for the next gathering," I say. "What topic would entice him?"

"The supernatural," she says without hesitation.

"Then that's what we'll discuss. Afterward, I'll speak to him discreetly on your behalf."

"Thank you, Angelica! I knew you'd understand." She thanks me at least six more times before the end of her sitting.

At our next gathering, Mary's pale face is unusually bright. Like a flower leaning toward the light, she sits near the door, awaiting the arrival of our special guest.

He doesn't appear.

After discussing the supernatural in history painting, the group debates the merits of various sketches thrown on the easel. Only after all the sketches have been critiqued and the last morsel of cake eaten, and everyone is set to leave, do we finally hear a knock at the door.

Mary welcomes a man in a heavily brocaded maroon cape.

"I may be late, but I couldn't pass up your invitation." He's speaking to Mary, but his eyes scan the group. They land on me.

Though not a tall man, Henry Füssli's manner of lifting his chin gives him the appearance of greater height. His eyes, set deep beneath bushy red eyebrows, are gray and watery. "I've heard so much about you," he says after Mary has formally introduced us.

"I trust it was pleasant," I say, hoping he isn't referring to the rumors of my disguise.

But he isn't. "I read David Garrick's rhyme about you in the *Public Advertiser.*" He tosses aside his cape, throws back his head, and recites, "'While thus you paint with ease and grace and spirit all your own, take, if you please, my mind and face, but *let my heart alone.*'" He turns back to me. "I'd count that as pleasant. But you must explain the last phrase."

Mary objects that it's unfair to expect me to answer for Garrick's poem, but I rise to my own defense. "David and his wife are my friends. It was all in good fun."

"Oh, I see." The syllables roll slowly off his tongue, as if he were trying to decide if he believes them. "I too know David. I sketched him as Macbeth." He looks around the room, then addresses everyone. "I have an idea. David is performing *Richard III.* Why don't we all go to Drury Lane and see it?"

Mary exclaims that she adores the theater.

I offer to check whether we can use Bridget's box, and Mr. Moser volunteers to serve as chaperone. Since most of us already meet in private, a chaperone is unnecessary, but we accept his offer so he won't feel left out.

After the others leave, I linger to see if Mary is happy with the outcome of our little connivance.

She is. In fact, she's all but forgotten Henry's late arrival and is abuzz about the outing. From her queries about Bridget's box, I gather she expects to sit beside him. "But you must speak with him alone," she adds.

I promise I'll do it as soon as the opportunity presents itself.

Bridget is all in favor of the outing. Feeling stronger and once again her personable self—our heated exchange about my prospects for marriage forgotten—she's eager to put her box to good use. Immediately she calls for her dressmaker.

"You must have the right outfit," she says, "even if I can't be there. All the more so because I can't be there."

I finger the crimson silk laid out on the sewing table. It feels like rose petals.

"This will be your most visible appearance thus far in London, and you must look your best." She runs the back of her hand down one of my cheeks, fussing over me as a mother cat might her kitten. "Be sure to wash your face with mercury water and apply white lead so your complexion is appropriately pale. Treat your hands as well. Remember, people must realize you're not an ordinary artist."

As the dressmaker measures my waist, muttering how impossible it will be to finish such an elaborate project in less than a week, I smile to myself. This time, privilege is not unwelcome. Though disinclined to powder my face, I have no objection to dressing stylishly while amusing myself at the theater with friends.

The impossible is accomplished, and the gown in all its crimson magnificence is ready on time. It fits perfectly over my new pannier hoops. The shoulder pleats have been pressed, the lace trim attached with a final stitch, and all the pieces securely pinned in place when the carriage taking me to the theater arrives at Charles Street.

To my surprise, Henry has come alone in a conveyance that comfortably sits only two. The others, he says, will meet us at Drury Lane.

As I arrange my skirt in the tight space between my seat and his—not easy with the large hoops—I try to adapt to this change of plans. I was going to draw him aside during intermission and inquire about his feelings for Mary, while at the same time convincing him he *does* have feelings. I hadn't figured out what to say. Now I find myself prematurely faced with just that.

As we chat about the weather and other trivialities, I observe Henry. It isn't obvious what Mary finds attractive about him. Perhaps the passion brewing in his watery eyes. Or his quick wit, even if it tends toward the sardonic. Possibly he has redeeming qualities I won't know unless I venture closer.

I inquire how long he's been in London.

"Long enough to know I prefer Italy," he scoffs. "Surely you do too?"

I tell him I have fond memories of my childhood in the Alps.

A cloud passes over his face. "I may prefer Italy, but there was nothing fond about my childhood." He explains that his father forced him to train as a priest. He shoots a dark look in my direction. "Can you picture me as a priest?"

I admit that would be difficult.

"Well, it's true. I was ordained by age twenty." He gives a short laugh. "After I wrote a letter exposing one of the magistrates, they threw me out. Now I do translations to support myself. And paint when I can." He pauses. "You must have seen my work."

I remember seeing some sketches in Mary's bedroom. The images were wild, supernatural, phantasmagoric. I wasn't able to fathom their meaning. Now I want to understand them, just as I want to understand the man who created them. *How strange*, I think as we pull up in front of the theater, *that we never met in Rome. Our paths must have crossed.*

When Henry and I arrive at Bridget's box, it is empty.

He assures me the others will be here soon. "You don't mind that we've had this time together, do you?" he says. The moistness is absent from his eyes; in its place, I see the glint of victory. He's proud to have me to himself. That must have been his plan all along.

I lean with both hands on the railing and watch the crowd churning below. He may think he's outwitted me, but he hasn't. Now it's my turn to outwit him. Yet when he joins me, standing so close he crushes my pannier hoops, I'm not sure what to say. How to pique his interest in Mary? I've never done anything like this before.

Then, with the speed of a thief in the night, his hand darts out. Before I can pull away, he has clamped down on my right hand and slid it, tight within his grip, off the railing and into the folds of my skirt.

In the same instant, I hear Mary and the others close behind.

"Angelica!" her voice rings out. I can only imagine what she must feel finding me alone with Henry, so close together, and well before intermission, not at all as we planned. "When we got to Charles Street, you'd already left. What were you thinking?"

I expect Henry to explain, but he seems to have taken a sudden interest in the chandelier.

It's Nathaniel who responds first. "We won't let her escape again," he says, striding toward me and claiming my left hand, still free on the railing. With a grip softer than Henry's yet too firm to evade, he pulls it into the folds of my skirt on the other side.

I stand immobile, both hands captive, and no way to free myself without causing a scuffle. Hundreds of heads below would surely spin on their necks at any sign of commotion. I can't risk that. Behind me, Mary is rattling on. I want to reassure her nothing unseemly has occurred, but any attempt to turn around will expose my predicament. With neither man willing to loosen his hold, all I can do is remain as rigid as a marble statue.

At last the curtain rises. Both men stumble over themselves to show me to the best chair and secure seats on either side. Mary and her father sit behind us. It's time for us to lose ourselves in Shakespeare's drama and forget our own petty one.

Nathaniel is sitting for me when a basket of fruit tarts is delivered. We both know who sent it.

"I realize you can take care of yourself," he says, refusing a slice of tart, though it's his favorite brandied pear. "But what about Mary? How should she handle this?"

I place a slice onto a plate for myself and avoid looking directly at him.

"Surely you saw how upset she was at the theater," he continues. "And yesterday when I stopped at Saint Martin's Lane, she'd shut herself in—"

"She's sick?"

"Sick at heart."

"I had no idea." Of course I do have an idea. But I'd prefer for him to think otherwise. The less he figures out about our theater fiasco the better.

"I thought you'd be the first to know," he says.

I hate misleading a man I consider a trusted friend, but I don't want to further betray Mary's confidence. So I simply point out I haven't spoken with her since Sunday.

But he persists. "Even if she hasn't said anything, we all know how she feels about that damned Füssli. And now for you to fall—"

"Wait!" I can't allow him to falsely accuse me. "I never encouraged Henry. He's nothing to me. My only purpose was to speak to him on her behalf."

"Really?" he says, with a final withering glance toward the basket. "If that was your intent—and if you say so, I believe you—I can only say it was noble of you." He goes back to his pose and waits for me to resume painting.

But impressions from the past week are flying through my mind. I fully expected to speak to Henry about Mary, yet all his actions and everything he said—and didn't say—made it clear he has no interest in her. Which rendered my task impossible. By the end of the outing, nothing had been said. I haven't had a chance to explain all this to Mary. Still, I'm certain she will understand. Most likely she'll make a witty remark, we'll both laugh, and then we'll come up with a better plan.

"Please excuse me," I say, "there's something I must do right now. It can't wait."

Without changing out of my painting dress, I order the carriage and drive straight to Saint Martin's Lane. I'm moved to tears. They're tears for Mary, because I see that she loves with a depth of devotion I don't know myself. And they're tears of remorse. I shouldn't have acted so thoughtlessly. Though I never gave Henry false hope, I didn't entirely reject him. I let my own freedom hurt a woman who doesn't enjoy or even want that same freedom. I'm prepared to confess all this to Mary if it can restore her health and our friendship.

Mr. Moser answers my urgent knock. If he knows why I've come, he doesn't let on. "Mary isn't seeing anyone" is all he says.

"But I must see her."

"She isn't well," he insists.

I assert with equal force that I have something important to say, something that will ease her suffering. We quickly reach an impasse. Then I see her watching from the top of the stairs. "Mary!" I cry. "There's been a terrible misunderstanding. Will you at least speak with me?"

More fragile than before, she glides down the stairs.

I help her to a chair and lift her feet onto the footstool. Mr. Moser withdraws after she asks to speak with me alone.

"You must believe me," I say, dropping to the floor at her feet. "I have no feelings for Henry. Whatever anyone told you, it's not true. Nothing happened. Nothing ever will!"

"Don't—"

She tries to stop me, but I have to make amends. I take her hands in mine. They're trembling. "This is all a mistake," I repeat. "You're the one who is close to my heart, not Henry. I was only trying to convince him—if he'd listen—to return your affections."

"Please don't—"

Again I shut down her protests. She has to realize there is absolutely no attachment between Henry and me. "I wanted to be your advocate," I plead, "as you asked me to do."

She closes her eyes and is quiet for a moment. It seems she has taken my apology to heart. But then misunderstanding folds over onto itself in ways I didn't anticipate. "Angelica, I know you didn't purposely betray me."

I pull my skirts together and perch closer to her, on the edge of the footstool. "So you're not angry? You don't fault me?"

"Not at all. I only fell ill because seeing Henry with you made me realize he'll never return my love."

I want to contradict her, to say that if we put our heads together we can come up with a better plan. But that wouldn't be truthful. Henry has declared his preferences. Much as I want to take her under my wing and protect her, I can't engage in any sort of pretense.

We sit in silence, friends once again, but with a new vulnerability between us.

"Will you do something for me?" she asks at last.

"Of course."

"Be good to Henry."

I want to object, but having just told her I would do whatever she asked, I must do it. So I promise to be good to him.

On the way home, I ask the driver to stop at the Church of Saint Cecilia. Inside, I offer a prayer for Mary, asking that her heart be mended. And a prayer for myself, that I may be forgiven. She has forgiven me, but I need forgiveness in God's eyes.

As I continue home, I marvel at the whims of love. This is something about which I as an artist and independent woman know little. Alluring though they are, even fearsome at times, the colors have not taught me this. Whenever the heart opens, I see now, it follows its own laws. It's not up to us to decide whom to love, nor whether our love will be returned. Mary, whom many consider weak, has the strength to love even when destiny is against her. Her devotion is so unshakable that she thinks only of Henry's happiness, even if she believes it must be with me.

Which of course is not what I want.

My vow to be good to Henry doesn't obligate me to keep his

company, but it will make it harder to reject him. For Mary's sake, whenever I see him, I will be kind. Yet I will reject him just the same.

As we drive down Charles Street, I recall the line Henry recited from Garrick's poem: *Let my heart alone.* Ironically, it is only by applying it to Henry that I can outwit him. Him and all the others. My heart lives in its own aloneness. That aloneness may not always be welcome, but in the end, it will be my strength.

Ten

My studio has become my refuge. Each day after my last sitter departs, I instruct the servants to turn away all visitors. I make sure the side entrance is locked and bolted. Then I pick up my palette and become lost in color. The tempest that is London, with all its glamour and gossip, innuendo and intrigue, may be roaring as loud as ever, but I am in a world of my own, untouchable.

Lady Spencer's portrait is finished, and the Society of Artists has accepted my painting of Arcadia, which means I'm free to start my next history painting. I'm about to do that today when a letter arrives, slipped under my door by a servant. The sender's name is in bold letters on the envelope: Henry Füssli. I pick up my paper knife to tear open the seal, but then I remember: *Let my heart alone.* I toss it unopened into the fireplace.

I turn instead to my new history project: a series on the Trojan legend. What could be greater fuel for an artist than love and war? In this case, a war waged over the love of a woman—Helen, stolen from her husband by Paris, the Prince of Troy—and instigated by the goddesses who requested him to judge among them. As I take out my book of myths to review the story, in walks Bridget. The idea that my studio might be a refuge hasn't occurred to her. After all, this is her house.

"Set aside your work," she says. "We're going out!"

I'm surprised, as it has been more than two months since she last left the house. Though no longer bedridden, her breathing is still labored and she can't walk without a cane. No one seeing us arm-in-arm now would assume we were sisters. They might even think she is too old to be my mother.

"It's not raining yet." Her voice is spirited, then turns grave as she pulls a newspaper from under her arm and brandishes it before me. "Have you seen today's *Advertiser*?"

I take the paper and scan the first page, my eyes falling on the phrase "we spotted Miss Angelica Kauffman." I look up. "It's about me?"

She nods.

"'In Lady W.'s box,'" I continue, "'dressed in crimson silk and indelicately sandwiched between two gentlemen.'" I read a little further, cringing with embarrassment.

Apparently satisfied, Bridget holds out her hand for the paper.

But my eyes have locked onto the ugly words. I can't stop reading. The article makes me sound like a common flirt. Even though, thanks to those wide hoops, no one noticed my captive hands and absolutely nothing untoward happened, it's a disgrace.

"How dare they?" I say under my breath.

Bridget could say she warned me, that I should have known better. That privilege is punishing me for taking up with the likes of Nathaniel and Henry. That I disappointed her and took advantage of her generosity. That I'm no longer welcome in her house. But she doesn't do any of that. Instead she snatches the paper and rips it in half. Then she throws the pieces into the fireplace—where they land on the ashes of Henry's letter.

Her gesture restores my dignity. I venture half a smile as I put on my cloak. "I swear I'll never go to the theater again!"

She looks skeptical. "*Never?*"

"Not if the king himself invites me!"

"Come," she says, glancing at the cuckoo clock. "It's already ten. He often goes out early."

Only after our carriage has crossed Piccadilly, turned into Leicester Fields, and pulled up before a large brick mansion does Bridget confirm our destination. However, the servant who opens the door informs us that neither Mr. Joshua Reynolds nor his sister is at home.

Bridget sighs. "I feared we might be too late."

"Perhaps," I say, "we can see his paintings anyway?"

Judging by the jab she makes with her cane, my request is ill-mannered. That doesn't stop me. As soon as the servant has opened the door wider, I'm following him down a corridor lined with pictures. Bridget is close behind. Chairs are arranged at one end so visitors can sit while they wait. The servant leaves us to view the work on our own.

Bridget goes straight to a chair, while I walk slowly up and down, looking at each painting—all portraits. The colors are rich and luminous, the brushstrokes light but confident. I stop before a woman in Grecian robes, pouring libations to a statue of the three Graces.

"She's Sarah Lennox." Bridget lowers her voice. "Trust me, her marriage to Sir Bunbury won't last."

Bridget may have the latest gossip, but what interests me is the work of this master artist, which I've so far only viewed in galleries. His studio door is ajar, so I wander in. On one easel, an arrogant young officer in scarlet stands before a stormy sky. On another, where a fresh palette indicates the artist has been working, a woman's face emerges from an otherwise unpainted canvas, her wide eyes like beacons shining through fog. I climb onto a chair for sitters, strategically angled in the middle of the studio to catch light from windows high on the wall, and gaze at her. Whether mortal or goddess, she is bewitching. *Can I*, I ask myself, *paint like this?*

Before I've reassured myself I can, the master of the house strides in, followed by Bridget. Though almost twice my age, Mr. Reynolds has a boyish manner and playful dimple that make him appear younger than his years. His face is soft, almost cherubic, like the guileless face of a monk.

"What a surprise!" he says, beaming.

I jump down from the chair and curtsy before him.

"Not so fast!" he says. "I haven't had a chance to paint you yet!"

"You won't find a lovelier model," Bridget chirps, "than Angelica Kauffman."

Such flattery, always annoying, is downright embarrassing here in Mr. Reynolds's studio. I want him to recognize me as an artist, not a model. Yet I sense the dimpling smile on his face is not because he has met a new model. There is an awkward pause as we search for more congenial meeting grounds. Bridget retreats to the far corner, where she stares at the insignia on the young officer's coat. Her ears, no doubt, are still fully engaged.

"I was admiring your work," I say at last, speaking loudly because I've been warned he doesn't always carry his ear trumpet.

"Yes, that's Emily Warren as Thaïs," he says, gesturing toward the bewitching face. Then he approaches a cabinet and pulls out some papers. "No one has seen my latest work," he says, laying the sketches on a table, before a bronze bust of Michelangelo.

They are lively, intricate, superbly rendered. Suspecting that one group of figures is the three Graces, I exclaim, "Why, I've been contemplating this very subject!"

"The Judgment of Paris?"

I nod, hoping it's not presumptuous to compare my ideas with those of a master.

But he doesn't take offense. He simply asks, "May I visit your studio?"

My answer is immediate: "Nothing would delight me more."

His response is equally immediate: "Would tomorrow be convenient?"

Bridget might expect me to counter with Monday a week. But she's left the room, so I follow my instincts. I mentally cancel any sitters as well as possible errands and say, "You'll find me there all day."

As we walk to the corridor, I feel we've formed an unspoken bond. All distinctions of age and experience have dissolved. Rather than relating to Joshua Reynolds as the lord of the London art world, I find myself speaking as I would to a trusted colleague.

"Tell me," I say, stopping before Sarah Lennox, "how do you mix your paints to get such rich color?"

"The trick is in the varnish."

I study the canvas more closely. The surface is brownish, creating an effect much like that of the Renaissance masters. "Fascinating," I say. "Don't you fear the colors will fade?"

"No. I've studied different mixtures. I'd be happy to pass on the results to you."

I tell him I look forward to that.

At the end of the hall, where Bridget is waiting, I notice a portrait I overlooked before. The heavyset man with wild curls and arching eyebrows bears a striking resemblance to Dr. Johnson. The weak brushstrokes and drab colors, however, are unlike Joshua Reynolds's style, leading me to wonder if it is a painting he did as a boy and hung for memory's sake.

Before I can inquire, he winks. "Don't bother with that one," he says. "It's only here to pacify my sister. Fanny likes to see her paintings on the wall."

"She paints?"

"Portraits." He shakes his head. "And not because I encourage her."

I tell him I'm surprised Dr. Johnson let a woman paint his portrait.

Mr. Reynolds gives me a perplexed look, then silently mouths a drawn-out *oooh* and says, "Perhaps he determined portrait painting an indelicate profession for women *after* Fanny painted his." He dimples at his own joke, and adds, "With his poor eyesight, I doubt he's ever examined the portrait."

"I knew he'd like you!" Bridget says, self-satisfaction etched on her face, as we drive home.

I explain I've never met anyone quite like Mr. Reynolds, so accomplished and wise, yet so humble. "He reminds me of a priest," I say. "I can imagine going to him as my confessor."

"Perhaps that's because he never married." Bridget laughs, then adds, "Of course, nothing says he'll remain a bachelor."

"He asked to visit my studio." I try not to sound too eager. "Do you think he will?"

"Angelica, that's wonderful! If he said he'd come, I'm sure he will."

"He said tomorrow."

Bridget makes no effort to hide her excitement. "I hope you agreed. Now you've finally met, he can't be kept waiting on any silly pretext."

I'm glad her etiquette is more lenient—at least in this instance—than I assumed. Mr. Reynolds doesn't seem to be confined by such rules.

"Any artist who enjoys his favor," she continues, "is guaranteed success. In fact, I wouldn't be surprised if he were knighted one of these days."

"*Sir* Joshua Reynolds?"

"Most certainly. I can hear the ring of it already."

And to think the day began with a shocking indignity. All that seems trivial now. With Joshua Reynolds as my mentor, no one will accuse me of being a common flirt.

"Henry told me Mr. Reynolds supports many of the young artists," I say.

Bridget gives me a pointed look. "In your case, it's more."

"Every artist wants a mentor," I say, ignoring her inference. There's no reason to suppose he has ulterior motives, especially considering his age is closer to my father's than mine. No, what matters is that London's most acclaimed artist is giving me the attention he accords Henry and the others. That I am a woman is of no consequence to him.

Bridget twirls her cane in silence for a moment. "I saw how he looked at you," she says. "Don't pretend you didn't see it too."

After we return from Leicester Fields, Mary stops by. As I pour milk into tea and hand her the cup, I tell her how marvelous it is to see her out again.

"Well, I didn't have time to paint my gravestone," she says with a toss of her head.

I'm glad she hasn't lost her sense of humor.

She says she's come to thank me for all I did on her behalf. And to offer me her support after seeing today's *Advertiser*. "If anything half as horrible were said about me, I'd fall apart," she says. "But look at you! You're so calm."

"I may look calm," I say, "but I have feelings too. Strong ones." Being an observer of the world, I explain, doesn't mean an artist is insensitive; quite the opposite: We can be artists *because* we're sensitive.

Of course, she immediately thinks of Henry. "Of all the young artists," she says, "he is the most sensitive. He's the most creative yet most unstable. Volatile, really. He needs your calm. He needs you!"

I remind her of the promise I made.

"I know you said you would be good to him," she says. "But I'm worried that may not be enough. Please, Angelica, be careful. Otherwise he'll be off to Italy. Or *worse*."

I'm not sure what she thinks would be worse. So I force a change of subject and describe my meeting with Joshua Reynolds. I make sure she understands how rapidly the horizons of my life are expanding, at the same time as demand for my work is surging. I'm not sure when I'll have time to meet Henry again.

After Mary leaves, I open my book of myths, ready to work on the Judgment of Paris. But it dawns on me that no one should have cause to speculate about what inspired my choice of subject. If Mr. Reynolds is working on the Judgment—even if he never turns his sketches into a painting—I must do something else. So I choose Penelope holding Ulysses's bow.

I begin by reviewing the sketches I brought to London. In some, she sits pensive near her loom—these were for a painting I did in Rome, in which she mourns her husband. She declares she won't remarry until she has woven his shroud. Each day for twenty years, she weaves a piece, and that night unweaves it. Thus she keeps her suitors at bay. I took great pains to capture her wistful look, echoed in the eyes of the dog at her feet.

My father was impressed that her eyes appear to hold tears though none are visible on her face. "How did you know to do that?" he asked.

I told him it was because he taught me well. I didn't want him to know I learned it by holding in my own tears after Mama's death.

The sketches of Penelope I did the evening Antonio and I argued in Venice are better than I recall. Even her thumbs are at the right angles. I need no further preparation to start work. This painting will show the pivotal moment: Penelope holding the great bow she intends to give to the suitor who is able to shoot an arrow through twelve rings. Only he deserves her heart. She is confident no one but Ulysses can pass this test. What she doesn't realize is that he has returned and disguised himself among her admirers.

I think about my own admirers here in London. New ones pop up everywhere. And now Joshua. I have to admit Bridget was right: He offers much more than Nathaniel or Henry. It took only one meeting to find a wisdom and maturity far beyond their flirtatious games.

Of course, that doesn't mean I will waver. No, I will remain independent, devoted to my art. My easel will be my loom, my paints the warp and woof, keeping me free of entanglements. Still, I wonder, *What if someone greater than all the rest is able to pass whatever test I set?*

Eleven

Joshua Reynolds arrives after breakfast, just as I'm getting a rough sketch of the new painting onto canvas. I've barely outlined Penelope's form when I sense a presence behind me.

"Oh!" I exclaim, unsure how long he's been watching from the doorway or how he managed to keep the servants from announcing his arrival.

"It's a good sign when an artist is fully absorbed. Then the painting will be a statement of truth. Except in my case," he adds with a grin as he steps into the room. "If I fail to notice someone, it's because I'm too hard of hearing."

I like the way he pokes fun at himself. And the way his gentle eyes melt when he holds my gaze as we laugh together. "I'm afraid there's not much to show yet," I say.

"You mentioned the Judgment of Paris." He tilts his head and looks askew at the faint image. "But this—?"

"Penelope with Ulysses's bow," I say, "the first of a Trojan War series. The Judgment will come later."

"Penelope in a Trojan War series? How unusual. I like it." He traces an invisible mustache along his upper lip as he studies the canvas. "Do we see her alone?"

Looking at her now, I see that she cries out for a counterpoint.

He says a contrasting figure would accentuate her mood.

"That's what I was thinking," I say. "I mean, after you mentioned it." He has a way of mentoring that makes me feel very much his equal.

"Her gaze," he continues, "and her whole posture are directed upward. Another figure will draw the viewer's eye down."

"A handmaiden," I say, building on his suggestion. "Obviously we can't see Ulysses."

"True. But by picking a scene prior to his return, you imply his presence." He picks up a brush and twirls it between his palms. For an instant, it looks like he might apply some paint, but he turns to me instead. "What other subjects are in the series?"

I pull out several sketches, without worrying they might seem too preliminary. "These show Andromache persuading Hector not to go to battle."

"Ha!" he exclaims. "Another woman left by her beloved."

I tell him I hope that won't hinder my ability to sell them.

He looks shocked. "You haven't sold them? Aren't they on commission?"

"I wish," I say, shaking my head. My goal, I explain, is to be a history painter, and I do have a generous patron, but it is still necessary to paint portraits to build my income.

"Maybe I can help," he says. A friend of his, he explains, has inherited an estate at Devon and is planning massive renovations. An architect is designing the grand salon, but he'll need an artist as well. "If it suits you," he says, "I'd be happy to make introductions."

"Suits me? Of course! I'd love to meet Mr.—"

"John Parker."

I laugh. "You wouldn't know this, but I painted his portrait in Rome."

He rubs his hands with glee. "So you must know about his estate, Saltram Park."

I explain that the portrait was some years ago. We haven't met since.

"Then allow me to reintroduce you," he says. "He's very generous with his commissions. I think he'll find your Trojan series perfect for Saltram Park."

Just then, a servant enters and hands me a note. Since it's marked urgent, I step aside and read: "I have missed your company. Perhaps we can meet tomorrow for tea? Ever yours, ND."

He must assume I'm still mad about that stupid Advertiser, I think as I scribble a polite acceptance and instruct the servant to have it delivered without delay.

When I turn back to Joshua, he is standing beside Lady Spencer's portrait. Careful not to touch the still-wet oils, he runs his hand over the surface, as if his fingertips possessed a magnetic energy capable of intuiting signs of life. "I'd like to give you a varnish that can be mixed with certain pigments for greater brilliance," he says when he sees he has my full attention again.

"One of your experimental varnishes?"

"One of my *secret* varnishes," he says, with a flash of his dimple. "I call it 'mummy powder' because it's made from the gum used to envelop mummies in Egypt. Not easy to obtain, but I have my sources."

"Ground-up mummies?" I search his face to see if he's joking, but he looks sincere.

"That's right. You'll find it has a very happy effect on paintings."

For a moment, we smile at each other, this remarkable man and I. Then tipping his hat ever so slightly, he takes his leave.

Joshua hasn't been gone for more than a minute before the door to my studio flies open and Constable rushes in, with Bridget close behind.

"He was here for an hour!" She can barely contain her elation. "Your face is glowing!"

I suck in my cheeks. She mustn't think I was flirting with Joshua Reynolds. Nothing could be further from the truth.

But Bridget is busy settling onto the sofa and coaxing Constable onto her lap, determined to make the most of the moment. "This is excellent!" she crows. "He could hardly have made his interest in you more obvious!"

I clarify that his interest is in helping me secure a commission from John Parker for my Trojan paintings.

But Bridget has other ideas. "I'm afraid you haven't had the guidance you need." She pauses. "I realize your father took good care of you. But some things aren't within the natural sphere of a father. Surely you know that."

If they're beyond the sphere of a father, I think, *surely they're also beyond the sphere of a patron*. Nevertheless, I don't want to appear ungrateful. So I simply nod.

"Perhaps," she muses, "I should arrange a ball. Or at least a dinner party. I'm strong enough for that now. We must make sure he feels at home here."

Dinner party or not, Joshua feels very much at home in my studio, judging by the fact that he shows up unannounced the following day. "I've brought something for your red pigments," he says, waving a small packet.

I hand him my palette, and he mixes a small amount of grayish powder into the crimson pigment, then tests it on a corner of my canvas. I look closely but can't detect a difference.

"Don't worry," he says. "The effect will be more pronounced after it dries."

I'm about to call for tea when he stops me. "Actually, my angel—I hope you don't mind if I call you that, because you paint like an angel—I came to see if you'd accompany me this afternoon. I'm having tea with someone special. This time I won't embarrass myself by assuming you haven't met."

I try to imagine who it might be.

"You painted his portrait in Rome. And I'm not speaking of John Parker."

He's waiting for me to guess, but there are too many names to choose from.

"I'm not trying to perplex you," he says after a moment. "Benjamin West!"

I explain that I painted him in Florence, before meeting him in Rome. "You had me fooled," I say. "I was thinking of my British patrons, not the American Quaker."

"So you'll come?"

I assure him I'd love to. And so, after I've left word with the servants to let any visitors know I was called away unexpectedly, Joshua whisks me off in his primrose coach.

Our tea proves thoroughly enjoyable, and even more edifying. After Benjamin and I explain how our respective travels led us from Italy to England, the discussion turns to the Society of Artists. Both men are members. They believe artists should have the financial freedom to paint more than just portraits. One means to do this is through the creation of an academy under royal patronage. So far, approval has not been granted.

I begin to sense why Joshua invited me. He understands my goals and supports them. I was the precocious young painter for whom it was an honor to be in the company of Benjamin West and other artists. Now he wants to reacquaint me with them in a new capacity, as an artist in my own right.

Though they agree about the need for an academy with royal backing that provides greater public support for the arts, they disagree vehemently about the particulars. Benjamin argues that William Chambers would be a better president for the Society than would James Paine. Joshua says engaging in such petty politics is a waste of time. He promises to pull out, no matter how much he favors the Society's aims, if they don't stop acting like children and start acting like artists. Benjamin says we have a responsibility as artists to resolve these issues, and that won't happen if Joshua withholds his support. The conversation weaves back and forth for hours, until the tea in its cozy has grown cold.

When I arrive back at Charles Street, it is past the supper hour. Not wanting to disturb the family, I go straight to my studio. To my surprise, Catherine is waiting for me. From the look on her face, something is amiss.

"Aren't you getting ready for bed?" I ask.

She ignores my question. "You're really late."

"That's why I came through the side entrance."

"I have to warn you, Mama isn't pleased. She went to her room without supper, and now the whole house is in an uproar."

I'm confused. "I thought she'd be very pleased. She's done nothing but encourage Mr. Reynolds."

Now Catherine is confused. "Mr. Reynolds?"

"Yes, he took me—" I start to explain.

But she interrupts. "No, no. It was Mr. Dance. When the servant said you'd been called away, he insisted you promised to meet him. Mama had to entertain him for hours before he finally left."

I groan, realizing what happened. "I did promise to meet him today, but when Mr. Reynolds showed up, it slipped my mind—"

Catherine is quite adult as she takes me by the arm. "Let's tell Mama. I'm sure once she finds out you were with Mr. Reynolds, she'll feel much better."

As the months pass, I find myself more and more amid the grandiose world of Joshua Reynolds. Not only are we at each other's studios, but he comes to Charles Street for dinner whenever Bridget extends an invitation. Which is often. His sister even comes once, which surprises everyone as Frances is known for being reclusive.

Joshua is anything but reserved. He maintains so many friendships I wonder how he keeps track of them—plus the literary club he started with Dr. Johnson, and the Bluestocking Circle meetings he likes to attend, as do I. And he's continually introducing me to new clients. More than once, he has persuaded a patron seeking a portrait by the renowned Reynolds to come to me instead. And as promised, he contacted John Parker, who immediately requested another portrait and expressed interest in four paintings from the Trojan series for Saltram Park. I'm busier than I've ever been.

Not only that, I'm making more money. Joshua didn't hesitate to point out my rates were too low. "My angel," he said, "you're worth more than the pittance you earned in Italy, more even than what you're earning here."

When I asked how much he thought I should charge, he said, "Twenty guineas! And by Jove, not a farthing less."

I wasn't sure people would pay twenty guineas for me to paint a portrait, but he assured me they would. And they are. Some even pay sixty guineas for a full-length portrait on a large canvas. Hopefully that will grow to the one hundred fifty guineas he himself commands for full-length portraits.

Although I sent Nathaniel two apologies for missing our

appointment, he didn't reply. I figured he was sulking, that he'd soon return with a bunch of peonies, and we'd joke and flirt again. Hoping to surprise him, I finished his portrait, without additional sittings.

How very hurt and jealous he actually is I only discover one morning when Bridget shoves the *Advertiser* in my direction. The page is open to a drawing in which a hard-of-hearing Joshua Reynolds pivots from his easel, one hand cupping his ear, while a caricature that resembles me diverts his attention. Nathaniel has drawn my nose so big it's hard to see much else. Except for the wedding ring he planted on my finger. It is the most heartless joke I've ever seen.

"How could he?" I cry, dashing the paper to the floor.

"People will gossip," Bridget says. "Doesn't mean you have to listen." If she blames me for this disgrace, it isn't apparent from her demeanor.

I can't let it go so easily. "When Joshua sees—"

"Nonsense!" Bridget cuts me off. "He's a perfect gentleman. He'll pay it no mind."

"All of London will see this," I wail. Usually I don't give a hoot what society thinks. The difference now is that I care what Joshua thinks.

But Bridget isn't concerned. "I'm sure they'll think nothing of it."

"They'll think I'm an ugly fool!"

"Nonsense," she says again. "It's Nathaniel Dance they'll see as the fool—as not worth another moment of your attention. Everyone knows you have a greater destiny."

I glance down at the picture. Suddenly my big nose strikes me as vaguely amusing. And Joshua is appealing in his monk-like manner. Bridget is correct: I have another destiny. I have my art, and it is thriving. If being a free and independent woman of privilege who is a successful artist means I have to cultivate greater toughness, I can do that. "You're right," I say, picking up the paper and tossing it into the fire. "People will see he's jealous. I won't give it another thought."

I'm spending even more hours in the studio. Between clients, I'm painting Joshua's portrait. He is painting mine as well. On days when I don't have time to drive to Leicester Fields, he comes here and sits for me. This quickly becomes my favorite time of day, especially when he lingers to chat over a cup of coffee. Though I offer tea, he brings his own pouch of Turkish coffee and sets it to brew while I paint. Tea, I learn, he considers a modern convention that should never have been allowed alongside coffee. He prevails on me to try his coffee, but one cup is enough to confirm that my tastes are incontrovertibly modern.

As I paint and we talk, one topic we return to over and over is the future of art and the important role the Society of Artists can play in that future. We must, Joshua says, look to the grand style of the Renaissance for inspiration. He doesn't see any inherent contradiction in going backward in order to go forward.

"I'm afraid," he laments one morning, "art has only gone downhill over the past two centuries."

"Which means," I say, "it's up to us to raise it to great heights again?"

"If not us," he counters, "then who?"

That gives me an idea. Although I've already made substantial progress on his portrait, I tell him I want to stop now and make a fresh start. I want to show that I can raise my art to greater heights, and I will do it by portraying him seated in front of the bronze bust of Michelangelo he keeps in his studio. Not only that, but I will darken the painting so the room is cast in shadows in the manner of the Renaissance masters. And of course I'll apply one of his secret varnishes.

He loves the vision. Then he gestures toward Penelope, resting on an easel in the corner of my studio, almost finished. Each morning as he takes his leave, he pauses to gaze at her. "You've already demonstrated your ability to paint like the masters," he says. "You realize that, don't you?"

Twelve

I don't know how Bridget does it. Unless Constable is a trained spy, she must be in the habit of hovering outside my studio. She always manages to appear within moments after Joshua exits. One day in early winter, her timing as precise as usual, she marches into the studio and goes straight to the bouquet on the mantelpiece.

"What delicate blossoms! Mr. Reynolds must have brought them this morning?"

"They arrived last night," I say, not diverting my eyes from the sketches of hands spread on the table. I'm trying to select the best pairs for Hector and Andromache.

"Lilies of the valley are hard to find this time of year." Arching her neck to sniff their fragrance, Bridget spots a note among the foliage. She plucks it and reads, "To My Angel." A slight frown crosses her brow. "Who calls you that?"

If she doesn't know, I'm not about to enlighten her.

She doesn't wait for my answer. "A letter arrived while you were occupied this morning, painting—or whatever you were doing—with Mr. Reynolds."

"Painting," I interject.

"Of course." She smiles as if that were not fully understood, then explains that his sister has invited us to dine at Leicester Fields Sunday next.

She sounds excited, so I tell her I hope her health will allow her to attend. Though we've been in London for almost half a year, her full strength has never returned. Some days, she gets about more or less as usual with the aid of her cane; other times, she's unable to leave her bed.

"I pray so," she says, "since this event is in your honor."

I turn abruptly from my sketches. "The invitation said that?"

"Not explicitly." She gives a short laugh. "What else could be the occasion? Everyone knows the Reynoldses rarely throw elegant dinner parties. This one's bound to be—let's just say I'd be surprised if it isn't the occasion we've been waiting for."

At the Reynoldses' dinner table, I'm surprised and slightly discomfited to find Henry Füssli seated to my left. Since our ill-fated theater outing, he hasn't returned to the Moser's gatherings, and our paths haven't crossed. He continues to send letters, none of which I've answered. If he's bothered by that, he doesn't let on now.

"Angelica," he whispers, "do you know how dazzling you are?"

I give a quick nod. He has no idea how many hours I spent getting ready. Not on his account, of course. Bridget learned at the last moment that the Spencers and Garricks were on the guest list. If she knew about Henry, she didn't mention it when she insisted I look my best. Despite her many donations and some purchases I've made myself, my wardrobe still falls short for a woman of privilege. I make up for it with my artistic talents. This evening, I wove gold silk ribbons into my hair, matching the gold embroidery on my stomacher. It took longer than anticipated but didn't go unnoticed by our host when we arrived. Now Joshua sits at the head of the table, catching my eye as often as he can.

When Henry has exhausted his flattery, he spears a slice of roast beef, then turns to me. "So," he says, "how is the amusing Master Dance?"

Months have passed, but the image of Nathaniel's cartoon in the *Advertiser* is fresh in my mind. Apparently it is fresh in Henry's as well. I glance up at Joshua. Bridget predicted he would never mention that incident, and he never has. Now, with his trumpet at his ear, he's straining to hear my conversation with Henry. I'm not sure how much he has caught.

"And how is Miss Moser?" I say, so Henry doesn't think he has the upper hand.

Before Henry can answer, Joshua interrupts. "My friend," he calls out, "I'm glad you're enjoying Angelica's company." On the pretext of better hearing Henry's reply, he springs from his chair, runs around the table, and positions himself behind my shoulder—where he remains as we discuss the flavor of the roast and merits of Yorkshire pudding, until Frances reminds him his food is getting cold.

I haven't been to many formal dinners in London, but enough to know this promises to be a long evening. While Henry babbles first to me and then to Mrs. Spencer on his left, my attention wanders. I have more valuable things to do. I could be in my studio working on the Judgment of Paris, deciding whether to show Aphrodite pleading for the apple or receiving it. I'm inclined toward the latter because it offers more dramatic tension.

After the second course, the servants clear the table, then lay out a fresh cloth, on which they place plates of fruits and cheese. They bring out clean goblets and pour port for the men, light wine for the women. There's a surge of energy as everyone begins talking at once.

Bridget holds up a goblet. "What exquisite crystal! I've never seen any like it!"

"Nor I," says Mrs. Garrick.

"Nor I," echoes her husband.

"Frances," Bridget continues, "thank you for gracing us with your finest stemware!"

Frances stands up, and all eyes shift to her. "Actually, the crystal tonight was entirely my brother's choice."

"Joshua's choice?" Bridget prompts.

"Yes. It's . . . an occasion he's been waiting for." Frances looks back at all the faces, then sits down abruptly, as if she's said too much.

But it isn't too much for Bridget. She smiles triumphantly at Frances. And even more triumphantly at me.

Henry's tone is anything but triumphant. "Let's drink to our rivals, shall we?"

Glasses rise all around, amid much banter and laughter. Even Bridget lifts hers, though only halfway. Clearly this isn't a toast to her liking.

Joshua is the last to pick up his glass. "To whose arrival, did you say, Henry?"

Suddenly the air feels as stifling as a midsummer heatwave. I plunk down my goblet as the realization dawns: Bridget intended from the moment the invitation arrived to make this evening about me. As if I were livestock, and she wanted to auction me off to the highest bidder. Frances shares this goal. Joshua knows nothing of their schemes, even if he selected the crystal. *Or does he?* It's insanity—this social spectacle in which everyone's speech seems to mean something other than what is said.

I look at Joshua, hoping his eyes will reveal what I need to know.

For once he isn't looking in my direction.

Bridget's manipulations I can handle, and I don't care what Henry or the others think of me. But the idea that Joshua might not be the trusted friend I believe him to be is enough to make me ill. I slide from my chair and tiptoe out of the room.

As the door closes behind me, I hear Frances say, "Of course you can drink yours any way you wish, my dear."

I hurry down the corridor, past the pictures, only glancing over my shoulder in case someone has followed. At the far end, the studio door stands ajar, the gaslights lit. I step inside.

As I walk slowly around the room, coming to a stop before the easel that holds my portrait, I calm down. Running out, I realize, was a bit disrespectful. But I'm here now, and rather than return to the dining table—which will call for contrived excuses and apologies—I decide to remain. It won't be long before Bridget appears. She'll place a hand on my forehead and conclude I've taken a chill and must be rushed home. Which means all her scheming will have come to naught. I can still salvage the evening by doing a few sketches by candlelight of Paris and the goddesses.

Footsteps sound in the corridor but without the added tap of a cane. It isn't Bridget.

"I thought I'd find you here."

I turn to see Joshua's smiling face. "I'm sorry," I say, "I didn't mean to be rude."

"No apology necessary!" The slur in his speech suggests he's downed a few too many glasses of port.

I cross the room and drop onto the sofa by the fireplace. "I must have looked silly."

He follows. "Not at all. But you left so suddenly, without a word. If something is the matter, you have to tell me."

"I'm fine," I say quickly.

"*Of course* you're fine."

He says it with assurance, but I see concern in his eyes. "You know," I say, "I find formal dinners an anathema. Sometimes they're so uncomfortable, I have to get away."

He sits down beside me. "I feel the same. These events are utterly tedious. That's why normally we don't organize them here. But this time, Frances insisted—"

"And you went along?"

"In spite of myself, I did."

I realize I was wrong to think he could be party to any sort of scheme concocted by Bridget and his sister. This is Joshua Reynolds, a kindred spirit who sees life much as I do. I can picture the two of us, secret conspirators, hiding in his studio on future such evenings. "I don't think I'll ever like formal society," I say. "I don't have the character for it. I'm afraid I am not at all like Bridget."

"Thank goodness!" He shakes his head, chuckling until his dimple springs forth, then adds, "Please don't misunderstand. Bridget is a dear friend, but she will never live in the same world I live in. Or you live in."

"As artists, you mean."

"Yes, as artists."

"Our art *is* our life. I'm so happy we share that."

"So am I." He pauses, then moves toward me on the sofa. He is closer than he's been at any time in the past months, close enough that I can smell the pungency of port on his breath. "It's more than that, my angel," he says, his words slurring not just from inebriation but from emotional intensity. "You *do* know that, don't you?"

I'm not sure what to say. I can't think of anything that could be more special than sharing art as we do. Abruptly, I stand up and walk back to the easel with my portrait.

He follows.

Coming up behind me, he lays first one and then the other hand on my shoulders, turning me toward him. "You must know what a difference your presence has made in my life."

Never in all our time together has he touched me like this, his hands lingering as if he assumes they belong on my body. His hold feels soft and warm, and its heat floods into my head. Before I can stop it, my body pitches forward.

He steadies me, steadies both of us. "Angel, do you understand me?"

I'm at a loss for words. If this were Nathaniel or Henry, I'd counter with a flirtation of my own. But this is Joshua. He isn't flirting. He doesn't speak that language—for all I know, he never did.

If my head is hot, his is hotter. Moist beads are forming on his forehead at an alarming rate and trickling down his face. "If I dare," he begins. "If I may ask—"

I stare at him. Is it possible that he, Joshua—the most revered artist, my special mentor, not to mention my most beloved friend—is proposing? To me? I can't believe he wants to marry me. He can't love me. Not like *this*. And so unexpectedly. It can't be true.

But as I watch a bead drip off his chin, I suspect it is true. He wouldn't expose himself like this if it weren't. He knows I've sworn never to marry, that I'm firm in my commitment to my art, yet he wants to share that life with me. He wants to propose a marriage between artists, a marriage more profound than any customary union between husband and wife. And he is waiting for my signal to proceed.

Suddenly my head goes from hot to frozen. All I can think of is the gossip that will whiz around London about the poor foreign artist who forced Joshua Reynolds into marriage. Who sought to be his wife—though he's almost twice her age—so she can siphon off his fortune and steal his fame. If I gave the *Advertiser* feed before, this would be fodder.

I must stop him—before he proposes and definitely before there can be the slightest temptation to accept. Even if Bridget and Frances didn't put him up to this and it's entirely his own initiative, I have to stay true to my beliefs. To myself. "What I know," I say, jumping back so his hands slip from my shoulders, "is that your art is your life. And my art is the same."

Perhaps he thinks I'm only being modest, because he reaches out and grabs my hand. "But art is not a living companion. Art isn't a friend. And surely not a . . . a wife."

His last word comes out as a whisper. But it couldn't hit me more strongly had he shouted. I back away, practically ripping my hand from his. "If any man were to become my husband, he'd have to be content with second place." I know my words must hurt but he has to know where I stand. "I belong only to my art."

He stares at me without replying. It's clear my response is not what he expected.

"Please," I say, determined to save him further humiliation, to show I'm the one capable of thinking with a clear head, and therefore he must listen to me. "I can't let you make such a sacrifice. I think too highly of you. Your friendship means too much. I never want to lose it."

There is an awkward moment between us. I look intently at Joshua and silently ask him to forgive me for any pain I'm causing. I am sincere in pledging my friendship. I adore him as a friend and mentor. I simply can't make a vow that goes further.

Then, as if neither of us said anything out of the ordinary, he clears his throat, walks over to a painting in the far corner, and begins to describe the new pigments he plans to try on it.

When we return to the party, all the guests have left except Bridget. Frances hooks my arm and steers me to her rooms for a peek at her latest painting. It's as poorly executed as the rest. Not wanting to leave Bridget alone with Joshua for long, I excuse myself, with the promise of a full critique on my next visit to Leicester Fields.

* *

Not a single word is spoken on the ride home. Bridget stares absently at the sprig of lily of the valley our host gave her as we were leaving. I've never seen her so sullen after a social event. Since she didn't follow me when I left the dining room, I expect her to ask—not that I'm eager to answer—why I ran off and what occurred in Joshua's studio.

Still she says nothing.

When we reach Charles Street, I offer her support, as I always do, as she starts up the stairs to her bedroom.

Instead of taking my arm, she whips around and shakes a finger at me. "Angelica Kauffman," she explodes, "your behavior tonight was insupportable!"

I stare at her face, pinched with hatred.

"I don't know whether you're stupid or just a fool!" She starts to lose her balance, then steadies herself on the railing. The lilies slip from her hand, but she doesn't pick them up. "I befriended you and brought you into my world. Into my family!" Her voice is so strident, I'm surprised the servants don't come running. "I planned the greatest of lives for you, as if you were my own daughter! And you betray me like this?" She picks up her skirts, and with a vigor she hasn't shown in months, hurries up the stairs to her room.

I collapse on the bottom step. I doubt Joshua would have told her about my refusal. In the few moments they were alone, she must have managed to pry the truth from him. It doesn't matter how she knows; all that matters is that she does. And that I'm no longer welcome in her house, no longer like family to her.

I closed a door tonight and must accept the consequences. I will begin in the morning to look for lodgings of my own. I have no other choice.

Thirteen

Dear Papa,

I received your letter and rejoice at the news of your good health. I'm delighted you feel strong enough to travel to England. However, much as I wish to see you, I think it would be best to put off your trip until spring. The climate is bad now, with dark, foggy days. Since you're unaccustomed to the smoke from the coal fires, I fear for your health—

I look up from the page, unsure what to say. The street lamp outside my window glows green through a soupy fog. Every evening has been like this, without hope for the bath of luminosity Papa trained me to look for. Lately, even afternoons have been too dark for painting.

Bridget's fury dissipated after I promised to find my own apartment. Much as she finds her life pleasantly unencumbered without the ambassador, she suggested I will thrive on my own. The day I moved, she kissed me on the brow and slipped a ring off her finger. "Angelica," she said, almost as if nothing had come between us, "I want you to have this."

I haven't taken off the intricately carved agate cameo since. It reminds me of the bond we forged and the comfort I feel now, knowing she is near. I decide stressing this comfort will make my father less likely to sense trouble. I never keep secrets from him. But some matters don't lend themselves to letters. I pick up my pen and continue:

I am living in a house on Suffolk Street, in Charing Cross, with excellent people, long-time acquaintances of Lady Wentworth, who recommended me to them as if I were her own daughter. It was such a good opportunity I didn't hesitate to take the apartment for the whole winter. I have four rooms. In addition to a bedroom and sitting room, there is a studio where I paint and another where I hang finished pictures. It's customary here for people to come and view the paintings without disturbing the artist. I pay two guineas a week for the rooms and another guinea for food and for the servant—whose clothes I must also provide. I couldn't manage without a servant. This might sound like a great expense to you, but I assure you under the circumstances, it couldn't be lower.

Again I sit back. This is the first time I've been apart from my father for so long. Half a year. Although we planned for him to join me by year's end, I'm not ready. It will take a full year to establish myself. If phrased this way, I think he won't feel I'm holding him off. I hastily finish penning the letter:

If you arrive during the winter, we'll have to lease a house, which will cost at least a hundred guineas for the year. And four hundred guineas more for furniture. Not to mention that everything costs more in the winter. Plus we'd need a manservant and maid for respectability. Please don't be disappointed if I ask you to wait. I will save money by staying here. I beg you to consider all this and not act hurriedly. May God preserve you in good health.

I remain until death your obedient daughter,

A.

* *

The winter proves to be solitary yet productive. Mostly I focus on portraits. Due to my new expenses, I have less time for history painting. Not
that I've given up on my goal. But it belongs to a more distant future.

I see Bridget only rarely. The combination of my dedication to
work and her fragile health makes meeting inconvenient. Though I
miss her, I'm not unhappy about the change. It means I'm fully independent and in charge of my business, an artist who knows how to
make her way in a man's world.

Henry still sends letters, long missives I skim through but never
answer. On the rare occasions when he stops by my studio, he's full
of flattery. If he noticed my move to new quarters coincided with a
certain dinner party, he has made no comment. Our talks are about
painting and what he calls "passion for life," which he says only artists understand. He insists true friendship is based on this passion.

Mary also visits occasionally—at different times than Henry of
course. We speak about our art and many other things, never about
him. Nathaniel is nowhere to be seen.

And there is Joshua. He too seems to be avoiding me, our vow
to remain friends and finish our mutual portraits notwithstanding.
Whenever our paths do cross, he doesn't meet my eyes. This pains
me. More than once, I felt as if slapped across the face when he gave
me the barest of nods and continued conversing with someone else at
a social event. So much damage was done all in one evening, so much
misunderstanding created.

One unexpected friendship has blossomed this winter. It began
on a rainy afternoon when Frances called unannounced at my studio.
Initially I dismissed this as out of character for someone so reclusive.
Not to mention someone who doesn't value a woman's full independence—neither her own nor mine. But she returned the following

week and stayed a full hour. It took her that long to tell me about her latest painting. Presumably she found me more willing to listen to her than her brother was to view the picture itself. Since then, she's been a frequent guest.

Today she arrives in her brother's primrose coach, with an offer to take me to Dr. Burney's for a musical party. "You won't regret the time away from your studio," she says as the footman shuts the carriage door behind me. "Dr. Johnson's friend Piozzi will be singing for us."

Knowing how much Joshua loves Piozzi's songs, I can't help but ask why he isn't here.

She leans closer. Though we're alone, she lowers her voice. "Angelica, I'm afraid my brother hasn't—how shall I put it?—been himself lately."

I lower my voice to match hers. "How so?"

"I've never seen him so sullen, so listless."

That doesn't sound like the Joshua I know. "Has he stopped painting?"

"Quite the contrary. He paints all the time. If anything, more than ever. I believe—" She hesitates but only for a second. "I believe he's lonely."

Suddenly it occurs to me she must have known all along that I refused Joshua. Yes, I've heard all about the portrait of George Selwyn he's painting, about how hard it is to get the pug to sit still on his lap, and about his plans for the Society of Artists, but neither of us has mentioned my last visit to Leicester Fields. Not once. I may never know whether she was part of a scheme to persuade him to propose, but that doesn't matter. For the first time, I see a possibility to fix this. Taking her hand in mine, I say, "I think there's been a misunderstanding."

I want to tell her it was more than a misunderstanding. I ruined the most special of friendships because I feared that breaking my vow not to marry would be a sign of weakness. Much as I prize my life as an independent woman, Joshua's companionship didn't threaten that. Accepting him wouldn't have lessened me as an artist. I want to confess that lately I've found myself expecting his familiar "hello, my angel," only to realize he isn't there to speak it. I anticipate seeking his advice about a painting, then have to proceed without. I want to tell Frances that Joshua is a good man, only I made the mistake of treating him as another Nathaniel Dance or Henry Füssli. He's so much more. He is the mentor I always wanted. Yes, my father provided unconditional support, but he wasn't a mentor. Leonardo was my mentor in spirit, but Joshua is a mentor in the flesh. He might even turn out to be the artist with bittersweet gaze I've long imagined. "You have no idea," I want to say, "how much I regret my mistake." Of course all of that would be too much for Frances.

As we pull up to our destination on Poland Street and alight from the carriage, she gives me a sharp look. "Perhaps I can help."

I tell her I'd welcome that.

To conceal my feelings, I pull out my fan. More than a few heads turn as I walk into Dr. Burney's house in my warmest coat and gloves, yet fanning myself as though it's a summer evening.

One of those who turns I recognize as Count Frederick de Horn, the man who was in mourning in Venice. He is no longer in black, and for the first time I can see how striking he is, with blond curls so thick he does not need a wig, and penetrating blue eyes. I'm pleased we finally have a chance to meet. I smile and lower my fan.

He approaches immediately. "Miss Kauffman, I'm honored." As

he bows, I see his ruby ring. At his side is an ornate saber, its handle also set with rubies.

I give a slight curtsy back. "How long have you been in London?"

"I just arrived."

"From Venice?"

"From Sweden," he says, pushing his temple spectacles higher on his nose. He's about to say more, but Frances takes my elbow and hurries me toward our seats.

A bouquet of forsythias is delivered to my studio early the next morning. "My brother sends these from his garden," the note reads. "He hopes to do the honor of calling on you this afternoon. Your faithful servant, F.R."

Placing the flowers in my most elegant porcelain vase, I have to give Frances credit. She must be aware of everything that transpired between Joshua and me and has been biding time until she could go about making it right. Now that will happen. The doors I shut through excessive caution will swing open again. Yes, Joshua is a good man. This time I resolve to meet him with equal passion.

His step when he walks into my studio is more dignified than I remember. When he stoops to kiss my hand, his lips barely touch my skin. His face has the same monk-like innocence, the same mild manner. The creases at each corner of his mouth, however, end with a distinct downturn. Although he looks genuinely happy to see me, it occurs to me his true feelings are a mystery.

There will be no more mysteries once I've let him say what I'm sure he has come to say. "It's a lovely day," I say gaily, settling onto the sofa by the fireplace.

Instead of joining me, he hangs back. "You know, Angel, I've often thought of visiting. But when Frances said you noted my absence at the concert, I knew I had to come today."

"I'm so glad you did!"

"I hope you're ready to sit for me again," he says. "It's been too long—"

I can sense him holding back, fearful of going beyond the safe terrain of painting. Which means I must lead the way. Some might see that as unbecoming for a woman, but I'm sure Joshua will appreciate it. "Yes, much too long," I say. "But now I can admit—"

It's his turn to stop me. "Please—"

Certain that all he needs is another chance to pose his question, I press ahead: "I'm ready to admit my mistake—"

"Please," he repeats, "you mustn't—"

But I can't be stopped. "It's not too late. We can still make amends, you and I."

He sits down—on the far end of the sofa. "I didn't come to speak about this. But since you bring it up, you must know that I acted inappropriately." His face is filled with compassion, yet his demeanor is commanding. "You were right in responding as you did. The truth is, I'd had one glass too many. We all know that port can make us spill what's hidden in the heart, even if we know it should remain secret. What I feel for you—" He falters, but only for an instant. "Perhaps, had we met earlier, things might have been otherwise. But at my age, how could I ask you to sacrifice so much for a friendship that will be yours regardless?"

I can scarcely hear all he is saying. I only know Frances was wrong to suggest anything could be fixed. And I've just made it worse by all but declaring my love. "You're right," I say. "I'm being preposterous. Let's never speak of this again." My face on fire with embarrassment at his rejection, I jump up and dash toward the door.

He follows me. "We're friends for life, aren't we, my angel? I'd never want to lose you."

My lips curve into what can only be described as a vacant smile. "Of course," I say. "We'll always be friends. It couldn't be any other way."

When the maid comes to light the lamps after Joshua has gone, I wave her away. For once I am unable to work. I sit alone, head in my hands, wanting to cry. Yet no tears come. Instead there is an ache in the pit of my stomach that surges upward in small spasms. Joshua is gone. Gone! His very words, that he doesn't want to lose me are the harbingers of loss.

Finally the tears fall. It is the recognition that this loss is irreparable that unlocks them. No matter if we remain friends, if we complete our portraits, visit galleries together, or meet at concerts, everything will be different. I cry like a child, sobbing as I haven't sobbed since I unburdened myself to the priest following my mother's death. This time no one is here to comfort me.

Fourteen

I awake with a pounding in my head, uncertain what to do next. In such a mood, merely putting my brush onto a canvas would ruin the painting. Not to mention the unappealing prospect of Joshua's bright forsythias taunting me as I work.

So, after applying a compress to relieve the worst of my headache, I dress, put on a coat and walking boots, and close my studio. I instruct the maid to remove the forsythias, cancel my appointments, and turn away any visitors. I especially don't wish to see Frances.

The day is cold and gray, as most are. As I wander through the crowds at Hungerford Market, dodging the hawkers and hagglers, sidestepping puddles and potholes, and then head north along Charing Cross, it starts to drizzle. But I keep going. Keep pondering. If only my mind could move as nimbly as my feet. I find myself wishing my father had come early, despite my instructions to the contrary, so I could go to him now for advice. But he didn't. And I can't. If I really want to speak to him, I'll have to pack my belongings and travel to Italy. Except—and it doesn't take me long to acknowledge this—I'm not ready to leave England. The climate may be dreary and I may miss my father, but there is still too much I need to accomplish here.

Which means I must figure out for myself what has happened. I've always been so certain I am an artist above all, so convinced art is all I need to sustain myself. How, then, could I have let down my guard with Joshua Reynolds, only to be shattered by his rejection?

Westminster Bridge is shrouded in fog, and I'm starting to feel chilled to the bone. As I turn toward home, I recall a similar chill—in the Frari, when Antonio mocked me for wanting to paint the sun. He shook my confidence, made me second-guess what I'm capable of. I'm afraid I've done that again. First I rejected Joshua based on my fear others would impugn my motives if I accepted his proposal. Then I wavered, and in a moment of regret—or maybe hauteur—tried to revive his proposal. I said no, and then he said no. I still don't believe he meant it; I think he simply felt I'd left him no other choice. Either way, it was not an act of confidence. I have not been painting the sun.

I recall visiting the Sistine Chapel, seeing Michelangelo's fresco in which God creates the sun. Artists usually only show the sun through reflected light. Otherwise it's too intense to view. Yet when I vowed to paint the sun, I invited that intensity into my art. Into my life. I committed to being true to myself as I am. To be an artist completely and consummately would be sufficient for me.

So, if Joshua was already a treasured friend, a mentor like none other, why should either of us need anything more? Why should our bond have to be contorted into something it is not? Why can't we be as we are? Isn't that enough? I should never have lost sight of that. Or, if I wasn't sure in the moment, at least I should have asked for more time to think about it. Now it's too late. Hearts have been wounded.

Returning from my walk, I encounter my maid in the hallway. "Oh . . . Miss Kauffman," she stammers. "You have a visitor. I'm so sorry. The others left when they heard your studio was closed. But Mr. Füssli insisted on waiting."

Through the open studio door, I see Henry pacing. My first thought is he must have finally discovered that the man he considered a rival is a rival no more, and rushed to see me. But his step is agitated, not like that of a man claiming victory. Then I remember Mary describing him as volatile. So I push aside my own troubles and approach with the intent of consoling him.

He glances up but continues to pace. "Angelica, I'm leaving for Italy."

"You are?" I say, struck by the irony of our similar thoughts.

"Tomorrow." He hesitates. "But I had to see you first."

I thank him for calling when he must be busy preparing for his trip. He still looks disturbed, so I add, "We'll talk when you return."

He stops pacing. "I'm not returning."

I stare at him. "I know how you feel about London, but this is your home now."

"Life here has become insufferable!" he says forcibly. "Unless . . . you—" He falters for an instant, but his gray eyes don't blink as he fixes them on me. "*You* are the only one who can hold me here."

I don't need Henry in London for my sake—we rarely meet as it is—but I can't ignore my promise to Mary. She'll be devastated if he leaves. "How?" I ask. "How can I help you?"

Before I know what's happening, he is on his knee, reaching for my hand. "I know you feel our bond. Don't deny it." His grasp tightens around my fingers. "Be my haven, my love—"

At the word *love*, I jump back. It seems disingenuous, a cruel joke. "Henry—" My tone is gentle, but the way I yank my hand from his is anything but. That yank, and the dismay on my face, hit him like a bucket of ice water. If I literally doused him, he couldn't rebound off his knee any faster.

"Fine!" He tosses his hair the way a dog shakes off water. "Then I leave tomorrow."

I reassure him that even if he leaves, he'll always have friends here. I hope he sees me as foremost among them. There's no need to feel like an outcast. He can return whenever he wants. Slowly I extend my hand.

Instead of taking it, he lashes out. "I was an idiot," he hisses, "to think I could count on you. Your haven, if you ever deigned to offer it, would be a pitiful place!"

"Henry—" I protest, dropping my hand, taking a giant step back.

"I've always hated clever women!" he cries as he retreats toward the door. "You think you're so clever, but you're no better than the spineless heroines you paint—alluring grace and nothing more!"

"For God's sake!" I say, clasping my arms around myself as if naked against his assault.

"And your heroes, what passionless men. But wait!" He gives a loud cackle. "Isn't that the only kind of lover you would accept?"

Without waiting for a response, he turns and is gone.

Never has anyone spoken to me with such vengeance, such vility. Antonio's words, harsh as they sometimes were, never came close. Surely nothing I said or did—not even anything I failed to say or do—justified such an attack.

To calm myself, I order tea, then sit and nurse it by the fireplace.

It's my pride, I realize, that was stung. Henry picked his weapon to match his target; he knew that attacking me as an artist is the only way to hurt me. Because my heart itself isn't vulnerable to him. Yes, I was attracted to his passion, flattered by his attentions. I even flirted back—perhaps a bit too much at times, but harmlessly. Still, Mary's friendship has always come before any bond that might have existed with him. Not to mention that my attention was wrapped up all the while with Joshua.

By the time I've drained my teacup, I have detached myself from Henry's criticisms. As a clever woman, I know they bear no reflection on my art. They're nothing more than the angry expression of a man who tried to stake a claim and lost, whose pain runs deeper than I imagined.

In the days that follow, I plunge into work. My friendships might be falling apart, but more clients than I can handle are knocking at my door. Shutting my studio for a few days doesn't deter them. Three new clients request portraits as soon as I reopen it.

I'm so busy I scarcely have time to take a walk, go for a drive, or play the lute. Nor a spare moment to indulge in any form of doubt.

When Mary stops by, she has to wait an hour because I'm painting the Duke of Devonshire. After he leaves, we have only a few minutes before my next sitter arrives.

"How could you let him go?" she demands.

Knowing she'll be even more upset if I describe the details of Henry's exit, I simply say, "Surely you agree I could never marry him, not considering how much you love him."

"But now he's gone," she wails. "I'll never see him again. All because you treated him poorly."

"He told you that?" I ask sharply, wondering what version of the truth he gave her.

"He didn't say much. But what am I to think, Angelica? Everyone knows he adored you. And now it is obvious how badly he's been hurt."

"I assure you," I say, "I didn't treat him poorly. He just didn't like that I refused him."

"But why? On account of Joshua Reynolds? Angelica, be reasonable!"

"I *am* being reasonable. Unreasonable would have been to marry him—Henry, I mean—when I don't love him." It's hard to explain myself since Mary isn't aware of all that transpired between Joshua and me, nor do I wish her to be. No one, not even my closest friend, needs to know how vulnerable I let myself be.

She looks at me in disbelief. "How can you be so cruel? You don't love anybody!"

Her words penetrate like daggers against which I have no defense. This isn't an attack on me as an artist or as a female artist. Or even me as a woman. It is an attack on who I am. "I thought the problem was I tried to love too many" is all I can say.

"No," she says, as the servant announces my next sitter. "The problem is . . . there are too many who love you. Don't you see that?"

Fifteen

Often over the winter, I'm tempted to book a passage to Italy. Certainly not to follow Henry. But so my father and I can start life afresh. I imagine being in Venice, in Naples, in Rome—all the places I love so much. Instead of checking the post each day for his letters, I could sit at his feet, tell him everything on my mind. Well, not everything. He doesn't need the burden of knowing about Joshua and that distressing turn of events. But we could talk about my career and make decisions together. Antonio's advice would be welcome as well. Too often I took him for granted. I see that now. Because of his peevishness, I overlooked how loyal he was.

Yet each time the temptation arises, I arrive yet again at the same conclusion: I can't leave. I came to London to fulfill a dream and I must stay until I've earned my success. I will work harder than ever, till I have the means to bring my father here.

By the early spring of 1767, I've saved enough money to rent a house of my own. I choose one with tall windows, on the south side of Golden Square, at the corner of Soho Street. As I cross the threshold for the first time, I know I've done the right thing. I belong in London. With this house, finally I've come home. The front drawing room, which looks out on a statue of King George II, is perfectly suited for my studio, with an adjoining gallery where visitors can view my canvases. The parlor is large enough for a harpsichord. I prepare one bedroom for my father, glad at last to have a place he can live in the comfort he deserves.

Clients flock to my studio. I have to paint faster than ever to keep up with all the commissions. Sometimes that isn't possible. Duchess Anna Amalia von Braunschweig-Wolfenbüttel, it turns out, has to return to Weimar before her first sitting. I'm disappointed, and not just because of the lost income. The one time we met briefly, I was fascinated by this woman who became a dowager duchess when she was widowed at nineteen and who now administers the affairs of state for her infant son, the grand duke. Her irrepressible laugh has the resonance of a cello. I hope someday we'll have a chance to meet again.

The most eminent of my clients is the Dowager Princess of Wales, the sister of King George III. She sent word asking me to paint her daughter, Princess Augusta the Duchess of Brunswick, while she's in London. It is to be a life-size portrait, holding her infant, and I have to work especially fast because she only has time for two sittings before returning to Germany.

Joshua always insisted skilled painters need not trouble with more than a single sitting. If the essential character of the face is captured, the details can be filled in later. All it takes is a bit of imagination. Though I've always been able to grasp a person's true character from just one look at their face, I didn't rely on that for portraits. Now that I'm pressed for time, I find it isn't difficult.

And I look for other ways to make my work easier. The more relaxed my sitters are, I've noticed, the more productive our sessions. So I'm learning to relax them. Often I stop a sitting to sing for them. Or I play my glass armonica. Some claim its sound can drive a person mad, but I find the opposite: When my sitters hear the musical glass, they feel soothed. It takes mere minutes to quiet them but saves hours of studio time.

When word gets out that the king's sister has been to my studio, all of London rushes to do likewise. Relaxed or not, I don't have time for them all. One nobleman was so dejected when I couldn't paint him that a group of his friends petitioned on his behalf. To avoid creating unnecessary enemies, I'll have to find a way to fit him in.

Every day, Golden Square is blocked by carriages—not just of those coming to see me but of those trying to catch a glimpse of my most famous sitters. The traffic gets so clogged that officers of the royal guard have to be called to help. Yesterday when returning from an errand, I almost lost my breath trying to squeeze through the crowd. I didn't notice in the crush, but a ribbon fell from my hair.

Later my maid told me two guards reached for it together. "They started to argue," she said. "Soon they were pushing and shoving. A third had to be summoned to break up the fight."

I told her I hoped no one was hurt.

"No," she replied. "But imagine, all for the sake of one ribbon from your hair!"

A particularly large coach arrives early one morning, before the street has become too crowded. The servant announces the Dowager Princess of Wales. Having commissioned her daughter's portrait, she wishes to see it for herself.

As she sweeps into the studio, I curtsy deeply and prepare myself for the formalities of a royal visitor. But Her Royal Highness sets a different tone. As might any mother, she coos over the image of the princess in a flowing white gown with blue and gold cape, her infant son resting on a pedestal before her. She wants to know all about it.

I tell her the pose is modeled after an ancient statue of Peace holding the infant Wealth.

She inspects the Grecian urn in the corner and asks about its inscription.

"It refers to the Duke's victory in battle," I say. "And to love's victory over him."

She smiles. "When he married my daughter, you mean."

"Exactly. And the figures of Mars and Venus holding the baby Cupid are a classical symbol for love's conquest over war."

She strokes my cheek. "For such a talented artist, love will surely conquer all."

No, I want to reply, *for me, art will conquer love.* But one can't contradict Her Royal Highness.

As soon as she has left, I run to the desk in my parlor to write my father: *Papa, you will be so proud of me! Today the Dowager Princess of Wales visited my studio! I've gotten nothing but applause for my work. Even the newspapers are full of verses in praise of me and my pictures.*

To other ears, my words may sound boastful, but I know they'll be welcome news to my father. If there's any boasting, it will be his as he reads my letter aloud to all the villagers.

As I finish writing, footsteps with a bouncing gait sound in the hallway. Perhaps because my thoughts are so strongly with Papa, the clatter reminds me of Antonio. Before I can add a postscript asking for news of him, I look up to see the man himself in my doorway.

"Antonio!" I give a little shriek. "Am I dreaming?"

"No," he says, grinning. "It's really me."

I smile back. "I'm so happy to see you!"

"And I, you." His grin grows even wider. "You're so elegant! Like the queen herself!"

I glance down at my burgundy dress with its burnished brocade trim, as if seeing it through his eyes. In fact, what I wear on an average morning here is fancier than what I wore to the grand ball in Venice. Antonio might have wished then that I remain simple and unspoiled, but now in his shabby jacket and worn boots, he is the one who looks out of place. "Don't hang in the doorway like you're about to run away," I tease. "Come and say a proper hello."

He needs no further invitation to stride into the room.

As he bends to kiss my hand, I look over his head toward the door. "Where's Papa?"

He doesn't let go of my hand as he leads me toward the sofa. "I came alone—"

I stop short, pulling my hand free. "But you promised to look after him!"

"I know. And I have, as if I were his son." As he settles on the sofa and I take a seat in the armchair, he explains he left my father in the care of Uncle Michel and his family. "He will come when the weather is warmer, but I couldn't wait any longer to see you," he says. "Besides, Robert Adams lured me to London to execute some architectural drawings. So here I am!"

"Here you are," I echo, trying to take in the news about my father and fully appreciate that the man next to me is flesh and blood.

"I found lodgings around the corner," he says. Suddenly his expression darkens. "Who was that man I saw here yesterday?"

"You came yesterday? Why didn't I see you?"

He gives a low growl. "I made it through all the traffic just as that tall man with spectacles was driving up. One look at his footmen with their ostentatious green livery and I decided to come back later."

Tall man with spectacles? Only one person I know fits that description. However, I haven't seen the man himself since Dr. Burney's concert. I assumed he went back to Sweden. But perhaps not. "That must have been Count de Horn. He didn't call, so he was probably just passing by. You remember him, don't you? We met him in Venice."

"*You* met him."

"Don't be so critical. The count has never been anything but friendly. Besides, in London one needs to hold onto one's friends."

Antonio shoots me a pointed look. "What's that supposed to mean? From everything I've heard, people here are mad over you."

"I do have admirers," I say vaguely. There is so much he doesn't know—and can't guess—about my life in London. "But it hasn't all been easy."

"If there are problems, you must tell me. Now that I'm here to protect you—" He stops abruptly and points to the hand he kissed a few minutes ago. "Who gave you that cameo?"

The Antonio I knew hasn't changed. His possessiveness, criticism, cynicism—all are as robust as ever. Yet I feel more forgiving. Secure in my own success, I don't need to react to each of his little apprehensions. "The ring was a gift from Bridget. And please stop worrying about me. I don't need protection."

"But you said—"

"No, no!" I laugh and move over to the sofa so I can shake the sleeve of his jacket. "Look at you. You're the one who needs help now."

He's about to protest again but stops himself. "I suppose I could use a new coat."

Not wishing to embarrass him, I don't say I will have several new coats sewn within the week. Let that be a surprise. Instead I say, "If Robert Adams doesn't keep you busy, it should be easy to find work. Engravers are in great demand. In fact, I'd love for you to engrave my paintings."

His eyes widen. "Your paintings are made into engravings?"

Our argument in Venice, when he rejected my suggestion he engrave my painting of Penelope, seems a lifetime ago. I explain there are other opportunities as well. "The queen commissioned my friend

Mary to paint decorative flowers at Frogmore Palace. We can ask if she needs anyone—" I hesitate, remembering how distant Mary has been since Henry left. Still, I don't see why she wouldn't help Antonio.

"I'd love to paint the palace ceilings!" His eyes grow even wider. "Have you been there?"

I tell him I haven't but the queen recently requested a portrait.

Antonio's face droops. "Compared with that, a ceiling isn't much."

"Come now." I tug playfully at his sleeve again. "I always dreamed of meeting the queen, and now it's coming true. Can't you be happy for me?"

When the royal summons comes just days later, I'm informed work will commence at once. I barely have time to prepare my canvas and pack all the necessary colors into my paint case before the carriage arrives to take me to Buckingham House. Queen Charlotte has chosen this palace, her place of retreat, for her portrait. I'm taken straight to the third floor, where she can sit for me and also be near the nursery.

The queen is several years younger than me, which helps establish rapport. As does her German birth, which means we can speak in her native language. One of the first things she says is "It pleases us to have a woman artist. We've seen too many of these men who think they know how to fashion a royal portrait."

When she says that, I know we'll get along.

I am to paint her holding her infant daughter, also Charlotte. Another babe—her fifth—is on the way, though of course not visible in the portrait.

As I work, we speak about the lace on the baby's christening gown, how my English is more fluent than hers, and the frequent showers that keep the gardeners busy. She invites me to walk among the mulberry trees, which were planted by King James I. He issued an edict promoting the cultivation of mulberries in the hopes England could produce its own silk. Regrettably, only black mulberries were planted, not the white variety used for silk. Still, she assures me, the ripe berries are delicious. I must return in the summer and try them.

The queen requires regular breaks to partake of a pinch or two of snuff. With pride, she shows me the miniature portrait of the king, set in a frame of rubies, that graces the lid of her gold snuff box.

Every day, I go to the palace. The queen, I learn, is a great lover of the arts, and music in particular. Her music teacher, she says, is a fellow I might know: Johann Christian Bach. When I explain he was the organist at the cathedral in Milan when I was there with my father, she claps her hands. She speaks highly of the child prodigy he introduced to her. "Mozart was only eight," she says, "yet he played like a master. We asked him to dedicate an opus to us, and he obliged."

In the end, she's pleased with the portrait. I'm happy too because I struck a balance—not making her overly glamorous, while doing all I could to dispel the rumors I'd heard from Bridget that the queen is ugly.

"One day," she says, "you must paint us as patron of the arts. We would appreciate that."

After I've finished the queen's portrait, the days grow warmer. My father will arrive soon. With money from the royal commission, I refurnish his bedroom and fill its wardrobe with a dozen new coats. I order them from the tailor who sewed new outfits for Antonio. I wasn't sure how my gift would be received, but he immediately discarded his old clothes and now wears only the stylish ones. I hope my father will do the same.

The prospect of seeing him has me singing in the studio. This is what we dreamed of—that I would be successful enough to support us both. Within one year in London, this has been accomplished, and then some. Not only am I basking in unprecedented glory for a woman artist, I finally have time for history painting. I'm free to immerse myself in the company of the goddesses, where my heart is always glad.

Once again I'm painting Ariadne. When I painted her in Rome, I focused on her grief at losing her beloved; now I intend to foreshadow the arrival of a new beloved, one who will immortalize their love. Immortalize *her*. I want viewers to believe love is more enduring than heartache, even if so many are drawn to the latter.

While the Titian in Bridget's Prussian blue room portrayed both Bacchus and Ariadne, I have made her my sole subject. My challenge lies in our dissimilarity. She's so unlike me. She does not crave what I crave. Nor would she ever make a vow that sacrificed her chances at love. Of course, to paint her, I must understand her. I must feel her heart, even if my own has little feeling left. I must know her sorrow as my sorrow. That, in fact, isn't difficult. Lately my tears have fallen as easily as hers.

Yet I have come to see and appreciate the blessing of not marrying Joshua. Or Henry or Nathaniel, for that matter. Regardless of how fond of one another we might have grown, and how supportive Joshua would have been, as his wife, I wouldn't have been free to paint with the uninhibited liberty I now enjoy. Marriage would have created too many conflicting demands. Not to mention, I wouldn't have been allowed legal ownership of my own paintings. Whatever the artistic merits of Frances's paintings, at least as a single woman she can call them her own. Yes, my life is fortunate in so many ways.

One of those ways is the freedom to go where I wish, to entertain myself as I choose.

In early summer, I decide to attend a concert at Dr. Burney's. Antonio isn't a music enthusiast, and though Frances and I are cordial, she no longer asks me to accompany her. So I go by myself. Some might deem it unbecoming for a woman to be alone at an event, but I don't think twice about it. After all, I'm here to close my eyes and be carried away by the music. No outer companionship is necessary. That I can feel so independent on a night I might encounter Joshua tells me my heart has mended. Indeed, I'm finally ready to resume work on our mutual portraits, as he's been pressing me to do for some time.

I arrive early to find the doors thrown open, a stage set under the arbor, and rows of chairs on the lawn. I take a seat toward the back and close my eyes as I listen to the musicians tune their instruments. The sound brings to mind how one prepares a palette before painting. Each color must be tuned, as it were, for the brush. Unlike music, however, dissonance doesn't arise with colors, at least not if the brush is kept clean. Just as I have this thought, someone slides into the seat beside me. I open my eyes.

"Count de Horn!" I exclaim.

"Frederick, please," he murmurs, leaning on the arm of his chair.

So Antonio was right: He *is* in London.

He adjusts his ruby-studded saber so he can lean closer. Our elbows are practically touching.

"I take it you're fond of Gluck?" I say, shrinking back so our elbows won't collide.

"Fond of—?"

"Gluck," I repeat, though I said it distinctly the first time. "I hear they've chosen selections from *Don Juan*."

"I'm very fond," he says softly, bypassing my explanation, moving closer to compensate for my retreat. He looks at me with such hunger etched in his blue eyes that I become slightly disoriented. He looks pleased to have that effect on me. "They can play whatever they wish," he whispers, "because I'm with the loveliest woman in London."

Sixteen

Frederick hasn't been around for months, yet now, like the London fog, he seems to turn up everywhere. When I attend the Society's latest exhibition, he's crossing the street just as I leave the gallery. Without saying a word, he offers his arm to shield me from the throngs pushing against my carriage. When I drive along the Thames after church, his coach is parked at a bend in the road. It's easy to spot with its footmen in green livery, the brightest in London.

He waves as I pass.

And I feel a little rush of excitement.

It's been so long since I flirted with Nathaniel or Henry or anyone else that I've almost forgotten how. In fact, I remind myself, flirtation doesn't have to lead to a social disaster. It can be amusing. It can be good fun. Not that I'm interested in flirting with Frederick. I'm just curious about him. I think it's because of his unusually handsome face. His classic features would be perfect for a history painting. Or perhaps I'm drawn by the desire in his eyes. I can feel it even when we pass at a distance.

Soon I'm anticipating meeting him whenever I go out, rotating my head a few extra degrees, in case he's near. If I don't run across him in town, I think about him later in the studio, wonder when he'll call at Golden Square. I'm surprised he hasn't already. Surely he must wish for a portrait. Everyone else of nobility does.

I can imagine him in the fourth painting of my Trojan series, which will be of Achilles. Since Achilles is always shown as fair, Frederick will be a fitting model. Of course, physical perfection isn't an indication of inner virtue. Every time we meet, I see the struggles of his soul shining through his eyes. He is a man of complexity. I can't wait to paint him.

By way of practice, I make some sketches from memory. In each, his finely sculpted face, with its porcelain skin and azure blue eyes, seems to leap off the paper. I want to keep gazing at it. The hunger in his eyes is a bit unhinging. But that doesn't stop me. I'm driven to find out more about him, the way one can't help but be curious about what one senses could prove dangerous.

Naturally I can't talk to Antonio about this. He'd see only cause for alarm. And not totally without reason: With all of London turning its collective head toward me, the last thing I need is for anyone to call me a flirt. I decide instead to call on Bridget.

As I step into her parlor, she lifts Constable out of the armchair by her side so I can sit and exclaims, "Come, tell me all about your new portraits!"

I begin with what she already knows—that Queen Charlotte and the Duchess of Brunswick sat for me. Then I describe the queue of clients waiting for portraits.

"Look at my protégé," she cries, quick as always to take credit. "I recognized pure gold when I saw it in that dreary church, didn't I?"

I thank her, of course.

"You must tell me when you're going to court again. Everyone's keen for stories about Snuffy Charlotte," she chortles. "The ambassador said that nickname has even spread to the Continent. The whole world knows how much she loves her snuff!"

I promise to let Bridget know if I'm invited back.

"Certainly you will be," she says. "If not soon, then later. That's how things are at court—if it isn't one delay, it's another. And now all that hulla-baloo over the colonists. I've heard talk Lord Chatham has taken ill again. He deserves it for supporting the American riff-raff." She pulls out her fan and begins pumping away. "Please don't let me get started on him."

That gives me an opening to bring up the count. Not that he's on par with Lord Chatham, but I do have some gossip about him. My maid is the source, though Bridget need not know that. "They say Count de Horn commanded a regiment in the French army."

"The *French* army?"

"That's what I heard."

This is new information for Bridget. She immediately excuses herself so she can relay it to her husband. Having befriended the count in Venice, he should be able to confirm or deny it. She is back after a few minutes to report he had little to add, except that he suspects the count is in London on a secret diplomatic mission for Sweden. "I'll keep my ears open," she says. "You'll be the first to know if I learn anything."

Though she doesn't inquire about my personal interest in the count, I know that's on her mind. So she doesn't get any wrong ideas, I tell her how eager I am to paint his portrait, how perfect he is for Achilles. As soon as he has become my client, which surely will happen very soon, I promise to bring her more news.

As I leave Charles Street—having assured Bridget I'll be at her masquerade ball next month—what should I see but Frederick's coach, stopped right across the road. He's staring out the window while his driver waits for another vehicle to get out of the way.

He spots me immediately and waves.

By now my curiosity has gotten the better of me. I stride up to him and ask outright what brings him to London.

I'm hoping for a direct answer to a direct question, but he only teases me before his coach moves on. "I followed you from Venice," he says, eyes blazing. "I'll follow you around the world if need be."

Frederick is a man of surprises. The day after my chat with Bridget, he pays his first visit to Golden Square. Instead of coming to my studio, however, he stops in the kitchen. I only learn about it from my maid the following morning. She saw him talking to the cook and assumed he'd gotten lost after visiting me.

When I mention this to Bridget the next time we meet, she gives me a quizzical look. "I was going to tell you he was riding beside the footman at the front of his coach," she says. "I saw them on Oxford Road. Extremely odd, don't you think?"

To me, these incidents aren't so much odd as charming. Perhaps it's my own modest background, but I draw comfort from what strikes others as odd. It impresses me that Frederick doesn't find it necessary to act like a count at all times, to flaunt his nobility. I just hope that won't keep him from requesting a portrait.

I soon discover we have more in common: We're both Catholics in a Protestant country. Though I've never seen him at church. Apparently he doesn't go regularly, as I do. But today, as I'm leaving mass, I notice him waiting inside the entryway.

He steps forward, extends his arm, and offers to escort me home.

"I didn't know you attended mass," I say, without taking his arm.

"I'm afraid I came late," he says. "Next time I will greet you when you arrive."

He sounds contrite. Besides, it's a long walk home and the sky is threatening rain. So I let him lead me to his coach.

Whenever I rode with Joshua, he entertained me with talk about art and literature and our mutual friends. With Nathaniel, such talk was laced with flirtation. Not so Frederick. Granted, he isn't an artist and we don't share many friends, nevertheless he speaks not a word as we cross the city. I wait for him to say something. When he doesn't, I sit quietly and take in his company. His stature is even more striking in such close quarters. His long legs stretch across the aisle, pressing against my skirts. While he looks out the window, I run my eyes from the bridge of his spectacles down the smooth slope of his nose, then along his jaw as it angles from his ear lobe to his chin. Mentally I sketch the curve of his lower lip, the hint of a natural pout. That last detail I missed when drawing him from memory.

As he turns from the window, his eyes meeting mine, it couldn't be more obvious that I'm staring. I explain that I'm planning his portrait.

The familiar hunger flashes in his eye.

"I hope," I say, "you'll let me paint one for your palace in Sweden."

When I offer that, his eyes dart to the window again. But only for a second. "Surely you can find more fascinating faces."

I think he must be joking, but his tone is deadly serious. I have to smile. His response is so unlike what I'm used to. It's free of the greed that makes clients say, "Paint *me* first. Make *my* canvas larger . . . *my* portrait the most magnificent." No, he is more concerned about my needs as the artist. In fact, I can hardly wait to paint him as Achilles, ready for battle, invincible but for one hidden vulnerability.

We ride the rest of the way in silence. It's possible, I can see, to become acquainted without speaking much. I attune to what otherwise might be overlooked: the breadth of his shoulders under his cloak, and the strength of his legs, which I sense through the many layers of my skirt. His limbs seem continually on the verge of motion, his body held taut, yet with an almost imperceptible vibration, like that of a bow strung tight. All this makes him seem unusually alive. It is hard to stop staring.

I only look away when we pull into Golden Square. A wagon is parked in front of my house, servants scurrying to and fro.

"It appears you have guests," he says.

I suggest that perhaps he can visit another day. We look at each other while his footman dismounts and comes around to open the door. Then I gather up my skirts.

Rising in his seat, Frederick catches my hand. "I can't let you go without a promise."

"What is that?"

"The first three dances at the event of the year—Lady Wentworth's masquerade ball."

"I imagine that could be arranged," I say, then quickly free my hand and step down.

As he drives away, I regret acquiescing quite so fast. I could have felt the pressure of his grasp a few seconds longer.

The old gray trunk with its worn cords and padlock sits inside the front door. When I see it, I know my father has arrived—before the end of the summer, as pledged in his last letter. I find him standing in the parlor, in his traveling clothes, undoubtedly the same jacket he's worn all the way from Schwarzenberg.

I fly across the room and into his arms. The scent of his sleeve as I bury my nose in it—a mixture of paint and tobacco, with a touch of onion—carries me straight back to childhood.

Wiping away tears, he leans back to look at me. "I scarcely recognize you!"

He too has changed. Though I don't point it out, new wrinkles cross his brow, deeper creases carve his cheeks from either side of his nose to the corners of his mouth. Never before did he carry a cane.

"Since Antonio showed us this palace of yours, we've been in a state of shock," he says.

I'm about to ask why he's speaking in the plural, when Antonio rushes into the room, followed by a young girl.

"Your cousin Rosa," Papa says. "Uncle Michel's daughter, in case you don't recall."

"Of course I do," I say, holding out my hands to the girl.

She takes them shyly.

"Rosa reminds me of you at her age," he says. "She's looked after me all year. Antonio taught her English, and she learned so fast Michel decided she should come to help around the house. When she's older, you can introduce her to society."

"We brought you gifts." Rosa's shyness vanishes as she reaches into the trunk and pulls out some large cheeses and a black lambswool shawl.

As I nibble the cheese, I tell her how excited I am. Right away we will replace her old frock with new clothes. And of course we'll take my carriage for a tour of the city.

Later, when Rosa is in bed, my father, Antonio, and I gather around the fireplace in the parlor. Papa props his legs on the over-stuffed stool, while I settle on the carpet, as close as possible. Except that the décor couldn't be more different, we might as well be in our old apartment in Venice. This is the family I've missed.

My father is ready to begin a new life, though apprehensive about how it might unfold. "Pray I can find some work to keep me busy," he says.

"There's no need for that!" I object. "My income can support us both and Rosa too."

He reaches down and strokes my head, tells me he couldn't be more proud.

"Then promise that whatever work you do will be for pleasure, nothing less."

Having stated it thus, I expect him to give his word. When he doesn't, I ask what's bothering him. It occurs to me his hesitation might be because, though I have managed my accounts with ease all year, he would prefer to do them again himself. But it turns out his worry isn't about finances. "I fear," he says, "you've made too great a sacrifice."

I bristle at that. Finances might be up for negotiation. Sacrifice is not. "Only sacrifices willingly made," I say.

He glances at Antonio, who's busy putting logs on the fire on this unusually chilly summer night, and sighs. "Seeing how mature you are reminds me I've done nothing to secure you a proper husband," he says, then adds under his breath, "Antonio is convinced you'll die a spinster."

When I hear that, I'm incensed. Antonio is entitled to his opinions, but this is none of his business. Then I remember the two of us haven't argued since he arrived in London. So I simply say, "You don't see me that way, Papa, do you?"

He frowns. "I don't think you can accuse me of pushing you toward a husband. Your happiness has always been what matters." He falls silent, and I watch reflected light from the fire dance across the new furrows on his brow. "Though," he adds, "at my age, I'm afraid I may never see—"

"Your wedding," interjects Antonio, aiming as always for the final word.

Seventeen

It is the day of the masquerade ball at Bridget Wentworth's estate. That grand event takes place unfailingly every autumn—except last year, when it was canceled due to her health. She isn't appreciably stronger this year but has resigned herself to directing the affair from a reclining chair, with two servants at her side to carry out orders and two more to fan her if her breathing becomes labored.

I leave the studio early, needing several hours to dress. The silver brocade gown Lord Exeter sent as an extra token of appreciation for his portrait lies across my bed. Next to it are an ostrich feather head-piece and mask. I will be stunning when I dance with Frederick, and all my other partners.

A tap at the door, and Rosa peeks into the room. "I wish I could go," she says.

"You will when you're old enough."

She approaches the bed and fingers the feathers.

"If you'd like," I say, "you can have the headpiece tomorrow."

"Won't you wear it again?"

"Oh no, one can't be seen in the same costume twice." I laugh at how incomprehensible such luxury would have seemed even a year ago.

A slight frown crosses her face. "What's Antonio wearing?"

"He won't be going," I say, turning away abruptly on the pretext of comparing two necklaces.

She follows and stands behind me. "You're going by yourself? To a ball?"

I remind her I've lived independently in London for a while and frequently go out alone. Besides, these are my friends. Antonio isn't well acquainted with them.

"You mean the count?" She gives a sniff of disgust. "That man makes me queasy."

I lay the chosen necklace, Bridget's silver beads, on the table and put the other into its box. "I don't see how you can say that. You don't know him."

"He called twice this week, have you forgotten?"

That's true. On both occasions, he arrived while I was playing my armonica to soothe a jittery sitter. We didn't have a chance to talk. He left a message with the servant, reminding me of my promised three dances. "Rosa," I object, "he stayed all of five minutes."

"Long enough to see he's a man with a dark secret."

"He doesn't have a secret, you silly! He's just quiet by nature," I say as I comb out my hair. "When you're older, you'll understand how that can be appealing."

"Well, I like Antonio the way he is." She peers over my shoulder at her face in the looking glass. "Why don't you introduce him to your friends? Then he'll be their friend as well."

I have to smile at her loyalty. "I'll remember that for the next ball," I say, giving her arm a playful squeeze. "Now I really must get ready or I'll be late."

As I make my way through the crowd gathered to watch the guests arrive at Charles Street, the first carriage I notice is the count's. It's the largest, with the most conspicuous footmen, standing like porcelain statuettes in their green livery, with huge nosegays and wands in their hands. Frederick is waiting in the foyer, dressed in a pirate's attire, with knee breeches, a black woolen cloak, and tricorn hat. His mask is a black patch covering most of the left side of his face. Taller than everyone, he's impossible to miss.

When he sees me, he rushes over. "I was beginning to think you wouldn't come!"

"I promised three dances, didn't I?"

"We've missed the first minuet," he says, taking my arm and escorting me toward the living room. "Fortunately another is about to start."

The room, empty of its usual furniture, has been decorated as a dance hall, with boughs of fir and sprigs of red berries hung all around. The music now isn't a minuet but a country dance, and it sends us prancing across the floor. Frederick is excellent on his toes, composed yet relaxed as the music speeds up. Even with a patch over half his face—and without the aid of his temple spectacles—he doesn't make a step that isn't graceful.

Out of the corner of my eye, I spot Joshua in an alcove, dressed in the hooded brown robes of a monk, talking to a woman in a Grecian costume whom I recognize from one of his portraits. I feel a wave of pride that everyone can see me—and they *are* looking, including Joshua—on the arm of such an accomplished partner.

At the end of three dances, we retire to the sidelines to catch our breath. By now it's understood we will dance a fourth.

Frederick is feeding me raspberry cake, trying not to get jam on my ostrich feathers, when Catherine grabs my arm. "It's my first ball!" she exclaims. "Did you see me dance?"

I admire the gold lace on her mask, while her partner, the ambassador—who is visiting in London and sporting sultan's robes and a turban he brought from Constantinople—strikes up a conversation with my partner.

"Have you seen the latest *Courant*?" I hear the ambassador ask.

"No."

The ambassador chuckles. "The editors are getting lazy. Their news is out of date. They're only just now announcing Count de Horn's arrival from Sweden on his first-ever visit to London. They think he'll be here soon!"

Evidently Frederick doesn't share the ambassador's sense of humor. "Ridiculous!" he mutters, with a vehemence that surprises me.

"Maybe you should set them straight," says the other, still laughing.

Before Frederick can reply, the music resumes, and Catherine tugs at her father's arm, begging for another dance.

As they glide away, Frederick throws down his tricorn hat and rips off his mask. He pushes back his blond locks, then dabs at his brow with a kerchief he pulls from a pocket under his cloak. "Is it hot in here?" he whispers.

"I haven't noticed," I say. In truth, I'm no warmer than usual after several rousing dances. But he looks distressed. "Perhaps," I suggest, "it would be best if you sit this one out."

"Yes, I'm afraid I've overdone it," he says, collapsing onto the Turkish divan behind us.

I bend beside him and cool him with my fan. It's disturbing to see such a vibrant man so suddenly undone. And for no apparent reason. Really, it isn't hot in here.

"Thank you," he says, glancing around, as if making sure no one noticed his faintness. "I'm feeling better already." He picks up his hat, dusts it off, and puts it back on. Then he folds his kerchief and tucks it back in his pocket, along with his mask. This is the first time I've seen him without spectacles. His face has a naked beauty like that of Michelangelo's statue of David in Florence.

I offer to fetch him some water.

"That's not necessary," he says, rising to his feet, then helping me up. "Just fresh air."

Assuming he wants to sit by an open window, I start to raise the sash of the nearest one.

But he shakes his head. "Let's take a stroll in the garden."

I hesitate. My promise of three dances is expanding much faster than I expected. Normally I have a dozen dance partners in one evening. My name is never joined to any man's. I've learned not to let secrets or innuendo circle around me, not to give anyone the slightest excuse to start false rumors. Not to let a flirtation lead anywhere.

Yet I've just seen a vulnerability in Frederick that touches me. The last thing I want is to let him walk away, perhaps stroll in the garden with someone else.

He anticipates my concerns. "There's a full moon. The garden will be brightly lit."

By way of reply, I slip my arm through his.

All the other guests are dancing, so we have the garden to ourselves. Its narrow pathways, bordered with low hedges, crisscross the flowerbeds and weave their way around a lily pond. Walking arm-in-arm along a path designed for one alone, we find ourselves unexpectedly close. I don't pull away—as I ordinarily would to avoid any hint of indecorum—so he can lean on me if he feels faint again. Besides, there is no one here to see us.

After a couple of turns around the pond, he has fully revived, and I begin to wonder if our absence has been noted.

I suggest we return to the ball.

But he isn't ready for that. Clutching me more tightly against his body, he steers me to a bench under a maple at the far end of the garden, where he brushes aside some dry leaves so we can sit. "My beauty," he whispers, "there is no jewel more precious than your face. Let me treasure it just a bit longer."

Perhaps it's the intensity of his words or the force of his breath on my face or the breeze that sweeps across the pond, but suddenly I shiver.

He takes off his cloak and lays it on my shoulders, then extends his arm around me to make sure it stays in place. As we sit in silence, the pressure of his arm across my back, much warmer than the warmest wool, burns through to my skin. Ignites something deep within me.

Under the heat of his arm, a lifetime of resolve begins to melt. Bridget, Antonio, Mary, and others—even my father—have told me I'm making a mistake, that I'm sacrificing unwisely. For so long I have resisted them, believing I know better because I am an artist. Could I actually be mistaken? Am I just stubborn, selfish even? Maybe, it occurs to me, there is something more satisfying than flirtation, something that can enrich my life as much as art does. In this moment, I wish nothing more than to be with Frederick, to sit just as we are.

"We must always be as we are tonight," he says, echoing my thought.

As I turn toward him, he leans in, and with his free hand, removes my mask. He runs a finger down my cheek until it comes to rest under my chin, then gently tilts my face toward his.

Briefly his lips brush against mine.

The few kisses I exchanged with young men in Milan and Rome were forgettable. Nothing like this. I'm ready to discover what a kiss can be.

However, Frederick pulls back. He sighs sharply and begins instead to talk about himself. Never have I heard him speak at such length. He tells me about Sweden, his military honors, his wealth. When I ask about his home, he describes a castle high on a hill in Huvudsta. "Someday," he says, his arm tightening around my shoulders, "I will bring you there."

Feeling his body so close, the force of the moment seems to affirm that, yes, this is possible. "Really?" I say. "You want me to go to Sweden?"

He counters with a question: "Will you come with me?"

I'm not sure exactly what he's asking. Sweden was never on our itinerary, but maybe my father and I could have a life of nobility and riches there, while I enjoy the freedom to paint as I wish. I feel again the elation I felt when Bridget invited me to London. One can't say no to such opportunities. Only this is much more than business. Frederick could be much more than a patron. Still, I can't commit to an offer so vague. "When are you going?" I ask.

"Soon," he says. "Very soon. But in the meantime, this must remain our secret."

Again, I'm reminded of Bridget expecting me to keep a secret. I didn't like it then either.

My unease must be written on my face, because he reaches for my hands. His grip is as convincing as his words. "It will only be a brief delay. I'm waiting for some documents from Sweden that I want to have in hand before I speak with your father."

The moonlight casts his face in shadow so I can't see his eyes, but I feel his strong intention. To make us inseparable. I too want that.

He tells me it will be worth the wait. "When my business is in order, I'll be able to give you the finest gowns and jewelry, a winter palace and a summer estate. You can turn any room into a studio. You can have ten studios if you want!"

I'm overwhelmed. We came out to take a stroll so Frederick could get some air. And now he is laying his world at my feet. "Is that really possible?" I whisper.

In response, he pulls me closer and presses his lips against mine.

Eighteen

At mass the next morning, I edge forward on the pew, my foot silently tap-tapping on the kneeler. Knowing I'll be here, how can Frederick stay away? Yet the mere thought of seeing him unnerves me. For the first time in my life, I'm keeping a secret from my father. In letters, it wasn't possible to tell him every detail, but I never deliberately withheld information. Never.

I sit beside him and pray for forgiveness.

At least a dozen times, I turn my head—slowly so as not to attract notice—and search the back of the church in case Frederick has come late.

He does not appear.

In the afternoon, having told my father that work demands my attention, I retire to the studio while he and Antonio take Rosa for a drive in the park. But I'm in no mood to paint. I stand by the window and watch for Frederick. If he sees my father has gone out, surely he'll want a few moments with me. Secret moments. Another secret kiss.

Closing my eyes, I feel again his finger lingering on my chin, his arm wrapped around me. And his lips. Beneath my skin, feelings I've never known are awakening.

At the same time, like a wild creature with a life of its own, this secret is struggling to breathe through my nostrils, scream through my teeth. I don't know how long I can contain it. Nor do I understand how I—a woman so determined to remain unmarried, who recognized the blessing of not marrying Joshua or anyone else, who values her freedom as an artist above all, who lives by the motto *Let my heart alone*—agreed to go to Sweden with Frederick. A man I barely know! It makes no sense.

My bond with Joshua grew out of friendship, out of our mutual love for art. I share none of that with Frederick. I don't think he even cares that I am an artist. Whether or not I'm talented or famous seems inconsequential to him. No, he sees me first and foremost as a woman. Which isn't how I have ever seen myself. Or wish to. However, it may explain the recklessness that overtakes me in his presence. I learned from Mary that the heart follows its own laws. Apparently being reckless is one of those laws.

When it's clear he isn't coming, I take out my portfolio and find the drawings I did of him from memory. Even on paper he excites me. My rough sketch of his face is enough to launch a thousand day-dreams—all carrying me from Bridget's lily pond to a stone castle in Sweden. Except daydreams aren't what I need right now. What I need is to understand why I am allowing this man to sway the resolve I've held onto for so long.

Voices sound in the hallway, and a moment later, Antonio rushes into the studio, followed by my father. I'm startled to see them so soon, not realizing I've been alone for hours.

"Where's Rosa?" I ask, snapping shut the portfolio.

"Upstairs dressing for dinner," my father says. "We've come with news."

"News?" I look up in alarm.

"Good news," he says. "Antonio and I have a plan."

Antonio explains the details: "With such high demand for your paintings, if John Joseph makes reproductions, they're guaranteed to sell."

My first reaction is relief the news isn't about Frederick. My second is to disagree. The notion of my father making copies strikes me as undignified. Besides, my own news—that we're about to come into more money than we'll know what to do with—renders their plan moot. My father will have to get used to a life of nobility. Of course, I can't tell him yet.

As we talk, I realize he simply wants to keep busy, to feel useful in his new home. In the end, we decide he'll come to the studio for a while each afternoon and work on copying my new painting of the Three Muses. When he hears I don't yet have a buyer for the original, he says we must find one. Reproductions won't sell well if the painting itself hasn't been sold.

"Finding a buyer shouldn't be hard," Antonio says. "All of London is mad for Angelica Kauffman."

"Let's start with that count of yours," my father says. "I should have spoken to him already."

"Please—" I pause, unsure how to dissuade him. Involving Frederick in a purchase is one complication I don't need at the moment.

But he is determined. "Clearly he's a man of great worth—"

"Monetary worth," Antonio snickers. "We don't know about the rest."

"Money is what counts here," my father says. "I don't understand why he hasn't requested a portrait. He must be considering it."

I try to steer the conversation back to reproductions, but my father goes on about the count: "When he does decide to buy—whether it's the Three Muses or a portrait or both—we must demand the highest price. One should always seek good money from those who can pay."

Antonio, however, has his own reasons for objecting to Frederick as a buyer. "Each picture has its own value—no more, no less. Why should Angelica sell her dignity along with her work by changing her price according to the buyer?"

I want to stop him, but it's too late. He is fuming about my predicament as an artist whose livelihood depends on her creative genius. Now that I'm making a lot of money, he insists my need for someone to handle my clientele is greater than ever.

"What do you think *I'm* here for?" my father counters.

At which point, Antonio accuses us both of not listening to reason and storms out.

All week, Antonio does not show his face in Golden Square. Nor does Frederick. Whereas before he seemed to be everywhere, now his absence is equally striking.

As the days pass, my desire to see him is replaced by doubt and misgiving. I run through the evening of the masquerade ball over and again in my mind. Yes, he invited me to travel with him and promised me great riches, but it wasn't a true proposal. Never did he use the words *wed* or *wife* or *marriage*. And definitely not *love*. Suppose I misunderstood? What transpired between us could have been mere flirtation in his mind. No more than a faint brushstroke on a blank canvas. A picture that was never meant to be painted. As a nobleman, it would be reasonable for him to have second thoughts about a liaison with an artist. When we next see each other, he may expect me to act as if nothing of significance has been said. As if all we did was indulge in a fanciful flight of imagination.

The more I think about it, it seems odd he was so suddenly faint at the ball, then recovered so quickly. Was all that a ploy to lure me outside for a kiss? When he invited me to Sweden, was he just toying with me? Or worse, trying to buy my favors?

But no, that is how Antonio thinks—always suspecting the

worst, always assuming I can be easily duped. That because I'm a woman, I'm helpless. I refuse to think that way. I can focus instead on Frederick's willingness to show vulnerability. On his gentleness and generosity. There is no reason to question whether I can paint him as Achilles in my Trojan series, then accept a place among Swedish royalty. I am worthy of that.

In the evenings, I distract myself from all the uncertainty by painting fans. I promise Rosa she can take one to her first ball. I listen with half an ear as she speculates about that event.

"You've been to so many balls," she says as I paint a peacock's tail across the folds of a fan. "You have so many admirers. Antonio says every man in London loves you. Why haven't you chosen one?"

She's just a child, so I humor her. "Whom would you have me pick? My printmaker, William Ryland, perhaps?"

"I see how much he likes you—"

"Possibly," I say. "But he's already married."

"I didn't know."

"Nor did I. He tries to keep it quiet. But he's very much married." I smile at her over the top of the fan and continue our play. "Would you prefer Jean-Paul Marat?"

She laughs. "The Frenchman who's friends with Antonio? He likes you too—but it's obvious he can't keep his eyes off any woman! Antonio—"

Before she can suggest Antonio himself, I hand her the fan and ask her to hold it so I can see its colors beside the hazel of her eyes.

A few weeks after the ball, Bridget shows up at Golden Square. "Luckily I was strong enough to leave the house," she says, leaning heavily on her cane as she moves past the servant and into my studio. "I instructed my driver to come straight here."

Lady Hyde, my next sitter, isn't due for an hour, so I follow Bridget to the sofa.

Declining an offer for tea, she gets right to her point. "I noticed how much attention Count de Horn paid you at the ball."

My instinct is to repeat what I've always said—that my art is all I care about. But she is aware of my interest in Frederick, so she will see through any denial.

When I don't say anything, she does her best to suppress a cough, then continues: "Considering all you've been through, I'm here as your friend to say you could hardly do better. After all, he *is* royalty."

I jump up from the sofa. Has Bridget, the master at uncovering every detail, uncovered our secret? If she knows, soon everyone in London will. If they don't already.

"It's true he exhibited odd behavior," she says, as I cross the room to my easel, "Riding with his footman was startling. But lately he's been quite the gentleman, don't you agree?"

I reach for a brush, not to paint, just stalling for time as I figure out what she does and doesn't know. The brush hasn't been cleaned, and a spray of scarlet shoots across the floor, narrowly missing Bridget's lowest ruffles.

"Look at you!" she says. "Even speaking of him now, you're aflutter. Can you deny it?"

Of course I can't. Not completely. But aflutter? That's for daffodils and fragile souls like Mary. I need to regain control by telling Bridget only what I want her to know. Nothing more. If I explain that Frederick has vanished, she will know how to find him. I return to the sofa, sitting closer this time. "He has—"

Before I can say more, she cuts me off. "Good! Then this is no mere dalliance." She leans over and wipes a smudge of red pigment from my wrist, as a mother might, with a corner of my apron. "It's time to give up your childish notions of remaining a spinster. Do it now, while you still have a chance at happiness."

I wince at her inference I don't know what's best for my own happiness. That I'd be amenable to a union in which I am a lesser partner. "You don't understand," I say. "He may have shown some interest, but he's disappeared."

"You haven't seen him since the ball?"

"Not once."

"Oh my," she laughs, "the ball wasn't that long ago! Give the man time. Think how busy he is, how much responsibility comes with his vast fortune. In fact, I hear he's staying at the Claridge. That alone says how wealthy he is."

Maybe, I think, *she's right.* As a celebrated artist and also a countess, I'd have the chance to do things no other woman has done.

As if she's heard my thoughts, she raises her head. "Last year you threw away the most favorable chance you'll ever have—"

It's the first time she has mentioned that night. "Joshua Reynolds?" I whisper.

"Yes. I was furious because you refused to heed my advice. Your imprudence almost cost us our friendship. If you make that mistake again, my heart will be broken. I hope you consider your options carefully."

I tell her I intend to do that.

"I don't mean to insinuate myself into your decision," she says. "But I had to speak before you came to a foolhardy conclusion."

"Nothing's been decided," I say, glad I've given Bridget some information, yet safeguarded my secret.

She clasps my hands firmly in her own. "You can have everything: your talent, your success—and a husband. I've always considered the count attractive. You could scarcely find a woman with a face as fair and free of blemish as his! Not all of us are so fortunate in marriage." With that last thought, a shadow crosses her face, but she quickly recovers. "Look what's become of the artist I discovered in Venice. Who'd have guessed she'd paint the queen of England and marry into Swedish nobility?"

"After dining with a goatherd," I say softly.

"Beg your pardon?"

Before I can explain, we're interrupted by the servant announcing Lady Hyde. In a white gown with a vibrant scarlet sash, she is ready for her sitting.

I don't have any time to reflect on Bridget's advice until I'm alone in my studio late in the evening, after my father and Rosa have gone to bed. As I prepare a canvas for tomorrow, I listen to rain lashing against the shutters and reflect on her encouragement. Ironically, Frederick might be the one in need of it now.

Just as I'm thinking this, footsteps resound in the hallway, heavy but muffled, unlike any of the servants. Not only is it too late for visitors, but the storm has kept everyone inside all evening. Instinctively, I back away from the door.

A second later, Frederick bursts into the room, his jacket unbuttoned and askew, his saber drawn.

My hands fly to my mouth, suppressing a scream.

Seeing me, he stops short. As I stand in the center of the room, hands over my mouth, he shuts the door, sheathes his weapon, and approaches me. "I'm sorry," he says. "I didn't mean to cause a fright. But I had to see you. Tonight!"

Nineteen

Slowly dropping my hands, I stare at the figure before me. This hardly seems like the man I danced with at the ball, kissed in the garden. Longed all week to see.

"What's the matter?" I say. "You look terrible."

"I'm afraid I have terrible news." He shakes the wetness out of his hair, then pulls out his kerchief and mops his brow. He stuffs it back into his pocket without folding it, his eyes all the while fixed on the floor.

I wait for him to meet my gaze, to explain.

"A letter came from Sweden." He looks quickly at me, then back at the floor. His voice is so faint I have to strain to catch the words. "My enemies are spreading lies. They've persuaded our king I'm conspiring against him."

I don't know what to say. "Perhaps," I suggest, "you can clear your name?"

"I'm afraid it's *much* worse than that!"

His words are so loud I have to hush him. "Surely there's no conspiracy?"

"None at all."

I realize how little I know about his circumstances. Didn't the ambassador say something about him being in London on a secret diplomatic mission? That's hardly a conspiracy. "Whatever happens," I say, "your friends here will stand by you. As will I."

He scans my face, as if judging whether I am truly a friend.

I look back steadily so he can see I'm sincere.

"I just heard," he says, glancing over his shoulder at the door, "the Swedish ambassador at the British court has orders for my arrest."

"They'd *arrest* you?"

He nods.

Hastily I circle the room and extinguish all the lamps, except one candle over the mantel. It seems the most immediate way to protect him. Then I rush back to his side. "It can't be true?"

For a moment, he doesn't respond, but the way his eyes dart about suggests he isn't exaggerating. "I'm afraid I'm near ruin. That's why you haven't seen me all week, and why I've come now. God knows, this isn't how I wanted you to see me!"

I try to absorb what he's saying, to imagine how such a powerful man could fall into utter collapse. And so suddenly. If no one else will, I have to help him. I say the first thing that comes to mind: "Stay here tonight."

He frowns. "I'm not asking for that."

"It's the least—"

He cuts me off. "Much as I'd like to stay, it wouldn't be safe for either of us."

When he says that, I envision the servants discovering him in the morning. Not to mention my father. How would we explain? "Then I'll find you a safe place," I say, "before the officials start searching—"

"They're searching as we speak."

"That's impossible."

"I swear it's true."

As the magnitude of his predicament dawns on me, I feel a new threat. Secret or no secret, these could be our last moments together.

If he is really in mortal danger, I can't ask him to stay for my sake. "Then you must flee London. Tonight! I'll help however I can—my carriage, my servants, whatever you need."

Again he stops me. "I have nowhere to go."

"Nowhere at all?"

"No. I'm afraid . . . there's only one hope."

"What's that?" If there's something I can do, I don't know why he hasn't told me.

Grabbing me by both arms, his hands still damp from the rain, he turns me so the candlelight falls on my face. "Thank God I found you in time," he murmurs. "My hope, my safety, is *here*—"

"But you just said it's not safe—"

"I mean here with you, as your husband. We must marry immediately."

I stare at him in horror. Yes, he invited me to go to Sweden, promised me great wealth, and I don't wish to doubt his sincerity. And yes, I'll do what I can to protect him. But the marriage he's proposing—one of secrecy, performed on the run, with no banns, as if we were sinners without blessing? It's unthinkable.

My reluctance only fuels his urgency. "If you believe in my innocence, stand up for me! With a holy bond uniting us, they won't dare send me to prison."

"I want to help. But—"

"Then marry me! Without delay. I love you and entrust my life to you. The queen will listen to you. Your influence will save me."

His declaration of love should touch me, but all I hear is his unfounded claims about the queen. "She scarcely knows me," I say. "You greatly overrate my influence."

"I overrate nothing," he cuts in. "You're the darling of London. You have influence over everyone. You can easily obtain grace for me." He falls to his knee and catches hold of my skirts. "If you marry me, I will owe you my life!"

The more he begs, the more uncomfortable I feel. I hate seeing him so humiliated. This man who offered me a life of abundance is groveling like a beggar before me, placing his fate in my hands. I have all the power. This isn't about what Bridget calls my "chance at happiness" or marriage in any usual sense; it's about my capacity to help someone in trouble. He continues to plead, but I motion for him to stand. "If you need my help," I say, my voice barely audible, "I will marry you."

"O Angelica, I knew you wouldn't forsake me." He clasps me so tightly I fear I'll pass out. Then he steps back. "But we must marry secretly and at once or I'm lost."

"Tomorrow," I say, catching my breath.

"As soon as possible."

"I'll meet you in the morning. We can be married by the priest at the little Roman Catholic chapel in the Austrian embassy. It's very private."

"Better Saint James's Church in Piccadilly."

I frown. Saint James's is an Anglican church. "No, our wedding must be before God, with vows spoken according to my faith—which is your faith too."

He opens his mouth as if to disagree, but stops. "So be it. We will marry at the chapel if that's my lady's wish—my lady, soon to be Countess de Horn." He seizes my hand and raises it to his lips. Then with a quick flick of his fingers, he pulls off Bridget's cameo. "Let this ring be your pledge." He holds it to the candle for us both to see. "If you give it to me now, I'll know you won't fail me."

His action is harsh, but his eyes are ablaze with a raw hunger that's hard to resist. I let him have the ring.

After he has slipped into the night to make arrangements for the morning, I stare at my naked finger. I've given my word. I will do my best to help Frederick. I can only pray that in so doing, my heart will be safe with him.

Twenty

Colors swirl in my head much of the night, making sleep impos-sible. Not destined to become paintings, these colors are shades of feelings too dark to meet the light of day.

But eventually that light comes. It's my wedding day.

My wedding! It's not the one I would have expected, had I expected a wedding at all. Still, I've often done the unexpected, made unusual choices. I'm a woman of independent spirit. And that's how such a woman lives. My father, of all people, knows this. He has always respected my choices. When he learns I was able to help some-one as eminent as the Swedish count, he'll be proud of me. Knowing I'm no longer alone in life, no longer a source of worry, he will forgive me for not telling him. Yes, he may still worry that this isn't a con-ventional marriage, but we can have another ceremony after all the trouble settles down.

I climb out of bed and throw open the shutters, scattering a flock of sparrows. Sunlight glistens on the rooftops, washed down by the heavy rain. From street to sky, everything looks as if painted with the finest varnish. *Perhaps*, I think, *it really is a day fit for a wedding.*

As I dress, there is a tap-tap at my door.

I jump.

It's only Rosa. "Angelica!" she calls out. "Why is your door locked?"

I send her away, saying I'm preparing for an urgent appointment.

It takes a while to find attire that won't arouse suspicion yet is suitable for a bride. After rejecting several elegant gowns, I settle on a summer dress styled like those I wear in the studio, only white. I tie my bonnet tightly so it hides my face when I look down. Then I throw a black velvet cloak over my shoulders. As much as possible I want to blend with the shadows.

When at last I go downstairs, my father and Rosa have gone for a drive. I'm able to leave through a back door, unnoticed by the crowds. I scurry down side streets, lowering my head as I pass Antonio's lodgings. If he were to stop me now, I'm not sure I would be able to go through with this. But he is nowhere in sight and I press on.

The Austrian embassy is not far from Golden Square. Even so, I've gotten such a late start that I half expect Frederick won't have waited. Cameo or not, he may have concluded I'm not good for my word.

To my surprise, the chapel door is ajar, and he pokes his head out as soon as he sees me. Not haggard like last night, he looks his usual handsome self.

"I feared you weren't coming," he whispers, steering me toward the vestibule.

"You know I wouldn't fail you."

"Do I?" he says sharply.

I tell him I hope he knows. I've given him no reason to think otherwise.

As he lifts the cloak from my shoulders, his anxiety gives way to adoration. "My gorgeous bride!" he exclaims as he hands me a small bouquet of white roses.

I hold it against my dress, white upon white.

He reaches out and touches my face. "This is how I'll always remember you. How fortunate I am to call you mine." Then he pulls me so close I can feel his breath in my nostrils. It sets off a sensation that shoots through my body, like liquid color blazing in my veins, head to toe.

"Remember our first meeting?" he whispers. "Something drew me to you in the church. Afterward I followed your gondola. Even then I felt you'd be with me forever."

As he leads me into the chapel, I'm suddenly focused on what is about to happen. "You made all the arrangements?"

"I persuaded the priest to marry us," he says. "We'll leave as husband and wife, and no one will know."

"And the witnesses?"

"Witnesses?" He frowns. "We don't need witnesses."

"It won't be a marriage without witnesses."

He stops me with a hand on my shoulder. "You insisted we marry here, not at Saint James's," he says in a low whisper. "It's illegal for a priest to marry two Roman Catholics—not to mention both foreigners."

He's referring to Lord Hardwicke's Act. By that decree, Roman Catholics must be married in an Anglican church. Our marriage here will be a crime punishable by death for the priest, and imprisonment for us both. That Frederick hasn't shied away from the risk shows how much he wants this.

We stand before the altar, beneath the painting of Mary Mediatrix, her heart stabbed by flames. The prayers, the blessings, the vows, our future together—all have the air of a dream. I keep my eyes fixed on Frederick's, and he doesn't break our gaze. If this is a dream, we are dreaming it together.

Toward the end, he produces the cameo and gives it to the priest, who touches it first to my thumb, then to my index and middle fingers, repeating, "In the name of the Father and of the Son and of the Holy Ghost." With amen, he places the ring on my fourth finger.

There is a rustling at the rear of the chapel. Frederick's hand flies to his saber, and the priest peers nervously over his shoulder. But it is only an old man come to light a candle. We quickly finish our vows.

I lay the roses by the altar, knowing I can't bring them with me.

Frederick hands the priest a small packet. The latter unrolls it and counts the money, then pulls Frederick aside. The two huddle together, while I wait by the door.

After a minute, he comes over. "I hate to impose," he says, shifting from one foot to the other, "but it seems I failed to bring enough."

I tell him not to worry. My purse is filled with guineas from a recent commission. It's a simple matter to pay the difference.

"I didn't know marriages cost so much," I say, handing over the coins.

"This isn't a usual marriage," the priest mumbles. "There may be more to pay later."

We leave the church separately.

Frederick promises to come to Golden Square this evening at the eleventh hour, after my father has retired. The idea of such a visit makes me nervous, but he reminds me we have joined our destinies. This is the way of husband and wife. He tells me how to distract the servants so he can enter undetected. I don't ask how he managed that last night.

As I step into the street, Mary and Mr. Moser are walking on the opposite side. They wave, but I pull my bonnet tighter and pretend not to notice. There's no easy way to explain why I was visiting the chapel at midday. To say I was seeing my confessor would only raise greater suspicion. Nor am I in a rush to return home. As soon as he sees my face, my father will suspect something. He knows me too well. So though the sun has gone behind clouds and a wind arisen—strong enough to blow through my velvet cloak—I take a circuitous route to Golden Square. When I finally arrive, I go straight to my studio and shut the door.

Immediately there is a loud knock.

Before I can answer, my father flings open the door. "You've been gone for hours! Where were you?"

"I'm sorry," I say. "I went farther than I intended."

But my apology falls short. "You didn't take the carriage. Never sent a messenger. What was I supposed to tell Lady Hyde? Rosa and I have been beside ourselves."

"I'm sorry," I repeat, summoning the power I've always had to calm my father with a word or smile, glad he isn't asking about the urgent appointment I mentioned to Rosa. She must have told him. "I didn't mean to worry you."

He softens. "I know you didn't. But I need to know what the matter is." He scans my face for clues. "You've been in such a mood lately—"

"I'm fine. Just chilled."

He takes my hands in his and rubs them. "Don't think we haven't noticed. You shut yourself in the studio. You don't come for meals. Please, what's wrong?"

When I don't respond, he presses further. "Are you worried about that squabble with Antonio? You know he'll be back sooner or later begging forgiveness."

"I'm not worried about him."

"Then is it the count? Did you argue?"

"No," I answer truthfully to his second question. "Why would you think that?"

"Because I'm certain he wants a portrait, yet he hasn't been here in a week."

It occurs to me to say Frederick is away on business, but I can't voice an outright lie. Instead I pull my hands free and begin sorting through some sketches, hoping my father will realize I have nothing more to say.

"I will call on him," he continues. "We can't lose his patronage."

By now our voices have drawn Rosa to the studio. She throws her arms around me. "Finally you're home!"

"I was just explaining to Papa," I say, hugging her tightly.

As she pulls away, my cloak lifts, revealing my dress.

"Today is much too cold for a summer outfit!" she exclaims. "You must be freezing."

I admit I am.

"Then I'll draw a bath right now." She turns to go, then pivots back, eyes half stern, half playful. "You look like a bride in your white summer dress. Angelica, what were you thinking?"

In the evening, I excuse myself early, saying I don't feel well. That's not entirely untrue. I feel slightly feverish and keep breaking into a cold sweat. I go upstairs and lie on my bed, without shutting my eyes. Waves of excitement and something close to dread wash over me in quick succession. I want to see Frederick, to be alone with him. To feel again that liquid color flowing within me. To become his wife in the most intimate way. Yet I have no idea what to expect, never having received this part of a mother's education. Not to mention, the risk of being discovered seems enormous.

It feels like an eternity before the clock strikes eleven.

Immediately I change into my bedgown and throw on a robe. The servants must get the impression I've been sleeping. I go downstairs and ask them to prepare mulled cider for my father and bring it to his room straightaway. It is a bedtime favorite of his, and I know he'll appreciate my thoughtfulness. Besides, its preparation will require the servants to go to the cellar—two of them because the keg is too heavy for one alone if it needs to be tipped. Frederick suggested this ploy before we left the chapel.

While they are in the cellar, I unlatch the front door, then dash back to my room.

Scarcely have I taken off my robe and climbed into bed, when the door opens and Frederick steps inside, boots in hand. It's hard to say who is more breathless, he or I. He drops his boots and jacket by the door, then sheds more clothes at my bedside. Without a word, he blows out the one candle burning on the night table.

We're plunged into darkness.

Now he is lying beside me, this man to whom I've made a sacred vow. This mysterious man with such power. I want to feel that power within me. That, I understand, is the meaning of my vow.

As my eyes adjust to the dark, I can see him by a shaft of moonlight streaming through the crack between the shutters. Again, I'm reminded of Michelangelo's David. Without clothes, his body is thinner and his shoulders bonier than I imagined.

I want to say something, to touch him with words.

But he hushes me.

He bends over me and kisses my forehead, his lips lingering until I raise my head to meet him. Suddenly everything happens very fast. As he kisses me, he is trembling. But it isn't the trembling of the gentle man who courted me with sweet words and white roses. He is breathing hard, his touch rough.

I try to relax into his arms, but he is struggling against me, muttering in a language I assume to be Swedish. I can't figure out what he is trying to do. Clearly, nothing is happening as it's supposed to. A desperate urge to push him away arises within me. Yet I don't.

The only thing worse than letting him have his way with me is the thought of my father or the servants hearing the commotion and bursting in on us.

Suddenly he jerks away, swearing under his breath—in plain English this time.

"What's the matter?" I whisper.

"Nothing." He springs from the bed like someone recoiling from a scalding bath.

"What did I do wrong?" Being so inexperienced in these matters, my first thought is that I'm to blame.

He reaches for his trousers. In his haste, he thrusts one foot into the wrong pant leg and has to stop and untangle himself.

I pull the covers tightly around me. "If I failed—"

He whirls around and stares at me, his face haggard. "Stop taunting me!"

"But I—"

"You what? Take me for a fool?"

His voice cracks, and I sense he's about to explode in fury. I shrink back into the pillows and close my eyes. I don't move until I hear the door click shut behind him.

My head is reeling when I awake. I try to sit up, but the room is spinning so violently I'm forced to lie back down.

When Rosa knocks on my door, I call out that it's open.

She rushes over and places her hand on my forehead. "My goodness, you're feverish! This must be from the chill you took. If I'd seen your dress, I'd never have let you go out."

Immediately she becomes my nurse. She applies a cold compress to my head, then fetches tea with brandy. I drink it slowly, propped on a shaky elbow, before settling back under the covers.

All morning I lie here, wanting to sleep but unable, watching wispy clouds drift across the patch of sky framed by my window, trying to understand what happened. I angered Frederick, that much I know. Our marriage has not begun well. I blame it on all the secrecy and sneaking around, the order for his arrest, the fear for his life.

By evening, the fever has broken.

A sense of calm descends. The important thing is that I'm married now. Not only that, I am royalty. I'm Countess de Horn. Frederick might not yet be my husband in all regards, but money was exchanged in the chapel. It may have been without banns and witnesses and a proper ring, but in the eyes of a higher authority, a marriage was decreed. We are united. It doesn't matter that no one else knows. God knows.

While I recuperate, my calm ebbs and flows. I struggle to reconcile my view of myself as a woman in control of her destiny with the fact that I've relinquished that power. What I vowed I would never do, I have done. In the eyes of the law, I no longer belong to myself. Yet, I ask myself, in the eyes of God, how could I ever belong to anyone else? It is I who paints, I who dream and imagine and create. It is I who love.

Or at least it is I who has vowed to love.

After he's sorted out his troubles, I tell myself, Frederick will return. He'll be his quiet yet commanding self again. He will be thankful I helped him in his hour of need, appreciate that it is my nature to be of help when someone turns to me. As Mary did. Of course, her needs were nothing in comparison with what Frederick asked of me.

We may still be strangers now, he and I, but we will learn to love one another, learn the ways of marriage. And we will lie together as husband and wife. Even if it feels unnatural, I will find that woman within myself. I'll breathe life into her so she can become the one who paints, who loves.

Other days, my mood darkens. I can't shake the notion Frederick's been arrested, even imprisoned. Or worse. As my fear grows, the fever returns. Lying here delirious, love turns to fear, then doubt. I can find no breath left for the woman I'm supposed to be.

After a fortnight, I feel well enough to return to my studio. As I stand among my canvases again, nothing looks quite as I remembered. I begin by reacquainting myself with the portrait of Lady Henderson. Her expression is decidedly insipid. I'm about to send a note requesting another sitting, when a servant hands me a letter. The messenger has instructions not to leave without an answer.

I tear it open and read: *Come immediately to Saint James's.* Though there is no signature, I know who penned it.

So he hasn't been arrested. He's alive.

I'm surprised how deeply this affects me. Just knowing he's safe, I could cry with relief. But the servant is watching, so I scrawl a one-word answer, reseal the letter, and hand it to him. Lady Henderson will have to wait one more day.

At Saint James's, Frederick guides me to a pew, where we kneel together and talk in whispers. Squeezing my hand in his, he says what torture our separation has been, how desperately he missed me. He makes no mention of his abrupt departure from my bedroom.

I whisper back how I feared for his safety, how thankful I am to see him.

He explains the documents he was expecting haven't arrived. He's been hiding at the Claridge, not going out even for food, praying to survive another day, if only to see me, his wife, again. "My creditors are pushing hard," he says. "They'll kick me out if I don't pay by tonight."

"Don't worry," I say. "I have enough saved."

"Oh please," he moans, "I can't take your money. Your father doesn't even know we're married."

"My money is yours." Legally, it is his already, but I want to reassure him.

"Then John Joseph must know the truth," he whispers.

Of course this is exactly what I should want. But the situation has become so confounded. "What will my father say when he hears I married without telling him? In a wedding without witnesses—"

Then it is he who reassures me. "I know. That's why I called for you. We're about to have a second ceremony, one that will please your father and in a faith the queen and British law will accept."

"Here?"

"Yes!"

Before I can ask more, he ushers me into the vestry, where the curate, Mr. Baddeley, is waiting. There is no time for a special dress, no bouquet of white roses. Within a few minutes, we have repeated our vows before the priest and again become husband and wife. The curate produces a certificate from the vestry book, and we sign it.

"And the witnesses?" I ask.

"Of course, of course." Frederick dips his pen into the inkpot and writes with a flourish "Richard Horne" and "Annie Horne."

I stare at the page. "Who are these people? *Where* are they?"

"My cousins," he says with a chuckle. "My British cousins."

I don't see the humor. My father won't either. "But you said—"

"Shh!" He lays a finger on my lips, pressing lightly on the lower one till his touch descends through my body. Suddenly the witnesses seem less important. Then he turns and dips the pen again. "The twenty-second of November 1767," he says. "A date you'll always remember, no?"

Twenty-one

The wedding at Saint James's notwithstanding, our secret remains a secret. Everything remains as it was. Frederick only enters my studio after he's seen my father go out. He never comes at night. And never stays more than a few minutes.

When I ask him to stay longer, he won't hear of it. "My safety aside," he says, "I won't endanger you or your family."

I tell him not to think that way. Anything he suffers I'll willingly suffer too. I made a vow to be his wife, and there is nothing I won't do to support him.

In response, he insists we inform my father of our marriage.

I want that too. If my father shares our secret, he can help us fix the problems. Then we'll be on our way to Sweden. Yet I know it isn't that simple. When my father realizes I betrayed him, he'll be furious. "We must find the right way, the right moment, to tell him," I say. It's hard to believe I'm the one advocating deceit.

Finally we decide Frederick will ask the priest who married us to speak with my father.

In the meantime, there's a more pressing problem. Having run out of the money I gave him, Frederick is again on the verge of being kicked out of his rooms. He says he will sell his saber and other precious items. I can't let him do that. Not if I, his wife, have the power to help. So I hand over the rest of my hard-earned savings.

The rumored order for his arrest hasn't materialized. Still, he feels it's only a matter of time before the authorities come after him. He urges me not to delay arranging an audience with the queen. Now that we've wed in an Anglican church—the same in which she married the king—he is convinced she will extend clemency.

I don't have to wonder long about how to arrange an audience. Within the week, an invitation arrives requesting another royal portrait. This time, I've been selected over many other artists to paint the queen as patron of the arts. I am to portray her as Aphrodite, and the young Prince of Wales as Cupid. She will be standing over the sleeping child, as suggested by the title: *Her Majesty Queen Charlotte Raising the Genius of the Arts.* This initial sitting will be at Saint James's Palace, where court functions are held. I'll paint the prince later, in his nursery at Buckingham House.

On the appointed morning, I cross Pall Mall, stepping sideways to avoid patches of ice, then pass beneath the arched gateway of the palace. Two pages—one carrying my box of paints and palette, the other my easel—escort me to the throne room.

As soon as they have positioned my easel across from the queen's dais, she sweeps in and takes her seat on the gold throne, beneath a red velvet curtain bearing the royal coat of arms.

When I look up from my curtsy, she greets me with a smile.

This should be a moment of pride. But I'm also here as a petitioner. It isn't every day a woman has the nerve to petition the queen. *How on earth,* I wonder, *can I present a convincing case when my artistry is with color, not words?* All I can do is begin work and hope the right words will come.

Though the queen is cordial, it is clear we won't be enjoying the intimacy we shared in her quarters. She comments on the chill in the palace during this unusually cold winter, and the many foreign dignitaries visiting London. She praises again my first portrait.

I look in vain for an opening to present my case.

At one point, a lady-in-waiting enters.

"Tell us what Miss Kauffman has accomplished," the queen says. Turning to me, she adds, "You will appreciate the observations of Mrs. Schwellenberg."

A stout woman with a ruddy face, Mrs. Schwellenberg bustles forward to examine my canvas.

"One must know something about art to understand a painting in its early stages," I say.

Mrs. Schwellenberg frowns. "Her Majesty's eye is small. One need not be a painter to see that."

"Maybe it's an effect of the unfinished work, as the artist suggests," the queen says.

Mrs. Schwellenberg's ruddy complexion turns a shade deeper. "If Your Majesty pleases, I'll keep my opinions to myself." Though the queen hasn't given permission, she turns to leave.

"Not so fast!" The queen seems amused by the little drama she apparently created to discipline Mrs. Schwellenberg's impertinence. She points to a paper on her side table. "Take this to the king. Remind him our audience with the visitor from Sweden will be in the council chambers."

My brush stops midway between my palette and canvas. A Swedish dignitary? That must be Frederick! I'm surprised he arranged an audience for himself before confirming I'd spoken to the queen. Then it occurs to me the visitor could be one of his enemies. I want to ask, but it isn't my place to question the queen about her guests. Besides, she has turned her attention to a page who handed her some documents. Could these be the papers from Sweden Frederick needs?

Or heaven forbid, the warrant for his arrest? With that thought, my brush slips and what I sketched in light lines is smeared with black. I know it can't be fixed till the oils dry, yet I don't want anyone to see the mess. I dab at it with a white brush, creating a larger smear.

After the page leaves, the queen is silent again in her pose.

I can't wait any longer. "I beg pardon, Your Majesty," I say, stepping in front of my easel.

However, she has a question of her own: "We meant to ask if the rumors are true, and congratulations are in order—"

I flush with gratitude. She already knows and is trying to help me.

"Among the artists, he is most prominent," she continues, "Mr. Joshua Reynolds!"

This certainly isn't the opening I wanted. "Oh no," I say. "*That* is not true."

She frowns. "There's someone else?"

"Count de Horn—"

"The Swedish count?" She looks confused. "He's marrying again? We had no idea."

"It hasn't been announced. We're still—"

By now she is completely perplexed. "You're speaking of the *Swedish* count?"

"Yes, Your Majesty."

"Then we will congratulate him when we meet today."

This is all wrong; my petition is happening backward. I have to set her straight. I rush forward, forgetting what Bridget once told me: The queen has an aversion to extremes of emotion. "Please," I exclaim, "Your Majesty must hear our story! Only your clemency—"

Her hand goes up to stop me. "When you've composed yourself, we may listen to your case."

I step back to my easel.

She rises from her seat. "Take some rest," she says more gently. "We'll appoint another sitting later." With that, she sweeps out of the room.

I stand alone, my breath coming in gasps. My husband is counting on me to let the queen know the charges against him are false. He will assume I've prepared her. Yet I haven't. If they meet now, she is bound to be unsympathetic. I must stop him.

Leaving my easel and paints, I throw on my cloak and run out of the room. None of the guards try to detain me as I rush down several hallways, then into a lobby with vaulted ceilings. A doorway at one end opens to a courtyard where, despite the light snow falling, a crowd has gathered. Peering between shoulders, I see a small procession. First comes a page ceremoniously carrying a sword. Then a tall man, bent with age, dressed in black, a cocked hat under his arm. Behind him is a secretary with a stack of papers. As they move toward the council chambers, I scan the crowd for my husband. He is nowhere to be seen.

"Who is the visitor?" I ask the nearest guard.

"The Swedish envoy, Count de Horn!" he announces, chest blown out as if the king himself were asking.

"*That* man? There must be some mistake—"

"No mistake, I assure you," he says and resumes his frozen pose.

As the crowd disperses, I spot Mrs. Schwellenberg. In any other moment, I wouldn't seek her out, but my need to know is stronger than my pride. "Please," I say, "who was that?"

She looks surprised to see me but eager for a chance to impress the queen's painter. "Count Frederick de Horn," she says, then lowers her voice. "I should know. I visited his castle in Huvudsta. He rarely travels but is here on business. Apparently an imposter stole money from him and forged his papers. He may even have married in the count's name. Can you imagine? Now he seeks the king's support in finding the fellow."

"An imposter?"

"Yes. May that rogue be put to death!" she exclaims. "Why, Miss Kauffman, you've gone pale. Are you all right?"

I can only nod and excuse myself.

I hurry across the courtyard and through an unguarded door into a garden. I'm shaking, my stomach threatening to empty itself on the spot. I lean against the wall, pulling my cloak over my head as the snow whirls around me, settling on the ivy and turning every color white.

Did Mrs. Schwellenberg just accuse my husband of being an imposter?

That can't be. Anyone who knows Frederick knows he isn't a criminal. I picture his face, so noble, so handsome. So fragile. A face like that is incapable of wrongdoing. Besides, if he were an imposter, I would have seen the signs—I who can take one look at a person's face and paint their true character. I've done that since I was eight. But even if that sense failed me, or if his charms blinded me, Bridget would have noticed. Or the ambassador. It's his business to know these things.

No, there must be some mistake. The man I know is kind, generous. I feel again his tenderness as we walked in the moonlight, recall his declarations of love, the thrill of his kisses. It is true he has his share of troubles. But he's been honest about them. As his wife, I vowed to share his burdens. I have no doubt he'd do the same for me. To turn on him now would be unconscionable. I refuse to betray him. I will not—cannot—believe such a heinous and blatantly false accusation. Until I've heard what he has to say for himself, I won't judge him.

I make my way back to my carriage, climb in, and draw the curtains tight. This is one time I don't wish anyone to notice as I drive across the city. I'm still shivering from the snowy garden. And perhaps even more so because I have failed my husband. Not only that, I've failed my father.

The more I mull it over, the clearer it becomes: I can no longer withhold the truth. If my father doesn't know about our marriage, he can't help me or Frederick. And it is better he hears the news from me than from the priest. Yes, I will tell him as soon as I get home.

In the meantime, huddling under the carriage blankets, I make myself as small as I can. I, the secret countess, feel like a child.

Twenty-two

When I arrive at Golden Square, my father is not in his usual chair in the parlor, where he likes to nap at midday. I find him in my studio—not working on the Three Muses but pacing back and forth, pounding his cane on the floor with each step.

"Angelica!" he cries when he sees me. "Have you lost your senses?"

I rush to him, but he brushes me away.

"My daughter, whom I've trusted over anyone in this world!"

His reaction is exactly what I feared, why I went to such lengths to keep my secret. Despite my resolve on the drive home, now I want only to shield him from the truth. That he may have learned it from someone else is all the more distressing.

He drops onto the sofa, hands over his face.

I fall to my knees at his side, my voice a whisper: "So, you know—?"

"What you've *done*?" He lunges forward, a burst of fury propelling him across the room, without his cane, then spins around to face me, his legs almost giving way. I've never seen him so angry. "You think I'm such a fool that you'd dare marry without telling me?"

I want to protest, to deny everything. But I can't. It's true: I married in secret. My actions are inexcusable. All I can do is hang my head.

"But you did it anyway! Didn't you?"

I feel his eyes on me, forcing the truth to out. Slowly I raise my head. "You talked to the priest?"

"Not the priest. His curate, Mr. Baddeley. He did what my own daughter wouldn't do. He told me—" He stops short and for the first time looks me straight in the eye. I can see the pain beneath his rage.

Springing to my feet, I grab his arm and guide him to the nearest chair.

He drops onto the seat, defeated. "I don't understand how you could do this. Or *why*."

That I don't fully understand myself. So how can I explain it to him?

"Time and again," he says, "you vowed not to marry. And now you marry a scoundrel?"

"He's not a scoundrel!" I object.

"And since when did you care so much about becoming a countess?"

"Papa, I don't!"

"So you're saying you love that man?" My father is incredulous. "A man who forced you to lie to me? Angelica, really!"

I swallow hard. Of course the idea of Swedish nobility is enticing. Having been a poor artist, how could it not be? But being a countess was never my dream. I don't need a palace or royal jewels. I've certainly never needed a husband. The truth is—I can admit it now— Frederick touched me deeply. If he hadn't, I would never have risked so much to help him. Still, that touch is not the kind of love my father is asking about. There are many kinds of love. These days, people like to marry for love, but there are still many kinds of marriages. And many kinds of vows.

Most important, though, I made this vow of my own volition. I must own up to that now.

I pull up a stool and sit beside my father. This time he doesn't push me away as I explain what I feel and what I've done. How I did all I could for Frederick, but now his fate is in the queen's hands. I say nothing about love. Nor do I mention what I saw today at the palace; I need to speak to Frederick about that first. "Please forgive us," I say. "We never meant to hurt you. Even if he has fallen into bad times, he is a gentleman."

My father isn't persuaded. "What sort of man marries without asking the father for his daughter's hand?"

"That was my fault," I say. "He wanted to go to you, but I wouldn't allow it. He is honorable, I promise."

"Honorable indeed," my father huffs. "Where's Zucchi now that we need him?"

"Antonio?" I bristle at the inference his absence is my fault too.

"He always looked out for you. Now we must seek help elsewhere."

"What help?" I say, still bristling. I may have created this mess, but I'm capable of looking out for myself.

"We know next to nothing about this man. Surely you see we need help," he says. "I will call on the ambassador first thing in the morning. Thank goodness he hasn't returned to Constantinople yet."

I object that Bridget is already satisfied with Frederick's character. She encouraged our engagement. After everything has been sorted out, I will tell her about the marriage and she'll be delighted. But my father is insistent. In the end, I concede no harm can come from investigating. It may be the fastest way to clear Frederick's name. And the only way to win over my father.

As soon as my father has left, Frederick appears. Bolting the studio door behind him, he drops his hat on the table and strides across the room.

As we regard one another in silence, I search his face. Does he know what I witnessed at the palace? Are there any telltale signs of his character I missed before? Any hint of contrition? All I see is the familiar hunger etched in his eyes.

He steps closer and runs a finger from the tip of my nose toward my chin. Parting my lips, his finger seeks my tongue. "My beautiful wife," he whispers. He draws me closer, as if no clothes separated us, and covers my mouth with his.

Much as I might want that, I have to pull back. There are too many questions for which I need answers. "The curate was here," I say. "My father is furious at you."

He gives a shrug. "That was to be expected. He'll come around. The important thing is you spoke to the queen."

I take another step back. "I tried—"

"You didn't speak to her?" he cuts in, a frown eclipsing the hunger in his eyes.

I want to ask about the imposter, demand an account that will vindicate him in my father's eyes. Yet I can't justify confronting him. If others are falsely accusing him, he mustn't count his wife among them. Worse yet is the possibility he has no worthy explanation. I'm not ready to face that. "I'm afraid we must wait for her next sitting," I say.

"Then I'd better leave," he says, still frowning.

I agree that would be best.

His frown fades as he reaches for my hand in parting. "You're wearing the cameo."

"I'll always wear it."

"Not *always*." He interlaces our fingers so my agate lies against his ruby. "In Sweden, you'll have a ring that puts this one to shame."

For the first time, I notice a hinge beneath his ruby. "Your ring is unique. It must be very rare," I say, hoping he'll divulge more about himself. Then we won't need an investigation.

"It belonged to my father."

"A family treasure?"

"Yes, a treasure. But not as you think." He disengages our hands, pulls the ring from his finger, and unhinges it, revealing a tiny chamber beneath the ruby. He holds it to the light so I can see inside. It's filled with a dark liquid.

"What is that?" I ask, bending closer. It doesn't smell like perfume.

With a flick of his thumb, he snaps the ruby shut. Then he tests the clasp to make sure it is secure and slides the ring back onto his finger. "You wish to know what it is?"

"If you wish to tell me."

"Why not?" he counters. "There must be no secrets between us." He puts his mouth to my ear and whispers, "It's poison."

I recoil. "Poison?"

"Yes, for my enemies. So deadly this small amount is more than enough."

Before I can ask any questions, he slaps his hat on his head and is gone.

At midnight, while everyone is sleeping, our house is shaken by pounding and rattling at the front door. Voices order us, in the name of the king, to unbolt immediately.

One of the servants is the first to reach the door. He opens it to two officers from the royal guard, swords drawn, demanding to see Count de Horn. I watch from the landing as first the servant, then my father, swear the count is nowhere on the premises. Only after I've thrown on a robe and come down to affirm we know nothing of his whereabouts, do they sheath their weapons and depart.

"What sort of trouble is that man in?" my father grumbles. "You said the queen was helping. Doesn't look like it."

I can't sleep the rest of the night.

I lie in bed, a ghost of myself, alone in the dark, trying to fend off an onslaught of wildly swirling colors. Much as I may have opened my heart to Frederick, welcomed his kisses, much as I have believed in his innocence, prayed for his safety, too many things aren't right. First the supposed imposter at court. And then his poison ring. And now the royal guard threatening our home.

By the time the first light of day peeks through the shutters, I've come to a decision. I have to be fully honest and forthright—with my father, but more importantly, with myself. Yes, in the eyes of the law, I am Frederick's wife, but I can't look at life through the eyes of a wife. Especially not now. I have to use my own God-given eyes, the eyes I've always relied on. If Frederick isn't honorable, I can't continue to defend him. And I certainly can't let myself be seduced by his touch.

When I go down for breakfast, my father has already left.

"He wouldn't take me," Rosa says. "He called it urgent business. What could that be?"

"We'll know soon," I say obliquely, surprised she slept through all the commotion.

When my father rushes into my studio a few hours later, he is jubilant. After learning of my marriage—and expressing concern the count may have duped others as well—the ambassador volunteered to launch an investigation. He even agreed to delay his return to Constantinople until de Horn's origins have been uncovered. With his vast diplomatic sources, that shouldn't be difficult to accomplish.

I have to admit I'm relieved. "No matter how bad the news may be," I say, "I'm ready to hear it."

"You won't have to face it alone," my father says. "I am here. And your friends as well."

I tell him I know he will support me. Always. However, I'm not sure about Bridget. "She may forget all her encouragement and declare I'm ruined. She may never speak to me again."

He shrugs. "If she does that, we can't stop her. But the ambassador didn't intimate anything of the sort. Really, I think these people love you as their own."

I give a slim smile, remembering he still doesn't know why I left Charles Street so suddenly last winter. Despite my intention not to keep anything more from him, this isn't the time to bring that up.

"Speaking of support," he says as he turns to leave, "you'll never guess who I ran into."

Only one person comes to mind. "Antonio?"

"Yes. And he promised to come over later."

I marvel at the ease with which these two inevitably forget their differences. "I suppose you told him about my marriage."

"I did. But he suspected it already. Apparently Mary Moser and her father saw you and de Horn leave the embassy chapel a few minutes apart. They speculated you were there for a private purpose, which our clever Antonio concluded could only be—well, you know."

All afternoon, I gird myself for the scolding I expect Antonio will greet me with. Honestly, I deserve it. But when he walks in the door, he doesn't do anything of the sort. He doesn't even mention the marriage directly. "The ambassador may be investigating," he simply says, "but I'm making inquiries of my own. I'm prepared to travel abroad if need be."

As we sit by the fireplace, I sense a distance between us that wasn't there before. It's clear how deeply my actions have hurt him. Even if none of those actions had anything to do with him. "Maybe we should enlist Mary since she has such sharp detective skills," I say, thinking that if I joke with him, we can make peace.

"You can't blame Mary," he says coolly. "She's concerned about you."

"Now all of London will share that concern," I say. Not that Mary is the gossiping type. I'm just trying to tease away the distance.

He stirs the fire with the poker and watches the flames flare. "Lucky for you, people are too worked up about all the other odd marriages."

This is news to me. "What marriages?"

He explains that Lady Strangways married an actor. And some other lady wed her footman. "Don't tell me," he says, "you were so busy falling in love you missed all that."

"If I was," I joke, "you're here to pass on the gossip."

He smiles, and I can see he's glad to be back in our home. "Gossip aside," he says, "opportunists and villains are at every corner. I've always said you need a good friend to watch over you. Maybe you've finally understood that."

In the interest of keeping the peace, I don't reply.

But I am beginning to understand something else: how much of my independence I have forfeited. I didn't notice it happening because it was so gradual. Like oils drying. When paint is applied, it's wet. And it's wet the next day. In fact, some of the pigments Joshua uses remain permanently wet. But the way I mix and apply paint, if you touch it after a few weeks or months, it will have dried. If you want to change that painting, you must begin anew. Similarly, mixing my life with Frederick's has eroded my independence in ways I didn't see until it was too late. Now I will have to fight to fix the damage, to get my freedom back.

The following day, Frederick arrives at Golden Square during Lady Henderson's sitting. Paying no heed to the likelihood my father, the servants—anyone—will see him, he storms into my studio, saber unsheathed, and insists she leave immediately.

Mumbling some excuse about rescheduling, I usher her to the door.

As soon as she's gone, I face him. "Why did you threaten my client?"

"Why is your father trying to destroy me?" he counters, his delicate face contorted with rage.

All his talk about never endangering me or my family, and now he dares blame Papa? "Put down your weapon," I demand. "My father did nothing to you!"

"He launched an inquisition against me!"

My hands clasped behind my back may be shaking, but I make my voice firm. "We need the truth—the truth you have withheld. All he did was approach a few friends."

"Those aren't friends! They're my enemies!" He speaks with a viciousness I would never have thought possible. "I forbid you to see them!"

His voice is so loud it brings my father to the studio. He stands inside the doorway and glares at Frederick. "Where's Lady Henderson?"

Frederick glares back. "She's been sent away."

My father turns to me. "What did—?"

But Frederick intervenes: "It was *I* who sent her. I've come for my wife!"

"Your *wife?*" My father chokes on the word. "She's not your wife. This marriage doesn't have my blessing."

"There's no need for your blessing. We're leaving!"

"Leaving?" Papa and I respond with one voice.

"Yes. Our bags are packed. We leave for Sweden tonight." He sheathes his sword and takes a step toward the door.

That he would run straight to his enemies in Sweden makes no sense. Besides, he always said my father and Rosa would come with us. "Surely," I say, "you don't expect me to go with you?"

"Indeed I do. Have you forgotten your vows?"

My father steps forward. "You can't force her!"

Frederick straightens his shoulders. At his full height, he towers over my father. "Your daughter married me of her own free will. It's her duty to go wherever I see fit!"

This is too much for my father. He hurls himself at Frederick with the force of a much younger man. Frederick's hat and spectacles fly off as he staggers under the attack. He's about to deliver a blow in return when Rosa appears in the doorway. She rushes past the men and buries her face in my apron.

The two men fall against each other, then scramble to pick themselves up. No matter how irate they might be, both are too ashamed to fight in front of a young girl.

Wrapping my arms around Rosa, I turn to Frederick. "If you think you can order me to leave, you're wrong. My father has always stood by me. It was I who betrayed him on your account. That will never happen again."

He takes a step toward me and reaches out a hand, suddenly meek.

I back away, arms tightening around Rosa.

"Angelica—" he pleads.

"No!" I stop him. "I have no idea who you are anymore. Maybe I never knew you. All I can say is I am staying here. Now, go!"

Frederick picks up his hat and dusts it off. His spectacles lie shattered on the floor. My father limps to the chair by the fireplace. Neither says a word.

"Go," I repeat with a power and a certainty I haven't felt in months. "I'm not going with you, not now—not ever."

Twenty-three

"I'm so happy to have my daughter back!" my father says as we adjourn to the parlor after supper. While I add oil to a lamp burning low, he selects a brandy from the cabinet and pours himself a glass.

I can't apologize enough for the pain I've caused.

He describes having worried for weeks that I was keeping something from him. "And then to learn you'd married that villain," he says. "It was enough to kill an old man like me."

Antonio comes in as my father is speaking. "Freezing out there!" he says as he shuffles snow off his boots, then sheds his hat and coat and sits down by the hearth. When we tell him about Frederick's visit, he shakes his fist. "De Horn is lucky I wasn't here. I'd have made mincemeat of him."

I suppress a smile as I sit beside him. "I'm glad you weren't here. He's a head taller than you. Not to mention his military experience."

"Taller yes. But that experience could be as false as his other claims."

"Well, I almost came to blows with the man," my father says, as he pours Antonio a brandy.

Now Antonio is the one suppressing a smile. "You did?"

"It's no laughing matter." My father is indignant. "You'd have done the same if you heard him order Angelica around."

I fill in the details: how Frederick expected me to drop everything and run to Sweden, as if a wife were just another item in a man's luggage. As if I would submit to his will and leave my father to fend for himself in London.

"At least you got rid of him," Antonio says.

My father frowns. "For now. We still don't have all the facts. Or know his next move."

Antonio says he's spoken to his artist friends, who've agreed to find out what they can.

"Artists know more than one might think," my father says.

"All it takes is one remark during a sitting," I add.

"The important thing," my father says, tilting back his head and downing the rest of his brandy, "is not to rest until that scoundrel is out of our lives for good."

"Agreed!" Antonio sings out, then stops short as Rosa enters the room.

"You've come two days in a row!" she says, running up to greet him. "I've missed you. Angelica has too. I know she has."

For a moment we're all silent.

"I'm sorry," she says. "I know I shouldn't interrupt you in the parlor."

I reassure her all of us are always glad to see her, then remind her of the lateness of the hour.

When she's out of earshot, Antonio turns to me. "Does she know?"

"No," I say. "And she mustn't. Though she did witness what happened today."

My father points out she said nothing about it afterward.

"You know," I say, "she didn't like Frederick from the start. She said so repeatedly."

"She's a smart one," my father says. "I wish you'd listened to her."

"Or to me," Antonio adds.

* *

The weather is warmer the following week when the queen calls me to Buckingham House for another sitting. This time, the Prince of Wales is with her, and our conversation is only about his latest model ships and insatiable taste for chocolate cake. After one session, I have all I need to complete the painting. I promise to deliver it within a fortnight. I want to finish quickly because the payment means more to me now than the honor earned from a royal portrait.

I'm working on it the next day in my studio when I sense someone in the doorway behind me. For a second, I freeze, thinking it might be Frederick. Though we haven't seen him, he could appear at any moment. As I turn, preparing to confront him and demand he leave and never show his face again, I'm pleasantly surprised.

The man watching me is Joshua.

We haven't spoken alone since finishing each other's portraits some months ago. Any hurt feelings between us are long forgotten. "After Mary told me—" He stops abruptly. "I hope it wasn't presumptuous of me to call unannounced."

I set down my palette and tell him I don't have any news. The investigation is ongoing.

"And I'm making inquiries myself," he says. "I never befriended that so-called count, but I heard the real Count de Horn embarked at Dover yesterday on his way home to Sweden—or perhaps you weren't aware he was in London?"

"I did know," I say, reminding myself I still haven't told my father what I saw at Saint James's Palace.

Joshua looks past my easel and surveys the room. "I see mainly portraits. Where are your history paintings?"

I acknowledge that portraits are in high demand. More than that, I need the money.

"Because of the . . . marriage?"

I nod. This is something else I haven't told my father. He will be upset when he learns how badly I depleted our savings.

Joshua sits down on the sofa, and I join him. "Promise me you won't give up," he says. "Once this trouble passes—and it will—your talents will receive full recognition. I'm so glad John Parker is using your Trojan series as overdoors at Saltram Park."

"Yes. I haven't forgotten you are to thank for that."

"No need to thank me." He dimples with characteristic humility. "Now I've come with another proposition. The Society of Artists is planning a private exhibition to honor the King of Denmark's visit. It would be marvelous if we could include your paintings—John said there are four—before they go to Saltram Park."

"I'd love that!" I say, though I haven't even begun the fourth, of Achilles.

"Even three would be plenty," he says after I explain.

"Then the three are yours."

"And there's more," he says. "The artists in this exhibit will be the first invited to show work when the new academy is formed."

I tell him I didn't realize the academy was finally materializing.

He claps his hands with the glee of a schoolboy. "We're so close! More than ever, I'm convinced an academy with royal backing is the only way artists can have support to pursue history painting, the only way to create a cultured public in this country."

If Joshua's strategy is to distract me, it works. As we discuss the value of an academy, I feel again the delight I've always taken in his company. Nothing is more thrilling than our talks about art, the giddy feeling that if we unite as artists, we can shape the culture of a nation.

Before he leaves, I invite him to visit my studio whenever he wishes.

As he puts on his hat, his tone turns serious. He tells me he has one concern. I think it might be a concern about our friendship, but his mind is still on the academy. "The Society's members won't stop squabbling over policies and procedures. Now Benjamin and some others are threatening to resign. If they do, I'll be powerless to stop them."

"Could it really come to that?"

"I fear it could."

I want to say something to bolster his spirits. Goodness knows, he's done that for me. "You never know how things will turn out. Ghastly as it sounds, their protest could be just what's needed to secure royal approval."

He stops in the doorway and regards me. "I like that. Yes, let's be optimistic. I'm stating here and now that I believe our academy will come into being within the year!"

"Good," I say. "If the first exhibit is within a year, Achilles will also be ready."

After he leaves, I feel more myself than I have in weeks. The freedom I feared was lost is mine now as much as it has always been. I don't need a husband or a marriage. I don't need to be adored as a woman, or even adorned as one; my paints are my jewels. I don't need a fancy castle; my studio is my castle. Here I can accomplish everything I want to accomplish.

The queen may be waiting for her portrait, but I can't resist starting on the painting I've already titled *Achilles Discovered by Ulysses Amongst the Daughters of King Lycomedes*. Of course, using Frederick as my model is out of the question now. But that doesn't matter.

As I'm roughing out the figures on my sketchpad, Rosa comes up behind me and peers over my shoulder. She wants to hear about the myth, so I explain that the central figure, with one hand raised holding a sword, is the hero Achilles. Deidamia is crouching by his side.

"Why does he look like a woman?" she wants to know.

"His mother," I say, "knew he would die in the Trojan War. So to outwit fate, she dressed him as a maid and sent him to care for the king's daughters. One—Deidamia—became his beloved. Then Ulysses disguised himself as a peddler and went to the court."

Rosa is confused. "Both men were disguised?"

"That's right," I say. "The heroes and gods didn't think twice about disguising themselves—as men or women. Ulysses brought jewelry, ornaments, and a sword. When the princesses viewed his wares, they chose pretty things. Achilles picked the sword."

"He revealed himself."

"Exactly. Which meant he had to go to war. Eventually he was killed by Paris."

Rosa looks pensive. "What happened to Deidamia?"

"She was heartbroken."

"But she knew when she fell in love how much she could lose."

I can't help smiling. "Since when did that stop anyone from falling in love?"

Early one morning, a messenger from the ambassador summons my father to Charles Street. He leaves immediately, forgoing his breakfast of spiced buns and ale. I can hardly cancel Lady Henderson, who's finally agreed to another sitting, so I do my best to focus on the curl of her fingers as they grip her gold brocade sash.

Antonio arrives before my father has returned. I can hear him pacing in the hallway; it's all I can do to keep from rushing out so we can worry together.

My father finally shows up as Lady Henderson is leaving. A

minute later, the three of us are alone in the studio. As I close the door and lock it, my father and Antonio both start to talk at once. I have to make them sit on the sofa and slow down.

"*Brandt*," my father snarls. "His real name is Brandt."

"Count Brandt?" I'm confused.

"Count nothing! The man isn't a count at all. Never was."

I stare at him.

"I knew it!" Antonio is triumphant, then glances at me and tempers his tone. "How do we know for sure?"

"The ambassador has many contacts among the Swedes," my father says. "Some were themselves deceived by this Brandt. Multiple sources have confirmed our suspicions."

"Is there more?" I say, sinking into the armchair, my voice flat, as if we were talking about someone else's life. It doesn't matter that I expected the worst, hearing how badly I've been duped comes as a shock.

"Oh yes," my father says. "Plenty more. His mother was a maid named Christina Brandt. She worked at an inn near the palace of the real Count de Horn. He frequented the inn, and a boy was born of their, ah, union. She persuaded the count to bring up the child at his palace."

"He knew the real count?" Maybe it's also true he was mourning his mother in Venice. Of course this in no way exonerates him.

"He spent his boyhood at the count's palace. That explains his gentlemanly manners and knowledge of the count's affairs."

"It could also be how he acquired the jewelry he gave Angelica." Antonio is quick to piece the story together. "Who knows how much he stole."

"Wait," I say. "Did the count acknowledge him as his natural son?"

"Apparently not," my father replies. "The boy was a servant. He only learned of his true identity when he was older."

I shudder. "Imagine finding out you were a servant in your own father's house. No wonder he's angry and vengeful."

"This isn't the time for pity—" Antonio spits out.

My father hushes him so he can continue. "Christina got her son to snitch a few items. But he stole as much as he could and then fled. For years, the count has been trying to bring him to justice. Supposedly he moved around, using a different name in each place, and married several women. In Sweden, he was known as Burckle and as Brandt. He worked as the count's footman under the name Buckle. In Amsterdam, he was Studerat. And in Breslau, he was Rosenkranz. Apparently he was in France too."

"My goodness!" I exclaim. "Why didn't the Swedish authorities catch him?"

"They were close. An order for his arrest was filed in London a few weeks ago." My father narrows his eyes. "That would have been about when he asked for your hand."

I admit it was.

"You mean you knew that?" Antonio is stunned. "And married him anyway?"

"If only you'd told us!" my father says.

I remind them of the night the royal guard awakened us. "Their search was what made me realize the danger," I say. "Before, I'd only heard rumors. And nothing about other marriages."

My father frowns. "The real count was just in London. The ambassador saw a notice in the *Daily Courant* about his arrival and thought it strangely belated. Now we know he came to petition the queen." He pauses. "I don't suppose you knew about that?"

"I'm afraid I knew that too."

As we sit in silence, the horrible details sink in.

"What do we do?" my father asks at last. "In the eyes of the church, you're still married."

I stare at the cameo on my finger. "If he isn't who he said he was, our vows were empty."

"But will he agree to end the marriage?" Antonio counters. "The man is a master of fraud and deceit. He has other wives. We can't assume he will listen to reason."

I pause. It's true the dissolution of marriage is no assured matter. Under coverture, husband and wife are one person, and that one person is the husband. With my vow, I gave up my power. I put myself at his mercy. "I don't know what he'll agree to," I say. "But let me see what I can do."

"What could *you* possibly do?" My father doesn't mean that disrespectfully; he's just acknowledging my lack of power in the situation.

"I can appeal to him in a letter."

"Where would you even send it?"

"He's been staying at the Claridge. It can be delivered there."

My father isn't convinced this is a good idea. Antonio is even more opposed. In his mind, a letter hurts my cause. As if the mere act of putting words on paper would enshrine my vows in perpetuity. In fact, I can see both suspect I'm still vulnerable to Frederick's persuasions.

"Please," I say, after they've made their case. "Let me do this my way."

As soon as they leave, I sit down at my desk. The reason I want to write to Frederick is that I believe, despite everything, he still loves me and will listen to me. I didn't mention this to my father or Antonio, because I knew they'd say, "That man is incapable of love!" And maybe they're right. But I prefer to believe that every human being is capable of love. And that if I appeal to him with that in mind, Frederick will respond with a letter of his own.

I pick up my pen and write a short note.

Dear Count de Horn,

I have heard many painful and upsetting rumors about you. You yourself said there must be no secrets between us. Please, I am open to hear whatever you can tell me about your history and position. Are you already married? Am I really your wife? As your supposed wife, I feel you owe me the truth. A letter of explanation is all I ask of you.

Angelica

As soon as he receives my letter the next morning, Frederick rushes to Golden Square. It is a reaction I failed to anticipate. I'm alone in the studio when he storms in, waving the letter.

"It's not your place to question your husband!" he shouts, tearing up the paper. "Pack your things! I've waited long enough. We're leaving for Sweden."

When I refuse, his fury increases.

"Go!" I demand. "Before my father sees you!"

He glares at me, then reaches for a porcelain vase on the table by the door and dashes it to the floor. Splinters scatter in all directions. "You want a separation?" he cries. "Very well, you will have it!"

I jump back, but he grabs my hand. For a second it seems he is going to pick me up and carry me off. Instead, he twists my arm so he can grip the cameo on my finger. Before I can wrench free, he has pulled it off and dropped it into his pocket.

The sounds of our struggle bring my father running.

But Frederick is past the point of argument. "You'll soon see who *I am*," he roars as he runs out the door. "And you'll be sorry!"

For three days, we wait to see how he will carry out his threats. Now that it is irrevocably over between us, I feel horror at the mere thought of seeing him. How his tenderness could have turned to such depravity is incomprehensible. And the possibility he might abduct me in the middle of the night—an action well within the law of the land for him as my husband—is terrifying.

It's hard to believe I ever felt anything for him. I can see now what I was blind to: He was never worthy of even a passing flirtation, let alone love in any form or color.

My father asks Antonio to move into the guest room. His presence is reassuring, but I doubt he'd be any match for Frederick if the latter is truly determined to do harm. The ambassador sends two men to stand guard day and night. If this causes a stir among the crowds, I'm too preoccupied to notice. The servants have strict orders not to admit the count under any pretext. Even so, I'm too agitated to be alone in the studio, and my father is too upset to work on the Three Muses.

When I go to bed, I lock the shutters with an extra bolt. I sleep in fits and starts, waking at the slightest noise, worried Frederick might force his way past the guards. And I can't get the image of his ring out of my mind. No doubt he wouldn't hesitate to use the poison.

On the fourth day, a wiry young man calls at Golden Square and insists upon seeing Miss Angelica. He claims to be legal counsel sent by Count de Horn. While the ambassador's guards hold him, swords drawn, he explains he's come to assert the count's rights. "You, Miss Angelica, must submit to your husband's wishes and join him at once."

"And if I refuse?"

"By law, he has rights over you and everything you possess."

"And if I dispute this so-called marriage?"

The young clerk looks at the ground. "Then the count will accept a fair settlement."

"What are his terms?"

"Pay five hundred guineas for a legal separation. You'll never hear from him again."

"Five hundred?" my father and Antonio bellow in unison.

"That's out of the question," I echo.

After the clerk leaves, having advised us to seriously consider his offer, my father and Antonio debate the conditions. My father wants to pay him off and be done with it.

Antonio is flabbergasted. "Paying him would mean we—she—accepts his dirty tactics. That bully doesn't deserve a ha'penny!"

Much as I value their ideas, I have to stop the debate. "We have no choice," I say. "I've already given him all my savings."

The only way to free myself from Frederick is to bring the case before a magistrate. The proceedings will take time. And we will need proof of his imposture. So with the ambassador's assistance, we dispatch messengers to courts around the Continent.

One afternoon, while awaiting the evidence, we receive a visit from the ambassador. My father ushers him into the parlor, frantically signaling the servants to fetch our most elegant goblets.

The ambassador declines any refreshment. "I've just learned about a plot of the most foul nature," he says. "I came myself because I couldn't trust a messenger. Angelica, your life is in danger. De Horn has engaged some ruffians to abduct you tonight. As we speak, their carriage is waiting. A boat will transport you across the Channel under the cover of dark."

"The house is already guarded," my father cries. "How do we stop this?"

"Don't worry," the ambassador says. "I've contacted the magistrate. The plot will be defused. In fact, something good will come of this: You'll be called to court before evidence arrives from the Continent. You should receive a summons within the week."

When we go before the magistrate a few days later, he rules that Frederick must provide proof of his nobility or be sent to prison.

Frederick counters by offering to have our marriage rendered null and void in return for payment of four hundred guineas.

When I refuse, he lowers it to three hundred guineas.

I'm ready to agree, having just received an equal sum from a commission. "Let's do this for the sake of peace," I say to my father.

"But the marriage most likely wasn't legitimate in the first place," he argues. "If we prove he was already married, it will be null and void without paying anything."

"I know. But I don't want the lengthy wait. Or the nasty publicity."

My father isn't swayed.

Nor is Antonio. "I don't care if it takes time," he says. "I'm opposed to giving that rascal a single farthing of our—your—money!"

The magistrate sides with my father and Antonio. "A criminal like this deserves to be punished. If you pay him off, you'll still be married in the eyes of the church, and he'll never go to prison. Don't do it."

In the end, it is my decision.

Whatever the truth turns out to be, I must free myself as soon as possible. A deed of separation will do that. I agree to pay three hundred guineas if Frederick will make no further demands on me, never again approach me or my property, nor make any attempt at reunion.

The deed is drawn up and signed on the tenth of February 1768, just shy of three months since we said our vows at Saint James's.

The next day, Antonio comes running into my studio, knocking over a bottle of varnish in his haste. "I got a letter from my friend in Germany! The man's bigamy has been confirmed!"

We summon my father, and Antonio reads the letter aloud. It says the man known as Brandt married a young girl in Hildesheim, Germany, in 1765. He won her confidence by claiming to be a colonel in Frederick the Great's army. Shortly after, he deserted her, leaving her destitute. She is prepared to come to London to testify against Brandt if I can pay her way.

"I knew you'd be vindicated," my father exclaims.

"Let's arrange for her to come immediately," Antonio says.

I remind them I already signed the decree.

"The money hasn't been delivered. This letter arrived just in time." Antonio sees me shaking my head but presses on: "You can't say it's too costly. Instead of paying Brandt, use the money to bring the woman here and pay the lawyer. You'll be free to marry again."

"Antonio is right," my father says. "End this marriage."

"You'll have your revenge!" Antonio is jubilant.

Their reasoning doesn't move me. Just knowing I've been granted a deed of separation, I feel my strength returning. I'm free! Free! No husband will ever have power over me again. *This* is the freedom I want, not the satisfaction of revenge. And certainly not the right to marry again. But with this freedom comes the responsibility to act honorably. "I refuse to act out of anger," I say. "If Frederick—I mean Brandt—is proven guilty, he will be sentenced to death. That's the punishment for bigamy in this country."

"So?" Antonio says. "I can't wait to see him hang."

I shake my head. "I may have been wronged, but I'm not a murderer."

Antonio stares at me in dismay. "Angelica, he must pay!"

I hold up my hand to silence them both. "Don't try to change my mind. I prefer to leave his punishment in God's hands."

Slowly my father begins to nod. He respects my moral decision. Antonio will have to accept it too.

I pick up an old painting rag and stoop to wipe up the puddle of varnish. "I have one request," I say. "Make sure I never see his face again."

Twenty-four

Nor have I seen him again. The ambassador told my father, who told me, that Brandt left the country. We're unlikely ever to meet, certainly not in London. There is no longer any reason to fear he'll try to force his will on me.

But there is another fear. The fear for my soul.

During the tumult of the past few months, I avoided going for confession. Yet I have always found sustenance in the church, so now I'm doing my best to make up for that lapse. Each time I go, I pray for forgiveness. I took vows without full respect for the sanctity of marriage, and without respect for my own father. Legally I've found resolution. Now I have to answer to God.

The priest explains it isn't enough to seek forgiveness for my own failings; I must forgive those who wronged me. "Can you do that?" he asks.

"I leave my husband's punishment in God's hands," I say. That faith drove my decision, and it still satisfies me.

But it doesn't satisfy the priest. "Everything is always in God's hands," he says. "What keeps you from full forgiveness?"

My father and Antonio have no problem calling Frederick's behavior unforgivable. For me, it isn't so simple. I do value forgiveness. Yet all the caring I would need to forgive Frederick has drained from my heart. Instead I feel only the desire to be rid of him forever. "My wish to end this marriage is what holds me back," I say.

"Yet you took sacred vows that have no end. Whether you like it or not, your marriage will continue in the eyes of God and the church until one of you meets death."

"Yes, that is what I fear. Help me to bear that."

"You can bear it," he says, "through forgiveness and by upholding your vows. You're fortunate your husband left, but you mustn't forsake him. When God chooses to do so, he will release you."

I leave confession with a heavy heart, but also with the renewed conviction I did the right thing. Loathsome as it is, I will uphold my vow. By so doing, I will forge a path to freedom no one can take away again.

My father can't understand how I could feel loyalty of any sort to a husband I have acknowledged to be utterly despicable. Antonio is also of that opinion, even more vehemently. But he has moved back to his own apartment, so I only hear his opinion on occasion. Night after night, my father and I have the same argument as he entreats me to, for God's sake, let the marriage be dissolved. For him, this is not a matter of faith but of dignity.

"It's up to you, Angelica," he says.

"It's not so easy."

"But the marriage was no marriage! There were no witnesses, no banns, no license. Your father wasn't even consulted. Besides, that devil was already married!"

"The bigamy hasn't been proven beyond a doubt," I say. "And there was a license. Remember, we were married in a Catholic chapel by a priest."

"A priest who knew it was illegal to marry two Catholics," he objects.

"When I took that vow, I was sincere. I was doing all I could to help Frederick. Now I must fulfill my vow, whether I wish to or not. There's no point discussing this further."

Antonio, who has stopped by on this particular evening, isn't persuaded. "Catholic laws regarding marriage may be strict," he argues, "but an urgent appeal to Rome can fix that."

"Please don't pressure me," I say. "It pains me to talk about all this."

My father takes my hand and strokes it, as if to caress away my pain. "A true painter's hand, such strong fingers," he muses, then stops short. "Where's the cameo you always wear?"

"I'm afraid he has it."

"Brandt?" He couldn't have dropped my hand faster had it stung him. "Why did you give it to him?"

"He forced it from me on his last visit."

"O Angelica!" he wails. "And now you're letting him force your heart as well?"

"That's enough!" I say. If I've learned anything, it is that only I and no one else can command my heart. That is the root of my independence. If I want to retain it, I cannot let anyone interfere. Not even my father. Without bidding them good night, I rise and leave the room. As I stand in the hallway, I overhear their heated voices.

"She's losing her mind," Antonio says. "Why else would she act this way?"

"She refuses to set herself free," my father replies. "I don't know whether it is a point of honor or just stubbornness."

"If she stays married to that fool, she'll never be free to remarry."

"I don't think she has any desire for that."

"Then you must convince her of her mistake."

"I've tried. She won't listen. Maybe you can persuade her."

"I've tried too. God knows I've tried."

There is a slight pause, and it seems the conversation might be over. Then Antonio speaks again: "More and more, I think it's time for me to leave London."

"No Zucchi!" my father cries. "Don't leave!"

"I have offers for work elsewhere, some very profitable. I fear I've put my own life aside for too long."

"What'll we do without you? What'll *she* do . . ."

Their voices trail off as I mount the stairs.

At midnight, long after Antonio has gone home and my father retired, after I've repeated my prayers several times over, I'm still unable to sleep. I made a vow out of what I believed was the goodness of my heart. Now letting that vow stand in a court of law is hurting those I love most. My vow, it seems, has become a sin.

Candle in hand, I slip down to the studio, no thought of painting, only wanting to sit quietly. In the flickering light, wrapped in my black lambswool shawl, I sit on the sofa. I sit and wait. For what, I'm not sure. As the flame grows low, my head droops and sleep overtakes me.

I must have dozed for some time. When I come to, the candle has gone out. Yet in the darkness, I have the distinct sense I'm not alone. I feel a presence in the room.

Immediately I know who it is—the man with bittersweet eyes I expected would one day visit my studio. I haven't thought of him in ages. Though I can't see him, he seems more real than a daydream. It occurs to me he's always been here, always with me, the way skin is beneath clothes.

I know you as I know myself, I say in my mind. *But who are you?*

There is no response.

You are the one who understands me. Who knows my heart in a way no one else does. When I paint or sing or play the lute, I want to share it with you. My laughter is for you. Even my sorrows are for you. Yet I have no idea who you are.

Still there is no response.

Finally, I climb back upstairs in the dark.

Whatever might be happening at midnight, work awaits with the light of day. After working on portraits, every spare moment goes to Achilles. Nothing can keep me from finishing it for the academy's first exhibition.

I'm painting dismay into Deidamia's eyes as she stares at her beloved, his raised sword belying his feminine guise, when Bridget appears unannounced one morning. Her face is so gaunt I have to conceal my shock.

"Angelica, how are you?" she says, pulling off her gloves and taking a seat by the fire. "I've been too ill to go out, but I came as soon as I could."

Common courtesy would have me call for tea and perhaps fetch another pillow. But I fully expect Bridget to declare me ruined—despite my father's assurances to the contrary—so I wait for her to unleash her judgment.

"To think he wasn't a count!" she continues. "And that I encouraged your relationship! Not to mention all the evenings he spent at our house. I shudder to recall it."

"We were all deceived."

"Weren't we, though?" She pats her chest rapidly, a signal that her nerves are frayed and she expects someone to provide water. I pick up the pitcher on the end table, pour a glass, and hand it to her. A few sips calm her enough to ask, "Have you heard the latest?"

"What latest? There are more rumors in London than layers to your petticoat."

She gives a little laugh. "About Joshua Reynolds, of course."

"What about him?"

"People are talking about his involvement with the count—"

When she says that, I stop her. "There was none. He never even met Brandt."

"He told you that?" She raises an eyebrow but doesn't wait for my response. "I think you should know what people are saying. Today's *Public Advertiser* says Reynolds himself masterminded the plot to discredit Angelica Kauffman. Imagine that!"

"I imagine nothing of the sort," I say. Perhaps Bridget doesn't consider me ruined, but this is worse. "How could you say such a thing? I thought he was a friend of yours!"

"Of course he is," she says between gulps of water.

"Then why repeat such a lie?"

Bridget's hand trembles so much she has to set down her glass. But that doesn't stop her from getting her story out. "They say he conspired with Nathaniel Dance and Henry Füssli to cause your disrepute after you rejected all three. They took it upon themselves to set up Brandt in London and arrange the marriage."

"That's absurd!" I'm practically shouting. "You know Henry left England. And Joshua doesn't bear me any ill will. Why should he? I wasn't the one who rejected him."

"You weren't?" Bridget doesn't conceal her surprise.

Immediately I regret mentioning that last point. Especially since it's only partially true. I sit down beside her and say more softly, "My friendship with Joshua is as strong as ever."

Bridget looks disappointed that I haven't substantiated her

gossip. As if venturing from her home were all for naught. "Well," she says with a grunt, "I don't know where such ideas come from."

With that, I relax. Others may talk, but Bridget won't be among them. I have made sure of that. As I pour her more water, I say in jest, "Perhaps you can blame my Italian critics. They're predisposed to be unfriendly toward British artists—you've said so yourself."

"So I have." A smile works its way across her lips. "I guess this means they no longer see you as Italian. You're a British artist now!"

"I suppose so," I say, smiling too. There is no doubt she means it as a compliment.

Though I've begun to feel like myself again, I'm not ready to go out in public. Knowing that, Joshua stops by regularly to update me on progress toward establishing an academy.

"A new plan has been drawn up," he says. "I'm hopeful all factions—not just Benjamin West and the dissidents, but the rest of the Society and our new president, Joshua Kirby—will accept it."

"That *is* progress," I say, noting how long all this has been in the works—since before I arrived in London.

Joshua explains that the king commissioned Benjamin to paint the departure of Regulus. Since it was Benjamin's first royal commission, it required many visits to the palace. "Initially they discussed the size of the canvas and other practical details," he says. "But Benjamin is a man of his beliefs. Soon he was talking up the value of a royal academy."

"And the king gave his support?"

"Indeed. He kept Benjamin till eleven o'clock to go over plans."

Accustomed to Joshua's humble way of telling a story, I probe further. "And what will *your* role be?"

"That's just it." He shakes his head. "They want me to be president."

"An excellent idea, if you ask me."

He stops to examine my painting of Achilles, then continues, "You know how much I dislike partisan positions. As president, I'd be in the thick of it."

"I've told you what I think," I say. "It's up to you to decide what's best."

Despite my advice, Joshua remains ambivalent. A few days later, he drops by to report with chagrin that the academy's future is still mired in politics. Several weeks go by without news, and I begin to think any appearance of progress may have been a mirage.

However, when he next appears in my studio, Joshua is elated. "We have our academy!" he exclaims.

I congratulate him and call for tea—with apologies that we don't have coffee—so he can sit down and recount the full story. I want every detail.

"I told you about Benjamin's painting of Regulus," he begins. "The king and queen wanted to see it as soon as it was finished. So he brought it to the palace. And—fancy this—Joshua Kirby just happened to be there."

I smile. "As president of the Society of Artists, he's Benjamin's sworn enemy. How did the king deal with their antipathy?"

"With royal cunning!" Joshua helps himself to a pastry, taking such a large bite he has to wash it down with tea before he can speak. "He invited Kirby to critique the painting, but without revealing who the artist was. Kirby gave his highest praise. He had to find some fault, so he said the frame should have been made by the king's gilder."

"How disagreeable."

Joshua chuckles. "Apparently the king thought so too. His reply was, 'When you're able to give us a painting of this quality, it will be framed by the gilder of your choice.' All Kirby could say was he hoped the painting would be shown publicly."

"He still didn't know who the artist was?"

"No."

"And Benjamin was watching all the while?"

"Yes. As soon as Kirby had committed himself, Benjamin stepped forward and said, 'I too hope it will be shown. But since I painted it for His Majesty, its exhibition will be determined by the royal pleasure.'"

"Perfect rejoinder!" I exclaim. "I bet the king liked that."

"He immediately agreed the work should be shown. Whereupon Kirby invited Benjamin to submit it to the Society of Artists for their next exhibition."

I shake my head. "What gall!"

"But listen to what the king did!" Joshua is practically leaping with enthusiasm. "He turned to Kirby and said, 'No, it will be shown at *our* academy—the Royal Academy of Arts!'"

I give a shriek of delight. "So that's how it was formed!"

"Yes, and it will exist under the patronage of the king. In addition to annual exhibitions, an institute will give free instruction to students of painting, sculpture, and design. It will be housed in Pall Mall."

"Is there enough space?"

He acknowledges that while the king has provided some rooms in Somerset House for teaching, the gallery will be only nine meters long. "Of course," he adds, "it's only temporary. The king has promised us more space within a few years."

"And your role?" I say.

Joshua is suddenly subdued. "Last night I had a visit from

Benjamin. He spent two hours trying to persuade me to join yet another petition to the king about forming an academy."

I'm confused. "Why petition the king if he's already agreed to it?"

"That's just it. Benjamin wanted me to come to a decision of my own accord, so he kept me in the dark about the king's proclamation."

"And since you didn't know, you continued to refuse to take a position?"

"I'm afraid I did. But eventually I agreed to accompany him to Joseph Wilton's house to meet with some of the artists. What I didn't realize," he says sheepishly, "was that thirty of them were waiting at Wilton's while I was speaking with Benjamin."

I laugh. "I can picture what happened when you entered the room."

He laughs with me. "They rose in unison and greeted me as their president."

"And you accepted?"

"What else could I do?"

I clap my hands, and he leans over and places his hands around mine. "And you, my angel, have been accepted as one of the thirty-four founding members! Isn't that the best news of all?"

Twenty-five

London, 1781

The soothing clip-clop of the horses lulls me to the brink of sleep.

Lately I've been tiring easily. Perhaps it's because I worked long hours to finish my entries for the Royal Academy—one fewer than last year. It's hard to believe I've been in London fifteen years, and a member of the Academy for more than a dozen. I continue to exhibit mostly history paintings, yet my commissions still favor portraits. That disappoints me. Despite its royal patronage and the inspiring leadership of Joshua—now *Sir* Joshua Reynolds—the Academy hasn't engendered wider support for history painting.

Nor has the Academy been without acrimony, even outright conflict. One artist, driven by envy, ridiculed Joshua's love for the old masters by depicting him as a conjuror. Anyone could see the little girl on Joshua's knee was meant to be me. And if that wasn't enough, the naked woman in black stockings dancing in front of St. Paul's Cathedral—the same church Joshua and I were selected to decorate with history paintings—was unquestionably me. I told the Academy I would withdraw all my submissions if they exhibited that atrocity. I wasn't sure they'd listen to a woman's objections. But they did, and the painting was rejected.

Because of all this and more, I think often of returning to Italy.

Not that my work isn't wildly popular in London. It is. And

so am I. As my engraver likes to say, "The whole world has gone Angelicamad!" Still, success doesn't have the far-reaching power I once imagined. It doesn't soothe the inner creases of the soul.

My father and I are traveling home to Golden Square, having visited Rosa and her husband at their estate outside London. I couldn't be happier about her marriage to Giuseppe Bonomi. She has, as Bridget would say, risen rapidly in society. Yet she's remained her pure-hearted self. I recall the eve of her wedding, six years ago, when I opened my jewelry box and pulled out a silver beaded necklace. I slipped it over her head and reminded her it had been a gift from Bridget in Venice. That was all the more special because she had succumbed the year before to yet another bout of ill health.

Rosa fingered the beads, and for a moment I thought they might fly across the room as they once did. Then she put her arms around me and whispered, "Since you never married—not really—tomorrow I'll do it for both of us."

"Angelica?" My father interrupts my reverie. "Are you awake?"

In answer, I reach out and take his hand. His skin feels like crisp parchment.

"I was dreaming of Schwarzenberg," he says.

I tell him it's comforting to dream of home.

"Especially with all the troubles here." He gives a shudder. "I wish Lord Gordon hadn't been acquitted. I fear it's only a matter of time before his crowd marches again."

I frown recalling the harsh realities of the past year. In June, incited by Lord Gordon, tens of thousands marched on the House of Commons to petition against the Roman Catholic Relief Act. In their minds, Catholics' allegiance to the pope makes us traitors to the king. The mob went on a rampage, looting and burning churches and offices and homes. Eventually, the king's forces quelled the unrest, but not before hundreds died.

We managed to escape to the Bonomis' estate, and when we returned, Golden Square was untouched. We may not be so lucky again. "If there are more riots," I say, "the Relief Act could be repealed."

"They still blame Catholics for starting the Great Fire. None of us are safe."

My fatigue dissolves as I grip his hand. "Then why don't we go?"

"Go where?"

"Home!"

"To Schwarzenberg?" He looks at me wide-eyed. "We'd be safe there."

"So let's go!"

The enthusiasm fades from his face. "Much as I'd love to go, I can't ask you to make such a sacrifice. You have commitments here. And I'm an old man."

"No," I say with fresh resolve. "I've done what I came to London to do. Besides, the climate is too rough for old age. Don't you agree?"

Instead of answering directly, he pulls his hand away and turns to look out the window. "My life is almost over. How can I leave with ease unless I know you'll be well taken care of?"

"Papa," I say reproachfully, "you still worry I can't provide for myself?"

"Of course you can. But I'm afraid that's not enough these days." He shakes his head, still gazing out the window. Rain runs down the glass in rivulets, blurring the landscape so it looks more like my palette than a painting. He lapses into silence for so long I think our discussion is over. But then he turns to me. "There's something I must ask of you so I can be at peace."

I reach out and take his hand again. "What is it?"

"Marry Antonio."

His words hit me with the force of cold mud flung from the car-riage wheels. I drop his hand and jerk away. "I can't."

"Why not? He's your most loyal friend. He'd be a devoted hus-band. Do you doubt that?"

I have to admit Antonio has been a good friend. Despite his threats to leave London, he has never gone far or for long. Sometimes I forget he isn't one of the family. But my husband? That has always been out of the question. "I don't love him" is all I can say.

"Then let's find another husband."

"There are no others." I stare at him in dismay. He's always respected my independence, and now he wants to push a husband on me? If he weren't so fragile, I would fight back. Instead I simply remind him I'm still married in the eyes of the church. It is an unpleasant fact we haven't discussed in years.

"You can change that," he says. "At least promise me you'll think about it."

And I do think about it. Each day—as winter turns to spring, and snowdrops sprout around King George's statue in the square—I turn it over in my mind. I recall the force with which the priest insisted I uphold my vow taken before God. That vow, he said, was without end. I know he'd say the same today. But I also know a priest isn't the highest authority. The church, and only the church, can declare my penitence complete.

Nor can I ignore my father's failing health. The longer we wait, the more difficult travel will be. Not to mention the risks of staying in London. Fortunately there have been no more riots, but tensions remain high between Protestants and Catholics. The uneasy standoff could end at any moment. Some nights I lie awake imagining flames at our doorstep, our house burning down. Not just my father, but I too may never have the chance to return home.

So, before the snowdrops have been supplanted by yellow crocuses, I reach a decision: Fourteen years of marriage is long enough.

I go to my father and tell him I'm ready to submit my plea to Rome, to see if the tie that binds me to Frederick can be broken. I'm not ready, however, to commit to a new marriage. He doesn't press me about that. Besides, we both know petitioning the Holy See is a lengthy process. If our departure from London depends on an affirmative answer from Rome, it may come too late. Nevertheless, the petition is drawn up and submitted.

In the meanwhile, we go on with life as usual.

In my spare time, I create designs for painted fans, more elaborate than those I used to paint for Rosa. It was Joshua who came up with the idea. He wants us to infuse our most sublime artistry into everyday objects. I pass my designs to a fan maker, who paints them on fans. People love them. Even the queen purchased one to show off on her birthday.

This afternoon, I'm working on a design with three gold medallions when my father calls me to his room. He is on his bed, as he often is these days. "This arrived with my letters from abroad," he says, handing me a brown packet. "It's addressed to you."

I tear open the wrapping, revealing a small case. Its red silk cover is faded around the edges, the clasp so rusty it's hard to unhook. When I finally open it and lift the lid, I gasp.

"My cameo!"

He nods. "What belongs to you has been returned to you."

I hold it to the light so we both can see without a doubt that it is the ring Bridget gave me. I slip it on my finger. It fits perfectly.

"There was a letter addressed to me as well," he says, watching my reaction.

"From *him*?"

"From a friend of his."

"Why now?" I say, dropping onto the bed at my father's feet. "Does he know about my petition? Is he—"

"He's dead."

"Dead?"

"He died after a short illness. Apparently his heart was weak."

"He didn't know about the petition?"

"No. It's pure coincidence."

I stare at the cameo, no longer the visible stamp of my vow, and let the reality sink deeper. Frederick is dead. My marriage is over. It's a moment I thought would never come. I can hardly think of what's next. "So there's no need to wait for a response from Rome?"

"No need whatsoever."

"I'm finally free."

"Yes, Angelica, you're free!"

Hearing those words, I begin to sob. These are tears of relief, not tears of grief for Frederick. Any sorrow I might have felt for him died long ago.

The next morning, I return to my father, having spent all night thinking about our future. More than ever, I want to return to Italy. And I want him to be at peace.

"Papa," I say softly, "I've reconsidered."

He breaks into a smile. Without my saying, he knows I'm referring to our conversation in the carriage that rainy night.

"I'm prepared to marry again."

His smile is unbroken, but he speaks with solemnity. "Only if you yourself are content. Otherwise I would never wish it."

I hesitate. But only for a second. "If we marry as companions, I can accept that."

"You will be forty next year. Antonio is fifty-four," he replies. "Of course, companionship is what would be expected."

"Then you'll speak to him?"

"I will speak to him."

And so it is decided: I will marry Antonio. I'm grateful there will be no formal proposal, no awkward moments. Instead, the two of us have a businesslike discussion about the arrangements. It will be in no way a marriage of coverture. Our finances will remain separate. All my earnings will be my own to use as I wish. A contract will be drawn up stipulating that as my husband he cannot use my estate to resolve any debts he might incur.

"This way," he assures me, "no one will accuse me of marrying you for your money."

I tell him I would not think that.

"I know," he says. "This way no one else will either."

A week later, Rosa comes to London with her two young children to help plan the wedding. She finds me in the studio busy with the Judgment of Paris.

Knowing it's my habit to revisit subjects, she inquires what intrigues me this time.

I tell her it's Paris's decision to give the golden apple to Aphrodite, who promised him the love of a beautiful woman. I want to capture the intensity on his face as he abandons his power of reason. He could have chosen a kingdom or wisdom, but he chose love. And I want to show the trepidation of the three goddesses, who know the price that must be paid for that love, because now the Trojan War is inevitable.

"Aphrodite must be your favorite," Rosa says. Never having seen Bridget when she was young, she doesn't recognize my model. "Her gossamer robes make her so feminine."

"Actually," I say, "Athena is my favorite."

I explain that while Paris and Aphrodite are male and female, Athena is their counterpart. Her power as a warrior and the goddess of wisdom is what I would choose for myself. The painting is meant to create a balance between the three of them, even if viewers will be too fixed on the gifting of the apple to notice.

But Rosa wants to focus instead on my wedding. "You're finally free," she says, "what are you waiting for?"

"Antonio comes to Golden Square every day," I say. "What's the rush?"

"I won't see Giuseppe for a week," she counters, "yet I miss him already."

"You forget I'm not a young bride," I say.

"But I remember when you were. I saw how mysterious you were, filled with your secret love."

I twist my lips. "What I remember is that there were too many secrets."

"I remember too. Especially the fight with Frederick you thought I didn't understand."

"You were aware of all that?"

"Yes. But to me, you were always as magnificent as"—she glances back at my painting—"Aphrodite with the golden apple. Except now you've paid the full price. Only love remains."

Our wedding takes place on the fourteenth of July. Although Rosa is disappointed, I wear only a simple dress and insist she does the same. Our vows are those few words required for a civil ceremony, nothing more.

Within a month, we've packed everything and are ready to sail for the Continent. At the last minute, Rosa and Giuseppe decide to accompany us so their growing family can escape the political tensions. Our carriages as we leave Golden Square at dawn are weighed down with the possessions of two households. Not only am I bringing my harpsichord but also several large unfinished canvases. I hope to resume work as soon as possible.

Twenty-six

Napping in my berth during our crossing of the Channel, I find myself walking a country road. It is twilight, and I hope to reach a friend by nightfall. Suddenly the colors begin to swirl around me, as they still often do at night.

So I leave the road, seeking a shorter route.

At first, the grass is soft underfoot, and I move with ease. Then the ground becomes steep and rocky. I hold my skirts high, yet I keep stumbling. Time and again, I have to pick myself up.

Finally I come to a crest that should be the high point, where my friend will be waiting. I rest against a weather-beaten pine, looking around for him. He promised he would be here.

But then I notice a higher peak ahead, so I resume climbing. The dusk is growing thicker, the terrain more treacherous. Soon it's so dark I have to crawl. I'm alone, utterly alone, seeking a friend whose name and face I can no longer recall.

Rome

Twenty-seven

Rome, 1786

Sunday, God's day. Instead of rushing to the studio, I make this a day of rest. In London, I worked every day, almost every hour of every day. Here in Rome, I find myself needing to pause and reflect so I can continue to create during the rest of the week.

Perhaps this slowing down is a sign of age, inevitable now I've passed my fortieth year. Or maybe it's the mark of married life. Not that married life has marked me in notable ways. Our wedding vows don't cut deeply, as I know vows can. In fact, this marriage has given me greater freedom than I would have had, had I remained alone. In our sprawling villa on Via Sistina, it's easy to all but forget I have a husband. Antonio and I often go the entire day without running into each other.

I worked hard in London to assert my independence. Each time I stumbled—which I did often—I picked myself up, dusted myself off, and continued on my way. Yet in the end, I wasn't as free as I expected, or as happy as I hoped. Even with an adoring public to hold me up, I felt let down. And over time, worn down. Now, instead of society, I find myself turning to solitude. I don't need much companionship if I have the company of the canvases in my studio. I don't need a husband's touch to pour liquid color through my veins; I have learned how to pour those colors myself. Nor do I regret never having had children; my paintings are my progeny. Yes, loneliness may creep in at times, but that's the price I pay for my freedom.

After church on Sundays, however, instead of retreating to my studio, I take the carriage and visit galleries. I look for new pieces to add to my collection, though never finalize anything without Antonio's consent. Not that I need him to judge a good buy, but that's one small way to keep the peace between us. Then I spend the rest of the afternoon in the garden, falling into a daydream. Age hasn't cured me of that habit. Nor has Antonio.

My daydreams are different now. No more fancies of painting the queen, of grand success. All the public success anyone could dream of has been mine. Nor do I let myself conjure up the artist with bittersweet eyes. For so long, I believed he would visit my studio. I thought he was real, and one day we would meet. But we never did. After Antonio and I married and settled in Rome, I laid all that to rest. Now my dreams seek something more intangible. Ineffable. As if I'd been painting with invisible oils, and only now realized there is no image. Most days, this doesn't concern me. But on Sunday afternoons, I sit here, with a fatigue deeper than flesh, and pray to see the invisible revealed.

Then, when Sunday evening arrives, I shake off my sluggishness and step out of my solitude. I pick fresh roses for the vase by the front door and prepare to greet our friends. Painters, writers, and lovers of art like to gather in our parlor. Many are foreigners on the Grand Tour, including some who came for that purpose but never left. Sometimes we have a musical performance, sometimes a dramatic reading, sometimes a discussion about the latest exhibit. Always it's a pleasure to be in the company of artists, as it was at the Mosers' years ago.

Though last night's gathering stretched into the wee hours because some regulars brought friends, I rise early, ready to complete my painting of Aeneas mourning the death of Pallas. I sharpen the edge of the shadow on Pallas's neck; a touch of midnight blue heightens the sense of his mortality. Then I paint the faint suggestion of an angelic face into the clouds. No one else will likely ever notice it, but my eye goes directly to the departed soul.

Only after I've worked for some time do I stop for breakfast. Sunlight streams into the dining room as I sit alone over tea and sweet rolls.

Antonio appears as I'm finishing and sits down across from me. He serves himself a sweet roll, then immediately wrinkles his nose. "These are ice cold."

I'm tempted to say that if he came earlier, he'd find them hot. But I anticipate his response: "I'm sixty, have you forgotten? I can rise at my leisure." Or he might turn the blame on me: "If you didn't insist on sleeping in that little closet over the studio, I'd hear you rise." Not wishing to hear any of this, I simply pour him a cup of tea.

He adds milk and sugar and stirs with a vigorous hand. "I thought you'd be in the studio by now. Didn't you promise to deliver Lady Foster's portrait?"

"I was in the studio," I say. "Now that Aeneas is finished, Lady Foster will be next."

He jerks the cup from his lips so quickly he almost douses himself. "Important clients should never be kept waiting while you fuss with history paintings!"

I've learned it's easier to calm my husband if I avoid confrontation. "Aeneas was commissioned by Emperor Joseph," I say. "Surely you consider him important."

Antonio doesn't dispute that. He runs a hand over his head, now entirely bald, and calculates how soon he can expect payment if he dispatches the painting to Vienna today.

228 JUDE BERMAN

"The emperor let me choose the subject," I remind him, "provided the work was done as fast as possible. That was two years ago."

"But he knew you had to finish work for Empress Catherine."

"Yes. And now the empress—"

He frowns. "She wants another painting? Why didn't you tell me? Angelica, how can I manage your affairs if you don't say when you get a new commission?"

"I was going to tell you."

His frown deepens. "It's out of the question. I won't allow it. If you take on more, how will you fulfill the requests you already have? The Duke of Gloucester, Sir Cecil and Lady Bishop, Baroness de Krüdener, Count Rossomersky, Prince Poniatowsky—it's hard to keep track of them all."

"And Father Jacquier."

"Pshaw! He should be struck from the list. You'll never take payment from him."

Antonio and I rarely agree on matters of art; we agree even less on matters of faith. I can imagine what he'd say if he knew I spend an hour in prayer every night. "It doesn't feel right to accept payment from those who have less than I do," I say. "Besides, I can't take money from the church."

"The church is hardly poor."

"That's not the point."

"You won't even take money from clients you befriend. Like that Venetian bride whose portrait you did."

"And look how that turned out. Her father-in-law gave me a present worth double what you wanted me to charge." I push back my chair and stand up before Antonio can mention Cardinal Ignatius, secretary of Pope Pius VI, who commissioned a painting of the Virgin Mary as a child. I did it for a pittance. The pope was so pleased he asked to visit my studio. In the end, he didn't, only because he didn't want to arouse the envy of other artists. But for me, his pleasure was payment enough. "I never said I'd refuse money from the empress. I'll make it clear she shouldn't expect her painting for two years. Or longer if I don't get back to work."

I walk to the door, then turn back. "Who was the foreigner with Tischbein and Reiffenstein last night?"

"The German?" Antonio looks up from his second sweet roll. "I heard him introduced as the baron-who-lives-opposite-the-Rondanini."

I laugh. "Strange name! I hope he comes again."

I have every intention of working on Lady Foster. But first I climb the stairs to the room above my studio—the space that, whether my husband likes it or not, is my sanctuary. A small painting on a walnut panel sits on a table at my bedside. Leonardo's *Saint Jerome* was a gift from my father. As I lift the veil with which I keep it shrouded, tears rise in my eyes. It has been five years since his death.

Our trip from London was strenuous. After a rough crossing to Ostend, we traveled through Flanders and Germany and on to Uncle Michel's in Schwarzenberg. With all of us packed into the farm-house, I found myself once again adjusting to a simpler life. This time though, I didn't mind. And I loved the costume with red-and-gold stitching across the bodice my aunt gave me. On Rosa's urging, I took out my easel and did a self-portrait.

When it was time to head to Venice, my father was reluctant to get into the carriage. It took all of us to persuade him to let us lift him in.

"The warm climate will give you strength," I said.

But he only grew weaker. While I set up my studio and painted portraits of the Venetian nobility, he took to bed. Rosa sent word to her mother—Papa's sister—who came to nurse him. Sitting by his side, my eyes closed, I saw a vast sky with clouds obscuring the sun, yet effervescent light shining through. Becoming absorbed in that light meant life as I knew it would be obliterated. *This must be what you're feeling*, I thought.

"Don't be afraid," I whispered. "I'm with you."

Even so, when the end came, I wasn't prepared. And if that weren't enough, my aunt followed her brother to the grave. Death had moved into our house. Though I made an effort to paint, the days were like empty shells of time. I could still see the inner sky I saw at Papa's bedside, only now it was filled with dark, brooding clouds. I put aside my other canvases and painted his death, portraying him as Leonardo, whose work he so admired. In London, I'd done a similar painting, and he liked it, as did all who saw it at the Royal Academy.

For once, Antonio wasn't against history painting. He brought a roll of papers to my studio and spread them out. "Do you recall François Ménageot?" he asked.

"You mean the French painter we met in London."

"Yes. He let me copy his sketches of Leonardo's death. You're welcome to use them."

The drawings were rough, but I thanked Antonio for his kindness.

As I painted the artist dying in the arms of his patron, King Francis, I looked for signs of my father's spirit, some hint he was still with me. But all I saw was the finality of his death impaled on the canvas. I didn't know how to go on living. Antonio became so worried about my health that he made plans for us to go south to Naples, and from there on to Rome.

I pull the silk over Saint Jerome and force back my tears. In truth, my own grief is dwarfed by the raw agony in his sunken eyes and hollow cheeks as he performs penance in the desert. It is all the more raw as Leonardo left the painting unfinished. And now . . . if Lady Foster's portrait remains unfinished, Antonio will have a legitimate grievance.

Since we've been in Rome, he has handled our household affairs so I can concentrate on painting. He purchases my canvases and frames, schedules my clients, manages the monies. He does his best to step into my father's shoes. And I am grateful. Except when he tries to tell me what to paint or how. Which he does frequently. "Angelica, Lady Foster's gown has too many folds. You've made her unfashionably plump," he'll say. Or "Why is the princess's left hand so small? It bewilders the eye."

Some of his criticisms are valid. But he delivers them with a peevishness that's annoying. And always there is our fundamental disagreement: I feel I've earned the freedom to do history paintings; he insists we can't get by without the income from portraits. And if I wish to collect art as well, he's quick to point out, a steady income is even more necessary.

Back in the studio, I darken Lady Foster's waistband to flatter her figure. No one will see her as plump. As I paint, however, an inexplicable urge arises, beckoning me to the Sistine Chapel. It becomes so strong that I put aside my paints and request the carriage.

"Signor Zucchi is out," the servant informs me. "Shall I ready the second carriage?"

I hesitate. Why stop when I'm making good progress on Lady Foster? I should wait till Sunday. But the chapel is calling. If I don't stay long, I reason, I can be back before Antonio. He won't know I've been away.

"The second carriage will be fine," I say, pulling on my gloves.

Twenty-eight

As soon as I step into the Sistine Chapel, I realize it was not a mistake to leave the studio. Truly, it's never a mistake to come here. Even for a few minutes.

I kneel toward the back and pray, then look up at the ceiling. Often when I do this, a particular element of Michelangelo's artistry stands out—such as the giant orange globe of a sun God has created, reminding me it truly is possible to paint the sun. Today, however, it is God's outstretched hand, majestic yet human as it reaches to create Adam. One finger with enough love to beget all of humanity. I long for its touch.

Then, much as it happened long ago in the Frari, I feel fingers of light lengthening toward me. They lift me up, transport me into the painting. Tucked under God's arm, where Eve was moments ago, I observe the church below. A man stands before the fresco of the Last Judgment, which graces the altar wall, scribbling in his notebook. *A lover of art*, I think. At the back, a woman kneels in prayer, head slumped forward. Just as I realize she is none other than myself, I'm back on the marble floor.

I must have been dreaming, more fatigued than I thought. As I gather my skirts and rise to go, I glance toward the altar. A man with a notebook is indeed standing there.

I walk toward him.

As he turns around, I recognize the baron-who-lives-opposite -the-Rondanini. "I beg your pardon," he says. "Have we met?"

"At our home last night."

His eyes widen in recognition. "Of course. Signora Zucchi—"

"Kauffman," I say. "Angelica Kauffman." I've never been comfortable using Antonio's surname. Fortunately he couldn't make an issue of it, since the public knew me as Kauffman, and changing names wouldn't be beneficial for business.

"Signora Kauffman, the painter!"

I wonder who this fellow without a proper name could be. Though his high forehead and long nose look aristocratic, the doleful expression of his eyes suggests a poet or scholar. "And you," I gently probe, "are a friend of Tischbein?"

"Yes," he says, "bonded by our love for art."

"Which you're enjoying here."

He breaks into a smile as he explains how obsessed he is with Michelangelo, so much so that he can hardly look at another artist's work. "Even my appreciation for nature," he says, "wanes in the presence of his genius."

I like the impassioned way he speaks. I tell him I too love Michelangelo.

He closes his notebook so he can focus on me. "What do you like most about his work?"

As I consider his question, I notice how the downward curve of his eyelids and the furrow between his brows lend a bittersweetness to his smile. As if he were at once delighting in his love for art and also on the verge of weeping. "I suppose his sense of color," I say after a moment. "Of course, people like to debate who's greater, he or Raphael. And some insist he owes everything to Fra Angelico—"

"Always a debate," he says, the furrow becoming a frown.

His reaction surprises me. "You don't like to discuss art?"

"Discuss, yes. Debate, not so much. Taking sides oversimplifies things."

I tell him I hadn't thought of that.

"Suppose," he says, warming to the discussion, "you declare a preference for one artist. If I then ask you to assess what I see as the greater merits of another, I'm doubling your work. The easiest response is to defend your view. In this way, debate robs us of valuable insight." He crosses his arms, satisfied with his explanation.

I can't resist pointing out the irony: "But you just stated your preference for Michelangelo."

"True—" He stops short and I expect him to refute my point, but his tone turns playful. "O wise critic, that's why I avoid debates! I'd rather directly observe whatever I find worthwhile."

His response is a world apart from what I'm used to. At such a juncture, Antonio would charge headlong into an argument. The baron doesn't care about being right; he's interested in meeting me mind to mind. I tell him I couldn't agree more: Direct observation is what makes art come alive.

There is a natural pause in our conversation. I'm about to take my leave when he says, "Tell me, what brought you here?"

"Actually," I say, "my husband thinks I'm working on a portrait right now."

"So you came on a whim," he says without a hint of reproach. "That's the best reason!"

"You think so?"

"Absolutely. Whims are the voice of nature. Following them can reveal her wonders."

I like how he plays with philosophy as an artist might play with paint. It moves me to speak more openly. I describe the lure of God's hand when I entered the church, how I felt myself flying to the ceiling. How I saw him standing below.

He looks up as if seeing the ceiling for the first time. Without changing the tilt of his head, he glances at me out of the corner of his eye and suggests we go up to the gallery for a better view.

I tell him I didn't know it was open to the public.

"It isn't," he says. "But that can be arranged."

He rushes off in search of a custodian, and a few minutes later, the gate has been unlocked and we're mounting the stairs. At the top, we cross a passageway leading to a narrow gallery. Much like me, the baron has no fear of heights. As we stand on the ledge, like two birds on the branch of a tree, observing God and Adam, I don't feel any need to comment, as I might with someone else. When we've taken our fill, neither of us suggests leaving; we just simultaneously retrace our steps.

"What a master," the baron says when we're on the ground again. "I wish I could fix his images in my mind."

"I think my soul just received his imprint," I say.

"An imprint should last." He laughs softly. "But just in case, I'm going to purchase as many of Michelangelo's drawings as I can afford before I leave Rome."

That takes me aback. "You're leaving?"

As he gazes at me, I have the sense he's about to reveal his identity. But instead he says, "Not yet, not when we still have so much to explore!"

"Then I look forward to it," I say. After we bid farewell, I realize his *we* in all likelihood didn't refer to me.

As I work on Lady Foster's portrait, I anticipate Sunday evening, when the baron-who-lives-opposite-the-Rondanini may return with his friends. Never have I met someone whose passion for art—for life itself—mirrors so well how I feel. Or at least how I used to feel. He has a youthful, independent spirit that reminds me of how I was in London, when I was so sure of myself and what I intended to accomplish, so unwilling to compromise my dreams. So unaware of how easily dreams can slip away.

However, he doesn't return on Sunday, nor the following Sunday. Tischbein and Reiffenstein don't come either, so I can't inquire about the baron through them.

The following Sunday is Christmas Eve. Antonio and I go to Saint Peter's to hear the pope celebrate high mass at midnight. As we're returning to our carriage, the street becomes clogged with people funneling out of the square, and we're separated. All I can do is let the throng carry me, like a log on a rushing river, and trust I'll reach the row of carriages.

Suddenly voices ring out: "Merry Christmas, Signora Angelica!"

I turn to see Wilhelm Tischbein, his round face illumined by candlelight, with the baron-who-lives-opposite-the-Rondanini at his side. After I explain the situation, Wilhelm volunteers to go in search of my husband. Since the crowd is starting to thin, he thinks it shouldn't take long.

As I wait with the baron, it is only natural to discuss tonight's mass.

"To be honest," he says, with a smile that's more sheepish than cynical, "when it comes to rituals, I'm a veritable Diogenes."

I tell him I take comfort from rituals.

"For a Catholic, I can see that," he says. "But for me, it's a distraction." He tells me he wasn't keen on coming tonight, after what happened when he and Wilhelm went to the Sistine Chapel for the blessing of the candles. "I was seeking inspiration," he says, "but all

I could focus on was the soot tarnishing my favorite frescos. I was so upset, I left before it was over."

I suppress a smile at the sensitivity that has him perceiving art as if it were a living being. "Where then do you go for inspiration?" I ask.

His response is instant: "Nature! Just show me the hills aglow at sunset, a rock praying in the dirt, clouds lit from within—" He gestures to the moon, peeking through clouds overhead. "And of course, the work of great artists."

"Like Michelangelo."

"Exactly. Art follows the same laws nature follows." He pauses, as if reflecting on the truth of what he just said, then adds, "I think of nature as the only book that holds something significant on every page."

There are a thousand questions I want to ask, but we are joined by Antonio and Wilhelm.

Only later, on the ride home, with my husband complaining all the way about the handkerchief he dropped in the crowd, do I realize I didn't manage to learn the baron's name. In the moment, it didn't even occur to me to ask.

As we enter the new year, what I neglected to learn on Christmas Eve continues to nettle me. This morning, my desire to find out who the baron is feels more pressing than the family portrait of six Russian noblewomen I'm composing from sketches sent by Prince Poniatowsky. I have to know who he is. I must see him again. I can't leave that to chance. The Sistine Chapel seems the most likely spot, so I call for a carriage.

As I enter the chapel, I feel a wave of elation. But it is instantly quelled. He isn't here, of course. I was silly to think he might be. I light a candle, then kneel and pray. When I raise my head again, I glance at the ceiling. What before I saw as the infinite love in God's outstretched finger now feels more like a scolding. A rebuke for leaving my six Russians. And an admonishment to return to them straight away.

As I hurry out of the chapel, I practically collide with a man striding toward me.

It is the baron.

So startled am I that I blurt out, "Who *are* you?"

He throws back his head and howls with laughter.

Not certain what he finds humorous, I apologize for offending him.

"No, no!" he says, hopping from one foot to the other, trying to contain his mirth. "Here we are, meeting again. I'm the offensive one for not letting you in on my secret."

"Then perhaps you should," I say.

He drops his voice. "Can I trust your discretion? You see," he says without waiting for my answer, "I've been traveling incognito. Only a few friends are in the ruse."

Despite his good humor, I wonder if he's in some sort of trouble. In my experience, secrets don't bode well. Especially if they involve going incognito.

He picks up my concern immediately. "It's all in pure fun! I wanted to travel as a supposed third-rate artist, but Hofrat Reiffenstein suggested passing myself off as a baron."

"The baron-who-lives-opposite-the-Rondanini?"

"That very one. But I assure you, I'm not an imposter."

A chill runs through me. "I hope not."

If he has any idea what that means to me, he doesn't say. "I needed the privacy to write, to heal my soul. Twelve years of service to the grand duke of Weimar have taken their toll." He pauses to see if I'm following.

Suddenly it dawns on me: He is none other than the German author and poet Johann Wolfgang Goethe—in fact, von Goethe since he was ennobled. Just a week ago, Antonio mentioned he was rumored to be traveling in Italy.

I start to laugh. "You had us all fooled! I couldn't imagine who this baron might be."

He laughs with me. "The disguise has been surprisingly easy to maintain. When some German artists heard I was in Rome, Wilhelm invited one who swore he knew me in Heidelberg to take a closer look. We figured the joke was up. But the fellow declared me a stranger with no resemblance to Goethe!"

"You wore no disguise?"

"None."

I smile at this man who has devised such an ingenious means to escape his admirers. "I'm delighted to meet you," I say. "Finally."

"My pleasure!" he exclaims. "Did you know the Germans call you Seelen Mahlerin?"

"Painter of the soul," I translate.

"They visit your studio as they would the Forum or Saint Peter's."

I invite him to do the same.

He eagerly agrees.

"Splendid!" I say, "Perhaps you can come—"

"Next Sunday?"

"That's what I was about to suggest!"

We look at one other with the amused bafflement of two people who've just discovered they share the same thought, however inconsequential.

Twenty-nine

"I see why they call you painter of the soul! To create like this, to pour out your passion, must be infinitely satisfying."

It's Sunday afternoon, and Wolfgang Goethe is squatting on the floor, engrossed in a pile of sketches strewn halfway across my studio. No one—not even Joshua, who was mostly concerned with the latest technique—has shown such an intimate interest in my work. In *me*.

"When I was young," I say, "I wanted to paint with my soul, paint for God. Yet I'm not sure I ever understood what that means."

He bends to look more closely at a sketch for a self-portrait in which one of my hands is holding a brush and the other is pointed at my breast. "Perhaps you understand more than you realize."

"Perhaps," I say. "Sometimes it seems painting is what allows me to keep breathing."

He uncoils himself and stands up, then wanders to the window and looks out over the rooftops. "We must recognize what sustains us as artists. Being in Rome has brought me back to life."

I follow him across the room and perch on one end of the window seat.

He sits at the other end. "In Weimar, my spirit was languishing."

I don't say anything, just watch the sunlight turn his curls golden. It's hard to imagine someone with such radiance falling into any sort of slump.

He takes my silence as an invitation to speak about himself. He arrived in Weimar at age twenty-six. Though already an author, he earned his living practicing law. One day, the grand duke made him the youngest minister in his court. "It was an honor," he says, but without the gusto I would have expected. "And of course everyone wanted to meet the man who wrote *The Sorrows of Young Werther*."

I tell him I read his book. It touched me deeply.

He shrugs. "It seems to have that effect."

I describe how Werther fever was all the rage in London. Young men wore his blue frock and custard-yellow trousers, bemoaned their pangs of unrequited love. I stop when I see consternation on Wolfgang's face. "I'm sorry," I say. "You already know all this."

"I'm afraid it's not amusing anymore."

I understand he's referring to all those who succumbed to Werther fever and committed suicide. Leaning closer, I ask how he copes with the burden.

His eyes come to rest in mine, and I feel his pain. "After easing my sorrows by turning my reality into art," he says, "others turned my art into their reality."

"How ironic."

He sighs. "The new edition has a warning that I'm afraid comes too late for many."

In the ensuing silence, I marvel at this man who has all but admitted he once considered taking his own life for the sake of love—the love of a woman who was married to another. I can't help but wonder if he loves her still. Not wanting to pry, I simply say, "You were speaking of Weimar."

He shifts on the window seat so he can watch me as well as the view outside and explains that life in the public eye made it hard to carry out his creative ideas. Inspiration was never lacking; the problem was finding time to bring it to fruition.

"So you came here."

A mischievous spark lights his eyes as he describes how he accompanied the grand duke to Karlsbad to take the waters. When everyone else was set to return to Weimar, he made his escape, boarding a coach in the middle of the night, bringing no servants or luggage. "I even left behind my name," he says, chuckling.

To require such a dramatic break, he must have a deeply personal reason—perhaps someone he feels a need to forget. Or someone impossible to forget. The love that inspired *Werther* could be only one of many in the life of this passionate man. Of course, I don't know him well enough to ask such questions.

"Fortunately," he adds, "I brought my manuscripts. My friend Johann Herder didn't let me leave for Karlsbad without them. Knowing how much I love geology, he wanted to make sure I didn't spend my whole holiday smashing rocks with a hammer."

"He sounds like quite the taskmaster," I say with a smile.

"A taskmaster is what I need," he says. "I have a naughty habit of beginning projects and then abandoning them when new inspiration strikes."

"So you're not patient." The more we speak, the more I see how he mirrors my own way of being.

He points to my sketches. "Neither are you. The ability to create so much so fast doesn't foster patience."

I laugh. "You're right. But tell me, how do you go about creating?"

It's a question that excites him. He paces the studio as he speaks. "I compose mostly in my head. That's how my muse works. My ideas come rapidly, often when I least expect." All of *Werther*, he explains, was written in four weeks. When a story arises, he's at its mercy. "It's as if whatever I write already exists in its full form. I'm just the servant holding a pen." He stops short and sits down, leaving a distance of only one pillow between us. "Is it like that for you?"

I tell him it is. When a painting is successful, I feel I did nothing to make it so. "Do you suppose," I say suddenly, "that's a sign I'm painting with my soul?"

He nods vigorously. "I'd even say painting is your natural means of confession. After all, what need does an artist with such a strong spirit have for a priest?"

There's something delightfully reverential about Wolfgang's irreverence. I build upon it: "If painting is confession, it's also prayer. When I close my eyes to pray, I often envision a finished painting, even though I have yet to start a sketch."

"And not wanting to lose it, you set straight to work."

I'm about to say I have my own taskmaster, acquired in marriage, who makes that difficult. Not wanting to admit how squelched I often feel, I ask instead about the manuscripts he brought with him.

He tells me he's working on a drama, *Iphigenia in Tauris*. This is the third revision, and the first in verse. Through her courage to tell the truth, his Iphigenia will show that a woman's words are more powerful than a man's sword. It's a revolutionary message, much needed in the modern world. He leans forward, chin on his hand, and regards me as he talks. It's as though we've sat together like this on a thousand occasions, caught up in the pulse of creation.

Having lost track of time, I'm startled by the servant announcing that Signor Zucchi is waiting for us in the dining room.

As the two men converse across the length of the table, I'm curious how their temperaments will interact, hopeful Wolfgang will feel welcome at Villa Zucchi.

After a long discussion about the Roman climate—during which our first two courses are consumed—Antonio raises his glass to our guest and declares his surprise at learning the baron's true identity. "No worries," he adds. "My wife swore me to secrecy."

Wolfgang clarifies that, with his drama almost finished, secrecy is no longer necessary.

As the syllabub is served, the talk turns to my husband's work. Architectural drawing, he says, suits him well, though trips to various castles keep him away from home more than he'd like. "No," he says when asked if he's also a history painter. "One in the family is enough."

"I'm often tempted," Wolfgang says, "to forsake words and sketch instead."

I'm pleased to hear his passion for art isn't limited to viewing. "Maybe," I say with a burst of enthusiasm, "I should write poems about my paintings."

"No, you shouldn't," my husband says quickly. "That's not your talent."

"Yet you might be a good poet." Wolfgang looks at me expectantly. "The reason I'm not an artist isn't, I feel, lack of talent. It's that I don't make the time to practice." He flashes me a knowing look. "Lack of patience, you might say."

"What do you sketch?" Antonio asks as we adjourn to the drawing room to await the Sunday crowd.

Wolfgang selects cognac over brandy for his digestivo and explains that his favorite subject is nature, especially rocks and trees. Sketching helps him fathom their essence.

"Then why not ask my wife for lessons?" Coming from Antonio, always so protective of my time—not to mention his habitual fits of jealousy—this is unexpected. It has the air of a challenge, almost a dare.

Wolfgang doesn't waste a second. "Please, Fra Angelica," he says, bowing playfully in my direction, "may I ask you to teach me?"

I laugh at the nickname and tell him I'd be honored to have him as a student. "If Michelangelo owed everything to Fra Angelico," I joke, "your success will be assured when you study with me." Then I give him an assignment: He is to take his sketchbook to the countryside and record the landscape, then return when he has something to show.

All week, I anticipate Sunday, when I hope Wolfgang will bring his first sketches. Though I've taught art to royalty, and many important people have passed through my studio, the prospect of instructing him excites me more.

In London, I was eager, ambitious, idealistic. Yet I was also inexperienced, fluttering in the breeze of so much attention, vulnerable in ways I failed to foresee. Age has altered all that. Now no one is watching me for signs of an unseemly entanglement, trying to soil my reputation. Nor will they call me a flirt. Ironically, marriage has made it easier for me to come and go as I wish, to meet whomever I choose.

Even so, I choose to spend most days alone in my studio. Except for our Sunday gatherings, most of my social activities involve pleasing one or another patron. To some, I'm "the British artist." To others, "the Italian artist." If they refer to me as simply an artist, they always mean a female artist. If I produced a thousand new paintings, that wouldn't change.

Perhaps I should be proud—as I was in London—of all my paintings, proud the public considers me practically royalty. And sometimes I am proud. But mostly I'm simply fatigued.

Now, though, that fatigue has been supplanted with fresh energy. I can't wait to start teaching my new student. Sunday evening can't come soon enough.

Nevertheless, Wilhelm arrives alone to our next gathering.

"Where is our mutual friend?" I ask, busying myself with some roses in a vase by the door so my question sounds more casual than it feels.

"Reading his new play to the German artists."

The tip of a thorn is sharp against my finger. "You must have heard him read it."

"Actually, I haven't yet." He hands his hat and jacket to the servant, then adds, "I think we should demand a reading here at Villa Zucchi."

I immediately ask him to extend the invitation on my behalf.

As I'm speaking, Antonio wanders over. "Whom are we inviting?"

"Herr Goethe," I say. "We'd like him to read *Iphigenia in Tauris* to us."

The next day, with Antonio's consent, Wilhelm asks Wolfgang for a reading. He agrees but says he prefers a more intimate weeknight gathering. I have no objection to that.

"Are you looking forward to the reading?" I ask my husband over dinner.

He tells me he has plans to go to Castel Gandolfo. Recently he purchased a villa overlooking Lake Albano, so I can take rest. It needs renovations, which he is overseeing.

I ask if he can postpone his trip. When he's noncommittal, I press him. I don't mind entertaining guests on my own, but because he encouraged my friendship with Wolfgang, I feel it only right he be here. His reluctance, I discover, springs from embarrassment over his poor recollection of the myth.

So I explain. At the start of the Trojan War, Agamemnon offered to sacrifice his daughter, Iphigenia, to appease the goddess. But a miracle occurred, and she was saved.

"Who saved her?" Antonio asks, his fork suspended over his straccetti.

I explain that the goddess sacrificed a deer instead and sent Iphigenia to Tauris. There, she was reunited with her brother, Orestes.

"They escaped together?" he wants to know.

"In the classic myth, yes. But Wolfgang has added his own creative touches. I can't wait to hear them." I look at the food growing cold on my husband's plate. "You'll delay your trip?"

"If you wish." He picks up his fork, then adds, "Though, you know I have no interest in these tales."

There is no point arguing; his cold food is proof enough. "I do wish it" is all I say.

Thirty

So thrilled am I to see Wolfgang that I scarcely notice he came without any sketches. All I care is that he's here with us—Wilhelm, Hofrat, Antonio, and myself. As he stands before the fireplace and reads his drama, I can't take my eyes from his face.

Hofrat also is spellbound. By the end of the second act, he's slapping his knees in appreciation. Even Antonio is riveted. The four of us keep begging for just one more scene—please, one more—until he has read the entire play.

We sit in awed silence.

"This will be a classic," Hofrat says at last.

"I love your Iphigenia," I say. "So courageous, so wise."

"But why," Antonio wants to know, "risk her brother's life? Why not escape with him?"

"That's what makes this so exceptional!" I say. "By telling the truth when she could have relied on deceit, she elevates her heroism. Her courage creates a more memorable triumph."

"You understand my vision!" Wolfgang beams at me. "Of course, later I thought of another plot, Iphigenia in Delphi, in which she confronts her sister."

"Why not write that next?" If he has forgotten my sketching assignment, I might as well encourage whatever project inspires him.

"I have so many inspirations." He sighs forcefully, as if trying to breathe life into yet another idea. "How do I find time for them all?"

It's almost midnight when our guests leave. Rather than follow my husband as he escorts the others to their carriages, Wolfgang lags behind. "You'll be happy to know, Fra Angelica, I have sketches for you. Hopefully you'll be pleased with your student." As he takes my hand and presses it for a second, I find myself flushing more intensely than I have in years.

Wolfgang brings his drawings while Antonio is at Castel Gandolfo.

I spread them out on the studio floor. One shows a country lane passing through fields, another a windblown tree. In a third, ancient ruins sit atop a rocky hillside. Though not subjects I would have chosen, they have been executed with a bold hand. I examine each before proclaiming he has talent.

"I draw what I love of nature," he says.

"But not people?"

"I write about people."

That seems fair enough. "Your impassioned technique gives life to each scene, but your objects could have greater solidity," I say as I copy his tree on fresh paper, rooting it more firmly, even as its branches are at the mercy of the wind. And I tell him what my father often repeated: "Whatever the subject, a painter is always painting themselves."

"I like that," he says. "It's the same with writing: No matter what I write, I'm writing about myself. All my works are one great confession. I just hope it isn't too transparent to readers." He sits beside me and adds a more solid rock below the tree.

"All you need is practice," I say after we've passed the pencil back and forth for a while.

He says he'll have time to practice while he's traveling.

"What?" I don't try to hide my shock. "Weimar is stealing you already?"

"Only Naples." He explains it's a chance to view the eruption of Vesuvius. He and Wilhelm will leave after the Carnival and return in a few months.

"Wilhelm is an artist. Maybe he can take over your lessons," I say, rubbing the eraser with extra vigor over the clouds to conceal my jealousy. Really, his departure comes too soon.

"I'm sorry to go when we've barely gotten acquainted," he says, leaning closer, his tone suddenly somber.

He is so close that the end of my braid swings against his chest as I set aside the paper and raise my head to face him. "You know," I say, "there are so few one can speak to about what truly matters."

"For that reason, we must make good use of our remaining days."

When he says that, my mood lifts. I'm not about to lose him. That's my fear, after all. I suspect he has ties—intimate ones—in Weimar who could tug on his heart and summon him at any moment. The fact he scarcely alludes to these ties makes them seem more capricious. If I don't want to lose him, I'll have to make sure he has reason to stay in Rome.

"I've been thinking," I say, "I'd like to illustrate your drama."

"A painting of Iphigenia?"

"A drawing. I can have it ready for your return." There is so much I want to share with him, yet so little time. On impulse, I run to my private quarters and return with Saint Jerome, which I place in his hands. "You've seen most of my collection, but this is the real prize."

His keen eyes take it in. "Leonardo?"

"I thought you'd recognize his hand."

He takes the little panel to the window and holds it to the light. I follow. "Extraordinary," he says. "Like being in the presence of the saint himself."

"I feel that way too." I pause. "Sometimes I converse with him in spirit."

"And does he answer?" he asks, a smile curving on his lips.

"He does. And always with the guidance I need." As Wolfgang hands the panel back to me, I feel suddenly self-conscious. "Now you're amused because I talk to a picture."

His smile becomes a chuckle. "Far from it. My amusement is merely delight at seeing myself in you. I also speak with angels and saints."

"Really?"

"Honestly I do. While writing *Iphigenia in Tauris*, I fixed the image of Saint Agatha in my mind and read scenes to her. If she didn't like a line, I didn't let my heroine speak it."

I sit on the window seat, cradling the panel on my lap. "So that's how you were able to give her such strength and wisdom."

"You could say it's my secret," he says as he sits beside me. "Artists, I believe, have a unique ability to see spirits. But," he adds playfully, "it's not just angels and saints. I also speak with ordinary people. I call forth a friend in spirit, ask them to sit down, then discuss what's on my mind. Invariably they respond in their own voice, offering their guidance. Of course, I have to be willing to take the advice to heart, or they won't continue to offer it."

"What a remarkable idea!"

"You say remarkable, but you just told me you converse with spirits."

I smile, realizing how natural it would be to speak with him in spirit. "That's true. But I've never admitted it to anyone."

"Understood. This isn't something one can reveal to just anyone."

"No. But do you ever let your friends in on what you're doing?"

He shakes his head. "Are you suggesting I should? Because I

suspect some would be shocked to learn how often they're involved in my private affairs."

The last flush of sunset has faded, but the lamps remain unlit in my studio. In the hour since Wolfgang left, I haven't moved from the window seat.

It's as if I'd been asleep for years, and meeting him shook me awake. Sitting here, knees bent, arms wrapped around my skirts, I'm certain of one thing: Never has anyone, man or woman, touched me so deeply.

Johann Wolfgang von Goethe. His name flows through me like a song. *Johann,* the sound is sweet on my tongue, like the finest liqueur. *Wolfgang,* such strength in those syllables; they hold me up from within. *Dear Goethe,* I think, *what a blend of gentleness and power.*

No matter that we were together an hour before, I want to whisper in his ear, in the most familiar way. Whatever his mother called him, I want to call him that. I want to know all there is to know about him. Every detail matters. Even the details of those unnamed ones he left in Weimar.

"Do you have a beloved in Weimar?" I ask.

"In Rome," I hear him say, "I have eyes only for Rome."

Which doesn't clarify much. It might be wise, I decide, also to keep my attention in Rome. Together, we can close our eyes to everything and everyone elsewhere, and be awake only here. Only to each other.

It is our last lesson before Wolfgang leaves for Naples.

As he enters my studio, he hands me a peacock feather he picked up at the Carnival. Then he describes a dream he had last night, in which his boat washed up on an island where peacocks ran wild. He lured some onto his boat, but after he reached the harbor and jumped ashore to find a place to unload them, he lost his way among all the boats. He awoke realizing he hadn't saved even one feather.

I brush the feather against my cheek, then hand it back. "At least you have this one."

"It's yours," he says. "When I saw it, I knew I must give it to you."

I thank him and promise to find a place to display it. Yet words can't convey all I feel. With a single feather, he has given me his heart.

After his lesson, he stays for dinner. "I'll miss our time together," he says as we walk to the dining room to meet Antonio. "It's clear how much I have to learn from you."

"And I from you."

"I couldn't agree more," says my husband, aiming for a smooth entry into the conversation.

Always the diplomat, Wolfgang addresses both of us: "I promise to sketch every day in Naples. I'll have plenty to show when I return."

"And I promise to illustrate *Iphigenia*," I say. "I've already started."

This isn't welcome news to Antonio, but he's careful not to object in front of our guest.

I keep my eyes on Wolfgang. "I will show Orestes awakening from his swoon to see his sister, her face radiating delight at their reunion. Everyone will see the love between them—" I stop, conscious of a deeper meaning to my words.

Wolfgang is too excited to notice. "You've identified the pivotal moment! But why didn't you show me in the studio?"

"I'll show you now."

"Your dinner will get cold," my husband grumbles as I jump to my feet.

When I thrust the sketch into Wolfgang's hands, he looks at it intently. "You've captured the essence with a few strokes of chalk. I could look at this image all night without finding any words to equal it."

I refuse to accept the compliment. But it gives me an idea. "When you return, let's visit galleries and discuss the art."

"I'd like that," Wolfgang says, making sure his glance includes my husband.

"Then I look forward to it," I say. "We can start with the Madonna in Crispino's gallery. She was painted by Andrea del Sarto, though he adopted Leonardo's sfumato so well that you'd think it is a work of the master himself." In fact, I tried to buy the painting, but Antonio didn't want to offer more than three hundred sequins. I said she was worth six hundred. He proposed buying instead an etching of Saint Anthony. I was adamant it be the Madonna or nothing. Our wrangling grew so loud, we had to step outside. In the end, I had to lower my offer, though it was my money being spent. I wasn't surprised when it was refused.

Evidently our fight is still fresh in Antonio's mind, because he steers the conversation in a different direction. "Have you been to the Carnival?"

"I spent most of today there," Wolfgang replies. "Men dressed as women—not to mention women dressed as men—I've never seen revelry that rivals it."

"The finale tomorrow is not to be missed," Antonio says.

I laugh. "My husband is telling you that. But he himself refuses to go."

"At my age, why should I?" he objects. "I've seen it so often. You must go without me."

"Then I'll arrange a party!" Wolfgang exclaims. "I'm sure Wilhelm and Hofrat would love it. You'll come, Angelica, won't you?"

Though I also haven't gone in years, I assure him nothing could keep me from it.

"Unless you leave early," Antonio warns, "you won't even get close to the Corso."

My husband tucks his napkin into his collar at breakfast. "He's lucky to have met you," he says.

"He?"

"Our German friend, who else?" Antonio reaches into the bread-basket and pulls out a roll. He slices it down the middle, spreads jam to the edge of each piece, and fits the halves back together. "Be sure to keep an eye on him tonight."

I'm mystified. My husband, always jealous of men who pay atten-tion to me, has repeatedly encouraged exactly that. It's almost as if he knows something about Wolfgang that overshadows even jealousy. I inquire what concerns him, what I need to look out for.

"Haven't you heard?" he exclaims, eyebrows shooting upward. "His behavior with young women has earned him quite a reputation. It would be a pity if his genius suffers as a result."

I suspect these rumors are based more on Werther's behavior than that of the author. "I don't see how you can say that," I object. "You—we—hardly know him."

Antonio shrugs. "If he stays in Rome, we'll have the pleasure of knowing him better. Not to mention the privilege of first audience for his dramas."

When he says that, I understand. He doesn't perceive Wolfgang as a personal threat but rather as a younger man well connected in German circles and all of Europe. Befriending him offers Antonio potential sources of new income.

I remind him I have no time for more commissions.

But he has already convinced himself of the advantages of a closer acquaintance with the famous poet. "Has it occurred to you," he asks, "to paint his portrait?"

Heeding Antonio's advice, Wilhelm, Hofrat, Wolfgang, and I get an early start for the Carnival. Nevertheless, when we get there, the Corso is already clogged. So we abandon our carriage and walk, moving slowly, hanging onto each other's arms and dodging the merrymakers, who pelt one another with sugar-coated almonds and small pumice stones covered with plaster. At one point, we hear the boom of mortars signaling the start of the race, but the crowd is so dense we can't see the horses.

With the growing dusk, paper lanterns appear on balconies, and footmen line the roofs of their carriages with candles. As Wilhelm runs to purchase candles from the nearest vendor, I explain to Wolfgang what's happening.

Wilhelm returns, carefully shielding a lit candle. "*Sia ammazzato!*" he taunts as he hands over the unlit candles. "Death to anyone without a flame!"

We light our candles from flames on a nearby carriage and the battle begins.

"Sia ammazzato, Signor von Goethe!"

"Sia ammazzato, Signor Tischbein!"

"Sia ammazzato, Signor Reiffenstein!"

Wolfgang is as swift as a wind spirit, making it difficult to keep a candle lit when he approaches. Even when Wilhelm and Hofrat team up, they can't outwit him. Fingers dripping with wax, they're forced to keep relighting. It is a battle to the death.

Wolfgang turns toward me. "Sia ammazzato, Fra Angelica!"

I do my best to defend myself, holding my candle behind my

back, then above my head, all the while trying to blow out his candle. Which is impossible because I'm laughing too hard.

He stands his ground. "Sia ammazzato, *la pittrice del secolo!*"

The painter of the century! Suddenly I'm motionless, candle extended before me. He too holds his candle at arms' length, its light blending into mine. Neither of us tries to extinguish the other's flame. In the frenzy all around, people are shouting, "Sia ammazzato . . ." But for us, it seems there can be no death.

After all the candles have burned down, Hofrat suggests we follow the crowds to the theater, on this last night before Lent. Wolfgang is all for it until he notices I'm hanging back.

I tell him it isn't my habit to go to the theater. I'm tempted to reconsider my vow, made to Bridget years ago, never to go to the theater again, not even if the king were to invite me. But I don't have to. Wolfgang nods as if I'd given the most logical explanation and advises Hofrat and Wilhelm to go ahead. He will accompany me home.

A few minutes later, we are instructing the driver to take us to Via Sistina. But I'm reluctant for the evening to end. On impulse, I ask that we first make a stop at the lookout point at the top of the hill.

The two of us get out of the carriage and walk over to a low stone wall, where we sit side by side, without talking as we take in the panoramic view. Puffy clouds of smoke from the fires below drift past us and into the sky; occasional shrieks from the revelers rise above the general din. With Wolfgang, I feel so carefree, so ebullient, so hopeful.

Suddenly he grabs my arm and points upward. But I'm already transfixed by the flash streaking across the sky. "Nothing," he says, "equals the revelry of the stars."

"Not even the Carnival?" I joke.

But he's serious. "I saw little genuine gaiety in the crowd tonight."

I tell him I noticed that too. "But why?" I say. "Everyone thinks they're happy."

He shakes his head. "Such is the folly of this world. Whoever seeks happiness at the Carnival will never find it. Nor at the theater nor a grand ball. Even the finest work of art is but a reflection—" He stops short and looks intensely at me. "Angelica, you're not happy, are you?"

I feel suddenly transparent, vulnerable as glass. I couldn't be happier than I am right now, sitting with him under the stars. But he can see beneath that. "What makes you say so?" My words come out in a whisper.

"I see it in your eyes."

Instinctively my hands fly to cover my face.

He gently peels back my fingers. "I'm sorry if that was too intrusive. I have no business prying into your private affairs."

"No," I say. "I'm sorry for trying to hide from you." And so I find myself speaking freely, unburdening my most secret thoughts, things I've never spoken about openly. Not just about the ambitions that drove me but about the disillusionment that came from recognizing I'd never be able to paint completely as I please. No matter how strongly I asserted my independence, there were always limits. And then I go further. I tell him about the hope I harbored of finding someone who truly understands my yearnings. Who understands me. I confess to the hollowness I feel married to Antonio. With age has come the disappointment that I'll never know what, if anything, could grant lasting happiness. Most likely I will die without finding it. In a flood of words, all comes tumbling out.

After I finish, we sit in silence.

Finally he says, "You must always paint what's in your soul."

His comment is about my art but I know he heard everything I said. "If only I had that luxury," I say. "But Antonio frets about our income."

"The fallacy of human desire," he scoffs. "As soon as one yearning has been fulfilled, a new one arises from its ashes. No one's ever satisfied. The wealthy especially always want more. They don't realize what is important in life is life itself, not the results of life."

I look out over the city and sigh. "I should be happier. Having been poor, I know that what I have now is more than enough."

"Still, you feel confined by your husband's wishes."

"I do."

"As an artist, you deserve more."

"Yes, I do."

"And yet you stay."

"Yes."

"Even knowing the price is your happiness, you stay."

I see now how that price has been slowly but inexorably squeezed out of me. Like coins I never expected to pay. My autonomy may have been inked into our marriage vows, but not even my husband's best intentions—which I believe were sincere—could guarantee it. Without freedom, what lasting happiness can there be? "I stay," I say, "because I know of no other place my life would be better."

He lays his hand on mine. "Angelica, you can always speak freely to me. I have faith in you. I will support your freedom."

Thirty-one

After Wolfgang has left Rome, I work each day on the illustration for *Iphigenia in Tauris*. I give Orestes, seated at the center, Wolfgang's curls, his large eyes. Having just awoken, he turns to look up at his sister, and their eyes bond, leading the viewer of the drawing directly from him to her. She stands over him, hand on her heart, comforting him. Keeping him safe.

Henry once faulted my female figures for being spineless. Not so this Iphigenia. With the power of love etched into every pore, no one will doubt her strength.

As I work, I question her.

She speaks to me in spirit. Life calls forth courage in unexpected ways, she says. Though experiencing loss is painful, it makes us wiser, teaches us to be true to ourselves. For this reason, it's best not to judge our hardships too harshly.

Even so, my own loss feels harsh. I miss Wolfgang. I miss the candor I enjoy with him, the recognition in his eyes that mirrors my own sense of who and what I really am. The night of the Carnival, I thought none of that would fade. Yet it has. The old fatigue has set in. I try to talk to him in spirit, but he doesn't answer. Day by day, his silence carves out a crater of loneliness in my heart.

"Will he return?" I ask Iphigenia.

I want reassurance, but she only adds to the silence, intensifies my worry that Wolfgang will forget me, that the rumors about his reputation may not be totally unfounded. Of course he's not a phi-landerer. Yes, he can be unpredictable and a bit impetuous, but I have no reason to doubt his intentions. Not toward me. Still, with so many enticing young women in so many places—Naples, Weimar, even here in Rome—I'd be foolish to think my company could sustain him as his does me. But then I catch myself; conjecture is pointless. So I stop trying to converse in spirit and concentrate instead on capturing Iphigenia's virtues in shades of gray.

Spring turns to summer. Iphigenia long since finished, I push aside my fatigue and focus on new projects. I regret it didn't occur to me to secure Wolfgang's promise to write. His travels, he told me, become richer when he sends details to his friends in Weimar. Those friends went unnamed. Now I wonder if anyone is treasuring his letters as I much as I would.

Then, one evening in July, Antonio mentions that Reiffenstein saw Herr Goethe at the Colonna Gallery. "Apparently," he adds, "our friend returned weeks ago."

I can't utter a word. How could I have believed he'd come back to me? The moments we spent together were moments in time. And time has moved on.

"He knows you were illustrating his drama," my husband contin-ues. "You'd think Villa Zucchi would have been his first stop."

"I'm sure we'll see him soon" is all I can say.

Excusing myself, I run to my room and close the door. I pull the silk off Saint Jerome and get down on my knees. But it isn't the saint's advice I seek; I want to hear from Wolfgang. Even if he didn't respond in spirit before, I need him to respond now. "Why haven't you come?" I whisper, but in my heart it is a scream.

There is no answer.

No matter how forcibly I question him, there is only silence. I begin to suspect conversations in spirit require a trust impossible in the presence of anger. And I am angry now. Too angry even to fall asleep, though I am exhausted.

I'm still exhausted the following morning, so much so I almost put off a trip into town. But I need to prepare for Rosa's visit in a few weeks. As I order pillows from my seamstress, I'm so distracted I forget to mention that one must be half size for little Ignatius.

When I return, Antonio meets me in the parlor. "You just missed Wolfgang," he says, then adds, "He didn't stay long, but he loved your Iphigenia."

"*You* showed it to him?" I'm not sure which I feel more: relief Wolfgang came or disappointment at missing him.

"Of course." Antonio frowns. "But it was a waste. He has no intention of purchasing it."

That transfers the frown to my face. The illustration was always meant as a gift. It can't be purchased, not for any price. Knowing my husband will never agree, I simply say, "I trust you invited him to return soon."

Wolfgang appears the next day, a bulging portfolio under his arm. I greet him coolly, without inviting him into my studio. "I hear you're satisfied with Iphigenia."

"Satisfied doesn't begin to describe it." He sets his portfolio by the door and breaks into a grin. "I'm *enthralled* with her!"

"You are?" I'm not sure why this surprises me, but it does.

"I positively am! However," he says, his lips drooping into an exaggerated pout, "I've been fretful, since your husband only allowed me the quickest of peeks."

As he wiggles his fingers, mimicking how Antonio held him at bay, I have to laugh. It's impossible to remain angry when the image he creates of my husband is so true to life. My guard comes down further when he says, "I was waiting to come till I'd put my affairs in order, so we could have more time together. I talked to you in spirit about it. Did you hear me?"

Instead of confessing I wasn't able to hear him, I place my fingertips on his arm and lead him into the studio so we can view the illustration together.

Or more accurately, so he can view it while I view him.

He bends over the picture, his tongue sliding forward, as if to help him digest what he's viewing. Apparently he senses how keenly I'm watching, because he turns and looks at me.

As our eyes meet, something passes between us. It's invisible, yet I can see it. More than that, I can feel it. It's not the emotion shared between brother and sister, like the two on the paper before us. Nor is it what I understand can occur between husband and wife. No, this isn't about a man and a woman. Or two of any gender. It's the recognition of who we really are, stripped of everything but spirit.

In this instant, there can be no doubt: I'm looking at the kindred artist whose presence I've sensed over the years, whom I've always known as deeply as I know myself, yet gave up all hope of meeting. The only question is why it took me so long to see this.

I wonder if he also sees it, but he has turned back to the paper. "You've drawn her just as I envisioned," he says.

"Her spirit grabbed hold of me, so it came naturally."

"As it did for me when I wrote the play. We were grabbed by the same spirit!"

"In that case, she's all yours," I say blushing, as if we're not just talking about a drawing.

"It's a perfect frontispiece!" he says, picking up the paper and holding it at arm's length, as if imagining a book. "I must show my publisher. Hopefully it's not too late for this edition."

Normally I would agree. But something in me says no, this Iphigenia belongs to Wolfgang, and to him alone. To give her to the world now would somehow lessen the bond we've just discovered between us. So I simply say, "She is my gift to *you*."

He abruptly lowers his arm and turns to me. I can feel him searching for the meaning behind my words. "In that case, she will enjoy a seat of honor on the desk where I'll be writing. And drawing too."

I point to his portfolio. "As it seems you have been?"

A moment later, sketches are splayed across the floor, and we're on our knees before them. Some are from Naples, others from Sicily, and a few from a trip to Tivoli he took with Wilhelm after returning to Rome. That trip, I realize, is why he didn't come immediately here.

He points to a sketch of Vesuvius with dark smudges of billowing smoke as his favorite.

I tell him the force of the eruption is palpable—especially as it contrasts with the delicate crescent moon high in the sky. When I have examined everything, I single out the sketch of a lone pine high on a crag. "Your pine has character," I say, "almost like a person."

He describes how the German artists have been gathering at Wilhelm's studio to share their work. "The portrait painters encourage the landscape painters to enrich the character of their rocks and trees," he says, laughing. "But when the landscape painters critique portraits, I'm afraid those faces will take on botanical features."

I'm tickled by that idea.

Wilhelm, he says, is painting his portrait. In it, he's wearing his wide-brimmed hat and white cloak and is seated on a fallen obelisk, with ruins in the background. Wilhelm has promised to include a miniature scene from *Iphigenia in Tauris* somewhere in the landscape.

"When the portrait is critiqued, I hope no one thinks you resemble a tree," I tease.

"I haven't sprouted leaves yet," he says, holding out his fingers as proof. "I think Wilhelm will create a good likeness, though he doesn't paint with your ease."

"Then you must allow me to—"

"Paint my portrait?" He exclaims before I can complete my thought. "By all means!"

Our lives fall into a deeply satisfying pattern. With Wolfgang, I can always be myself. It's not as if freedom were something I didn't have that he could give me; rather, it arises naturally in the world we share together. I feel I'm growing younger, as if the years have reversed their course. As if a crimson sun were rising in late evening.

Whenever he can find a spare moment, he drops by to sit for his portrait.

With so much to discover in Rome, he assures me, he'll stay at least through next winter. As he explores the city, his art collection is growing rapidly, including several busts of Juno. The first is a cast of the Juno Ludovisi. She was his first love in Rome, he says. Now he has three Junos, lined up side by side at his door.

"*Three* loves?" I say, as if it were not clear that more is better.

He shoots me a knowing look. "That's what happens when we fall in love: We think we must do it again and again. Instead of something rare, we end up with what is merely ordinary."

Our friendship is anything but ordinary. It isn't a flirtation. Or infatuation. It's not one of those mindless games of sentiment men and women play—games I spent so many years resisting because I refused to let my life be created by someone else's brushstroke, with colors from someone else's palette. Nor is it falling in love in the way Wolfgang spoke of, where more is always needed. I don't want more; this is all-consuming.

Alone in my studio, I can think of nothing else. Even if I'm exhausted after hours of work, I have the vitality of a child. There are no more craters of loneliness in my heart. I wonder if Wolfgang is thinking of me too. When I close my eyes, I feel his hand on my shoulder, warm as a living hand. I dare not turn and look, so much do I reject the possibility he might not be here.

"You know it is I," I hear him whisper.

"But you're invisible."

"The essence is visible." His voice blows through me like a summer breeze.

This is more than a conversation in spirit. It is the most perfect of embraces. There is no man, there is no woman. There is only spirit.

Thirty-two

Marriage and motherhood haven't dulled Rosa's keen perception. She sits in my studio, cradling Ignatius on her lap, as I work on a portrait for Father Jacquier and we catch up on the ebb and flow of our lives. Time has eroded the difference in our ages, and we speak as equals.

"Your letters had me worried, but I'm glad to see you rejuvenated," she says, then adds, "Marriage has been good for you, hasn't it?" When I neither confirm nor deny, she hoists the baby to her hip and wanders over to inspect the canvases lining the wall. She stops before an unfinished portrait on an easel in the corner. "Who's this?"

"Johann Wolfgang von Goethe."

"The German poet? How exciting! Is he in Rome for a while?"

"We hope so," I say ambiguously. "In fact, he was here last night."

"That man with a portfolio who was getting into a carriage when I arrived?"

"Yes." I explain he often brings sketches to share with me, sometimes stays for dinner. No doubt she will meet him soon.

She studies the portrait, then frowns. "It was dark, and I couldn't see him clearly, but this looks like another man." My cousin isn't a painter, but she grew up around artists and her eye is trustworthy. When she voices criticism, it holds weight. "This Goethe sings like a canary—"

"That's charming."

"Yes, charming. But the man I saw looked like he would roar like a lion."

I stare at the canvas. She's right: Something is lacking in this Goethe. I tell her he's not a canary, but I'm not sure how to fix that.

"Well," she says, "I guess you'll have to spend more time together, won't you?"

When Wolfgang comes for his next sitting, I share my frustration over the progress with his portrait and ask what he thinks of it. "Please," I say, "be honest with me."

He approaches the canvas and stands before it in silence. I'm not sure whether he's mulling its merits or just how best to break the bad news. "Don't be upset," he says finally. "He's a pretty fellow. But I see little of me."

I groan at his confirmation of Rosa's critique.

He, however, makes light of it. Not only is everyone enamored with Wilhelm's portrait, but now Alexander Trippel is producing his likeness in a marble bust. "The world doesn't need yet another Goethe," he jokes.

Of course, this plethora of Goethes only increases my desire to salvage the painting.

"We're never satisfied with the portraits of those we know best," he says. "That's the nature of friendship."

"Perhaps," I say. "But people should at least be satisfied this is a portrait of *you*."

"I'm certain you'll find a way to make that happen." I expect him to take a seat so I can get to work, but instead he says, "I'm also certain I won't be a pretty fellow for long in this sweltering heat. Let's go to Villa Farnesina. It will be cooler there."

So I close my studio, and we spend the rest of the afternoon in the

Farnesina. While Wolfgang wanders through the galleries, enjoying the originals of paintings he saw in Weimar as reproductions, I study Raphael's frescoes of Psyche. Then he joins me, and we crane our necks to view the paintings on the vaulted ceiling. I note that Psyche and Cupid are hidden on the far side, forcing one's eye to search for them. Wolfgang speculates it's because Raphael didn't want the owner of the villa, who commissioned the frescoes for his wedding, to feel outshone by the divine couple.

On the way home, he asks if I'm planning to paint Psyche.

I describe my ideas. Unlike the grandeur of Raphael's frescoes, I would prefer to capture an intimate moment. "Perhaps," I say, "the instant the light of her candle falls on Cupid's sleeping form, and she sees his beloved face for the first time."

"Or maybe," he suggests, "the next instant."

"What? When wax drips on him, and he wakes in a fury?"

Wolfgang chuckles. "No. When he flees, and she regrets her lack of faith."

I'm not convinced. "You'd prefer to see her suffer on account of love?"

"I'd never wish that on anyone," he says. "But Psyche is the goddess of the soul. Her suffering is divine discontent. As artists, if we elevate suffering and let ourselves be shaken by its naked truth, I believe we can create greater work, live a greater life. Love more fully."

I tell him what he says makes sense, but I'm no closer to understanding my subject.

"Love is elusive," he muses. "As soon as we try to shed light on it, it slips away."

I can hardly disagree. That, after all, is Psyche's story.

"The mind," he continues, "thinks it perceives love, but only the heart can do that."

"Sometimes love is even imperceptible to the heart."

He sighs. "Or perceived by one heart yet imperceptible to another."

When he says that, I'm not quite sure whose hearts he is referring to. So I steer us back to the myth. "It's only natural for Psyche to want to see her lover."

"True. Never seeing one's beloved would cause discontent in any heart." He is pensive for a moment. "As the artist, the choice is yours. Think about what will make the best painting."

Alone in the studio, after Wolfgang leaves, I consider burning his portrait. I've never burned a canvas before, never even considered it. But I've also never failed to achieve a proper likeness. I, painter of the soul, am unable to paint the most beautiful soul I know. This portrait, which should be my best, is a failure. Instead of emitting light as they do when we're together, his eyes stare back mournfully. This isn't the Johann Wolfgang von Goethe I know.

Yet there is a certain familiarity.

On a whim, I go to the cabinet and take out an old portfolio. I sift through a stack of drawings, many done years ago. I'm not sure what I'm looking for. But toward the bottom, I come across a sketch I did in London for a self-portrait. As I hold it against Wolfgang's portrait, I see an exact likeness: the same eyes, same nose, same gentle expression. The same melancholy. We're even seated in the same pose, staring out at the same angle. I shake my head as I compare the two.

He looks back at me silently, like my reflection in a looking glass.

"My friend," I say aloud, "I've painted you as myself."

This explains the familiarity. And the failure.

Since both Antonio and Rosa know the self-portrait I painted from this sketch, I'm surprised neither spotted the likeness.

Fortunately that self-portrait hangs in a London gallery; this painting of Wolfgang, if I don't burn it, will hang in Rome. No one will ever have occasion to see the two together. My secret is safe.

Over the next week—during which time, Wolfgang is conspicuously absent—I continue to debate with myself. Should I destroy the portrait? Start over? Would more sittings help? Why did I paint him as myself? If I see myself in him, wouldn't he also see that?

When the door to my studio finally opens and he walks in, he apologizes for not coming sooner. He has been working, he says, long hours on a play he began over a dozen years ago. *Egmont* is a tale of resistance in the face of authoritarian rule. The first act is finally done.

"It's a good feeling," I say, "when one completes a work."

He immediately understands I'm alluding to my lack of success with his portrait and reminds me of all the other portraits everyone loves. If I think another sitting could make a difference, he'd be happy to oblige. "And I'd be honored," he adds, "if you would do the frontispiece for *Egmont*."

I tell him that would be *my* honor. And it will be published for the whole world to see.

At this point, I can't deny the futility of trying to fix his portrait. Nor is there any reason to tell him about my self-portrait hanging in London. However, since he has hopped onto the sitter's chair, I dab at the canvas while we talk.

He tells me he almost came to Villa Zucchi last night. He was on his way when some neighbors invited him to a dance in their garden.

I wince at the thought of him dancing the night away with one or another young woman, while I fretted over his portrait.

"In the past," he says, "I would have partied till the end, but last night I left early. The moon was bright, so I took her company and wandered around the city."

I stop painting, and we look at one another.

"The moon is a faithful friend," he says. "She never misjudges me."

I realize he noticed my wince and felt my jealousy. My lack of faith in him. He wants me to know it isn't warranted, that no one else holds the same place in his heart.

As a gesture of good faith, I put down my brush and announce I'll stop work on the portrait. I'm ready to call it finished, and we can agree to quietly retire it. That will leave me free to begin a frontispiece for *Egmont*.

He is pleased but wants to be sure this won't keep me from history painting.

Which leads to a discussion of Psyche. My latest idea, I say, is to paint Cupid using a strand of her hair to wipe away her tears. But I worry that would make her appear weak.

"We tend to see suffering as weakness," he says.

"You don't?"

"No. It only becomes a weakness if we don't realize the root of suffering is seeing ourselves as separate. None of us are separate beings. It is pure folly to assume otherwise," he asserts. "Nor do I believe God is separate from us, as we think. He exists wholly within nature, within the world, within each heart."

I take in his ideas. They are so expansive that I don't quite know how to bring them down to earth. "Yet often the heart is filled with pain. You said as much yourself."

"True. But I think we feel pain because we don't perceive the divinity within a human heart. We deem ourselves more isolated than we are—not only from God but from one another."

I don't say anything, just watch his eyes. The pain of which he speaks is reflected in their depths, as if divinity were just out of reach. "You know this personally, don't you?" I say softly.

He looks away, and I'm not sure he will answer. We aren't speaking of art or myths anymore. But then his reply comes slowly, as if rising from deep within and only caught in the last instant by his lips. "I've always sensed there is one I am so close to in spirit that no matter how far apart we are, I'll never forget, never lose, her. Because we aren't separate beings."

"She was your inspiration," I say, wanting finally to hear about this one he considers his beloved, yet at the same time wanting to know nothing about her. "When you wrote *Werther*, you thought you'd found her?"

The front feet of his chair rise as he leans back and closes his eyes. "I thought so. But I was mistaken. It was mere infatuation. I was young, and my heart was boiling over. This happened more times than I care to admit. Now I see it was the foreshadowing of a truer love."

I tell him I too fell for infatuation. "It felt irresistible, but in the end it was devastating."

"That's because we don't know the true measure of love," he says, eyes still closed. "It's not a passing passion between a man and woman; it's a profound recognition by the soul. It's the union not of personalities but of souls. When we experience this, we feel no one has ever really loved before us, and no one will ever love in the same way after us."

"And now," I whisper, "you've found that?"

His chair drops abruptly, and his eyes return to me. "You know I have."

I look back at him, something in me pressing to expose more. "How do you know?"

"The familiarity, the comfort, the simplicity, the knowing of you as myself—" He stops and gives a slight shrug, suggesting all this is beyond the need for words.

We sit in a luminous silence, filled with the light of what is shared between us.

Then the light fades, and doubt creeps into my mind. I can't help but recall the rumors about his reputation, imagine a parade of young women, all offering their hearts. "If you know this now, what is to say you won't know it more later, with another?"

He leans closer, the natural furrow in his brow deepening. "Why must you always—"

Before he can finish, Rosa bursts into the studio, followed by Antonio. They have just returned from an errand. I can only guess their thoughts as they behold the two of us sitting so close, so inconveniently close.

The moon is full, its silver rays streaming like cool sunshine across my pillow. It's impossible to fall asleep, so I throw on a robe and go out into the garden.

I kneel on the grass by the rosebushes and gaze up at the sky. Wolfgang's faithful friend is beckoning me to walk with her. I consider getting dressed and wandering around the city, as he did the other night. As I'm sure he often does. I'll be back before dawn. No one need know.

But before I can stand up, without warning, my heart explodes with love. This is not the love of a person, but of the moon, of the stars, of the universe. It shoots forth from within me like a thousand rockets—far more brilliant than the girandola I saw at Castel Sant'Angelo on Easter. Suddenly, I have no doubts. If a love of such magnitude exists, then he and I are not separate. It isn't a fantasy. It is the most beautiful love imaginable, vast and free. And I understand something else: Not only is this love not mere passion between a man and woman, as Wolfgang said, it's also not just between two souls. Because those two souls are one. He and I are one.

What is to become of us?

By the light of the moon, my heart may soar, but I know the harsh light of day will define me by gender. As it always does. When I sit down to breakfast, I'll be an aging married woman with a well-ordered life, dining with my husband—or waiting for him to join me—knowing how oblivious he always is to the state of my soul, how blind to my loneliness.

Yet now there is no loneliness. There is only oneness. All I can do is kneel beside this rosebush and pray this love is never lost.

This summer is hotter than any I recall. Everyone moves slowly, and work comes to a halt even before midday. Only after the sun sets does anyone venture out. Nevertheless, Wolfgang manages to come to Via Sistina almost daily and often brings his drawings for critique.

"Tell me about these," I say when he hands me some landscapes drawn with a firm hand.

He asks instead what I think they are.

"The public gardens?"

He shakes his head.

"Pompeii?"

"No."

I look from one sketch to another. "Near Naples?"

"Not that either."

He pauses for another guess, but I have none.

"They're moonscapes."

I realize the orb in each, which I took as the setting sun, is the full moon. The faithful witness that listened to my prayers in the garden.

He smiles. "I love to sketch when it's too hot for sleep. These were done near the Palatine Hill. Do you like them?"

I compliment his ability to create the otherworldly.

"Angelica, do you realize?" he exclaims. "My brain is filled with otherworldly ideas—ideas that make moonscapes seem mundane."

"Tell me," I say. "I must know."

"Not everything can be put into words."

"Then show me."

He nods, and for an instant I see an entire universe of ideas within his eyes. "Come walk with me in the moonlight on the Palatine," he says, "and I'll show you."

Thirty-three

I sit between Antonio and Wolfgang in the carriage taking us to Rondanini Palace, where Wolfgang suggested we go for our Sunday outing because he wants to view the bust of Medusa. Neither man looks directly at the other. They haven't spoken since the afternoon my husband and Rosa interrupted us in the studio.

"I'm too old for this heat," Antonio grumbles, while Wolfgang stares out the window. "We should go to the countryside. Why else have a villa there?"

I remind him I first have to finish the commission for Empress Catherine.

"Then we should make Villa Zucchi cooler. Perhaps a new fountain. Or heavier curtains on the south windows."

While Antonio speaks endlessly about trivial matters, Wolfgang keeps his eyes on the scenery. I glance at him, but his attention is elsewhere. Finally, I give my black lace purse a slight shove, so it falls off the seat.

Instantly he reaches down and swoops it up.

I also bend over. For one long instant as he hands it back to me, our eyes lock.

Now Antonio is silent. Until we reach the Rondanini, he is the one gazing out the window.

I'm in my studio, waiting for a coat of varnish to dry, sitting on the sofa and reflecting on the uncertainty of my future. Wondering how to live in a world that will rebuke me if it figures out I'm a married woman who loves a man who is not her husband. That our souls are united won't matter; I will be that woman.

My reverie is interrupted by a tapping on the studio door, open to let in the cooler evening air. I turn to see Wolfgang, smiling ear to ear.

"How long were you standing there?" I ask.

"A minute or two." He apologizes for interrupting when I'm so busy.

"You say that as if you'd found me hard at work."

"Our most important work," he declares, "is done in such moments."

He hasn't moved from the doorway, so I invite him in.

"You'll never guess where I've been," he says, walking toward me. "I'll give you a hint: It's the perfect oasis in this scorching weather."

Knowing how much he enjoys little guessing games, I play along. "The seaside?"

"Much closer."

"The Palatine?" I frown, not wanting to hear he went there without me.

"No. The Sistine Chapel. Did you know it's cool even on the hottest of days?"

I admit I didn't.

He sits on the window seat and explains that Count Fries commissioned Friedrich Bury and Heinrich Lips to paint a reproduction of the Last Judgment. They invited him to come along for the fun of it. "We had the whole chapel to ourselves," he says.

That surprises me. The chapel is a popular destination, regardless of the weather.

He grins like a schoolboy. "I tipped the custodian so he'd keep the public away. We had our midday meal under the altar. Afterward I snatched a nap on the papal throne."

I know him well enough to know he isn't joking.

He doesn't stay long. As he's about to leave, he says, "I thought you'd be interested to know Count Fries purchased the Madonna that attracted you a few months ago."

"The del Sarto?" I feel a twinge, recalling how much I wanted that painting.

"Yes."

"What did he pay?"

"Six hundred sequins."

"My husband insisted we offer no more than four hundred fifty. Of course we lost out."

"I would have advised offering the full amount—" He stops abruptly. "Angelica, you love collecting art. So do I. I'd own an entire museum if I had the money. You, however, can afford anything you set your heart on. Please, don't deny yourself the pleasure."

And so begins another dimension to our friendship. When we aren't discussing art or sketching or visiting galleries, we are planning purchases. Our first project is a painting of the *Burial of Our Lord* by da Volterra that Wilhelm discovered, owned by the monks of Porta del Popolo. They're willing to sell for one thousand scudi, which is beyond Wilhelm's means.

Wolfgang proposes I buy it, with the understanding Wilhelm will repurchase it when he can afford to do so.

I like the idea but doubt Antonio will give his consent.

"Then remind him of the Madonna by del Sarto," says Wolfgang with a huff.

I do exactly that, with the result that the painting acquires a

home at Villa Zucchi. Not only is the work exquisite, but it is one
more tie bringing me closer to Wolfgang.

Although it seems like Rosa and Ignatius just arrived, they leave for
England tomorrow. But first we have a special event to attend. Ever
since Wolfgang heard I don't go to the theater, he's been promising
a performance for me in his apartment opposite the Rondanini. The
arrival of Philipp Kayser with his violin has finally made it possible.

At the appointed hour, Antonio, Rosa, and I follow a trail of col-
ored lanterns up the stairwell. The three Junos, wreathed in holly for
the occasion, greet us at the door. Inside, more lanterns line the ceiling. Refreshments wait on trays by the windows. Most of the guests
have already taken their seats, but Wolfgang has saved the best chairs
for us.

"Our guest of honor is here!" he cries as he ushers me to the front
row and sits beside me. Antonio and Rosa take seats behind us. "Let
the music begin!"

The performers play selections from Cimarosa's latest opera.
With the windows wide open, our music floats into the street. Soon a
crowd has gathered. Orchestral musicians in a passing carriage stop
to serenade us with an aria from the same opera. Everyone loves it,
and their applause draws an even larger crowd.

Wolfgang is aglow. What he intended as a gift for me has become
a night to be remembered by many.

It's past midnight when Rosa knocks on my bedroom door.

I was dosing off, lulled by refrains from the concert and the
memory of sitting beside Wolfgang all evening, but Rosa is leaving
and this is our last chance to speak alone, so I motion for her to sit on
my coverlet. I ask what's on her mind.

THE VOW

"It's not what's on *my* mind," she counters. "I've watched you all the while I've been here—you and Wolfgang Goethe. Be honest, what's happening between you?"

"Is it that obvious?"

"Not to anyone else," she assures me.

"Good," I say, though I have to wonder what Antonio sees.

As we sit with arms around one another, I tell her my secrets—hesitantly at first but more freely as I feel the relief of finally having a confidante. I search for words to describe my feelings for this man who is as much a dreamer as I am, who's probably the only person on Earth more like me than I myself.

Rosa showers sympathy. She only cares about my happiness, in whatever form it might take. "What will you do?" she asks. "And what about Antonio?"

I tell her I don't know. His support for this friendship has only made it more complicated.

"That's odd," she says. "He was always the jealous one. If anyone even mentioned the count's name, he flew into a fury."

"This is different. He respects Wolfgang. He doesn't feel threatened by him."

"Perhaps he should," she says with half a smile.

"Perhaps. But—"

"But what?" She doesn't understand why I would falter, when I just described finding something so special. "Do you think there could be another woman?"

I'm glad she has clarified the issue so I don't need to. "Antonio thinks there are many women. The irony is he sees me as a good influence because I keep Wolfgang from flirting with all of them, and thus protect his reputation."

Rosa looks dubious. "If such women exist, where are they?"

"That's just it. It's all rumor. As far as I can tell, there is no one in Rome." I shift uneasily on the bed. "In Weimar maybe." I tell her that since Wolfgang doesn't reveal much about his life there, I can only speculate.

"Still, you're afraid he's fickle."

I flinch at the thought. Really, how could such a wise and sensitive soul be fickle? How could his head turn so easily? And why, if two souls are united, would one be unfaithful? Or the other jealous? I run my hand back and forth over my coverlet, smoothing out the wrinkles, as if it were a hot flatiron that could erase all my worries.

"Trust your feelings." Rosa pulls me closer. "A woman knows these things."

Resting in her embrace, I explain that, for me, it's not what a woman knows; it's what the soul knows. "What exists between us is extraordinary. It's not just my imagination. He will say the very thing I'm thinking. It's uncanny." The doubts I was feeling ease as I speak. "And the way we find humor in the same things. We're always laughing together."

She acknowledges noticing that.

"His ideas make sense," I continue. "He believes we're all alive not just as humans but also in spirit. We can experience this directly if we keep our eyes and ears open to nature. And to art—" I stop when I see Rosa's eyelids drooping. "But enough. You must rest before your trip."

At breakfast, Rosa asks Antonio to accompany her on the first leg of their journey. He agrees to go as far as the inn where they will change horses at nightfall. He will sleep there and return home tomorrow.

As I'm going into the house after they leave, a carriage arrives. The horses whinny when the driver reins them up short. Wolfgang leaps out.

"I realize it's last minute," he says. "I'm going with Wilhelm and Friedrich to examine a statue unearthed near a church on the Tiber. Join us?"

With Antonio away, I'm accountable to no one. So I fetch my parasol, and off we go.

The statue turns out to be less intact than originally reported. We're joined by a carriage full of Wolfgang's artist friends, who also heard about the statue and who are likewise disappointed when they see it. However, they've brought ample bread, cheese, and wine, which they lay out under an olive tree beside the church.

At one point, the conversation turns to the merits of various artistic giants. Wilhelm argues in favor of Titian. I'm surprised to see Wolfgang dismiss his usual distaste for debate and extol the talents of Michelangelo. "His paintings cast such a spell," he raves, "that when I stand before one, I'm dumbstruck."

"Being dumbstruck inspires you to create?" one of the artists asks with a chortle.

"Just the opposite," says Wolfgang. "I'm ready to toss away my pencils."

"Now *that's* dumb!" jokes the artist, to a roar of laughter.

"Tell us," says another, "how do you manage to keep the pen in your hand when writing a drama?"

Amid more laughter, Wolfgang gets up and walks away.

I know discussing something as precious as his writing with such a raucous crowd is repugnant to him. In fact, his departure ends the discussion. Tipping their hats over their noses, some lie down for a nap in the shade, while others wander off to explore.

I decide to follow Wolfgang. Circling the church, I find no sign of him, so I head up the rocky hillside behind. I pick my way between the stones, lifting my skirts to keep from stumbling. I raise my parasol against the sun, then realize it's more useful as a walking stick. Halfway up the hill, I see Wolfgang propped against a tree growing in the crevice between two large rocks.

When he sees me, he moves over to make room in the shade.

We sit in silence, surveying the river valley. There is no need to say anything. When he realizes I'm not carrying a fan, he takes off his wide-brim hat and fans me with it. I close my eyes and feel the caress of air on my skin. Then I take the hat and fan him. He likes the breeze on his forehead, so he reclines, his head resting on my knee.

"You have such a high forehead," I tease. "Is that to house all your ideas?"

He laughs. "I believe you just replaced all my ideas with air."

That prompts me to set the hat down. Ever so softly I lay my hand on his head. I can feel the blood pulsing in his temple. "I want to know all your ideas," I whisper.

He reaches for my hand and brings it down to his lips and kisses it. Then he spins around so he is seated again on the rock, facing me. I think perhaps he feels we've gotten carried away, and it's time to leave. But he makes no move to get up.

"Tell me," I say, "have you always believed in spirit?"

He assures me he has. "Artists are the seers of spirit. We're the dreamers. The lovers."

"You spoke of two souls who aren't separate. I want to believe such love possible."

He moves closer on the rock, where our patch of shade is fast retreating. "It is," he says. "When I truly love someone, I disappear and only one person remains."

"So there aren't really two souls after all?"

"Not in the usual sense."

"In what sense then?"

"In the sense of pure spirit, they are one," he says, eyes growing wider as he looks at me. "You could say love is like a death. Or better yet, love transcends death. The ancient Egyptians believed this. They thought it possible for two people to spring from the same soul. And they performed magic so those two could return to this world and reunite." He explains he knows this from reading secret documents discovered in the East. "However," he adds, "one can't speak publicly about such ideas in this modern world. People won't understand."

"But you believe them?"

"I do. Unfortunately the sacred alchemy was lost over the ages." He stands and extends a hand to help me up. "All we have is Faust, for whom alchemy is a bargain with the devil."

As we head down the hill, I ask if he plans to write a drama about Faust.

He tells me he started one years ago but couldn't finish it. He rebelled against the idea that greed could prevail. Instead of a Faust who sells his soul to the devil, he wants his Faust redeemed. "I think," he adds, "I'll struggle with that story for the rest of my life."

When we reach the church, the others are waiting. Since no one wants to return home, they decide to reconvene at a nearby café for music and food. I see another side of Wolfgang as he frolics with his friends, drinking and joking until the wee hours. Still ever the sage, he is boyish, uninhibited, even impish. Yet all the while, he gives me his full attention, whispering in my ear, seeking my opinion, heeding me when I chide him for some outlandish behavior. If there is a younger woman in his life, I must be her. I couldn't feel more youthful.

Though I don't know what was said between Rosa and Antonio on their day's journey, it is hard to mistake my husband's sudden interest in our social life.

"We must repay Wolfgang," he says. "I want to plan a surprise. We won't be outdone."

I ask what could possibly improve upon the concert at Wolfgang's apartment.

"Only one thing," he replies with a sly smile. "You."

"Me?"

"I will arrange a concert, and you must sing."

I'm taken aback. "I haven't sung publicly in years."

"That's just it. You'll take everyone by surprise."

In the end, I agree to call the tuner for my harpsichord so I can begin practicing. And I see a reason to be excited: Wolfgang has never heard me sing. As soon as the harpsichord has been tuned, music I thought I'd forgotten flows through my fingers and bursts from my lips.

When Wolfgang stops by, Antonio meets him at the door and informs him I'm hard at work on a special project.

"No questions," I hear him say. "You'll find out in due time."

I understand why Antonio, who never showed interest in my music, wants me to perform. The way he manages my career, he now aims to manage my friendship with Wolfgang. But he can't manage my heart. In it, I am preparing my own surprise.

When Sunday evening arrives, the evening of the performance, my harpsichord sits in the sunroom, at an angle beneath the palms. Lit only by tall candles, this will serve as the stage, while the audience listens from the parlor. Antonio scurries around, helping everyone find a seat. He makes sure Wolfgang has the most comfortable armchair. I can't greet him myself as I wait behind the palms, but I can see the anticipation on his face.

After Antonio has welcomed the crowd, murmurs of appreciation arise as I step forward and take my seat at the harpsichord.

I'm too nervous to look up as I sing the first song. Images flood my mind, starting with the open-air concerts Raphael and I gave at the Count of Montfort's castle. And then the songs I sang to relax my sitters in London. These memories fade as the last strains give way to applause. Everyone is so enthusiastic that my stage fright dissolves. I look straight at Wolfgang and sing the second song for him. And the same for the next song, and the next. I don't even glance toward my husband to see if he notices.

After two encores and more ovations, the group's attention shifts to the patio, where a minuet is being organized. Rather than join in, I linger at the harpsichord, silently fingering the keys, humming to myself.

Instantly Wolfgang is at my side. "I had no idea," he gushes. "Your voice! Those songs!"

I thank him with a smile.

"Really, Angelica, I was in heaven." He pauses. "Has anyone ever called you an angel?"

"Years ago."

He leans against the harpsichord, his elbows on the lid, head close to mine. "And now you are my angel." Abruptly he straightens up, as if he has said too much. I sense he's about to turn away. But suddenly he is speaking so fast it's hard to catch his meaning. "You can't continue like this. You can't spend your life waiting for . . . for God knows what. It'll destroy you. You must *do* something!"

"Do what?"

"Leave." He looks at me intently. "For someone such as yourself, it's the only way."

As his eyes hold mine, I see a new and pressing sense of exigency. Hearing me sing has moved him—and not in any way Antonio had in mind. No, he wants me to leave my home, my marriage, to put aside everything that keeps me bound. He's challenging me to step with both feet into my independence, to be more true to myself than I've ever been.

"But what would I do?" I counter. "How would I live?"

"Come with me."

"And go where?"

"Naples? Venice?" He throws up his arms. "Austria? Does it matter?"

"Of course it matters." I stare at him. I want this more than he knows. Yet it's not as easy and obvious as he seems to think.

"What matters," he counters, "is being true to ourselves. We share that vision, don't we?"

"Of course we do."

"So you'll come?" He leans closer, so close I feel the urgency in his breath. I can see he's serious. This is the Wolfgang I adore, whose passion matches my own. That I've always dreamed of a moment like this, while he may only have thought of it now, is irrelevant. He sincerely wants me to leave with him.

"I can't."

"Of course you can. I know you want to!" He grimaces with the realization I may not agree.

"I *do* want to," I say. "But consider my circumstances."

"I know your circumstances. You're unhappy. Even with all your talent, all your success, your marriage is empty. You admitted as much to me. And Antonio is—with all due respect—he's not a husband to you. Never has been."

"I know, but—"

"But nothing. You deserve to be free. You deserve to paint, to travel, to live, to love, to follow your dreams, to—" He stops when it becomes apparent his words aren't swaying me.

"You're fortunate to enjoy such freedoms," I say. Really, he must know how different our circumstances are. As a man, he can let his soul lead him through the world. He can go where and when he wants. No one will stop him.

"Yes, I'm fortunate," he says, "and I want the same for you. Trust me!"

Trusting him couldn't be more tempting. Yet I know that if I agree to go with him—wherever that might be—I will be giving up my independence, losing the freedoms I already have. "Can't we," I say, trying not to sound defeated, "just let things go on as they are?"

"Why would you want to do that, even if you could?" He can't hide his exasperation. "What's the point of such a sacrifice?"

Our deadlock is broken by a servant passing the harpsichord on his way to the patio with a tray of refreshments. Wolfgang looks steadily into my eyes, as if doing so long enough will change my mind. "Have compassion for yourself," he whispers. "Will you at least think about it?"

Thirty-four

More than a week has passed since the concert, and I've taken time to think. It's easy to imagine traveling with Wolfgang, letting our fancies guide us, exploring centers of art as well as lakes and mountains. Painting and sketching and writing and talking and laughing and singing and dancing. And more. Because I'm a dreamer, I can see all this as clearly as if we've already left Rome.

Still, I can't ignore reality. What if Antonio tries to stop me? What if he finds me and forces me to come back? And then retaliates by taking away my paintings? Or what if I become ill and can't keep up with Wolfgang? What if his whims lead him elsewhere? Or to someone else? If he lets his heart turn to one or another young woman, it won't matter how strenuously I refused to believe that could happen.

In a myriad ways, I could forfeit the independence I've worked so hard for. Ironically, the very freedom Wolfgang is proffering could itself rob me of my independence.

When he comes next to my studio, he doesn't mention his proposal. "I was determined to finish *Egmont* so I could send it to friends in Weimar for their review," he says, thrusting a morocco-bound volume into my hands and shifting foot to foot as I untie the leather strings. "That's why you haven't seen me."

I open to a blank page where the frontispiece would go. "For my etching?"

He nods.

I'm proud of him, of course. But now he has one less reason to remain in Rome. Reading the manuscript will inspire me to work on the illustration, so I ask to borrow his copy.

"It's a gift!" He couldn't, he says, have completed it without my support. "Nor would *I* be what I am," he says, with a long look that says he hasn't forgotten his proposal.

I set the volume on the mantelpiece and suggest we celebrate with an outing. If he's leaving soon, we should take every chance to be together.

His eyes light up. "What better than the ruins?"

Since Antonio isn't expected until evening, we take Wolfgang's carriage to the Palatine. The heat wave has broken, and we're cooled by a breeze as we walk around the palace, meandering between fluted columns, fractured urns, and fragments of bas-relief. When we tire, we sit on the stadium lawn, mostly silent, occasionally bantering about the artifacts around us. Neither of us says anything about our future.

"We must come here in the moonlight," he reminds me.

"Yes, we must."

Then he suggests it might be prudent to go home. Antonio could return early.

"If you're ready," I say with a smile that says I'm not.

Apparently he isn't ready either, because he calls out to his driver to stop near some ruins along the way. A fence has been erected to keep the curious out, but Wolfgang takes my hand and helps me through a break in the slats. Nor does he let it go as we pick our way among the piles of dirt and granite to reach a giant stone lying on the ground at the far end.

"The obelisk of Psamtik II," he says, dropping my hand so he can push aside some weeds, revealing rows of sphinxes at its tapered tip.

I run my finger over the carving. "None of this was created for the human eye. Only the sun's rays could touch it."

"Which means," he says, "we're among the few to receive the sphinx's direct blessing."

"Isn't that a dubious blessing?"

"How so?"

I remind him that the Greek sphinx killed wayfarers who couldn't answer her riddle. Finally Oedipus knew, and the sphinx was forced to kill herself.

"That's right," he says. "I knew it, but it's slipped my mind."

"What creature goes on four legs in the morning, two at midday, three in the evening?"

He answers immediately: "As children, humans crawl on all fours. As adults, they walk upright. And in old age, they use a cane."

"You do know it." I laugh with him. "Better yet, you've outwitted the sphinx!"

"Fortunately the Egyptian sphinx wasn't merciless like the Greek sphinx," he says as we retrace our steps to the carriage. He describes how the sphinx of Giza protected the dead, how the soul was thought to travel to subtle realms after leaving the body. "We must learn to see death as a means to touch eternity, to immortalize love," he says, "not as a cause for sorrow."

I describe my grief at my father's death. Though I know he is in heaven, I still miss him.

"You wouldn't be human if you didn't," he says. "Nevertheless, I believe no one has ever really left us or will ever leave."

"If my father never left, why can't I talk to him in spirit and receive his guidance now?"

Wolfgang considers for a moment. "Perhaps he was here to guide you in youth, and now you must draw guidance elsewhere. Or for that matter, give guidance to others in spirit."

That takes me aback. "Me? Give guidance?"

"Why not? I'm sure those who speak as spirit can guide through spirit as well. Whether we're aware of it or not, I believe we all make vows to help one another, now and forever."

"If we aren't aware of it, how could it happen?"

"Because our spirit is aware. It can't help but go in search of those we love. And not just the ones we love most; I suspect it will guide all those it encounters who are in need."

"Well," I say, "I'm sure I will always seek your spirit, whether there's a need or not!"

"And I yours," he replies, his hand resting lightly on mine.

"So it's our souls' vow?"

"I believe so. When two souls are pledged to each other, not even the angels can undo their vow."

As the carriage pulls up in front of Villa Zucchi, I sense he is still no more ready than I for our outing to end. Nonetheless, the servant throws open the carriage door, so it isn't possible to say more. But the vow I give Wolfgang as I step out is wordless, spoken heart to heart.

"When will you finish that commission for Empress Catherine?" Antonio asks at breakfast. It doesn't matter that I said last week she would have it before the end of August. He thinks if he inquires more often, I'll finish more quickly.

I offer a sweet roll, piping hot on a morning that is already so warm my husband has to repeatedly wipe his brow with his napkin.

"You always work fast," he grumbles. "Why is this taking so long?"

I remind him I have many projects. I don't mention Wolfgang's frontispiece, though I was up at dawn reading his play. "The empress's commission would have been finished by now if the grand duke of Tuscany hadn't requested a self-portrait—"

"An honor you obviously couldn't ignore," my husband insists.

"So why does it bother you now?" I ask, trying to be reasonable.

"Because it's keeping us in Rome."

I frown. Rome is exactly where I want to be.

He puts down his knife, roll half buttered, so he can wipe his brow again. "I want us both to go to Castel Gandolfo to escape this intolerable heat."

I sense weather is only part of his motive; this is another ploy to direct my social life. I point out that renovations on the villa aren't finished. "If you can't abide the heat here," I say, "why not go yourself and oversee the work?"

He stares hard at me, as if trying to judge whether I'll be safe alone in Rome.

"I'll follow when my painting is finished," I say, not indicating when that will be. In fact, I don't see a rush. My husband's departure will give me more time with Wolfgang.

And it does.

After Antonio leaves, Wolfgang visits more frequently, and at different times of the day and evening. In the evening, he often comes ready for an outing. It is the fashion to go to museums at night and view the art by torchlight. Antonio scoffs at this, calling it "another insanity of the tourists." But Wolfgang wants to make as many pilgrimages as possible.

One night, after the heat of the day has subsided, we take a carriage to the Capitoline Museum. Illuminating one statue after another in quick succession creates the impression that each has come alive and is moving around the room. Wolfgang is especially interested in a Juno that's poorly lit by day. When he shines our torch on it, he decides he must obtain a cast.

"Where will you put it?" I ask. His apartment is already crammed with three Junos, several Jupiters, the Medusa from the Rondanini, and many smaller items.

"I guess I'll need a larger place."

I stop short. "In Rome?"

"Yes."

My heart thrills at what I think he's about to say. "So you've decided to stay?"

But he turns it around on me: "Are you ready to leave?"

I know he's been giving me time to think, not pressing me to make a decision. But vow or no vow, when it comes to the practical realm, I still don't have an answer.

"Don't worry," he says. "I won't leave without letting you know."

I'm putting the finishing touches on my painting for the empress when Wolfgang shows up, much too early for visiting a gallery. He circles the room as if it were a cage and he were locked inside. Before I can ask what's wrong, he blurts out that several letters came from Weimar. His friends are criticizing *Egmont*. The most upsetting is from a woman. "You're a woman," he says. "What do *you* think?"

Pushing aside my curiosity about who she might be, I ask what her objection is.

"She wants to me to change the dialogue to include a direct expression of Egmont's love for Clara."

"Sometimes it's best not to speak of one's love," I say, wondering if he sees the irony.

"You think so? His dream before being executed is meant to reveal his love for her."

"It does. As does the scene where she comes to him as Liberty, and they unite in their passion for freedom. She will watch over him for all eternity. It's perfect."

"So you advise against changing it," he says, relaxing enough to sit down.

I ring for the servant to bring tea. "His dream is the most memorable scene. When I've finished the frontispiece, I'd love to paint it." I explain that will have to wait until I return from Castel Gandolfo. Antonio is expecting me now that I've finished the empress's commission. I have run out of excuses to stay in Rome.

Wolfgang tells me he has a standing invitation from the British art dealer Thomas Jenkins to stay at his estate, which happens to be next door to our villa. "Why don't we rendezvous there?" he says. "We can have a sketching party at the ruins near the papal residence."

I like the idea. Finally I have a reason to be excited about going to the countryside.

After Wolfgang leaves, I begin preparations to join Antonio, with the expectation Wolfgang will soon follow. It will be a serene and restful time, the perfect opportunity to finally settle our future. I can hardly wait.

Thirty-five

Shortly after I arrive at Castel Gandolfo, Antonio and I are invited to dine with Mr. Jenkins and his niece. Curious to see where Wolfgang will be staying, I ask for a tour of the estate, which has the dimensions of a hotel, with more bedrooms than I can count, several parlors, a ballroom, and a maze of covered walkways that crisscross the garden. Since Jenkins has opened his doors to everyone wanting to escape the heat, the place is full. Knowing Wolfgang's proclivity for privacy, I wonder how he will take to it.

My suspicions are confirmed a few days later.

"This place is a public watering hole," he hisses, with no hint of his usual humor, as we stroll along the walkways. "Everyone comes for a social encounter they can talk about for the rest of the year. It's nothing but a world of folly. I'll never get any sketching done."

I suppress a smile. "You're welcome at our house if you need a rest from your holiday."

"Antonio won't object?"

"He's always been cordial to you. That hasn't changed," I say, wondering how we'll find any time to be alone. Fortunately Antonio is fond of long naps.

However, several days pass without Wolfgang following up on my invitation. So I decide to visit him again. Most likely he will have found a quiet spot in the gardens to be alone and read. But when I inquire, neither the guests nor servants have seen him. Only after wandering around the entire estate, do I locate him in a far corner of the upstairs parlor, at a table with two young women. An older woman sits by the door, with her embroidery. The threesome are too engrossed in lotto to notice me.

My impulse is to rush in and give Wolfgang a piece of my mind: *This is why I haven't seen you?* Not wanting to embarrass him, I stand silently in the doorway.

The girls make a study in contrast. One has dark hair and eyes, pale skin, and a brown frock. She doesn't speak much, but when she does, her eyes blink rapidly. The other has fair hair piled a bit too high for fashion, blue eyes, and a rosy complexion almost the shade of her dress. Her upturned nose conveys an innocence that could easily be mistaken for insolence. Unlike her friend, she talks and laughs nonstop.

Wolfgang has teamed up with the dark one. They roll the dice together, voicing their bets against the fair one, who appears to be losing. I can't help but notice that though Wolfgang is aligned with the dark one, his attention is riveted on their opponent.

If we're so close in spirit, I think, *why haven't you noticed me?*

But he hasn't.

Since I came uninvited, I figure it would be best to leave.

As I'm about to slip away, the older woman looks up and greets me.

Wolfgang quickly turns. If he's surprised to see me, he hides it by making introductions. "Maddalena Ricci," he says, pointing to the rosy one, "just arrived from Milan."

"We haven't stopped playing lotto since I got here," she says with a giggle.

"Ceci and her mother are from Rome," he continues. "They come every summer."

"So do I," interjects Maddalena. "My brother is Mr. Jenkins's clerk."

"Mother and I have known—well, known *of*—Herr Goethe for a while," Ceci says.

"They live near my apartment," he explains. "We've passed on the street."

"We figured he was a rich milord after that concert—" the mother says.

"And to learn he's a famous poet!" Ceci's eyes blink so rapidly I wonder if it's painful.

"Let's finish the game." Wolfgang is eager to be through with introductions.

I stare from one to the other, hardly believing my eyes. Does he really prefer their company to his books and sketches? To *me*?

"Make yourself comfortable," the mother says, indicating an empty chair beside her.

When Wolfgang echoes her invitation, I find it hard to refuse.

In truth, I can't tear my eyes away from the trio. Clearly, Wolfgang is enjoying himself. And he's enjoying Maddalena—vapid as she may be. The look he gives her is not the same look he gives me. That much I can tell. But is it a look I would want him to give me? The more I watch, the more it seems this is finally the proof of his rumored disrepute. Antonio must have been right all along.

Maddalena has devised a method of rolling the dice that involves twirling until she is dizzy enough to require a hand to sit down—which Wolfgang supplies. But her antics aren't enough to win. "Two against one isn't fair," she wails as she again comes up short.

"All right," says Wolfgang, feigning reluctance. "We'll switch and play one more."

I assume he'll take on the two women, but to Ceci's chagrin, he aligns with her friend.

"Maddie!" I hear her cry as I excuse myself. "If you applied yourself, you wouldn't lose."

"Be a sport!" says the other, now twirling entirely for Wolfgang's benefit. "It's all good fun."

Wolfgang shows up at the villa as we're finishing supper. Antonio offers brandy, while I fill an awkward silence by describing the lotto game—careful not to sound too reproachful because, while his flirtation may have disturbed me, he did nothing wrong. As I ask who won the final game, I try to catch his eye, hoping he can reassure me he deserves the benefit of the doubt.

But he's staring into his brandy. "Not I, that's for sure."

"Well," I say, "I don't see why any of that matters."

"It mattered to Ceci's mother," he says. "She accused me of forming an improper attachment with another young woman after showing interest in her daughter."

Antonio is confused. "You're interested in her daughter?"

"They teamed up in lotto," I say.

"So, a minor attachment?" Antonio offers our guest more brandy.

"Very minor," says Wolfgang, accepting the refill with more than his usual gusto.

"Minor or not, convention dictates you carry through with the appropriate courtesies, at least for this season." Antonio turns to me. "Wouldn't you agree?"

"I suppose," I say, wondering when my husband became an expert in such matters.

"Her mother made it clear," Wolfgang says, "she was protecting her daughter and educating a foreigner." He polishes off the second brandy but refuses a third.

"Did you stand up for yourself?" Antonio wants to know.

"I said that being a foreigner frees me from such conventions, because in my country, we're equally courteous to all women."

Antonio roars with laughter. "My friend, with that attitude, you'll be in endless trouble!"

"Then I'm afraid Angelica will have to keep me out of it," Wolfgang says, turning to me.

After Wolfgang leaves, I bid a hasty good night to my husband, saying I want to get a little air on the veranda before turning in.

It's a serene, moonless night. A breeze blowing off the lake rustles the leaves of the olive trees, cools my skin. Normally this would be enough to lull me toward sleep, but now all I can feel is a fever of disappointment.

I believed in you, I whisper. *I defended you. I adored you. I probably always will. But what's the point of pledging our souls if you're going to act like this?*

Though I speak to him in spirit, I don't expect an answer. I'm not speaking to his soul; I'm speaking to the man—and a very human one at that. I've always known he has Werther's tendencies, known he is susceptible to passion, vulnerable to infatuation, unwisely impulsive at times. Still, I never wanted to believe any of that defined his character. Or could decide our future.

Now, finally, I have the answer to his question. I know exactly why I can't leave Rome with him. If the likes of Maddalena can turn his head, I hate to think of the temptations that exist all over Europe.

As the breeze dies down and the olive branches still, I don't move from my seat on the veranda. The future I had hoped to begin is over before it even started. Everything I so vividly imagined has been obliterated. It as though an artist pretending to be me threw a thick layer of gesso grosso onto the canvas of my dreams, then painted their own chosen image instead. No one looking at it, not even a hundred years hence, will ever suspect my original vision was entirely different.

When the messenger from Jenkins's estate brings a note from Wolfgang requesting our presence for dinner, I tell my husband we're entitled to decline, having dined there last week.

But he wants to witness our friend's ordeal firsthand.

At dinner, I'm seated next to Wolfgang. The chair on his other side is empty but doesn't stay so for long. Maddalena, adorned in yellow, ribbons and flowers woven into her hair, is about to join Ceci and her mother when she spots the opportunity. The alacrity with which she slides in beside Wolfgang causes even Antonio's eyebrows to bobble.

As we eat, Wolfgang directs all his comments to me. Maddalena can hardly be expected to speak about the authenticity of Roman artifacts. Normally I'd warm to the topic, but her attempts to get his attention through dice-shaking maneuvers with her napkin ring are so distracting that the discussion remains one-sided.

When her subtle maneuvers produce no results, Maddalena tugs at his sleeve. "Have you forgotten your prize pupil?" she demands. "Isn't that what you called me this morning?"

He spins around. "Of course not," he replies all too quickly.

She leans forward to catch my eye, her tresses almost wiping the butter off Wolfgang's bread. "You can't imagine the fun we had—even grander than lotto." She explains it started when she saw Mr. Jenkins's British newspaper. "Girls in Milan," she says, "aren't taught to write for fear we'll turn our pens to writing love letters."

Her revelation surprises me. "You can read, can't you?" I say, looking past Wolfgang and meeting her eyes. They have the unfathomable blue innocence of an infant.

"Only what we learn for our prayer books. And definitely not any foreign languages. When I heard you and Herr Goethe speak English, I was sad because I couldn't understand."

"I told her English is easy," he says. "So I picked up the newspaper—"

"You should have seen his kindness!"

"I found an article," he continues, "about a woman who almost drowned. I read it aloud and asked her to follow my finger, word by word. Then I translated the nouns and tested her. She caught on right away."

"Yes," she boasts, "he made it so much fun, I couldn't help but remember."

"After that, we did the verbs and adjectives—"

"Like solving a puzzle—"

"Until she'd read the entire story." He makes a bow that is both deep enough to convey approval and curt enough to indicate the end of this topic.

Oblivious, Maddalena launches into a full analysis of the article. Did the woman fall in the water by accident or intend to drown herself? And who rescued her: her fiancé or her lover?

Antonio and others who also read the story join in, including one man who insists the drowning is evidence of the Werther phenomenon. A lively debate ensues, during which I rise from the table and walk out into the garden.

I'm sitting on our veranda before breakfast, looking out at the lake, exhausted after rehashing last night's dinner in my mind instead of sleeping, when Wolfgang appears, knapsack on his back.

"I was hoping I'd find you alone." He throws down his sack and drops onto the step at my feet. "Oh god, I've made an utter and complete fool of myself!"

Seeing how distraught he is, I push aside my own feelings and ask what happened.

After Antonio and I left, he explains, he went out to watch the sunset. He found himself in the company of Ceci's mother and several other women. "They offered me their seat of honor," he says with a groan. "I couldn't refuse."

"It sounds as if you were most proper. What could be taken as foolish?"

"They were discussing a trousseau. They went through all the items: cutlery from the grandparents, linens from an aunt . . . and whether it could be assembled in time." He rolls his eyes. "I was bored to tears."

"Justifiably so," I say, still waiting for a sign of foolishness.

"Then they dissected the bridegroom's character. He seemed reputable enough, if a bit youthful. Any flaws will be offset by the graces of his new wife—"

"But who *is* this bride?" I ask, becoming impatient.

"Exactly my question! I waited for the right moment to inquire. Finally, as the sun dipped below the horizon, I found a discreet way to do so."

"And?"

His answer is so mumbled I have to ask him to repeat it.

"Maddalena."

I'm confounded. "Maddalena is engaged?"

"Her fiancé arrives any day."

This should be good news, but Wolfgang doesn't see it as such. In fact, I'm surprised by the intensity of his reaction. Yes, flirting with a bride-to-be would make him appear foolish. But he seems to be suffering from more than foolishness. "Come now," I say, speaking as one would to a child. "Is this really such a calamity?"

"I don't know what came over my heart," he moans.

When he says that, my stomach lurches. Everything he's ever said about the union of two souls, about disappearing into the one he loves, about a love that transcends death flashes through my mind. "The girl is certainly amiable" is all I can say.

"Amiable, yes," he says, hanging his head. "But not an excuse to let the fate of Werther pursue me. Angelica, you must think me an utter fool! You of all people. I can't bear that."

"Don't be silly." My voice is suddenly sharp. "You know how I feel about you."

He raises his head, his eyes meeting mine.

As we gaze at one another, I see two Wolfgangs: one is the image of Werther, the other of my own soul. Both are true. Both sets of eyes hold tears. And I realize—unexpectedly, considering how angry I've been—both are dear to me. Of course, I wish the former would dissolve into the latter. But that isn't up to me. Wolfgang will have to reckon with his own heart.

"You have your knapsack," I say finally. "A walk in nature is always good for the soul."

"You're right," he says, picking up the sack. "I was thinking not to return until late."

"Do you have a sketchbook?"

Having forgotten it, he asks if I can lend him some chalks and paper.

Fortunately I brought extra supplies from Rome. "If you make yourself scarce for a few days," I say, handing him paper and my fanciest pastels, "any foolish behavior will be forgotten. In the meantime, I'll do what I can to dispel any misconceptions."

"You'd do that?"

"Of course."

"How can I ever thank you enough?" For a brief moment he clasps my hand. Then he slings his knapsack on his back and is gone.

I have no desire to see Maddalena's pert face and be reminded of Wolfgang's roving eye. Nevertheless, I gave my word, not to mention my soul's wordless pledge. I wait a few days, then head to Jenkins's estate.

I have no trouble finding her. She assumes I'm looking for Wolfgang and informs me no one has seen him. She is delighted when I ask her to walk in the garden.

Inquiries about her fiancé yield a more subdued response. His arrival is a week overdue, and he has sent no word.

"Perhaps he's been delayed," I suggest.

"Perhaps," she echoes, curling and uncurling a ringlet. Further inquiry unleashes a storm of confusion. He is from a good Roman family, and she was grateful to better herself through their union, but now she's worried. "If he even suspects I entertained another's attention, his pride will never let him forgive me."

"Did you give him any such cause?"

"I never meant to." A tear slides down her cheek. "But Herr Goethe was so kind—" She stops, afraid this is a forbidden subject, but I urge her to continue. "I couldn't help myself. And then he offered to instruct me—"

"All of which was harmless, I'm sure."

She grabs onto my words. "Entirely! And I haven't spoken to him for days."

In spite of myself, I find my heart going out to Maddalena. Perhaps it's on account of Wolfgang's liking for her. Whatever he likes I can't find it within me to dislike. Or maybe it's my desire to help a young woman—she's young enough be my daughter—who can benefit from the strength of my independence.

So I wipe away her tears with the fringes of my cloak and tell her there's no point feeling guilty over something so trivial, something Wolfgang himself has already forgotten. Something her fiancé never need know about. She can always unburden herself to me, I say. I even invite her to stay at Villa Zucchi when we return to Rome.

Wolfgang decides to cut short his holiday at Castel Gandolfo, but not before thanking me profusely for helping him wriggle out of his little debacle.

I assure him I did nothing out of the ordinary.

"I don't know what you did or said," he replies. "All I know is I was headed for disaster, and you saved me." In the meantime, he explains, he got into a tiff with Jenkins over some mushrooms he gave to the cook. It's already been resolved but gives him a convenient excuse for returning to Rome.

He asks how soon I will be back.

"Very soon," I promise.

However, when I tell Antonio I'm ready to go home, he insists I take care of my health. Grudgingly I admit the past weeks have taken a toll on my well-being. So we stay on.

For once, I don't miss my studio. I sit on the veranda and gaze at the changing colors on the lake as the sun moves from horizon to horizon. Some days, I only observe; other days, I take out my sketchbook and capture the light falling on the olive trees.

I try not to think about Wolfgang. A chasm has opened between us, creating a distance where before there was none. I don't know how to close it or if it will ever close again.

Thirty-six

We've only been back in Rome a short while when I receive an unexpected visit from Ceci. This time, her eyes are wide and unblinking as she pleads, "Signora Angelica, you must come. Maddalena's been asking for you. I'm afraid she's deathly ill!"

As I reach for my cloak—the weather has turned chilly—I remember the young woman's vibrant smile, her rosy cheeks. Not someone who'd be on her deathbed. In the carriage, Ceci explains that some mean-hearted friends of Maddie's fiancé spread rumors about her attachment to Herr Goethe. No matter how minor it was, when the young man heard about it, he severed their engagement. This threw Maddie into a state of shock. "That was weeks ago," Ceci says. "Mama and I have been with her day and night, but she's slipping away."

When I enter the sickroom, I see immediately this isn't an exaggeration. I sit on the edge of Maddie's bed and coax her not to give up. I describe all the things we will do together when she gets well. I'll take her to dances and parties where she'll meet new friends. She'll have new dresses, new hats, new ribbons. "I'm sure you'll recover," I whisper, "when you realize someone dear to you does care." I say this knowing it may save her life.

When I finally leave her bedside, she is sleeping soundly, a smile on her lips.

I run immediately to Wolfgang's apartment. We haven't seen one another since Castel Gandolfo. As our eyes meet and I see his soul once again looking back at me, it seems there is nothing to say. Everything has already been said. Everything there is to know between us is already known.

Yet he does need to know what I have come here to say.

He smiles and tells me he's missed our talks and outings.

Before he can describe the plans he has for us, I interrupt to tell him about Maddie. "You must go," I say. "It can't wait."

"Are you sure?" He looks dubious. "What will Ceci's mother think?"

"Don't worry about her. Just bring flowers and ask after the girl's health."

He says he can do that.

"If she's asleep," I instruct, "make sure they tell her when she wakes that you inquired about her."

A few days later when I visit Maddie, I find her sitting up.

"You were right," she says, greeting me with a hug. "I'm already better." She points to three bouquets on a table across the room. "He does care."

I visit her almost daily, and each time there are fresh flowers. Her favorite moment of the day, she says, is when Ceci relays Herr Goethe's greetings. "I fully accept our friendship will never go further," she assures me. "Nor should it."

I find myself telling her how a great lady befriended me when I was a poor young artist. Now it's my turn to repay that debt by introducing Maddie to society. I have the satisfaction of knowing—though I don't mention it—that I am doing this for Wolfgang's sake. And for the sake of all young women in need. Years ago I naively believed my independence gave me the wherewithal to help Mary, that my vow not to marry meant I couldn't be caught up in any such dramas. But I was. More than once. Now I can do better.

After she has recovered, Maddie comes to stay at Villa Zucchi.

She accompanies me wherever I invite her: a Christmas pageant, a New Year's ball, a tea party at the embassy. I choose events Wolfgang isn't likely to attend, which means I myself rarely see him.

On the final night of the Carnival, she rides in my carriage. If it weren't for Maddie, I would have avoided the madness, contenting myself with memories of last year. When we reach the Piazza Venezia, where the line of coaches begins, it's already so crowded our carriage is forced to halt. As the merrymakers shower us with confetti, I spot Wolfgang at the edge of the throng.

He also notices us and makes his way over.

"Look who's here," I say to Maddie. She hasn't seen him since before her illness.

"I'm glad," she whispers. "I was hoping for this."

I lean out the window to greet Wolfgang, then withdraw so he can see who's beside me. *How ironic*, I think, as they gaze at each other, *if I'd agreed to leave Rome with him, this wouldn't be happening.* When they still haven't said a word, I break the silence. "Let me act as interpreter," I say, speaking to him but looking at Maddie. "My friend can't find words to tell you how grateful she is. She wants you to know her recovery was due to the kindness you showed her."

"What Angelica says is true." Maddie reaches across my lap and holds out her hand.

Still without a word, Wolfgang thrusts his arm through the window and grasps her fingers. Then the carriage jolts forward, forcing them apart. As Maddie falls across my lap, I look over her head and out the window. But he has already disappeared into the crowd.

I have the opportunity to purchase a Titian I've had my eye on for a while. Antonio goes with me to the gallery and this time doesn't object when I name my price. It is the most expensive painting I've ever bought.

As we hang it in the drawing room beside the *Burial of Our Lord*, I have to concede it is the star of my collection—except for Saint Jerome.

On Sunday, Wolfgang comes to Via Sistina, his first visit in some time.

I immediately show him the Titian. "I'm already incorporating Titian's techniques on my newest canvas," I say as he studies the painting. "Especially his use of light."

Then we go into my studio so I can show him the new painting, *Ariadne Abandoned by Theseus*. She sits by the wide expanse of the sea—his ship in the far distance, sailing toward the horizon—as young Cupid weeps at her feet. But she is not weeping. The light on her breast, exposed between the folds of her gossamer chemise, will outshine even the brilliance Titian painted into his Bacchus. I explain that I've painted her numerous times, but never accompanied by a collapsed, grief-stricken Cupid. Here, her outstretched arm and radiant breast will highlight the courage with which she faces her own pain. All women, I believe, need such courage.

Wolfgang tells me about his own discoveries. A friend who is an art dealer has a rare statue of the Muse, and Wolfgang has set his heart on it. But though the price is low, he can't afford it. "I was wondering," he says, "if you'd consider an arrangement like what we worked out with Wilhelm for the *Burial of Our Lord*."

"You mean I'd purchase it and keep it till you can buy it from me?"

He nods. "If your husband approves."

A few weeks ago, I would have indulged Wolfgang, made sure he could secure any treasure he set his heart on. But things between us are different now. So I tell him the need to restore statues makes them riskier investments than paintings. Plus there is the fact Wilhelm has yet to claim his piece.

"You think I should give up on the Muse?" he asks regretfully.

"I'm afraid so." I explain he is likely to provoke the ire of professional dealers if he meddles with rare items. As I discourage his involvement in the art trade, I realize I'm loosening one of the last holds that can keep him in Rome.

In fact, when I see him next, he sits beside me on the window seat in my studio and tells me what I have expected to hear for some time: His departure is imminent.

"I spent longer in Rome than I planned," he says. "My heart planted itself here, and now it's time to uproot it again. I'm ready to follow the path revealed by my muse." He describes how he will travel through Italy, stopping in Florence, Milan, and wherever his fancy leads him, with the intention of returning to Weimar by summer.

Tears rise in my eyes as I realize this is the journey we could have made together.

He reads my thoughts. "I will take you with me in spirit."

"That's small consolation for the mind and body."

"Angelica!" he says, his voice suddenly stern. "I did my best to convince you—"

"I know you did," I say quickly, not wanting him to think I blame him for leaving without me. After all, I am the one who made that final decision. And it was the right decision. I tell him I will miss our time together, but I'm not willing to uproot myself.

"Nor should you," he says, his sternness softening, the familiar bittersweetness in his eyes telling me he shares my regret. "It's obvious your home is here."

Which it is. Still, I hate that his departure sounds so final, that I have no way of knowing when I might see him again—*if* I will ever see him again. "Surely," I say, more tears rising, "you won't be able to stay away forever."

"How could I when this is where I finally found my true self?" he says, with a deep look that tells me he considers me indispensable to that discovery.

"So you will come back?"

"Within a few years, no doubt." He says he intends to convince friends in Weimar to go on the Grand Tour, as he did. He takes both my hands and holds them firmly. "In the meantime, Fra Angelica, I promise to write."

"You promise?"

"I promise." He gently places my hands in my lap and adds, "If you prefer, I can send letters through Hofrat so it will be discreet."

I think of my husband's habit of reading all the mail that arrives before I see it. "That would be wise."

Friedrich will move into his apartment, he says, and Wilhelm will use the studio, so his furniture is spoken for. But he needs homes for the objects he collected that can't be shipped to Germany. "I want you to have my most prized treasure," he says, looking suddenly shy.

"Your Juno?"

"Yes."

Suddenly I am laughing through my tears. "The original, the Juno Ludovisi?"

"No other!" He laughs with me. "Or would you like all three?"

"Since the Juno Ludovisi is your favorite, she's mine too. I'd love to have her. She will stand at the entrance to my studio, the way she did at yours."

As he walks toward the door, he tells me he will have the Juno sent over in the morning. He opens the door, then turns back. "I have one more gift for you. It's a surprise. I won't bring it until the day before I depart."

Thirty-seven

It is April twenty-third, and I'm at work on a history painting entitled *Virgil Reading the Aeneid to Augustus and Octavia*, commissioned by the king of Poland, when Wolfgang appears. He is carrying a large bundle wrapped in brown cloth.

As soon as I see the bundle, I throw down my brush. "You're leaving tomorrow?" My words burst out with the full force of denial. "You can't be!"

"Early tomorrow morning." He walks past the Juno Ludovisi, newly installed by the door, and sets his gift in the middle of the floor. Pulling the cloth away, he reveals a small plant in a pot.

"This is your surprise?" I don't know what I expected, but this isn't it.

He nods. "A pine tree. I hope you like it."

I kneel beside the pot. "Where did you find it?"

"In the botanical gardens," he says, squatting beside me.

I stroke the soft, young pine needles. The little tree is hard not to like. "Something alive," I say, "something to take care of—"

"Yes," he says, "something to remember me by."

"I'll remember you, no matter."

His gaze tells me he knows I will. "We're going to plant it together."

"You mean here?"

"In your garden, so you'll see it every day." He jumps to his feet. "Let's do it now. Do you have a spade handy?"

I fetch the garden tools, and we take the little tree outside. "Where shall we put it?"

We look at one another, then both turn our eyes toward the same spot, by the rosebushes—the bushes by which I've kneeled and prayed on more than one moonlit night.

While I loosen the plant in its pot, Wolfgang digs a hole between two large bushes. Only a shallow hole is necessary for such a small tree. We work slowly, without speaking. When the hole is ready, we pick the tree up together, our fingers overlapping, and position it in the ground. We pack the dirt around it with our hands, as if covering a small child in its crib.

After we water it, we stand back and regard the tree nestled between the roses. Someday it will likely be the tallest plant around. I can't conceive of such a day. Can't conceive of years passing without Wolfgang.

I turn to face him as I break the silence. "What is it that binds two people?"

"It is eternal." He looks deep into my eyes, as if to absorb all the passion within my question. "Don't you know it?"

"I'm not sure I do."

"It is what makes this tree grow." Without taking away his eyes, he gestures toward the sky. "It is what draws water to the earth. What lets the clouds roll by. What moves even the planets."

"It is what is taking you away," I say bitterly.

Now he is the one speaking with undisguised passion. "My angel, don't you believe we will meet again?"

It is some moments before I can reply. Finally I say, "Yes, I think we must."

"Then we will, one way or another. I promise you."

"I have your word?"

"My solemn word."

With that, he turns and strides back into the house. I want to follow, but I'm rooted here, like the tree we've just planted. When I can finally move, I go inside. But he has left.

Thirty-eight

I take my supper in the studio so I don't have to explain to Antonio that Wolfgang has left, and then listen to whatever he has to say about it. I eat a few bites, then lie down on my bed, close my eyes, and drift into a dreamless void.

At midnight, I jolt upright, awakened by the clock striking. I can't recall what day it is or what is happening in the world. Then I remember: Wolfgang leaves in the morning.

I cannot let him go.

Nor can I stay here without him. All the freedoms I've safeguarded will be worthless if I never see him again. My independence will be a sham, an empty display of stubbornness, like paint that won't submit to the painter's brush and instead dries up—cracked and useless but independent—on the palette.

It isn't too late. We can still take this journey together. It doesn't matter if a thousand Maddalenas wait in every city. It doesn't matter where we go or what we do when we get there. We will figure something out.

There isn't a minute to lose. I throw on a dark dress and over it a dark cloak, then tiptoe down the stairs and out the door into the garden, past the rosebushes and the little tree we just planted, and out the back gate.

At this hour, I can't take the carriage. The only way is on foot. It doesn't bother me that my cloak is thin, that a sharp wind is blowing.

That a woman would never walk alone through the city after midnight. I half run, half walk, my mind devoid of thoughts. Having made my decision, there is no point in thinking.

Near the Rondanini, a pigeon roosting on a post awakens as I pass by. It flies into the air and lands on my shoulder. For a few seconds we walk together, unlikely companions. Then I shake it off.

"I am free," I whisper over my shoulder as I walk on. "Finally free!"

When I reach Wolfgang's apartment, the front door is unlatched. I push it open and peer inside. All is dark. I wait for my vision to adjust. There is a stub of candle by the door, where the Junos used to stand. I light it and enter the living room.

The furniture is still in place, but all his belongings are gone. My mind begins to race. I wonder if, after we planted the tree, he changed his plans and left in the evening.

I call out his name. Softly at first. Then louder.

There is no answer.

I walk into his study. The bookshelves that lined the walls are bare, floor to ceiling. The desk looks desolate without its usual array of pens and papers. Only a green glass lamp remains, waiting to shed light for the next occupant.

Pushing aside any hope he might be asleep upstairs, I climb the dark steps to his bedroom. With each step, the emptiness of the house echoes in my soul. I run into his room and throw myself onto the bed.

Thirty-nine

Each day stretches into the next, each more gray than the one before. I stand in the studio, staring at my canvas, accomplishing nothing. My painting of Ariadne should have been finished by now. But all I see when I look at it is the ship disappearing into the distance. All I feel is the heartache of a woman abandoned. The courage to face her own pain? I must have been dreaming.

Perhaps I've forgotten how to paint—not just the lofty goal of painting for God but the simple act itself. Perhaps I'll never finish another painting, never wander lighthearted through another gallery. Never see him again.

Never. I can't think like that.

I pull myself together and walk out, past the Juno Ludovisi and into the garden, where I sit by the little pine tree. Already it is showing signs of new growth. That gives me hope. I remind myself Wolfgang promised to keep me in his thoughts. Promised to write. Promised we'll meet again.

I content myself by composing letters in my mind. All day long, I write letter after letter. Whether I'm in the studio, the garden, or my bedroom, each letter says the same thing. Since nothing is committed to paper, there is no need to tear it up.

Antonio is concerned. Except after my father's death, he's never seen me too low in spirit to work. If he suspects the cause of my mood, he doesn't say. He only alludes to Wolfgang's leaving as a loss for all of Rome. He finds the pine tree amusing and suggests replanting it farther from the roses so it won't take over the flowerbeds. When I say I'm happy with it where it is, he shrugs and shifts his focus to convincing me to go to Castel Gandolfo. "I bought the villa so you could take rest," he argues. "Please be sensible and let's go."

He doesn't realize Castel Gandolfo is the last place I want to be.

The moment of falling asleep each night is my salvation. Because I can dream. Vibrant dreams cause the loneliness of my days to fade. Hopeful dreams allow me to forget. Loving dreams begin to heal the fractures in my soul.

After some negotiations with Trippel, his newly completed marble bust of Wolfgang finds a home in the corner behind my harpsichord. Its features are so lifelike that whenever Antonio enters the room, he calls out a greeting to "my friend Herr Goethe."

I sit at the harpsichord and sing what I sang the night Wolfgang begged me to leave Rome. Over and over, I sing the same songs. Each becomes a prayer for happier times. A prayer to transport me to Weimar. Yet I don't know what I'd find there, how many women awaiting his return. Like Maddie, they could smile at him in any parlor, flirt over any dining table. While he was here, I reassured myself no one else could offer what I offer him. I can no longer do that. Now my mind fills with the kinds of worries I've spent a lifetime pushing aside as too petty for someone like me, someone with loftier goals, to heed.

I search backward for a point when life could have taken another course. What if we'd met in London before I married Antonio? Or before I was duped by Frederick? Still, the entire chain of events seems to have been inevitable; at no point was I free to alter the outcome. No greater assertion of my independence would have made a difference. The only way I can picture another outcome is in the parallel world of spirit Wolfgang made so familiar to me.

A fortnight after Wolfgang's departure, Hofrat brings a letter from Florence. After he leaves, I can't tear the envelope open fast enough. As I read about his travels, the friends he's met, the paintings and music that inspire him, I know without his saying so that he still feels we're together in spirit. He includes an address in Milan, so I pick up my pen to respond. I know my words will be emotional. Yet I must write them. I can't hide what I feel, not even if it reveals how weak and weepy I've become.

10 May 1788

Dearest Friend,

Thank you for your letter from Florence, which I looked for with such longing. A few nights ago, I dreamed I received some letters from you. In the dream, I felt consoled and said, "It is well he has written, or else I soon would have died of grief."

Parting from you has penetrated my heart and soul with sorrow. The day of your departure has lodged itself in my memory as one of the saddest of my life. Since that last and fatal day, I have been as in a dream from which I can't rouse myself. The lovely sky, the most lovely scenery, even the divine in art—everything is indifferent to me. My Sundays that once were days of joy have become the saddest of days.

Now I won't write more sad words. I am content to know you are well. May heaven keep you thus. I am sure you have seen many beautiful sights you'll one day tell me all about.

Antonio thanks you heartily for your kind remembrance of
him and desires to continue in your recollection.

Please let me have the only satisfaction I can now enjoy,
that of hearing from you often. When I know you are well and
content, it's easier to reconcile myself to my fate.

Farewell, dear friend, keep me in your thoughts.

Angelica

I reread Wolfgang's letter every evening before going to sleep, and many times in between. With the energy it gives me, I gradually return to painting. Not quite ready for Ariadne, I start with Virgil. Besides, the king of Poland shouldn't be kept waiting any longer. The focal point is not Virgil but Octavia, as she faints from grief upon hearing a verse about her dead son. I don't have a son, yet I can feel her grief.

Everything I do, I do with the thought of eventually sharing it with Wolfgang. In the meantime, I know I'm doing what he would have me do: believe in the reality of spirit. Still, it's hard to subsist on spirit alone. I'm continually thinking of ways to make our contact more physical. For example, taking a cutting from the pine and sending it to Weimar. We would have sister trees of remembrance! Of course, it is too small for a cutting, so I'd need to get one from the botanical gardens. And there is the issue of how to send a living tree so far. I decide instead to have a cast made of the muse Wolfgang wanted to purchase before he left.

After only a week, I receive a second letter, though he hasn't yet received my first sent to Milan. Again I answer immediately. And again without trying to conceal my feelings. Honestly, if I have any strength left, it is the freedom to write exactly what is in my heart.

17 May

I thank you a thousand times, my dear friend, for the joy your letter has given me. As you asked, I have handed your commissions over to Hofrat and made your excuses to him. He loves you dearly—but who could help doing that?

I'm not pleased to hear Philipp Kayser has left you alone and prefers the library to your society. If only I were in his place. Ah, how I envy him! It is true that in spirit I am often as close to you as your own shadow. But no matter how strong the power of imagination, it remains only an imagination.

I hope to hear you're now comfortably lodged in Milan. Everything about you interests me. Your health and well-being are as near to my heart as my own.

If you haven't already, you will find my answer to your first letter in Milan. But I couldn't leave this latest without any answer. Though I admit I've forgotten much of what has happened since you left. When I think of you, I grow confused. I sit with pen in hand, have much to say, and would wish to say it all to you. Yet every pulse of my heart suffers and complains.

But what use is all of this? Nothing I can say will bring you back to me. It's better I remain silent. Your feeling heart can imagine the rest.

A

Antonio continues to insist we go to Castel Gandolfo. When I refuse, he becomes moody and suggests we sell the place.

"Very well, sell it," I say. Of course that's unfair. It isn't Antonio's fault I feel as I do.

In addition to Virgil, I put my energy into several commissions for British patrons that were arranged by Thomas Jenkins. I find myself working more slowly than before, as if what weighs on my heart also holds back my brush.

I don't want to part with the *Burial of Our Lord*, despite my arrangement with Wilhelm. It has taken on too deep a connection with Wolfgang. I tell Antonio I wish to buy back Wilhelm's option at a higher sum. I'm pleasantly surprised when he agrees it is a good investment and proposes we meet Wilhelm at Wolfgang's apartment to discuss it. The bittersweet pain of going there is offset by a letter that greets me upon my return. I stay up late composing an answer.

28 May

This evening when I came home, I found your letter on the table. How my heart beat as I opened it. And how much I thank you for the contents and for your friendship, of which you gave me proof by sending those dear lines to help make my weary days less hard to bear. May heaven reward you for this and keep from you everything that would annoy you.

I look forward to receiving your manuscript of Tasso. Every word you've written will be precious to me because it is yours.

Today I went with Antonio to visit your apartment. (What took place there I will tell you when it has been con-firmed.) I could hardly tear myself away. I remembered the lovely music Philipp once played there for you and me. Ah, those happy days!

I live such a sorrowful life because I can't see what I most desire. I fear I am caught on the outer edges of that folly of which we often talked. In the other world, I hope it will be arranged that all dear friends meet, never more to part. And so I look for a happier life above.

I must stop, and I beg your pardon for allowing my pen to run on so wildly. Antonio desires his most friendly remembrance, as does Hofrat. Whenever we meet, we speak of you. I'm looking forward to the letter from Milan you promised.

Your Angel

After a fortnight, I still haven't mailed the letter. If I'm waiting to get another before sending mine, it appears I'm waiting in vain. So I add a postscript and send everything to Weimar.

P.S. Pray forgive the length of this letter and the disorder with which it is written. My mind was half distracted when I wrote.

Not a line from Milan! Have you forgotten your kind promise? Hofrat may have received letters by yesterday's post. But he is away in Frascati, so I won't see him until next Monday. Therefore I will wait no longer. Since you gave me permission to write you at Weimar, I will do so. I trust you have arrived there by now.

I'm happy to say I have the Burial of Our Lord *here at Villa Zucchi. I couldn't bear to part with such a treasure. I talked the matter over with Antonio, who agreed to negotiate with Wilhelm. Now the masterpiece is ours, wholly and entirely. As long as I live, I shall look at it. It is kept in its case so only those who're capable of truly appreciating it will see it. I am telling you all these details because I know they will give you pleasure. When will we see it together? I live continuously between fear and hope—alas, more fear than hope.*

Tomorrow is Sunday, once such a longed-after day. The only consolation left is the hope you keep me in your

remembrance. That you may always be well and happy is the
sincerest wish of your devoted

> *A*

At the end of the summer, Wolfgang writes about his return to Weimar. He continues to send letters, though less frequently now that he's immersed in his duties again. I scour each for signs of a beloved, someone with whom he might be communing as he did with me. Even so, I refuse to succumb to jealousy. I've seen its ugly face on my husband too often. Jealousy will only taint the love of spirit; it won't bring Wolfgang back. This I know.

He writes that, as planned, he is encouraging friends to visit Rome. Through them, he hopes to revive the arts in Weimar. Philipp will arrive soon with his violin, followed by Johann Herder, the man I jokingly called Wolfgang's taskmaster when he described his trip to Karlsbad. The Dowager Duchess Anna Amalia von Braunschweig-Wolfenbüttel is also planning to winter here. He says she and I have much in common. What he doesn't know is that I met her in London but couldn't paint her because she had to leave to fulfill her duties for the grand duke.

This morning I'm in the studio with the first light of day to put finishing touches on Virgil. But before I can begin work, I have to write to Wolfgang.

5 August 1788

> *Dreaming again, you'll say.*
>
> *But I know you forgive me.*
>
> *I dreamed last night you had come back. I saw you a long*
> *way off and hastened to the door. I seized both your hands,*
> *then pressed them so close to my heart that I awoke from the*

pain. I was angry because my joy was so great it curtailed the happiness in my dream.

Still, today I am content because I have your letter written the nineteenth of July. It doesn't surprise me that in spite of your many distractions, you often find yourself here in spirit. That you think of me is proof of your goodness, for which I'm grateful. I rejoice that you are well and wish you an unbroken course of happiness. For me, I live only in hope of a better life.

I am now in possession of your muse and will send it to you. You asked what I'm working on. I'm finishing Virgil. The chiaroscuro has given it a great deal of strength, and the colors are brilliant. You would be pleased. Soon I must think about another commission for Empress Catherine II. I have done nothing yet, because I want to make it as good as possible. For this, I will imagine it is Sunday and you're coming to my studio. Ah, the past.

I am glad to know Philipp, Johann, and Her Excellency the Duchess of Weimar are coming. But you are not—that is my everlasting sorrow and lamentation. Dear friend, Rome is beautiful, but no more so for me.

Farewell, be happy, and do not forget me. I honor and esteem you with all my heart.

Angelica

Returning home late one afternoon, I find Friedrich in the drawing room with Johann Herder at his side. Bowing deeply, Johann tells me how much he's anticipated our meeting. Wolfgang promised our friendship would be a highlight of his visit to Rome.

"I hear you're the poetess of the paintbrush," he says with a grin, "who works with the verve of fifty men—"

"And the gentleness of a hundred angels," adds Friedrich.

"Please," I say, "hyperbole will only disappoint."

Though his manner is more subdued, Johann's passion for the arts and brilliance of intellect immediately remind me of Wolfgang. Unfortunately he and Friedrich decline my invitation to stay for dinner because they already have plans for the theater.

The following day, Hofrat delivers a letter, so I pick up my pen to answer.

21 September 1788

How joyful I am on the days your letters arrive and I learn of your well-being. I'm glad the muse has reached you, that my little remembrance has given you pleasure, and that you consider it a small proof of my true and unutterable esteem for you. That it arrived by coincidence on your birthday makes my heart happy. I pray I may live to keep that sacred day with you again.

Last night, Friedrich introduced me to Johann Herder. It gave me great joy to meet this excellent man, your friend. The visit was short, but he assures me he will come often.

It will shortly be the season when we were together at Castel Gandolfo. I will only spend a few days there this year, but in my imagination I will see you everywhere, as I do here in Rome. With such memories, how can I hope for pleasure in the present?

Your letters console me with the hope of a future. I try to relish that hope, for it makes the present more bearable. The garden has produced nothing wonderful this year. Your pine tree grows among the roses. You would laugh over my anxiety about it when a storm is brewing. As soon as I see the sky

darken, I rush out to the garden and cover the young plant so
it won't risk injury. All the other plants I leave to their fate.

    A

"What a perfect likeness!" Johann exclaims on his next visit, when I show him Trippel's bust, which I've just had moved into my studio. "How happy Wolfgang must be to have a permanent place among your paintings."

This time, he stays all evening. As we talk, I'm aware of how readily we understand one another. He is one of those rare individuals with whom one can dispense with formalities and converse about significant matters—hardly the taskmaster I imagined.

"When I was young," I find myself saying, "I dreamed of an extraordinary life."

"As you have had," he says. "Think of all you accomplished. The entire Continent—the whole world—loves Angelica. It's the love affair of the century! Angelicamadness they call it."

"The world out there maybe," I say.

He grasps my drift. "Over the years, how many fell in love with you?"

"Those were ordinary loves," I say. "Only one was extraordinary."

I mention no names, but he knows. "Of one thing I'm certain," he says, glancing at the bust. "He didn't want to leave you."

"Yet he's gone."

"You have regrets?"

"I'm afraid so," I say, thinking of the night I hurried across Rome only to find an empty apartment. No one will ever know that. "I wonder if I should have had greater faith."

"Our love doesn't perish with us," he assures me. "At least you can have that faith."

I allow myself a smile. "That's what he said."

Before he leaves, Johann asks me to paint his portrait. "It will be interesting to see how you view me," he says. "I'm sure you're incapable of painting an impudent face."

I laugh. "You consider yours an impudent face?"

He feigns a scowl. "That was meant as a compliment about your skill at rendering faces."

"In that case," I say, turning serious, "perhaps you can help me solve a puzzle." I explain that a commission from the church requires me to paint the face of God, and I'm not sure how best to do it. "What do you think?" I ask. "If I conceal his head in a veil of mist, would that create a truer depiction than, say, Michelangelo's method of painting?"

He shrugs and gestures toward my sketches. "All your faces are the epitome of grace. I have no doubt you'll create a most gracious God."

His confidence in me is welcome. But suddenly I wish I were speaking with Wolfgang. He'd understand why Michelangelo painted as he did, and would offer insight into my dilemma. I tell Johann I plan to leave subjects beyond human imagination for when I'm in heaven. If indeed it's possible to paint there.

Painting Johann's portrait gives us time to talk. I want to know everything he can share with me about Wolfgang's life in Weimar, especially details Wolfgang has avoided. "Tell me about his beloved," I say as nonchalantly as I can.

Johann gives a startled cough. "We're speaking of a very private man."

"Private of course. But you don't deny there is a young woman?"

This causes Johann to pivot from his pose. From the way he scrutinizes my face, it seems he is gauging how much I already know. The less I know, presumably the less he needs to say.

"Please," I say. "I must know everything."

"There is no young woman. Charlotte von Stein is your age."

That is unexpected. I had presumed another Maddalena—young, attractive, yet incapable of offering the depth of intimacy Wolfgang thrives on.

"She is like you in some ways," he admits when I press for details.

I frown. "An artist?"

"No. Her passion is writing. Like you, though, she has a marriage of convenience. Her husband is frequently away on business. She's been Duchess Anna Amalia's lady-in-waiting for years." He reminds me the duchess will arrive in Rome this week.

I'm in shock. I've gone from knowing nothing about this woman to the prospect of meeting her within days. However, when I mention this, Johann tells me she isn't accompanying the duchess on this trip.

As he resumes his pose, I pick up my brush and dip it in the white pigment I'm using for the ruffles poking out above the top button of his fur-lined jacket. "He didn't hide the fact that he came here seeking refuge," I argue. As if that could somehow change the reality that he is in Weimar with his beloved. "He was running from something—from someone."

Johann acknowledges that to be true.

"All the while," I say, "he insisted his heart was nowhere but Rome."

"I'm sure it was."

"Still, he constantly wrote to Weimar."

"He did write often—"

"Every day."

"Perhaps."

"And whatever he writes, you know he pours his heart into—"

"Angelica, please!" Johann says with such force that the top button on his jacket pops open. "By no means am I maligning our mutual friend. He may be passionate, but duplicitous he is not. Besides, it's my understanding he broke off the relationship after his return."

I skip straight to his last point. "They're no longer together?"

"As far as I know," he says, as he re-hooks his button, "you have no cause for worry."

Duchess Anna Amalia arrives a few days later, and Johann makes sure we meet right away. Her physique has filled out since our brief encounter in London and her hair gone gray, but she has the same irrepressible laugh, still with the resonance of a cello. I find it remarkable how looks can change over time, yet the sound of a laugh endures.

She says she remembers me as well and is looking forward to renewing our acquaintance. She wastes little time in requesting a portrait.

My work on it progresses quickly, as does our friendship. Rarely have I enjoyed such closeness with a woman my age. She is brilliant and also creative. Having ruled Weimar until her son came of age, she now devotes herself to the arts and social activities of her choosing. Her circle includes nobility and artists alike, even the pope. Music is a particular fondness of hers—not just listening but composing as well. Soon she has me singing arias from Wolfgang's *Erwin und Elmire*, which she set to music, while she accompanies me on the harpsichord. In turn, I take her to museums and galleries and introduce her to dealers of art and antiquities. She hopes to bring many items back to Weimar and wants me with her as she selects them. At times, I feel I'm retracing the path I took through Rome with Wolfgang.

It is only natural that we speak of him.

I want to ask about Charlotte von Stein, but that will have to wait until our friendship is on more intimate grounds. Initially, we talk about the obvious: Trippel's bust; the three Junos; the manuscript of *Tasso*, which both of us are impatiently waiting to read. We often take our tea in the garden near the roses, and she is quick to notice how special the little pine is to me.

So I tell her its history.

She immediately understands what is in my heart. "I have an idea," she says. "When I bring the portrait you're painting of me to Weimar, it will mark a new era for the arts. I think you should be there. Don't you agree?"

"I'd love that!" I exclaim.

"Then I invite you and Antonio to travel with me when I return," she says, adding, "Circumstances permitting, of course."

Any hypothetical circumstances seem irrelevant. All I care about is having an ally who will help reunite me with Wolfgang. Plus I continue to believe he can be enticed to join us in Rome, even if only briefly. After so many months apart, I'd be glad for a single day's visit.

As soon as Anna Amalia leaves, and before speaking to my husband, I rush to write Wolfgang.

11 November 1788

Do you know, my dear friend, that I am coming to Weimar? Have you ever dreamed of such a thing? The duchess has invited Antonio and me to accompany her. How could we refuse such a gracious proposal?

My thoughts so often fly to Weimar. Will I really see it and see you there? And I still hope that even before then, we may see you in Rome.

The duchess and I often speak of you. When we do, such joy fills my soul. A few evenings ago, she took her entourage to the Pio-Clementino Museum and I had the honor of accompanying them. It was quite a festive night, yet some-thing was lacking for me. When we were in the Hall of the Muses, someone spoke your name. I looked all around, but I only saw you in spirit.

As we were standing before the statue of Apollo, Johann pro-posed we each offer a prayer to the god. He said we should ask for something dear to our hearts. My prayer to Apollo was that he inspire you to come to Rome—and before I go to Weimar.

O that my wish be granted!

However, the circumstances Anna Amalia alluded to make themselves known as soon as I bring up the trip with Antonio. He is unwilling to consider it. "Surely your portrait of the duchess can travel to Weimar without us in attendance" is how he phrases it.

When I try to convince him otherwise, he dismisses the entire matter. Nor is my going alone an option. The invitation, as stated, was for both of us.

Anna Amalia takes a side excursion to Naples over the summer. Upon her return, she rents an estate bordering our property so we can spend as much time as possible together. This inspires me to have a gate installed at the far end of the garden. Soon we're visiting at all hours of the day.

Our conversations often turn to life in Weimar. Despite Antonio's refusal to travel, Anna Amelia is convinced he will come around; I just need to be patient.

At this point, I feel we're close enough that I can pose the intimate questions I've been waiting to ask. Over jasmine tea in the garden, I broach the subject of Charlotte von Stein. I begin by saying I've heard about her relationship with Wolfgang. I leave an opening for Anna Amalia to respond with any details she cares to offer.

However, she averts her eyes and simply confirms what Johann said: That liaison is over.

Not satisfied, I push for more. After all, whenever we speak about Wolfgang, Anna Amalia is never reticent.

This time, she pushes back. "Angelica, why are you pursuing this? I told you the relationship was inconsequential. Besides, it only existed in spirit."

When she says that, I feel both relief and disbelief—relief their union really is over, disbelief it took place on the level of spirit. I don't want to believe Wolfgang could be connected to another in the special way he is connected to me. Then it occurs to me that "in spirit" may be nothing more than her way of saying their relationship was platonic.

Before I can reply, Hofrat steps into the garden. He declines an offer to join us for tea; he just stopped by to deliver a letter, which he hands to me.

As soon as he leaves, I tear it open and begin to read.

Anna Amalia clears her throat a couple of times and asks if it's from Wolfgang.

I confirm it is. "Please excuse my rudeness," I say. "Why don't I read it aloud?"

I assume she's eager to hear his news, but she is more interested in Hofrat's delivery. "How," she demands, "could he be in possession of something as private as a letter from Wolfgang?"

"We asked him to serve as intermediary."

Anna Amalia is a brilliant woman. On numerous occasions I've witnessed her instantaneous comprehension of the most complex ideas. Yet she stumbles over this. "Wolfgang doesn't want your husband to read his letters?" she says, as if that weren't obvious.

"Correct."

"So . . . you found someone trustworthy."

"Correct," I say again. "Wolfgang felt we could trust Hofrat."

"I see." She pauses, then adds under her breath, "Like Charlotte."

Immediately I picture Anna Amalia in Weimar—perhaps in a garden, as we are now—talking with her lady-in-waiting when an intermediary delivers a letter from Wolfgang. I can't help but wonder if Charlotte tore her letter open as eagerly as I did mine. Hoping to draw out more details, I say, "I'm sure Charlotte didn't want her husband to read Wolfgang's letters."

She knits her brow. "Baron von Stein travels often. He wasn't around to read her letters."

This confuses me. "Then why did they need an intermediary?"

"I never said that." She gives a vehement shake of her head. "My point was that Charlotte is trustworthy."

"Trustworthy?"

"Yes, trustworthy in the same manner that your Hofrat is trustworthy."

"I see," I say. But I don't see. I again picture the scene in Weimar, this time with Charlotte as the intermediary. To whom does she give the letter? To herself? She can't exactly be her own intermediary. Does she give it to one of the many others who are present? Really, none of this makes sense. I stare at Anna Amalia, unable to come up with the right question to unravel her story.

Nor is she waiting for me to do so. "Come," she says, "don't keep me in suspense. I must hear what Wolfgang wrote!"

I set aside my confusion and read the letter aloud. When I glance up between sentences, Anna Amalia's eyes are closed, her head nodding ever so slightly. The beatific smile on her lips suggests the sentiments of one receiving the holy sacrament.

When it comes time to part company, I pluck the last pink rose blooming on the bush along the stone wall and hand it to her. She inhales its perfume, then takes my arm so we can walk together to the gate. She chatters on about an art dealer she wants me to visit with her, as if we've spoken of nothing else all afternoon.

But when we reach the gate, instead of unhooking the latch, I stand squarely in front of it, blocking her path. "When you said Charlotte was trustworthy," I say, "what did you mean?"

She twirls the rose in her fingers, frowning down at it, then puts both hands—and the rose—behind her back and regards me. "Please, my friend," she says, "I hope you'll understand when I say it's better we never speak of this again."

Forty

Now that it's spring, Wolfgang's friends are on their way back to Weimar and I find myself resuming a solitary life. Johann is the first to go, having promised his wife, Caroline, he wouldn't linger amid the fascinations of Roman antiquity.

"Take this as a remembrance of our time together," I say as we part, slipping a thin gold chain onto his finger, "a token of the friendship I feel for you and Caroline."

Anna Amalia plans to leave soon. We haven't spoken again about Charlotte von Stein. I have too much respect for the duchess's wishes to broach the topic. Of course, that doesn't keep me from thinking about it. Constantly. I can only come up with one explanation: She is hiding a secret about her own relationship with Wolfgang. Now when I replay that scene in the Weimar garden and picture Charlotte arriving with a letter, no one else is present when she hands it to Anna Amalia. As a dowager duchess who is always in the public eye, she would want the kind of vigilance an intermediary could provide.

I also recall the emotion she displayed when I read his letter. Did I miss similar signs during all our time together? And what about Charlotte's own relationship with Wolfgang? Was it just a screen to shield the duchess? Or was Antonio right when he insisted Goethe had liaisons with multiple women? In the end, especially considering how implausible it seems that the duchess could be Wolfgang's beloved, I can't come to a solid conclusion.

When we meet by the garden gate one morning in early May, Anna Amalia announces she is proceeding straight to Weimar on account of a pressing family matter. She adds that while she still believes Antonio could have been persuaded to make the journey, her change of plans precludes the possibility. She looks sincerely sorry as she relays this news. "I've grown so attached to you," she says. "You must promise to tear yourself from your easel long enough to write me. At least once every fortnight."

Then she casually mentions that the grand duke is sending Wolfgang to fetch her.

"Here?" I exclaim. "He's coming to Rome?"

"Why yes."

"But you didn't—"

"I didn't mention it because I assumed you knew already," she says, her eyebrows rising. "In fact, he should be here by this time tomorrow."

"Tomorrow?" I echo.

"Yes. We'll have a few days before heading to Weimar." She reaches across the gate and pats my arm. "You will have a chance to meet your dear Wolfgang again."

This should be welcome news, but all I can feel is shock. "I had no idea," I say.

She looks befuddled. "I thought you'd be more pleased."

I am in turmoil all night. My prayers have been answered—and so unexpectedly. Yet the reality seems anything but a blessing. I try to envision meeting Wolfgang again. The light in his eye, the expression on his face. What each of us will feel and do and say. And what we will not, cannot, say.

I long so much to see him again.

I want to experience the communion we shared and the irresistible freedom to be myself that I felt whenever we were together. I want the liberty to love as my heart sees fit. I want to serve him tea in my studio and go out to the garden and show him how much the little pine has grown. I want to talk with him about art and my latest paintings—show him Virgil and Ariadne, both now finished. I want to talk about books and intriguing ideas, and about freedom itself.

In this moment, it occurs to me, my most treasured freedom is the ability to make decisions for myself. As I anticipate this meeting, the wisest decision comes as a surprise: I mustn't allow it to happen.

The destiny that bound us is as strong as ever. I can feel its pull, like a golden noose that promises nothing but the pain of another parting. And another parting will be inevitable. However close our souls, our lives have taken separate paths, and Wolfgang will return to Weimar without me. For this I have forgiven him. And in forgiveness, I have earned a semblance of peace I can ill afford to have shattered.

I see only one option.

So I rise from my bed and pack a couple of bags. I write a note to Antonio explaining my sudden decision to go to the countryside for a few days of rest, inviting him to join me when time permits. He'll be happy I am finally taking advantage of Castel Gandolfo.

Before sunrise, the coachman loads my bags onto the carriage, and we slip away while the rest of the household is still asleep.

However, after only a few bends in the road, it becomes necessary to re-bridle one of the horses. While I wait for the coachman to fetch a new harness, I spot Anna Amalia's carriage approaching from the opposite direction. I'm surprised to see her out so early.

She notices me as well and motions for her driver to pull over.

"I'm so glad to see you," she says, pushing aside her lace curtains.

"I was afraid we wouldn't meet again before my departure." She glances at my luggage, and confusion registers on her face, but she doesn't ask where I'm going. She has something more pressing to say: "I received word that I must immediately tie up my business here. I leave for Venice today."

Now I'm confused. "Venice?"

"Yes. Wolfgang traveled no farther than Venice. I will meet him there." Her abrupt tone tells me she herself does not know why he decided against coming to Rome.

To me, however, his motive is as clear as my own: to spare any further pain. Whether this pain is his too or only mine, I can't say. All I know is that this is not how or when his promise that we'll meet again will come true.

Epilogue

Rome, 1807

It takes all my strength to make it down the stairs from my bedroom to the parlor, weighed down by this bundle of old papers. I sit in my chair by the fireplace and unwind the twine that has kept them together. Carefully I lay all of Wolfgang's letters before me. Because there are so many, even one from this year, they overlap on the hearthstones.

I pick up each in turn and strain my eyes to read it once again.

It is time to burn them. I've known for years this is what I must do. What will happen to the letters I wrote him isn't up to me, but at least I have power over his. The world shall never know what sweet words they contain.

I gather them up again and for a moment hold them to my heart. Then I place the pages one by one onto the flames. As I watch the papers ignite and disappear, it almost seems none of this ever happened—as if no words, thoughts, or dreams ever passed between us. Yet the memories are indestructible.

One memory stands out above all: his promise we will meet again.

When originally he said it, I believed him. Even when it became clear our paths had diverged for good, in my heart of hearts, I never stopped hoping.

As the fire burns low, my hope becomes a vow. I will find him again—as spirit seeks spirit, as spirit unites with spirit, as spirit loves spirit. *Whatever it takes, I will do it.* So many times I pledged myself to one thing or another, only to have it later nullified by life. But there is a greater vow that goes beyond life. I believe the vow of spirit can succeed where all the vows of flesh have failed.

I toss in the few remaining letters and watch them burn. My body is so tired, but I don't call the servants to help me upstairs. Not yet. As I stare into the fire, I promise him: *I will be your guide, your guardian, your protector. Your angel. This is my last and final vow. My most true of all vows.*

I must have fallen asleep by the fireplace because I don't remember being carried upstairs. When I awake in my bed, I am so weak I can't lift my head. The room is dark, except for a candle on the table by the window and a faint moonbeam on my pillowslip. I can't tell if it is still the same night or if a whole day or even a week has passed since I burned the letters.

The priest stands by my bed and inquires how I am, bending close to hear my answer.

I whisper that I wish to hear a verse by Saint Gellért, a favorite of mine I know can ease the pain of any illness.

He takes a seat at the foot of the bed, where the candlelight is brightest on his prayer book, and begins to read.

But it isn't the verse I requested. It is "Ode for the Dying."

I try to repeat my request. "Father!" I summon all my strength. "Father, please!"

But he can't hear me.

How can I explain what is happening now? Was the candle snuffed out? Did the moon pass behind clouds? There is only darkness and more darkness, as memory merges with memory.

I struggle to orient myself. On the strength of my vow, I float beyond the darkness, over rooftops and trees, cathedrals and lakes and mountains. Like a river of paintings, each creating and recreating itself, the memories flow all around me. Just when it seems I've become lost in the details, blue light fills me. Blue turns to gold, and gold to white. These are no longer the hues of a painting or even of dreams. Or of human emotion. No, this is the very light that fabricates existence.

And then I remember. I know exactly what I must do. There is, in fact, nothing to do. It all happens of its own accord.

Immediately I find myself with Wolfgang. He is sitting alone in his library. The flames leaping from the logs in the fireplace light the room with an unearthly glow. It seems so familiar somehow, permeated with the musty scent of old volumes, like a sentient incense filling a sanctum of knowledge. I could swear I've been here before.

I draw near so I can observe him more closely as he sits lost in thought, an old man now, hair thin, legs wrapped in a woolen blanket against the evening chill. The poet is at work—or is he? His quill isn't moving, and the page he holds on his lap is blank.

Then he slumps forward. His quill falls from his hand and his paper drifts to the floor.

I move closer and embrace him, arms of light surrounding him. And then—wonder of wonders—I feel his embrace in return.

"Can you feel me?" I whisper. "Can you hear me?"

"Who's there?" He raises his head and peers around, disoriented. "Christiane?"

I stay by his side, realizing I'm powerless to make him recognize me.

He sits up straighter, blinks his eyes. "Angel?" he says tentatively. "Is it . . . is it you?"

"Yes!"

He shakes his head in disbelief. "I must be dreaming." He shivers as he pulls the blanket higher on his knees. "God knows, the damp cold has seeped into these bones."

"My friend," I whisper, louder now as he can hear me even if he can't see me, "this isn't a dream. All these years, I've spoken with you often in spirit. Now I'm here with you!"

Suddenly he becomes animated. A spark of light flashes in his eyes. "Of course! You're the one who'd understand. You always understood—often before I did myself."

I smile, sensing I've come at a moment of need.

With a sigh, he holds out his blank page. "I have nothing to show for my efforts at the end of what has been a decidedly vexing day."

Why is all this so familiar?

The story of Faust has haunted him for decades, he says. Now he is determined to finish his play, yet it eludes him. "Suppose," he says, "we could satisfy all our desires for pleasure and knowledge, even if it were to cost us our very soul. What would we learn? And how could such a drama be enacted so the power of heaven prevails over the power of darkness?"

We talk about the play he is laboring to write, just as we used to talk—our thoughts intersecting, our words building upon one another. To someone else, it might sound as if we were constantly interrupting each other. But it doesn't feel that way. It is more like a single river of ideas we are riding together. Nor does our boat have a gondolier; it knows exactly where to take us. Simply because we are in it together.

He stops suddenly. "This is amazing. It's as if not a day has passed since we last met."

"You're surprised, but didn't you always speak with your friends in spirit?"

"That's right." He laughs. "I'd almost forgotten the little game I used to play."

I don't laugh with him. "Well, I'm here to remind you it is more than a game. It's a true means of guidance."

When I say that, he also turns serious. "I'm afraid a lot has been forgotten."

At another time, it would have meant so much to hear him express regret, to know he too suffered as a result of what was lost between us. Now that no longer matters. It is more important to guide him toward what I know he values, toward what can sustain him, can sustain us both.

"The world of spirit was always part of you," I say. "Surely it still is and will forever be."

He sighs. "It seems the years have stolen some of the best parts."

I want to reassure him nothing has been lost. Love can be immortalized. Our being together now is proof of that. "You always told me two could be one in spirit," I say.

"Yes," he murmurs. "And guide one another. You're reminding me of that as well. And your timing is perfect. This is what I was most in need of recalling."

He begins to doze off, as if it is too great a strain to continue our conversation.

I doze with him. In the world of light, it is apparent all I need do is think of my dearest friend to enter into his life. With no effort at all, I can be right beside him, closer than I ever imagined. It is so simple. If he is reading a book, I am reading it too. If he is taking a walk in the forest, I'm walking with him. If he looks up at the sky, so do I.

My thoughts are no longer just my thoughts but his as well. My very heart and soul are forever one with his. Angelica, yes, I can see now what she has become: a rainbow from God's palette that embraces and is embraced by all that she loves.

Author's Note

In telling Angelica's story, I drew inspiration from Anne Thackeray's *Miss Angel,* in *The Works of Miss Thackery,* Vol. 8 (London 1893) as well as from Goethe's *Italienische Reise* [Italian Journey] (Insel-Verlag 1913). The letters written by Angelica are adapted from translations in Frances A. Gerard's *Angelica Kauffmann: A Biography* (Harper, 1875).

With minor exceptions, all names, dates, and historical circumstances are true to fact.

Book Club Questions

1. Angelica made more than one vow over the course of her lifetime. Which vow do you see as the most important? Why?

2. Have you ever been taken in by a con? What allows someone to be conned? What can you do to safeguard yourself?

3. How good a judge of character do you feel you are? Have you made any assessments of others that later turned out to be wrong? If so, what happened?

4. In what ways do you see the struggles women faced in the eighteenth century as still relevant to women now?

5. Do you feel we've seen sufficient progress in women's rights? If not, what changes are needed and how do you think they can be achieved?

6. If you were Angelica, would you have married Antonio? Why or why not?

7. If you were Angelica's friend (or her guiding angel), would you have advised her to leave with Wolfgang? Why or why not?

8. Do you believe people are better off with a partner/spouse than single? Why or why not?

9. How would you describe the differences between women's friendships in *The Vow* and women's friendships you see or experience these days?

10. Do you believe love can endure beyond a lifetime? Either way, how do you know?

11. At the end of your life, what records (letters, documents, social media) do you want preserved, and what records do you want destroyed? Why?

12. What is the most important vow you have made in your life? Have you stuck to it? Why or why not?

Acknowledgments

My deepest thanks to those who, each in their own way, were companions on this journey over three decades, including especially Alan Crisp, Laura Duggan, and Penelope Shackelford. Great thanks and admiration to Brooke Warner of She Writes Press/SparkPress for her revolutionary vision and contributions to the publishing world, and to Shannon Green and all the dedicated members of the publishing team. Many thanks also to Julia Drake of Wildbound PR for everything she does to get my books out into the world.

If you enjoyed this book, please consider leaving a review on your preferred site. New authors, indie authors, and books like *The Vow* can only thrive with the support of wonderful people like you who take the time and energy to let others know about them. Feel free to spread the word in whatever way feels good to you.

About the Author

photo credit: Jude Berman

Jude Berman grew up amid floor-to-ceiling shelves of books in many languages. In addition to a love of literature, her refugee parents instilled in her a deep appreciation for cultural diversity and social justice. Jude has a BA in art from Smith College and an EdD in cross-cultural communication from UMass Amherst. After a career in academic research, she built a freelance writing and editing business and ran two small Indie presses. She lives in Berkeley, CA, where she continues to work with authors and write fiction. In her free time, she volunteers for progressive causes, paints with acrylic watercolors, gardens, and meditates. She blogs at https://judeberman.org.

Looking for your next great read?

We can help!

Visit www.shewritespress.com/next-read
or scan the QR code below for a list
of our recommended titles.

She Writes Press is an award-winning
independent publishing company founded to
serve women writers everywhere.